D0338287

Tables

Tables

A NOVEL BY

JOHN LUCAS

LITTLE, BROWN AND COMPANY
BOSTON TORONTO LONDON

Copyright © 1990 by John Lucas

All rights reserved. No part of this book may be reproduced in any form or by any electronic or mechanical means, including information storage and retrieval systems, without permission in writing from the publisher, except by a reviewer who may quote brief passages in a review.

First Edition

The characters and events in this book are fictitious. Any similarity to real persons, living or dead, is coincidental and not intended by the author.

Library of Congress Cataloging-in-Publication Data

Lucas, John
Tables: a novel / by John Lucas. — 1st ed.
p. cm.
ISBN 0-316-53519-2
I. Title.
PS3562.U237T3 1990
813'.54 — dc20 89-48372
CIP

10 9 8 7 6 5 4 3 2 1

Designed by Robert G. Lowe

BP

Published simultaneously in Canada by Little, Brown & Company (Canada) Limited

PRINTED IN THE UNITED STATES OF AMERICA

For Frank

Tables

THE *MAN* who had once been enormous sat up against the headboard of a bed that still was. He had been very fat, more than three hundred pounds, until very recently. Now he weighed less than half that, and his skin fell around him, like the robe he was wearing, in loose, useless folds. If he had chosen this, if he had ever found the willpower to shed so many pounds voluntarily in such a short time (he had resolved, many times, to do exactly that, but he always fell off whatever diet was fashionable that year), then of course he would have exercised for hours every day to keep his "tone." As it was, the cancer that had first taken root in his lungs, that now seemed to be growing in every direction at once, had prevented all but a few exhausting laps in his beautiful pool. And the last time he'd managed that had been weeks ago.

Because he was a rich man, he had at least been given the option of dying at home, and surrounding him now were all the paraphernalia for monitoring and regulating and nourishing that a hospital room would have provided. In his nostrils were the pale blue plastic tubes that led back behind him to the torpedo of oxygen. In his arms were lifelines leading up to clear plastic pouches dangling above him on a stainless steel tree, like fruit that was just out of reach.

The bed itself, canopied and hung with side curtains, which were now pulled back to allow access to the machinery, was a sore point. Every doctor or nurse who encountered him — and there had been dozens of them — wanted to wheel in the single hospital bed that waited out in the hall at this moment. Easier to change, they said. Easier to get to him for all the poking and probing they needed to do. Easier to raise his head or his legs or — for all he knew — his hips, with marvelous electric buttons. He refused. He wanted to die in his own bed and he was paying enough for that privilege, wasn't he? The medical profession always backed down when he said that, because indeed he was, but it never totally gave up trying.

The nurse who came in now made a great show of grunting when she reached across to arrange his pillows and smooth the blanket across his legs. Then she straightened up and said good-bye and take care; she was going off her shift and the night nurse was here, not to worry, just downstairs talking with the cook for a minute so they could think up something yummy to tempt him to eat. The man in the bed growled that they were certainly *not* talking about his dinner because he hadn't eaten anything solid for days and what they certainly *were* talking over and drooling over was which yummies they wanted for their own fucking tummies. She laughed delightedly: he was such an amusing, such an original man! He curled his lip.

This sickness, this dying, formed an island at one end of a big, lavishly furnished room. In an armchair just offshore, watching the interchange and patiently waiting for the nurse to leave so they could resume their conversation, sat a visitor who knew the man very well and who understood why he was snarling now. The man had been known for his wit; he'd been famous for it; and it was paining him that a little sour sarcasm would be mistaken for it and that his audience, hour after hour, day after day, was so incapable of knowing the difference.

When they were alone, the man in the bed gestured for his visitor to move the armchair closer. The odor of the cologne that permeated the room was that much stronger here: a clean, spicy, slightly bitter scent from the blossoms of the linden tree. The man had discovered it in a little shop in the rue Royale just before the war, had used it exclusively ever since, and was now trying to hide his own dying smells from himself with it. He began to talk. The cancer had spread to his esophagus, which was the reason he couldn't swallow solid food, and the reason the strange rasping sound he made now was nothing like his own voice.

"Christ, I'm surrounded by well-meaning cows. And the next one's even . . ." He broke off and smiled with more gentleness than all but a handful of people had ever seen in his face. "But you've been here, thank the Lord in whom I decided I may as well better start believing. And that's what I was trying to say, before the changing of the cows just now. How much I appreciate it, how much it's meant to me. How much *you've* meant to me."

A few tears appeared in his eyes and began to trickle down his face. He wiped at them angrily, forgetting about the oxygen tube, and the time it took to get it back in position was long enough for him to recover himself. When he spoke again, his voice was weaker, barely above a whisper, and his visitor had to move the chair much closer to the head of the bed.

"I'm leaving you something *extra,* something I couldn't very well put in the will. None of the rest of them would know how to handle it. . . ." He smiled. "None of the others have the brains or the ambition or the . . . *balls* to handle it. Secrets. I'm leaving you secrets that belong to other people, a whole lot of other people, but I paid dearly for them one way or another, and so now they belong to me too. I never did anything with them, though," he said with an odd combination of pride and regret. "I never needed to, but I loved collecting them and having them and *knowing* them, and I suppose . . . soon, I guess . . ." He took a deep breath. "Soon, I'm beginning to hope, they'll belong to you."

He'd been gazing off across the room as he talked, fiddling with a cologne-drenched washcloth, but now he looked straight at his visitor and he spoke very slowly and deliberately. "They are things these people would never, ever, want anyone else to know. But you'll know them. Better yet, you'll be able to *prove* you know them. And the *very* best thing of all is that these people are all rich, at least as rich as I am and most of them a lot richer. And if you're very, very clever, my love, my beauty, and you are or I'd never have bothered with you, you'll be able to live very, very well for the rest of your life."

1

MARIO FERMI came down the steps of his apartment house and turned west on Eighty-first Street into the buttery afternoon sun that blessed even the buildings on his block and allowed them to be mellow for a little while instead of merely old and shabby. September often served up exhausted reruns of August's brown, wet heat, but the city had been spared today: the air was warm and dry and just faintly crisp; sleepy and softly buzzing at the same time. It was the beginning of fall, and fall was Mario's favorite time of year in New York.

Feeling pleased with himself because he didn't have to be at work for another hour, he pitied any of the eight million souls who had to be inside on an afternoon like this. He liked to think the sunshine would melt even the hardest cases — his boss, for instance, who thought New York weather was either something to be kept out or escaped from — but, thinking about it, he wasn't sure the man would recognize a beautiful day unless he'd spent a lot of time and money and effort to find it, unless it was the Caribbean in February or the Hamptons in August, and he thought that was a shame.

He started to whistle "Autumn in New York" but when he couldn't remember more than the first five notes, just the falling scale of the title, he switched to "The Best Things in Life Are Free" and then he laughed at himself because he knew — or, rather, he'd been told a hundred times — that he couldn't carry a tune. People passing him on the sidewalk stared, and he wondered if that was because he was laughing or because he was hurting their ears.

He was comfortable and he thought he looked fine, but it occurred to him that he wasn't dressed the same as anyone else. Maybe that was it? He could see how a nice pumpkin-colored cotton sweater and some ivory corduroy pants and a pair of tasseled moccasins with no socks might be more acceptable. He was, in fact, wearing a black T-shirt, a loosely tailored, rather wrinkled, black linen suit, and black high-top basketball shoes. He wasn't at all depressed and he wasn't trying to make an eccentric statement of any kind: it was just that black was his favorite color, and so he only bought black clothes and he never had to think about what matched and what didn't. He made an exception for squash and jogging, when he wore all white.

He was tall and thin, with dark Italian features and black hair that he slicked back. Maggie, the girl he loved, tried to get him into other colors by telling him he was handsome enough to wear anything and look good. She bought him green sweaters and blue shirts, and when he returned them she called him a closet anarchist, a Sicilian widow. Her other campaign, also a lost cause, was for contact lenses instead of the wire-rimmed glasses he always wore, and she was particularly mean about the flip-up sunglasses he clipped over them on days like today.

At Third Avenue, he stopped at a deli for a pack of Winstons, laughing again — guiltily this time — when the woman behind the counter frowned and wagged a finger at him. She knew he'd given them up for a few weeks and now he was obviously back on them again, so he waited till he was out of her sight before he tore open the pack and lit up. He felt like a second-class citizen these days because he smoked; even this nice old babe — who must make a good profit on all the tobacco she sold — managed to make him act like a naughty schoolboy.

A single-engine plane droned overhead and, blocks away, a helicopter circled Central Park. Film crews, he thought, and he wished them luck at getting this day, this city, in a can. He remembered all the weekends he'd come in from Princeton, checking into the Chelsea and roaming everywhere and anywhere for hours with a camera. He'd moved here seven years ago, he still took long walks, but he didn't take pictures of the city anymore because he was part of it now and he didn't need to capture it and he wasn't sure he wanted to try.

The neighborhood grew cleaner and richer as he walked along. His own block, between Second and Third, had always been respectable but never very fancy. As he headed west, crossing Lexington and then Park, the real money began to show itself — elegant town houses, substantial old apartment buildings with doormen trying to look like admirals, and parking garages that rented slots for as much as a decent one-bedroom apartment would cost in most towns. It was part of what he'd always loved about New York, the way it changed so fast from block to block, and this rags-to-riches transition today was gentle compared to walks that took him along Twenty-eighth Street from wholesale flowers to furs to junk jewelry in five minutes, or up one of the streets on the Lower East Side from China to Israel to Puerto Rico to Italy in fifteen.

He turned onto Madison Avenue, the street that did its best to absorb whatever money anyone in the world happened to have in abundance, and when he sniffed the air he imagined he could actually smell its bouquet of leather, wool, oil paint, rich foods, and the exhaust fumes of well-bred limousines. There were other streets in the city where he could stroll past elegant shops — a few blocks of Fifth Avenue, of course, and those newly gentrified neighborhoods of the Upper West Side and Soho that really had much more charm than this — but nowhere else was there this concentration of wealth in such a small area, and it fascinated him for precisely that reason.

He zigzagged down the street, crossing whenever there was something he wanted to see in a window on the other side, ignoring red lights like the native New Yorker he'd become. There was much more traffic, the sidewalks were far more crowded, than the last time he'd taken Madison, and that was only a week before. Summer was suddenly over; it was official; everyone was back in town from wherever they'd been. He watched the women who walked slowly or briskly in and out of boutiques and galleries. Behind his dark glasses, he could stare at them a little longer than usual — a tweedy young matron coming out of Ralph Lauren, a dazzling South American beauty waving for a cab in front of Valentino, an older blonde woman holding a skirt up to the light in the window of Saint-Laurent. Sometimes he mentally undressed them, sometimes he only tried to guess what their lives were like, who their husbands were, who they loved and why they loved and whether they loved at all.

He bought a couple of books in the Madison Avenue Bookshop and, a little farther along, he treated himself to a silk shirt — black, it went without saying — at Gianni Versace. His last stop was in Sherry-Lehmann. Putting on the kind of thoughtful expression that was appropriate to a serious wine shop, he had a short talk with the assistant manager and ordered ten cases of a Château Pichon Lalande he'd tried a few nights before. Whenever he had a little extra money, he bought wine in quantities like this and had it delivered to a storage place in Brooklyn that kept it at the right temperature and humidity. The few people — two, altogether — who knew what he planned to do with it called it his hope chest.

Out in the sunshine again, he turned off Madison to head east on Sixty-second, walking fast as far as Second Avenue, where he paused before crossing the street and going into work. In just a few minutes, he'd left behind some of the most valuable real estate in the world and arrived at this block that consisted of a pizza parlor, a supermarket, a tanning salon, a Korean vegetable stand, and the corner building that waited for him now. It was an ordinary gray walk-up tenement with a typical New York mixture of tenants — old Greek and Polish couples, a floating stewardess arrangement, some single secretaries, a chorus boy, a methadone addict. The ground floor had once been a funeral parlor, and its only windows were small, discreet ovals on either side of the wide door, painted over with the same dark green as the walls and the awning that stretched out to the curb. It looked as if the building had been dipped in paint up to the second floor and only the brass poles and the plant boxes had been cleaned off and polished. On the sides of the awning and diagonally across each window, a white signature spelled "Rudi's."

To someone who didn't know better, Mario always supposed, it must look like a dozen other places on First or Second or Third — well-maintained, probably rather expensive, nice enough but no big deal. In fact, in the ten years since Rudi's opened, it had become more than a restaurant and bar; it was now an institution. No review had ever awarded its food more than two out of four stars, *Architectural Digest* had never done a spread on its decor, but its clientele was as much a cross-section of the rich and the talented and the powerful and the beautiful as any restaurant in town. If it wasn't, literally, a club, it was very close to being one, but it was unique because it catered to no one element, no single crowd. Sardi's had theater folk; "21" had chairmen-of-boards and real estate lords; Four Seasons had politicians, publishers, and advertising czars. Rudi's attracted all of these and more. The cast varied, of course, because these people were nothing if not mobile and someone was always off to London for a taping or a house party in Palm Beach or a screening on the Coast, but this had become home base. Photographers were banned; outsiders were heavily discouraged; it was a place to relax.

Mario was partly responsible for this rich mixture of elements because he'd been the manager for five years now, after a year as a waiter and another year as a captain. The core group had been the people Rudi knew and liked and fawned on best: Old Hollywood, privileged wives and their eunuchs, fashion powers, and the very, very rich. Mario had stirred in his friends, the people who interested him — artists and their dealers, writers and their agents, dancers and their choreographers, actors and their directors — and now it was livelier and, up to a point, more democratic.

After scooping some cigarette butts out of the planters and tossing them in the gutter, he pushed through the door. The foyer, where he could still picture relatives standing and receiving condolences, was kept deliberately bare — rest rooms off to the left, coat check to the right, and two low couches for people to wait for friends or cabs or limousines. It was a dead space, a buffer zone between the street and the bar, a place to leave Second Avenue behind. He smiled at this month's coat-check girl — the tenth in the past year — and remembered her name just in time to use it. She was reading a paperback and looking a little bored, an actress-between-parts who was actually very pretty under too much makeup. He would never have hired her as a waitress — Rudi's only hired waiters, anyway — but he thought she looked exactly the way a coat-check girl ought to look.

He sent her in to make sure the ladies' room was empty before he checked it out, and then he looked into the men's. A busboy tidied them every hour or so; the restaurant wasn't even open yet and the bar had only been serving for half an hour; but they were the first stops on the tour Mario always made. A small mess, a tiny rudeness, the staff knew by this time, could make him as angry as a far bigger disaster. There were few enough places in New York where frazzled, creative, spoiled people could buy comfort and courtesy at any price, was his reasoning, and he was determined that as long as he was here, Rudi's would be one of them.

The big room that would be jammed with drinkers in a little while was nearly empty at this time of day. A few couples lounged on the tufted leather banquettes lining one wall, but no one sat at the tables that filled the center and only four solitary men hunched over their drinks at the U-shaped bar that bulged out from the other side. Covered with autographed photographs of Hollywood and Broadway stars, dead and alive, watercolor costume and set designs, and signed exhibition posters, the walls here made up for the starkness of the entrance space. Nobody except the occasional stray tourist ever looked at them very closely, but there was a sense that they were a natural accumulation of Rudi's life, and that was exactly the impression Rudi wanted to make.

He waved to the bartender and continued on through the room. Until six, when the first dinner customers were seated, the archway between the bar and the dining room was closed off with louvered doors. Just beyond them was an alcove that held telephones, credit card terminals, a cash drawer, and, perched on a high stool — like a parakeet, Mario often thought — Lillian. Lillian was not only the cashier, she was the Voice of Rudi's for most of the dinner bookings that came in. She was sixtyish and tiny, with bright, shrewd eyes peeping out from under a cloud of hennaed hair. She'd been here from the beginning and by now people only asked for Mario or Rudi if they needed special favors or if their membership in the club had somehow escaped Lillian, but she was practically never wrong about who should be blessed with a reservation. Daily, she devoured "Suzy Says," "Liz Smith," James Revson's "Social Studies," "Page Six" of the *Post,* and *Women's Wear;* weekly, she skimmed *People* and *New York;* monthly, it was *Vogue, Town & Country,*

Vanity Fair, and *Interview.* She was always able to give unknowns the impression that she'd love to book a table for them but that it just wasn't possible for the next few weeks.

She adored Mario and she was far more loyal to him now than she was to Rudi, who treated her nicely some days and not so nicely on others. Today, passing on the message that he'd gone for the day, that he'd be playing bridge, that he could be called at home in an emergency, she snorted. Mario laughed and spun the reservation book around to look at it. It was nearly full, of course — it always was. She'd bring it in to him later, and they'd sit with an erasable plastic table plan to figure out the seating. In the meantime, he read quickly down the neat columns for a sense of how the evening would be shaping up.

He walked on into the dining room, glancing into the smaller rooms on either side that could be used for overflow when they weren't reserved for private parties. Chairs and banquettes were covered in velvet that matched the dark green on the building's outside, and the off-white walls held a few second-string Impressionists that Mario had always found uninteresting but inoffensive. At this time of day, the room was an empty stage and the track lights bounced off the shiny wood surfaces of the two-tops along the sides, the square four-tops and the round six-tops in the center. Vases of white rosebuds and stacks of dark green tablecloths and napkins waited for the all-important seating arrangement.

Beyond the swinging doors, the noise level in the kitchen was about the same as Second Avenue at rush hour. Powerful exhaust fans whooshed above the ranges as other fans pumped fresh air back in; pots and skillets clanged on the stoves and in the dishwashing sinks; walk-in refrigerator doors were slammed; heavy knives chopped; heavy mallets pounded meat. Eighteen voices competed for attention in English, French, Italian, and Spanish. Mario was always surprised by the quiet that would be descending as soon as the first order came in. This was prep work, and for some reason prep work was supposed to be noisy.

He had to speak to the chef first, of course — the one time he hadn't, every knife had frozen in midair, every spoon had stopped in midstir. Louis turned to him from the pots he was watching, one with fish heads and skins that were being sweated with a little oil and wine for a stock, another with the asparagus peelings from the night before that would go into a roux for soup. He was Alsatian, pear-shaped, balding, and rather mournful. He was in complete charge of the kitchen, but of course he worked for Rudi, and Mario spent what he considered far too much time as their referee. Louis was happiest when there was a private dinner in one of the small dining rooms because then he could show off his very real genius. The regular menu here bored him and so did the two or three nightly specials. Rudi didn't allow him much scope, and Mario knew that, after only a year here, Louis was looking for another job. The four sous-chefs would all like to fill his shoes, and their rivalry was sometimes friendly and sometimes bitter. Then one of the three cold-side cooks, who were in charge of salads and appetizers, might be elevated to sous-chef level, and one of their assistants might replace one of them, and one of the floating apprentices might move up, and so on down to the dishwashers. Mario thought he'd feel right at home in the Kremlin.

Louis was presenting him with only two problems today, and Mario was relieved. Rudi had insisted on changing to new fish suppliers because they were a little cheaper, but they had no bay scallops today, Louis refused to make his Coquilles Louis with chopped-up ocean scallops, so what good was a new supplier if they couldn't give him what he needed? And the produce man was giving him trouble because his bills weren't paid fast enough. Mario promised to see what he could do, and then he slowly made his way around the kitchen, finding a word for everyone in one language or another. In the dishwashing room, he turned down the volume on the disco-blasting radio and smiled at the two Puerto Rican boys who were bent over dirty pans in the huge sinks, knowing — because it happened every day — they'd turn it up again as soon as he was gone. He climbed down the staircase, so steep it was almost a ladder, to the storage room, and then he backed up the stairs and crossed the kitchen to the office.

Behind the double thickness of glass it was quieter, and he sank gratefully into his chair. He spent a little while with the secretary, a sweetly efficient Haitian woman, and then Lillian brought the reservation book in and it took another half hour to sort out the table arrangements. She quietly corrected him when she saw him put a particular publisher at a table next to a particular ballerina's table. Hadn't he seen that blind item a few days ago, the one about his wife and her husband? Mario shook his head and smiled; Lillian, who knew none of these people personally, never failed to amaze him.

At five, changed into his tuxedo, he met with the two captains, the twenty waiters, and the ten floating busboys in the dining room. It wasn't a roll call, exactly, but he expected them to be on time and he made a point of embarrassing anyone who was late. He told them what the specials, the soups, and the desserts were, in enough detail so they could describe the ingredients and the way they were prepared to anyone who asked. He delegated waiters to tables, explained the seating chart to the captains, and left the setup to them while he went back to the office to deal with more paperwork.

It was the time of day when he sometimes looked up from his desk, gazed out at the busy kitchen, and indulged in running daydreams. He was a Napoleonic general whose aides-de-camp awaited his decision about those cannons over on the right flank; he was the director of a Broadway musical; he was captain of a destroyer in the Philippines in 1942. Today, he was the tough old editor of a big city daily, looking out through the glass to the frantic newsroom, running his eagle eye down a freshly printed menu, sending a reporter back to the murder scene to check on some facts.

After a few minutes, he dove back into his In box. It didn't take long for his fantasies to dissolve into thin air, for him to start grinding his teeth. Clipped to a note from the fruit and vegetable wholesalers that asked for prompter payment — the problem he'd just told Louis he'd try to sort out — was a memo from Rudi: "Mario: Don't like their tone. Find someone else?" At the bottom of the florist's bill for the month, Rudi had scribbled "Mario: This seems *awfully* high." Attached to a bill for six cases of a champagne that Mario had always considered overrated, a bill that clearly showed delivery to Rudi's home address, was a memo saying "Mario: Run this through our books."

The produce people were the best in the city, no more expensive and probably far more patient than their competition would be. The florist's bill was exactly the same every month and it was minimal for a place of this caliber. The champagne for a party at Rudi's town house would take an hour or two of somebody's time to get in and out of the restaurant's inventory and it would worry the accountant because it was exactly the kind of dumb trick some IRS auditor would love to catch.

Mario had been swearing softly under his breath, but now he spoke aloud to the empty room, just a single word. "Someday," he said.

2

SWINGING OUT through the big revolving doors of her apartment house onto Eleventh Street, Maggie Wetherby hesitated for a moment and decided to walk down to her appointment at Jim's instead of taking a cab. It would make her a few minutes late, but she'd been on the phone all morning at home and she'd be inside for the whole afternoon, first at Jim's and then at the gallery. She wanted a short swim in this beautiful, liquid afternoon.

She was wearing high-heeled Maud Frizon lizard pumps but she walked fast, clicking down Fifth and into Washington Square, under the white triumphal arch and past the big, empty fountain. Squirrels skittered through the first few dead leaves; pigeons shoved sparrows away from old ladies' breadcrumbs; and drug dealers lounged on benches, chanting their little speeches one by one as she passed them.

"Dime bags," they mumbled. "Coke, crack, ups, downs." She always wondered how they could all make a living. Everyone she knew who bought any of these things — herself included, although that was only for a little bit of pot every few months — had a private dealer. These guys, who were periodically run out of the square but who always reappeared, must exist entirely on the teenage tourist trade, she decided, like all the tacky head shops and T-shirt shops on Bleecker Street. As businessmen, they rarely came on to her, but there were plenty of loiterers who did. A great variety of suggestions were made, along with appropriate sucking and slurping sounds, in both English and Spanish. It was hard, sometimes, not to make the mistake of smiling. She agreed with them today, as a matter of fact: she'd lost a couple of pounds and she felt sexy in a new white Donna Karan jersey dress, her blonde hair pulled back into a little ponytail.

Once she was out of the park and on La Guardia Place, she tried to concentrate on the problems ahead of her. Problem, singular, she corrected herself. Jim Wilkins was a sculptor whose reputation, at thirty-one, was just beginning to take off. He'd already had three exhibitions in New York, but the gallery she ran was about to show him for the first time. His work was hard to classify, but she thought of it as California Minimal — enormous upright panes of subtly iridescent glass that he arranged in odd, atmospheric configurations. It was Maggie who convinced Max Silverman — her boss, the man who owned the gallery — to lure him away from his old dealer with a fatter contract. Now, along with fifteen other artists and half a dozen employees, Jim was her responsibility: Max had just had an operation, a bypass — triple? quadruple? she wasn't quite sure — and he'd be recuperating for at least three months. She was very fond of Max, but, after all, it wasn't fatal and she secretly thanked God, because it put her in total charge, a couple of years shy of thirty, of one of the most prestigious galleries in Soho.

The problem was that Jim was one of the biggest bastards in the art world and that he was more trouble than the whole rest of the stable put together. On top of that — something Max didn't have to worry about — he never failed to make a pass at her. His show would be opening in two weeks and she could already predict the crises it would bring with it, but today she had to talk to him about something that was just as important as the exhibition itself, a commission that was practically in the bag. It would be a huge exterior piece, bigger than anything he'd ever done, on the plaza of the McKinnon Bank headquarters that was being built on filled land next to the World Trade Center. Before he signed with Max, she knew, Jim had screwed himself out of a smaller commission by demanding too much money, and she couldn't allow that to happen this time. The McKinnon Foundation, which chose all the art work for the bank, was too rich and too important. She'd have to be firm with him, she decided, standing outside the door of his building after pushing the bell. That was as far as she got in her thinking, that she would need to be very firm with him.

He lived and worked in a big loft on the eastern edge of Soho, a building he'd been smart enough to buy into just before the real estate boom began in that neighborhood. When he buzzed her in, she stepped directly into the old freight elevator that slowly carried her up, creaking and shuddering when it stopped at his floor. Harry the Doberman was waiting and he leaped up on her, his tongue lolling, as soon as the elevator door opened. He was only being friendly, but she was afraid of dogs, certainly big Gestapo dogs like this one, and her fear excited Harry even more. She'd forgotten about him, and she was annoyed. This wasn't the kind of entrance she'd wanted to make.

"Get down, Harry," Jim said nonchalantly. "Knee him, Maggie. He smells those fucking cats of yours."

"Right. It couldn't be Harry's fault and it couldn't be your fault for training him so poorly, so it must be my fault or my cats' fault?" When she brought her knee up, hard, into the dog's chest, he yelped and sat back, puzzled but still willing to play. She brushed off her dress and glared at Jim. Tall and thickly built, with red hair and a heavy red beard, he was leaning against the wall, grinning and puffing on a cigar. He wore a dirty terry-cloth bathrobe that had once been blue, loosely tied at the waist. It was apparent that there was nothing under it.

"Your little outfit is heaven."

"I just got out of bed."

"So why is your disgusting cigar half smoked and why can I smell coffee?"

"Let's say I thought maybe we could combine business with pleasure."

"To coin a phrase. Did you used to get a lot of mileage out of lines like that with all those Idaho farm girls?"

"We do pretty well," he said, looking down at himself. "Big Mac and I, we haven't had any complaints yet."

"I don't have time for this," she said coldly, walking past him to a window and standing there, telling herself that, really, it was no worse than what the creeps in Washington Square were saying just now. She looked at her watch. "Everyone at the gallery is waiting for me. I want to fill you in on the commission and then we've got to go over the price list for the show. I'd like your undivided attention for the next hour, and then I want to get out of here."

"All right, all right. Never hurts to try. Coffee?"

"Yes. Black," she sighed. Why did they always have to get this silly sexual skirmish out of the way before anything could be accomplished?

She sat down heavily at a long picnic table that was strewn with dirty dishes, dirty clothes, old newspapers and magazines, and cleared a place in front of her for the notes she'd brought. Looking around at the big open space, she realized she hadn't visited him here for a few months. There had been a pretty girl with long dark hair living with him then, and it had been cleaner, much cleaner. He never talked about that part of his life and he always came to the gallery alone, which didn't necessarily mean anything because he treated his women like concubines and never took them anywhere. Anyway, the girl certainly wasn't around these days. Jim and Harry together had turned the place back into their kennel, although — appropriately, considering Jim's preoccupation with light and reflection — the tall windows were spotless. She didn't see how he could work in the middle of it, but there were big sheets of glass leaning against the wall at the far end, and there was the enormous machine, like an iron lung for an Amazonian race, that treated the glass with a metal particle vaporizing process that she didn't completely understand.

She never failed to wonder at the contradiction in Jim, that out of all this slovenliness, out of the big filthy machine — not to mention the big filthy mind — came the delicate panes of tinted glass, organized into beautiful patterns that a critic for *Artforum* had called "Oriental in their atmospheric quality." There was no art other than his own anywhere in the loft — naturally, she thought, since he never had a kind word to say about or to any other artist, living or dead. His newest passion was all around her, though: black-and-white, blown-up photographs of vintage planes, and big models of others in Plexiglas cases.

He was rattling dishes back in the kitchen, presumably rinsing out dirty cups for them to use. "I gather Rosa bit the dust?" she yelled.

"Sure as shit did. Stupid Polish cunt was beginning to talk about our relationship. Only big word I ever heard her use. Relationship. When she moved her sewing machine in and started putting up curtains, I told her to go screw herself."

"You have such a way, such a winning way, with women."

"She'd already exceeded the three-month limit, anyway."

Harry came up to sniff her. "Fuck off, you ugly Nazi mongrel," she snapped at him. His tail drooped and he slunk away. She wondered idly if it was possible he had feelings. "It's beginning to look like the Smithsonian's Aviation Wing in here."

He came out carrying two mugs in one hand and a battered enamel coffeepot in the other. "Did you notice the Staggerwing?"

"The one that has pride of place, with the funny wings?" The biggest enlargement was tacked up over his bed, a bulbous biplane in the air, its top wing set farther back than its lower one. It was strange to see Jim's face grinning out of the side window like the Red Baron. She assumed there were people somewhere who specialized in photographing owners of planes in flight.

"That's my baby. I didn't have that picture the last time you were here." The only time he ever showed this kind of boyish enthusiasm for anything or anyone was when he talked about antique planes, particularly his own plane. He'd made a deal with a client a year or so before, trading him two of his sculptures for it.

"I thought you had a Beechnut."

"Beechcraft, bitch, and it is. They made these; the Staggerwing was their first enclosed model. It's incredible, Maggie. You've gotta come up with me sometime."

"Thanks for getting dressed, by the way." He'd put on sweatpants and a sweatshirt. She couldn't help noticing how things flopped around under the soft material. My God, she said to herself in the next instant, a few minutes ago you were repulsed by it and now you're — what? faintly titillated? Just because he's covered it, them, up? You're evidently working *far* too hard and you're not seeing *nearly* enough of Mario.

"You're welcome. Listen, if you're nice to me I'll take you up."

He was tapping a little mound of cocaine out of an amber-colored bottle onto a piece of mirrored glass.

"Gosh, what an offer. First I get to be nice to you, whatever that means, and then I get to go twenty thousand feet up in the air with you, alone?"

"That's about twice as high as she'll go," he muttered. Now he was chopping with a razor blade, like a chef mincing parsley. She wondered if he'd offer her some; she wondered if she'd accept. There was something so depraved about doing coke in the middle of the day — she only did it very occasionally, maybe once a month when someone else had some, never with Mario because he was violently against it. Still, it would make this meeting a little more bearable. . . . If he didn't offer her any, she decided, she was damned if she'd ask for it.

"Well, knowing you, you probably put it on automatic pilot and . . ."

He laughed. "Automatic pilot. On a 1937 plane. Of course." He divided the coke into four long lines and passed the pane of glass over to her with a short length of plastic straw.

"Um, thank you." She only sniffed one line, half for each nostril. She didn't have enough experience to really know, but she thought it was so smooth that it must be very high quality. He snorted all the rest of it, and it occurred to her for the first time — she knew he did it but she'd never actually *seen* him do it — that he must have a pretty heavy habit.

"I really care a lot about you," he said then, leaning down to pull Harry's ear. "I wish you'd believe that."

"Jim." Which was worse, the heavy macho posing or the fake sincerity? "I assume you mean me and not Harry, but it's impossible. How many times do I have to say it? I like you, for some unknown reason. I respect your work and I even respect this mania you have for your Beechcraft, but I'm not interested in you that way. I think *you* think I'm playing hard to get, like some cute little Doris Day gal-on-the-go, but you're just not reading it right. I have a man, a lover, whatever you want to call Mario, and — for the thirty-fourth time — you and I are not going to wind up in bed together. Got that?"

Without acknowledging anything she said, still playing with

Harry's ear, he suddenly reverted to type, the Jim Wilkins she was used to, relentlessly — but, at least, predictably — egocentric and greedy. "So what do they want from me?" he asked, as if someone were demanding something unreasonable.

She sighed with relief, sat back, and pushed her notes, neatly typed up by her secretary, toward him. "Read these over, and here's their court architect's rendering of what the plaza area will look like. Of course, you'll have to go see it, but I don't ever want you dealing with Frederick McKinnon himself, if you don't mind. I prefer keeping you away from our more important clients."

"Okay with me, Maggie. That's what dealers are for, to protect me from assholes like Frederick McKinnon."

"No, darling, it's to protect assholes like you from themselves. And since you've never met him, I don't see how you could know what he's like. He's very knowledgeable and very civilized and very important, and that's exactly the reason I'd rather you dealt with his assistant on this. She's young and sweet and she'll probably be impressed by you for a few minutes until she figures out what a shit you are. And I suppose you'll have to meet the architect or someone from his office at some point. Anyway, I need exact estimates from you in the next couple of weeks — in time for the opening, say. I've already told them it would be around a hundred and eighty, which must mean about eighty, clear, for you after materials and installation and our cut, no?"

He had enough questions and objections and smoke screens to use up the whole hour she'd allotted for this, but with the extra little edge from the coke, she was ready for everything he could throw at her. She was waiting for the elevator, congratulating herself on the commission she'd be getting from this — ten percent of the gallery's profit — when she remembered the price list. His show wouldn't be opening for another two weeks, but there were a couple of collectors and one museum director who were reserving pieces in advance on the basis of photographs. They were pressuring her for quotes, she couldn't put them off much longer, and she hadn't come to an agreement with Jim yet.

"We could argue about prices if you have dinner with me tonight," he said. She realized he'd probably dragged out the talk deliberately, but she couldn't help that now.

"Okay. Your treat. Pick me up at the gallery at seven. I'll book."

"And you'll want to go to Rudi's, naturally," he snarled.

"Naturally." She knew he hated Rudi's, but then, he hated every restaurant in New York except a couple of downtown art scenes where they treated him like a star. "Take it or leave it," she said, as the elevator door banged open behind her. "You're jeopardizing three sales if you don't." She was half bluffing, and of course he realized it, but he agreed. He'd be about an hour late, she thought, just to show her who was boss, but she'd already figured on that. She had so much to do at the gallery that she hadn't planned to leave till eight, anyway. Round four hundred and ninety-eight to Maggie, she said to herself when she was back on the street again.

3

THE *WOMAN STOOD BY HERSELF,* gazing out over the East River to Queens and up to the housing projects of Harlem. Because this was an apartment building that dated from the twenties, there was a real window she could open onto the soft autumn day, the first day of this extraordinary weather. Warm air caressed her and made her a little edgy at the same time, as if something should be happening but wasn't. She was having a moment to herself, turning her back on a party that was buzzing in the big room behind her, occasionally dipping her cigarette into the tiny Lalique ashtray she'd brought with her to the windowsill. When the breeze blew the ashes back onto her skirt, she absentmindedly brushed them off.

Mrs. Hamilton McKinnon, Frances Lambetti McKinnon, was very beautiful. She admitted it to herself and she knew she was lucky, but she was actually a little tired of hearing it. Her last name had been McKinnon for more than twenty-five years, but no one could mistake her for anything but Italian. Her coal-black hair contrasted sharply, startlingly, with a pale white, transparent complexion that was faintly blue when she was tired or cold. Her large dark eyes were set far apart under a high forehead. Her perfectly straight, rather narrow nose was softened by a generous mouth that just escaped being too generous. People who saw her for the first time sometimes thought of early paintings of the Madonna, but today, with her hair pulled tightly into a knot at the nape of her neck, she looked more like a lady of ancient Rome, the wife of a prominent senator, virtuous and rather severe. She usually dressed with flair, with a sense of humor, even, but because this was a family occasion, her husband's family, and because her husband's family was what it was, her style was understated. Under the light gray Chanel suit that she kept in the back of the closet for exactly this kind of event, she wore a pale pink blouse and a double string of pink pearls.

The party she was temporarily escaping was being held in her sister-in-law's apartment at Ten Gracie Square, all the way east between Eighty-third and Eighty-fourth. Dorothy McKinnon Clough, Hamilton's sister, had gathered a collection of McKinnons and Cloughs and Armitages — the last were her son-in-law's family — here this afternoon after the christening of her first grandchild at Saint James's, the Episcopal church on Madison Avenue where what's left of Old New York commemorates itself. The little baby girl, Sarah, was being carried around the room by her grandmother. Everyone had to say something to her, but she only frowned more deeply when their huge faces loomed up in front of hers. There was a long line of baby-drool down the front of her Belgian lace christening gown.

"Darling little thing, and already so much hair!"

"Tiniest little hands!"

"You were a good little girl at the church today, Sarah!"

Frances took a deep breath, put out her cigarette, and took the ashtray back into the room, exchanging it with a maid for a cup of tea. Baby was promptly brought up to her. Short, overweight, and overdressed, Dorothy was perspiring in her heavy blue silk suit from the effort of carrying her. Why couldn't she leave well enough alone? Frances wondered. That absurd Queen Mother flowered hat or the mass of dyed reddish-brown curls (glowing faintly with a purplish shimmer), but not both; the ugly diamond-and-pearl brooch or the big matching earrings, but not both.

"Now, smile for your Great-aunt Frances, Sarah. Maybe you'll be as beautiful as she is when you're all grown up."

Frances liked babies, but she loathed these three-way conversations in which they were talked to and answered for. She spoke directly to her sister-in-law. "She's awfully pretty, Dorothy. You must be very proud. I was thinking how sad it is that Spence isn't here to see her." Frances knew Spencer Clough would have been much more excited by a new polo pony than by a new granddaughter, but she was in her automatic family mode and she could murmur the right things to his widow.

"I know. Of course. I thought about that too." Dorothy's speech was just slightly slowed down, Frances noticed, and for all her fluttering, there really wasn't very much expression to it; her words were delivered in a kind of monotone. Ever since Spence died, she knew, she'd been on mood elevators — no, antidepressants was what they called them — and tranquilizers as well, she was sure. She felt genuinely sorry for Dorothy, she knew what a hole his death had left in her life, but she wondered if it might not be better to somehow stumble through this period without pharmaceutical help. She'd never been very close to her sister-in-law, but it looked like there was a danger of her turning into one of those matronly zombies, and she — who never took anything stronger than aspirin — was a little concerned.

"It's helped me so much to have this precious little thing just now, just almost a year since I lost Spence. I'm so glad you came along when you did, Sarah, and you've been the best little baby what ever was!"

Frances's irritation came back, stronger than ever after her moment of sympathy. She hated euphemisms for death: people *died;* when they were *lost,* she was always tempted to look under the sofa for them. I'd better get out of here, she thought. Soon.

"Oh, Ham's signaling for us to go," she said brightly, suddenly. It wasn't true, but Frances smiled over Dorothy's shoulder to Hamilton's back at the far end of the room. She thanked Dorothy for a lovely party, stroked little Sarah's amazingly silky hair for a moment, and excused herself. Ham would need only the slightest nudge from her to know she couldn't stand a minute more, and he'd make all the excuses himself so her manners wouldn't look so bad.

Hamilton McKinnon, a big, heavy man who carried himself rather stiffly, was awkwardly balancing his cup of tea and stooping down to hear something a little girl was saying. He was distinguished, more because of his manner than because of any real handsomeness, although his face seemed to suit him better now, in his late fifties, than it had when he was younger. His hair had been gray for years, but lately — to his fury — it was receding back from his forehead, which called attention away from an ironic, amused, but rather thin mouth to pale blue eyes under gray brows. They were very intelligent eyes and he was a very intelligent man. He'd tripled the McKinnon fortune since it came under his control, and he was respected on Wall Street as very few men were.

For all his power, and for all the weight of the McKinnon name, there was a shyness, a reserve, that had always been there in him. It was seldom broken, except by Frances, by his brother and sister, and by children. He relaxed with children. They responded to Frances because she always treated them like adults, but in Hamilton they sensed an odd, quirky childishness and they loved him for it. The charity to which he donated the most time and money was a network of foster-care and day-care centers all around the city, in all the boroughs, and one of his favorite things to do when he found an extra hour or two was to visit one of them and talk to the children. Frances was touched and a little saddened now, seeing him with this little blonde girl who must be one of the Cloughs. She and Hamilton had no children of their own.

Together, they said good-bye and congratulations again to little Sarah's parents, Dorothy's daughter Peekie and her husband, and made their way to the elevator. The car was waiting for them downstairs, and Danny held the door for them. Frances sank back against the creamy leather, told him to take her home first and then to take Mr. McKinnon back to his office, and pushed the button to raise the glass partition. As the big old Bentley dipped into Eighty-third and purred west, she turned to Hamilton.

"Great-aunt Frances," she sighed. "There's probably one in Dickens somewhere, an old, old prune. . . ."

He smiled. "Let's stop and ask someone on the sidewalk if he thinks you look like a prune."

"No, let's not. I'm sorry, it's my usual post-Dorothy complaints. Her branch of the family makes me feel so *old* — even older than usual, because they never change, I suppose. That apartment, exactly the same as twenty-five years ago: when a slipcover wears out, she replaces it with the same pattern, and it's all in such good taste it makes my teeth itch. And all those Cloughs are even stuffier, and the Armitages are the worst of all, and that poor little baby — is she two months old? She doesn't have a chance."

"Is that what you were thinking when you were over by the window?"

"Oh, you saw me. I'm sure they all thought, 'Frances is being strange again . . . such an odd, foreign-looking woman.' "

"I'm sure they didn't, Franny. Anyway, it wouldn't matter what they thought. They're only in-laws of in-laws."

She lowered the window to let in the gentle air. "Well, I'm sure she sides with them. She tolerates me, darling, because I'm married to you and there isn't anything she can do about it, but she doesn't like me and she doesn't understand me and she never did and she never will." She knew Ham would like to pretend it wasn't true when she talked like this, but he was too honest to deny it. They were quiet for a moment.

"Actually," she said, "I was thinking how ugly her view is — it's been a long time since I was there in the daytime. I can't understand why people pay so much money to turn their backs on Manhattan. Looking out to Queens, it might as well be Chicago. And she can see Harlem, too, and Harlem can see Dorothy, and I wonder if she ever thinks about it. It's a lot of pretty lights at night but . . ."

She trailed off, realizing what a cheap irony it was and how unfair. Every year, millions of McKinnon dollars went to medical research, to the arts, and especially to programs that filled some need the government agencies had missed. Hamilton and Dorothy were far more concerned than many of their friends were, but their generosity was institutionalized in the form of the McKinnon Foundation. Their brother, Frederick, the eldest, more outgoing and easygoing than Hamilton, ran the Foundation. It was Frederick who was known as the philanthropist. His wife had died many years ago now, and as Frances's only real friend in the whole family, he was often her escort for openings and parties that Hamilton either didn't have time for or didn't care about. Frederick had been out of town today, and she'd missed him.

"In any case, that crowd shouldn't make you feel old, my dear. They *are* older than you, or at least Dorothy and the other grandparents are."

"But I'll be forty-seven next month." She knew she was fishing, she knew exactly what Hamilton would say, but she had to hear it anyway. She seemed to need reassurance more and more often these days.

"My God, Franny, I've got twelve years on you, or you've got twelve years on me, whichever it is, and how many times have people thought you were my daughter, to my complete mortification? You're one of the most beautiful women in the city and you know it, when you're honest with yourself. You have more life in your little finger than that whole roomful of people combined. It never ceases to amaze me that you worry about your age at all."

She pressed his hand. "Thank you, Ham. You always know what to say when I feel this way." She looked out the window and laughed softly.

"The godmother," Hamilton mused. "She kissed me and called me 'Uncle Ham,' but for the life of me . . ."

"Peekie's oldest friend. Jan, um, Franklin. You haven't seen her since she was little, and now she's all grown up and Frenchified. She's something cultural in the embassy in Paris."

"Oh. That explains her cologne. Linden blossom. But I would have thought it was for gentlemen. . . ."

Something in his voice caused her to turn from the window and peer at him, but his face reflected nothing of what she thought she'd heard. "Those lines aren't so rigid anymore," she said slowly, wondering when Ham had ever learned to tell a linden blossom from a lily blossom, surprised once again by the odd bits of information he tucked away in his mind. "Are you definite about tonight? You're going to that dreary dinner and sit around and smoke smuggled Havanas and argue about mergers and splits and takeovers and things?"

"And enjoy myself. And you?"

"A thing at the French Institute and then dinner with Trish. I don't know where she's booked. Rudi's, probably."

"Is that the place in the Village? I've never been there, have I?" Hamilton knew, not because it mattered much to him but because the knowledge was in his blood, which Van Rensselaer had married which Vanderbilt, but sometimes Frances went off in very different directions, and he didn't always remember the places and people in her world.

"It's on Second Avenue in the Sixties and no, I don't think you have." They'd pulled up in front of a concrete and glass building. "Have a good time and say hello to any of those old robber barons who remember me." She was fishing again.

"They all remember the beautiful Frances. I'll have to listen to all their stories about where they saw you last and how stunning you looked."

She kissed him and hopped out. "Once again, you picked up your cue."

The lobby was high-ceilinged and simple, lined with warm, pale yellow marble. There were three spherical light fixtures, custom-designed by a firm in Milan; a vast pale blue Chinese carpet that had been woven for a merchant's Peking mansion in the early twentieth century; a grouping of Mies's Barcelona chairs covered in ivory-colored leather around the low glass table that was their companion piece; and a Henry Moore figure that reclined quietly in a shallow reflecting pool. Frances always congratulated herself on the Moore: it was smaller than the one in Lincoln Center but it was generally considered a finer example of his work. She had reason to be proud of the lobby and everything in it, because she had designed it. This graceful, apparently random selection of elements from different periods had been a public debut for her ideas about interiors — before then, she'd only worked for herself and Ham, for family, and for a few friends — and she'd been ecstatic when it was praised by critics and photographed for architectural magazines.

Until the past fifteen years, the site of 888 Fifth Avenue had been occupied by the McKinnon house, built in 1905 and nearly the last private house remaining on the avenue. It was about the same size as the neighboring Frick mansion, without including the Frick's gallery and library wings, but with its dark sandstone facade and massive Beaux-Arts ornamentation it seemed even bigger. Hamilton's father had been dead since before Frances's time, but his mother had held on in this place. After she died, he bought out Frederick's and Dorothy's shares in the house, signed the deed over to Frances, and told her to do whatever she wanted with it.

She first thought of leaving it as it was on the outside and ripping out the interior to form modern, light spaces, but then she changed her mind. It was such a conspicuously wasteful use of valuable property; nobody lived that way anymore; and, most important, the big pile of granite and sandstone had always oppressed her. It really had no particular redeeming artistic merit; it was just huge. She decided an apartment building was more appropriate; they'd sell off all the other floors and keep the top two for themselves.

She shopped for architects and finally decided on Stephen Bingham, a sober, Yale-trained man in his mid-thirties whose projects had mostly been houses in the Hamptons. He'd just opened his own office and this was a spectacular opportunity for him, an eighteen-story apartment building on Fifth Avenue with an enormous budget and all the publicity that would come with the McKinnon name. Frances and he worked closely together for a year and a half on the plans, hammering out all the small custom design elements like doorknobs and window frames, details that make the difference between an important architectural statement and merely another expensive building.

She and Hamilton moved down the street to the Pierre for the next two years while the old mansion was razed and the new building rose in its place. She was very selective about what she wanted to keep from the house to which first Hamilton's mother and then she herself had come as brides. Except for the wing that had been hers and Hamilton's, most of the house had been decorated in a heavy, dark, late Victorian nonstyle. Three of the ground-floor rooms, though, were very fine examples of rococo, brought over intact — paneling, tapestries, chandeliers, and furniture — from a Paris *hôtel de ville* at the beginning of the century. Now they were disassembled once again and given to the Metropolitan. Frances could stand the fussiness of rococo only in very small doses.

She saved certain pieces of furniture and very little of the art. Hamilton's parents and grandparents had been known for their musical evenings and for their lavish patronage of the Metropolitan Opera and the Philharmonic, but never for their art collection. There were a few decent Hudson River School landscapes, one extraordinary Rubens that a dealer had convinced them to buy at some point in the 'twenties, and a pair of Gobelin tapestries from the baronial entrance hall.

The only actual *piece* of the old house that she kept for the new building was the pair of massive bronze doors that were commissioned in Italy by Hamilton's grandfather for the main entrance. Surrounded by a heavy framework of garlands and wreaths was an enormous monogram, *Mc* superimposed on *K*. The McKinnons might not have a coat of arms, but they had had the biggest monogram on Fifth Avenue. Frances was superstitious about them; they'd been so intimidating, so symbolic of the wealth she hadn't grown up with, when she first stood in front of them. She used these panels now, in effect, in the same way: with the help of a complicated system of tracks and pulleys to handle their great weight, they became the doors to the McKinnons' private elevator, one sliding behind the other when it opened. It was usually set on self-service unless they were entertaining, and she took herself up to seventeen. She constantly rearranged furniture and art in the apartment, and the elevator itself was a victim of her restlessness. Today, an Abstract Expressionist watercolor by de Kooning hung above a low gold-and-white settee that might or might not have belonged to Pauline Bonaparte Borghese.

That had become Frances's trademark as a designer, her signature: she was known for combining pieces from wildly different periods and all corners of the earth, putting them next to one another or on top of one another to see what happened. In her foyer, at the moment, a tall Giacometti sculpture from the mid-'fifties was placed on a Shaker chest. When Marianne, the housekeeper, opened the door to her, she stood for a moment in the hallway to admire the Warhol "Marilyn" silkscreen she'd hung above a Louis XV marquetry shelf like a pier glass.

She hadn't always been so confident. She wasn't born into this world of marquetry and parquetry, and for the first few years of her marriage she'd relied on other decorators — Billy Baldwin and Sister Parish, mainly — to help her with the rooms in their wing of the old house. But while her sister-in-law and her postdeb set were gossiping over lunch tables and bridge tables, Frances was quietly giving herself the education she'd never really had. She'd sign up for a class at Columbia on Tudor history or she'd audit a class at Parsons in recaning chairs. She'd spend an entire day reading about Catherine the Great or the Chinese export trade of blue willowware. She pored over Hamilton's collection of eighteenth- and nineteenth-century caricatures and political cartoons until she could tell him things he hadn't known about them and until, finally, she could help him expand it. For years, she set aside an hour every day for one contemporary gallery or another on Fifty-seventh Street or Madison Avenue and then eventually in Soho. She wandered through the auction houses, the big ones and the obscure ones, and then she sat through a hundred auctions before she finally raised her hand to bid on a Meissen cachepot she'd fallen in love with.

There was no single moment at which she suddenly decided she could make a move, and there would never be a point at which she thought she could stop educating herself, but she gradually came to trust her own instincts and she began to relax and have fun with it all. Along the way, because her mind had soaked up so many kinds of things that interested her, she had come to know not only a genuine Queen Anne chair from a fake, but what Queen Anne herself had looked like and who her favorite prime minister had been and what kind of poetry she had read. She understood the political climate out of which the Bauhaus had sprung. She knew where Napoleon III's mistresses had lived. That wasn't true of very many designers, and of course it wouldn't have done her any good if she hadn't had an "eye" in the first place. But she did.

And of course Hamilton was there, every step of the way, quietly suggesting, never lecturing, and very often discovering new delights along with her. There were periods and artists he knew in great depth, apart from the great caricaturists in his collection like Hogarth and Daumier. He had an amazing collection of small bronzes, for instance, from the Mannerist period, that odd movement that sprang up between High Renaissance and High Baroque. He also had a beautifully developed ear for music, and although Frances never did become very sophisticated about early twentieth-century composers like Scriabin or Satie, she at least came to love what she could share with him in Beethoven and Mozart. In the same way, he had trouble looking at anything painted after about 1920, and she could point things out to him — that the abstracts of Mondrian were sometimes based on the overall composition of Vermeer, for example, or that there were sly references in Rauschenberg to Leonardo and Michelangelo — that helped him appreciate at least a few of the contemporary canvases she adored.

Still, his family could always make her remember how gauche she used to feel, and today — she couldn't help it — she needed to go through the apartment to reassure herself, to reclaim herself from them. Marianne — short, fat, rosy, and talkative — was ready to give her all the important messages and all the news, but Frances quickly cut her off with a smile, promised to meet up with her in the kitchen in a few minutes, and began to wander around the main rooms.

The other apartments in the building, one on each floor, were spacious and beautifully designed, but because the McKinnons had kept the seventeenth and eighteenth floors for themselves, the bedrooms could all be relegated to the upper floor and the seventeenth could mostly be devoted to a few spectacularly proportioned spaces. From the elevator foyer, she crossed the wide corridor into the living room on the front side of the building, by far the biggest room. Its great length of floor-to-ceiling windows looked out across Fifth to the entire park and all the towers that bordered it on the north, the south, and the west. The expanse of glass was broken every ten feet by the half curve of a single fluted wooden Doric column. These columns were painted as faux marble now — she'd done it herself and she was thrilled with the effect — but there had been times when they were white or deep green or speckled faux granite. The three layers of translucent silk draperies echoed the exact gray and ivory shades of the columns. Frances hated tinted glass in any form in any environment except offices or airports — it made her claustrophobic and she always wanted to scratch a hole in it to see what color the sky *really* was at that moment — so the entire building was obliged by contract to use pale-colored drapes for privacy and to filter out the afternoon sun.

The room was so big that it was necessary to break it up into smaller areas, but this was where Frances experimented the most, and she was forever expanding or contracting them, changing the flow around them and the treasures that might be found within each of them. The carpeting was a pale, neutral taupe, but some of the groupings were defined by rugs laid on top of it. At the moment, the area in front of the enormous white (real rather than faux) marble fireplace, which had come from an antebellum house in Charleston, was overlaid with a big late nineteenth-century Aubusson in pale pinks and greens. The furniture there at the moment was a grouping that Frances had designed and had even thought of marketing: armchairs that were a kind of homage to the Mission style, their clean, comfortable lines updated in oak bleached nearly white, their cushions covered in deep green leather. Over the fireplace, between the pair of pillars that mirrored the ones along the windows but which were painted with dull reddish gold leaf, was a brooding Rauschenberg assemblage from the late 'fifties that had bits of wooden toys swept into folds of stiff canvas.

She straightened these chairs now so they were in perfect alignment, and then she removed one browning blossom from among the white camellias that floated in a shallow, bright green Fiesta ware bowl on the cubed table. In another part of the room, she plumped the monkey fur pillows of a gilt Louis XIV armchair and smiled again — a little meanly — at how appalled her mother-in-law would be if she could see one of her favorite coats put to this use. She rearranged two robin's-egg-blue velvet Charles X chaises longues so they were side by side, facing out to the park with a Frank Lloyd Wright wrought-iron floor lamp between them. They were only excuses for her to touch these things, to get reacquainted with her home again.

Italian seventeenth-century double doors — painted in trompe l'oeil to give the illusion of an endless vista of gardens and fountains — led to the dining room, the other room on this floor that faced out to the park. She ran her hand along the satiny surface of the enormous rosewood slab that was supported by four cast aluminum eagles that had once perched on the four corners of a WPA post office in a little town in Illinois. She stood back from the Rubens that was hung over the long Sheraton sideboard and wondered for the millionth time if this kind of pink-and-white overblown fleshiness was ever going to be considered desirable again — and hoped not. Then she passed on through the serving pantry and into the kitchen.

She was only halfway through the swinging door when Marianne began to talk. Jean-Yves would be here at five-thirty instead of five. The cleaners smashed a button on one of Mr. McKinnon's jackets. The delivery boy from the market dropped his pack of cigarettes and a reefer rolled out. She followed Frances down the corridor and upstairs to her bedroom, accounting for everything that had happened since noon, both in her own domain and — because she traveled up and down the service elevator all day — most of the other apartments in the building.

Marianne and her husband, Danny, had worked for the McKinnons since before Frances's marriage. They lived in a comfortable three-room suite that opened off the kitchen, and Frances considered them part of the family, but she sometimes wished she could be one of those ladies who treated their servants like so many electrical appliances. It was a constant argument she had with herself. Jean-Yves, for instance, her hairdresser, was usually late, and most of the women she knew would have thrown a tantrum on principle. She simply allowed for an extra half hour every time he came and it worked out fine, but she didn't think she should be letting him get away with it.

Finally alone in the bedroom, she stripped off the Chanel suit and the blouse and threw them in a heap on the floor, pretending for a minute that she really was a splendidly spoiled creature instead of boringly considerate. She bathed quickly, wrapped herself in her favorite heavy silver silk kimono, sighed, picked up her clothes, and hung them in the section of the closet that meant Worn: Check Them Over to the woman who came three mornings a week to look after them. Then she went into the sitting room that connected her bedroom with Hamilton's, got herself a Diet Pepsi from the little refrigerator, and went upstairs. Above the duplex, forming a very partial nineteenth floor, was a single room that was basically a glass box. The only access to it was through her bedroom, up a spiral staircase, and it shared the roof with a cleverly disguised water tank and a terrace filled with shrubs and trees.

Steve Bingham's office was just a few blocks away, and Frances had her own staff of three installed there, plus a couple of his people she could use for drafting or researching or "resourcing." This, though, was where she often worked, a refuge meant just for her, sparsely furnished with a drawing board, a desk, and some files. There was also a big, overstuffed chair, covered with a chintz pattern that was very different from anything else in the McKinnon apartment. It was a bit of nostalgia from her childhood, when she used to climb onto it to read and daydream for hours. She curled up there now, skimmed through some papers, and picked up the phone to return the most urgent calls.

4

JUST BEFORE SIX, Mario toured the kitchen again quickly and then made his way through the dining room, where the lights were lowered and the stage was now set, to the captains' station. The first meals would be pretheater (or preballet or preopera) suppers, usually not very elaborate, and the room wouldn't really be filled until a little later. For the next couple of hours he was able to have a word or two with everyone, to confer with Lillian whenever she needed him, and to do a little more work in the office. By eight, though, he was on the floor full-time, circulating effortlessly, leading people to their tables when both captains were busy, chatting, congratulating, or commiserating like the best kind of host at the best kind of party.

Straightening up from the group he was advising on wine, he saw Maggie come through the bar with Jim Wilkins in tow. She was stopping every few feet to say hello to someone, and when she caught sight of him she gave him a tight, tired smile. Her white jersey dress clung slightly, showing off her full breasts and hips and her cheerleader legs. Most of the men she was passing knew she was half of a couple, but that didn't mean they couldn't and didn't appreciate her. She wasn't a classic beauty, but she had the kind of fresh, all-American looks that would sell millions of bars of soap if she'd chosen to sell soap instead of contemporary art — glowing skin with a few freckles, brilliant blue eyes, and corn-silk hair.

She spent a little longer with a deeply tanned man who was sitting at the bar, until Jim lost his patience and pulled her up to the dining-room entrance. When she kissed Mario, it was one of their public, cheeky kisses, but he whispered in her ear, "I thought I'd come down tonight after work?"

"Yes. Please. Goody," she breathed. "But I can't promise any, um, spectacular action, after the day I've had and after dinner with this drainer."

He held out his hand to Jim. "How's it going? Maggie says your show's going to be beautiful."

Jim shrugged. "Maybe. She changes her mind every five minutes about which pieces to use and her jerk-off workmen are so retarded they're bound to fuck up the installation, but maybe it'll go okay."

Maggie made a face at him. "They're not retarded, and you should be happy you've got a dealer who's a perfectionist." She turned back to Mario. "Where have you put us? I didn't give Lillian much notice, but I'm starved."

He led them to a small rounded table that fit snugly into a curve of the banquette, halfway along the left side of the room. He started to move off when the waiter came up for their drink orders, but Maggie stopped him.

"Chuck's out at the bar," she said, no longer smiling. "Did you notice?" Chuck was her brother, and of course Mario had noticed and he knew exactly what she meant.

"Saw him, but don't worry. Nowhere near his limit."

She rolled her eyes. "Yet. He had that *look,* y'know? Like he was settling in for the night?"

He promised to do what he could — they both knew that was probably nothing at all — and with a nod to Jim he left them alone. Maggie tried to concentrate on dollars and cents. At his old gallery, the prices for Jim's work had been very gradually raised, but now he was determined to use this show as a pretext for a sudden jump and she was just as determined to keep the level at what she instinctively knew was right for this point in his career. She waited till their drinks came and they'd ordered dinner before pulling a crumpled piece of paper out of her purse. Jim wasn't ready yet.

"You could do better than that dumb Italian faggot," he said.

She was next to him on the banquette, and she turned her head slowly without moving her shoulders. "You're dead wrong on two out of three, but you've been clever enough to pin down his ancestry." The day suddenly caught up with her, and she wanted to cry. Coke early this afternoon at his place, adrenaline all afternoon and into the evening at the gallery, then seeing her brother just now, well on his way to another drunken scene. She was crashing, and she didn't think she could get through either dinner or the price list without a little artificial help. "I'm going to go powder my nose, if you'd be so kind as to lend me something to powder it with. When I come back, please, can we talk about money? Please?" Under the tablecloth, he wordlessly passed her the vial, its tiny silver spoon linked to it with a thin chain, and helped her push the table away so she could get up. It wasn't much — it certainly wasn't an apology — but she chose to believe it was a concession of some sort.

* * *

From the back of the dining room, Mario watched a young couple stop at Maggie's table for a moment before moving on to their own. The man was tall and painfully thin, with curly sandy hair, blue eyes, and a bony face that was undeniably Irish, handsome and monkeyish at the same time. Under a brown corduroy suit, he wore a tattersall check shirt and a knitted wool tie. A few people recognized him as he ambled along with his hands in his jacket pockets behind the girl and the captain, but he didn't seem to be noticing.

The girl, on the other hand, was trying a little too hard to show she didn't care about where she was or what kind of entrance she was making or whether anyone was recognizing her date. Mario didn't like her; even if he hadn't already met her once for a few minutes, he'd have known he didn't like her. She was holding her chin just a shade too high; she wasn't moving her head from side to side quite enough; and he was sure her pale eyes were peripherally appraising the room and comparing herself with everyone in it. She was pretty — very pretty, he decided, to be fair — and slim and beautifully poised. Fine, sun-streaked blonde hair fell straight to her shoulders in no particular style. She was about his age, but her clothes — Ralph Lauren, he guessed — were what suburban matrons bought so they could look like her, not what girls her age usually bought for themselves.

Patrick Mahoney, a writer who'd just made a big splash with his second novel, had been Mario's closest friend since college days. Judith — Chesterfield? No, Davenport, he thought, and of course it was one of those *Social Register* names — had the kind of vague public relations job at Sotheby's that rich girls sometimes had, but he was sure she didn't buy those clothes and all that turquoise-and-silver jewelry on the starvation wages auction houses paid. Maggie knew her slightly and had introduced her to both Mario and Patrick at a Martha Graham dance benefit a few nights before. He hadn't talked to Patrick since then, but he'd suspected something had clicked, so he wasn't surprised to see them together now.

Knowing how hard it was for his friend to pick up the phone and ask someone out, he was at least glad for him on that account. But hell, he thought, why can't Patrick ever date a different *type* — a Jewish sociologist or a French rock singer or even some equally talented and neurotic writer? At Princeton and then in New York, Patrick had consistently fallen in love with one Judith after another. Mario couldn't even remember their names now because they were all alike: blonde, pretty, smart enough, and — as far as Mario was concerned — totally uninteresting. If they weren't actually debutantes, it was only because they'd decided coming out was out that season.

Patrick had a reputation as a loner who was so wrapped up in his writing that he couldn't be bothered most of the time with women, and only Mario knew how unhappy he made himself over his goddesses. They were impressed by him, they basked in the reflected glow of his brilliance, and they were happy to celebrate with him when his short stories were accepted by the *New Yorker* and then when his first novel was published. But when he worked himself up to telling them how he felt, they inevitably said it was impossible or that he had to grow up or that they were seeing someone else. He was their token poet, and Mario finally got him to admit they were tokens to him, too, like all obsessions. They represented something golden and unattainable, something completely alien to the blue-collar Irish block in Baltimore where he was raised. His finest writing was tough and realistic, grounded in what he knew best. He wasn't in the least bit impressed by wealth as wealth, but in spite of himself he was dazzled by the kind of girl that generations of it produced.

Anyway, he hadn't been seeing anyone at all for a few months, and this was obviously going to be the current model and Mario might as well get used to it. Patrick was his good friend. Mario was his host and therefore he was Judith's host. He moved toward their table.

* * *

"It'll be close," Frances said to Trish. They were on a banquette against the right wall, lingering over coffee and dessert. "I can't tell you for sure till tomorrow 'cause I'll have to call a couple of the suppliers. The carpet should be okay, but I'm not positive about all the custom cabinets. They promised the glass for the tenth. . . ."

She wrote in a little notebook while Trish — Patricia Green — puffed on a cigarette, ran a hand through her spiky salt-and-pepper hair, and looked out across the room. She was short, overweight, and, until she smiled, a little tough looking, a handsome, no-nonsense woman but not a beautiful one. Everyone assumed she was older than Frances. She never corrected them — she was a loyal friend and not particularly vain — but, in fact, they were exactly the same age, closest friends since high school. Tonight, they'd been to a reception at the French Institute for a show of Poiret dresses from the 'teens and 'twenties, and then they'd gossiped all through dinner, putting off business till now.

Trish's name in the fashion world was well established for her classic suits — one of which she wore tonight — and her sumptuously beaded evening gowns, but she was about to take the plunge into ready-to-wear. Frances was designing the extra twenty thousand square feet Patricia Green Incorporated had taken in the 550 Building on Seventh Avenue. That was going according to schedule, but the trouble now was the boutique, which Frances was also doing, where the new line would make its debut. It would be on the Designer floor at Bloomingdale's, and the people there had suddenly asked Trish today if she could open earlier than planned.

"I hate to admit it, but I think they're right," Trish said. "The Bloomie's brass. I'm not going to have two free minutes to rub together till December first, but it's better to open before Christmas when the store's jammed and people can get used to my name being there, and then when they really do heavy buying for spring they'll remember me."

"But you'll still open with the resort collection?" Trish nodded. "And you want me to promise I can get it done? All right, I promise. It'll cost you, though, in overtime and rush shipments."

"That's okay. Really. But what about your idea? You said you had an Idea, in capital letters."

"I did. I do. I was thinking you need a pinch of flash, just a little sparkle somewhere. We don't want all the bleached wood and soft colors to put people to sleep."

"I like that look," Trish protested. "I don't want that stainless steel and glass crap a lot of the others on that floor have."

"Don't worry. We had the right idea and I'm not going back on it. We certainly want a contrast to their spaces, but there's a danger of looking a little drab. That's the problem with having a dozen boutiques together: you have to look at what everyone else did with their spaces."

"I'm sure you're right. I mean, I'm paying you to be right, aren't I?"

"Through the nose. But let me tell you. It's just a matter of a couple of details and there's still time. The draperies on the dressing rooms —"

"— are going to be that print with my logo, dark green on pale green."

"Well, we'll use that fabric at 550 somewhere. At Bloomie's, I want copper lamé — no, it isn't copper, exactly, it's sort of a bronze color I have in mind. We'll still have the logo — some people in Germany do that kind of custom work, and they can weave it dark on light, and on the other side it'll be light on dark. It's perfect, sort of 'warm glitter,' if that doesn't sound too dumb. But the material will be twice as heavy and we'll have to order stronger tracks or else . . . just need . . ." She wrote quickly, and then she snapped the book shut, sat up, and poured more coffee for herself.

Trish had smiled and nodded to a table across the room. "Why does she look so familiar?" Frances asked.

"She's Max Silverman's director. Maggie . . . Westerly? Wetherby. Max probably swoops you up himself whenever you're down there, but she's helped me once or twice. Did you hear he'd been sick?"

Frances shook her head. "A bypass, I think. Something like that, but he's all right now. Maggie's running it for a while, and I'll bet she's worth her weight in gold. She's smart and she moves fast and she could sell — what? — menorahs to the Iranians?"

"And who's Redbeard?"

"Jim Wilkins. Poor thing. Not him, her. He's a real old-fashioned son of a bitch. Reminded me of Josh, in fact, the one time I met him." Josh was the second of Trish's three husbands, three sons of bitches in different ways. Trish had symmetrically had a child by each — all in college or graduate school by now — two boys and a girl, who somehow turned out well in spite of their fathers. Frances loved them and spoiled them and envied her for having them. Trish now had a long-standing, separate-apartments relationship with a handbag manufacturer who laughed too much but whom she considered — and Frances agreed with her — by far the best of the lot.

"The Foundation's probably going to commission him to do a piece for the Bank, did I tell you? But haven't I seen Maggie . . ."

"Yes, you have." Trish noticed Mario approaching before Frances did.

"Shall I send the dessert cart over again?" he asked Trish neutrally.

"You saw me snitching her éclair, didn't you?" He nodded, smiling.

"It's an old trick." Frances laughed up at him. "First, she gets me to order some unbelievably sweet thing I don't want and then she tries just a bite and then all of a sudden it's not there anymore."

Mario looked at Trish. "It's true," she sighed. "It never tastes as good when I order it myself, because then there's too much guilt mixed in. But, hell, I'm a hardworking babe and I've had a long day, and yes, please send it over. Frances wants another." He bowed solemnly and moved off.

"I like that man," Trish said when they were alone. "And he has the good taste to be smitten by you, which of course doesn't make him unique. . . ."

"I was *about* to ask you if I haven't seen her, Maggie, at things with him. And thank you — you're my biggest fan club and morale booster and peanut gallery — but you're mistaken."

"Yes, you have seen them together. Yes, they've been an item for a year or two, I think. No, I'm not mistaken. *You* may not be aware of it, and maybe *he* isn't even aware of it, but he's been hovering around you like an Italian helicopter all night, and I noticed he remembered what you drink. He didn't remember what *I* drink, and I come here at least as much as you do." The dessert trolley arrived then and took all of Trish's attention.

* * *

It was just after midnight when Mario saw the captain showing Carole Todd and her group to a table in the center of the room. She was with another woman and some men, six of them altogether, but it was Carole who was the focus of attention for the whole restaurant. It happened everywhere she went, even with the crowd at Rudi's. It wasn't only that she was striking and that heads would have turned in any case, but because she was Carole Todd, a brilliant actress and an amazingly clever (and demanding) manager of her own career, who'd somehow been able to straddle the great gulf between Broadway and Hollywood as almost no one else had ever done. Thirty-five now, she'd already collected two Oscars, two Tonys, and a reputation as one of the more difficult talents on either coast. She took chances, she played wildly different parts, but there was something of her that came through in all her characters without smothering them. She was a star who happened to be a great actress, or vice versa.

Mario was just as glad Maggie had already left because she was unreasonably jealous of Carole. It wasn't appropriate — the time he'd spent with Carole had been before he knew Maggie — but she'd become one of those ridiculous symbols lovers throw at each other in arguments. "I suppose *Carole* doesn't do it that way," she'd say, or "I'm sure *Carole* wouldn't think so, but . . ." The affair had been fun, short, and (except for one display of temper, which left him with a scar that might be visible someday if he ever went bald) painless. Carole had gone back to Hollywood and met a commodities trader and then a rock producer and then someone else; he'd stayed in New York and met Maggie. Now, even though they didn't see one another very often, he considered her a friend — a complicated woman, mercurial, unbelievably selfish and then suddenly so generous and loving that it was easy to forget the rough edges.

She looked very different from the last time he'd seen her, but he'd discovered she never stayed the same for more than a few months. Her chestnut hair was longer, coiled on top of her head with a few wisps allowed to fall down around her face. She wore no makeup that he could see from where he was standing, but her coloring was extraordinary, a high, healthy beauty with eyes that were a rare green. Her nose was sharp and slightly cleft at the end, and her mouth was full and wide with teeth that were a tiny bit crooked. She'd refused to have them capped, and she'd been right. With her high cheekbones and her strong jawline, the result was fascinating instead of only perfect.

After he threaded his way to her and leaned down for a kiss, she waved vaguely at her table. "You all know each other, don't you?" she asked in her famous whiskey voice, which Mario knew came from genes and training rather than whiskey. Everyone smiled and nodded as if everyone did, but in fact Mario had met only the other woman, who was an older character actress, and one of the men, a director. They were involved in an argument about stage lighting, and he had Carole to himself.

"These are my buddies. For the run of the show, anyway. We're starting previews next week, you know. Opening in a month, knock wood." She rapped on the table, then looked under the tablecloth.

"It's wood," he laughed. "But is it necessary? Is there trouble?"

"No, not exactly. Just jitters, because it's a revival of a revival and the backers are all so nervous we have meetings about twice a day. But tell me about you. I haven't seen you since . . . May?"

"June? I'm okay. Same old stuff, except there might be something on the horizon, but . . ."

"But this isn't the time or place. We could have lunch, maybe? If I ever get myself sorted out? I'm staying at a friend's for now, but I bought an apartment over on Central Park West and I'm feeling like really *nesting* for the first time in my life. I want Frances McKinnon to do it."

"I'm impressed."

"So am I. And scared, I can admit to you. Da lady and da showgirl. We've made an appointment, but I haven't met her yet."

"She was here awhile ago. You'll like her. She's nice, she's beautiful, she's not . . . anything like you'd expect."

She squinted up at him. "Uh huh. And how's Maggie?"

"Fine. Blooming, in fact, because her boss is sick and she's stepped into his shoes. She was in tonight, too."

"Oh, I'm sorry we missed each other," she said with no particular inflection. She had made a rather halfhearted attempt to be friendly to Maggie at first, but Maggie had decided she was being patronized and she'd returned the overtures with a coolness that Mario suspected had surprised Carole and maybe even hurt her feelings.

"I'll send you tickets for the first night, and there's the inevitable Sardi's thing afterwards. Will you come? With Maggie?"

"Of course I'll come. I can't speak for her, but I'm sure she'll try. Will you be, uh, escorted?"

"Do you mean 'How's my love life'?" Her face softened, and so did her voice. She glanced at the rest of her table, but they weren't listening to her. "Oh, Mario, something amazing has happened, but I can't tell you about it yet. Not here, anyway."

He looked at her closely. That was what was so different about her, of course, that she seemed happier and less frantic and more . . . open, vulnerable . . . than he'd ever seen her. "It's very becoming, whatever it is. Whoever he is," he said, and she smiled shyly and squeezed his hand.

A couple on their way out passed near them just then — first the woman, one of the most powerful literary agents in town, and then a rather stocky blond man. Carole's expression changed from milky softness to cold, cold marble as he went by, her nostrils flaring as she took a deep breath. *"Who is that?"* she hissed, her hand now clutching Mario's.

"That is . . ." He had to wait until the man's head was turned. "That is John Ashton. No. Ashenden. He's a big cheese in English publishing. Why?"

"Mmmm. Doesn't matter. He can't be . . ." She relaxed her grip and then glanced at the nail marks she'd left on his wrist. "I'm sorry. Just a Pavlovian response to something."

Mario didn't think she could have seen anything but the back of a head, and it wasn't such a distinctive head, so . . . he wondered if the very faint whiff of Ashenden's cologne could possibly have anything to do with her reaction: her head had gone up and she'd sniffed the air like a thoroughbred pointer. The scent was familiar to him, too, and he remembered there'd been a French guy in his freshman dorm at Princeton who'd worn it. Linden blossom? Yes, but why . . . He forgot about it in the next instant, when he saw who had just arrived.

"If you'll just casually glance at who's coming through the bar right now," he said under his breath, "you'll be looking at the possible something on the horizon I mentioned that I'm not supposed to mention. And his wife."

She immediately threw herself into it: draining her bourbon and water; looking around for a waiter; noticing someone nonexistent in the bar and waving. Then she whistled. "If you mean Radnor and whatsername — Susan? — then it would be an unbelievable chance for . . ."

"It *could* be," he said, straightening up and going to meet the short, slightly plump man in black tie and the blonde-maned woman in blue Lacroix flounces and sapphires who towered over him. They were standing calmly with fixed smiles on their faces at the captains' station, but Mario estimated that the few seconds it took for him to reach them were just about the limit of their patience. Rick Radnor and his very social, very pretty, nearly anorexic wife didn't *wait* for things to happen, they *made* things happen. They were a phenomenon: he, at just over forty, controlled a big piece of the Monopoly board of New York real estate; she, at just under forty, had done the same thing socially.

Radnor's head start had consisted of ten stories of offices in Times Square that his moderately successful father left him. Building his own apartment buildings and office complexes, buying and renovating others, he now owned more of Manhattan than any single man in the city, maybe in the history of the city, and lately he'd begun to branch into baseball teams and television stations and anything else that took his or Susan's fancy. Newspapers interchangeably used the words *tycoon, czar,* and *mogul* to describe him. Mario favored words from the animal kingdom like *tiger, shark,* and *piranha*. The Radnors disgusted him and fascinated him, but they seemed to like him and it was just possible they could be very, very helpful.

They'd been vague with Lillian about what time they'd be getting here after the opera tonight — she was on the board at the Met, of course; she'd wrangled her way onto every important board in town — but he'd held their favorite table and he led them to it now after an overly firm handshake and an airy, don't-smear-the-makeup kiss.

"Lively crowd at the bar tonight," Radnor said as Mario pushed their table snugly into them. He wasn't making small talk; he was lodging a complaint, and he was right: the noise from the bar was spilling over into the dining room and it shouldn't have. It was only the latest of the small, dissatisfied sounds he and Susan had been making lately about Rudi's — the crowd, the wine list, the service — and Mario was always put in the position of either agreeing and apologizing or excusing and defending. In fact, he knew exactly what they meant: there *were* a few moth holes and stains in what should have been the seamless fabric of Rudi's, the sort that Mario couldn't do much about.

Radnor's subtext was, of course, that they'd take their business elsewhere if only there were an appropriate elsewhere. The sub-subtext had consisted of extremely general hints that Mario himself ought to be getting out and providing that alternative and that maybe there would be some way they could make that happen for him. So far, though, all of Rick's and Susan's talk had centered around the need for spectacular new restaurants in two of Radnor's projects. One was a gigantic office/apartment/retail complex over on the East River that wouldn't be finished for at least a year and a half. The other was a blue mirrored-glass tower on Fifty-eighth Street that was nearer completion but that Mario privately thought was one of the ugliest buildings New York had ever seen.

He was chatting with them about the new production of *Maria Stuarda* they'd just come from, keeping them company till the waiter brought their drinks, when there was a crash of broken glass in the bar, followed by a thump, by more broken glass, and finally by silence. The Radnors looked up at him with identically cocked eyebrows. He excused himself, got to the front as fast as he could without running, and found exactly what he'd expected. Chuck Wetherby, Maggie's brother, was on the floor, one foot twisted in the rungs of a fallen bar stool. Shattered bar glasses and ashtrays lay around him and under him, and his hands and face were bloody. A bewildered man with a drink running down his face stood over him.

Half an hour later, after wrestling Chuck into a cab with the doorman's help and then stopping at nearly every table in the house to apologize, Mario retreated to his office for a cigarette. Much as he'd like to, he couldn't put Chuck on the doorman's *non grata* list and he couldn't tell the bartenders not to serve him. It was Rudi's restaurant, and Chuck was Rudi's boyfriend; or, rather, Rudi was infatuated by Chuck, but it wasn't clear, even to Maggie (probably not even to Chuck), how he felt about Rudi. He'd lived in Rudi's town house for two years; he shared Rudi's bed, presumably; but he didn't talk about it and he was anything but affectionate to Rudi in public. He used Rudi's credit cards, too, and Mario knew that the expensive tennis lessons he gave at the Metropolitan Athletic Club only provided him with pocket money. Chuck was in his early thirties now, his waist was thickening and a capillary or two had blossomed in his face, but the golden boy was still there somewhere. When he was relatively sober, he charmed women and men and it was easy to see Maggie in him. When he was drunk, he reminisced about the tennis circuit and picked fights with anyone who didn't believe he'd been at Forest Hills, which was what had happened tonight.

Just as Mario was picking up the phone to call Rudi and explain, he saw him coming through the kitchen from the delivery entrance, heading straight for the office and brushing past everyone. He opened the office door carefully and closed it behind him just as carefully, as if he were barely controlling an urge to throw it open and slam it shut.

"Chuck was dumped in the foyer by some Irish thug of a cabdriver like a sack of potatoes," Rudi said. "He was bleeding in about twenty places and he was yelling about the manager of this classy little establishment. Now, let's have an explanation, please." He began softly, just as he'd closed the door softly, but the last few words were delivered at full volume. As always when he was excited, he lost control of his voice and his Yugoslav accent. Mario looked at him calmly. Rudi, pushing sixty, worked very hard at maintaining his body and his dark good looks. He went to a gym every day and a tanning salon twice a week. Tucks had been taken around his eyes and plugs of hair had been moved around his head. The usual effect was a caricature of impersonal handsomeness with just a suggestion of dissipation, but tonight nothing was quite in place. His face was distorted in anger and his hair wasn't combed carefully enough to hide the transplants. The white cashmere turtleneck he wore had a few spots of blood on it. His hands were clenched in the front pockets of his tailor-made khakis, stretching the fabric to its limit.

"Is Chuck okay?" Mario finally said.

"How fucking *dare* you ask me if Chuck's okay! Why didn't you bring him home yourself if you're so goddamn concerned if Chuck's okay?" Rudi was looking down at himself. "Chuck was bleeding and this is his blood on my sweater and you did it." Now the squeak had become a whine.

Jesus, Mario said to himself, trust Rudi to get hysterical in any situation where Chuck's concerned. He buzzed the bar on the intercom for glasses and Courvoisier, and then he motioned for Rudi to sit down. When the bottle was brought in and Rudi had tossed down a couple of shots, he seemed to be a little more in control of himself.

"I don't see why you had to handle it that way, Mario. It's never happened before."

"Never happened before? I can think of about five times lately when someone had to help him to a cab."

"But this time he was hurt."

"Yeah, he was hurt because he broke a bunch of glasses and then lost his balance and fell on them. After throwing a drink in Norm Epstein's face, by the way. I wasn't even there when it happened. Give me a little support, for Christ's sake!"

"Chuck says you insulted him." His voice was back in its normal range.

"I told him not to do it again. If that's insulting him, I insulted him. If you want Chuck to make his own little Kristallnacht in here once a week or every night for the next year, it's your business, Rudi. Just don't expect me to stick around to watch you go broke."

"You don't know how to handle him."

"Rudi." Mario gripped his glass. "You obviously pay more attention to Chuck than I do. It's been pretty busy tonight and you weren't here and I didn't have time to check up on Chuck's intake every ten minutes. You're right, though; I don't know how to handle him and neither does anybody else, because he's a drunk. He'll listen to you because you live together, and you can usually beg him to go home. You think it'd help if *I* begged Chuck? When you're not here, the only thing I can do is ask him to leave. If he won't leave when I ask him, then . . ."

"I think Chuck hates you, Mario."

"I can't do anything about that. I've been pretty decent to him, for your sake and for Maggie's sake. He's made a career out of ruining himself. What do you want me to do?"

"Just try to understand him."

Mario sighed. He was tired and hungry and he was more than bored with Rudi and Chuck. He promised to try to understand him.

5

THE *SOFT MEOWS* outside the bedroom door started up as soon as the alarm went off, and Maggie realized before her mind was really functioning that Mario must have spent the night. Her kitties would usually be sleeping with her, two at the foot of the bed and two up near her face, but Mario was one of those people who didn't like cats, and she had to keep them away when he was here. Then she sensed Mario himself. The bed was big and they weren't pressed together, but there was a scent, a weight on the other side of the bed, a warmth under the covers, and the very faint sound of regular breathing. She opened one eye a crack to look at him. He was sprawled on his back with the blankets up to his chest, one arm flung out in her direction and the other lying along his side. He became a child again when his features relaxed in sleep, and she could see what he must have looked like when he was a little boy. She thought it was probably true of everyone until they were old; then, she supposed, people start to look the way they will when they're dead.

Her head felt thick. When she stood up, she was so groggy she nearly fell back onto the bed, and she remembered she'd taken a sleeping pill the night before. She rarely needed one — certainly not for the past couple of weeks, when she'd gone to sleep as soon as her head connected with her pillow — but now Jim's show was about to open, tomorrow night. So yesterday had been the longest, most brutal day yet, because it had included a heavy dose of Jim. She calculated an even dozen arguments with him about how the show would be installed, and she'd probably overindulged herself, just a little, with the coke he kept laying out. Her mind was still racing at two this morning, so right after Mario showed up she'd taken this pill.

She staggered once or twice on her way down the hall to the kitchen, the cats following her and rubbing against her legs. Nice, Maggie, she said to herself while she was grinding coffee beans. Next time take half a pill and take it earlier, so you get something like a full night's rest. Today's going to be even heavier than yesterday; tomorrow will be the worst of all; and your mind is about as sharp as a wooden spoon, just to borrow a little kitchen imagery. She started the coffee maker, and then she reached behind the nutmeg in the cupboard for the little vial of coke she'd hidden there. It was the first time she'd ever actually bought any, and the dealer Jim sent her to had sneered when she asked for only two grams. It made her feel wicked and criminal and somehow grown-up at the same time, even if it was just a little emergency ration and she'd barely touched it in the week she'd had it. This can certainly be considered an emergency, though, she said to herself as she took a little in each nostril and immediately felt her head clear. I need help getting through today and tomorrow, just till the opening — well, maybe including the opening — but after that I won't buy any more and I won't accept any more from Jim or anyone else.

Back in the bedroom, after brushing her teeth and sniffing a drop or two of water to clear her nose, she looked down at the bed, feeling powerful in the rush from the coke, watching over Mario lovingly as if his life were in her hands. As always when he was here in the morning, she wondered why they didn't spend more nights like this, or why they didn't just start sharing a place. After two years, they'd settled into a routine of two or three nights a week, always at her apartment. Neither of them took much vacation time, but whatever weeks or long weekends they could arrange were spent together. If it's good some of the time, she wondered, why can't it be good all the time? Later in the day, she knew, back in her own life, she'd change her mind. She made herself list the reasons now, while her impulse was to wake him up and suggest it.

We're too complicated. We're preoccupied with our work. We're difficult in different ways. It wouldn't work for me because I'm too independent. Face it, I'm downright selfish. Mario is actually nicer than I am; he's willing to compromise; he'd like to live with me and — be fair, she thought — he wouldn't try to run my life: he doesn't try to now. For some reason, even though I expected all sorts of Italian attitude when I first met him, it turns out he's so comfortable with himself that he doesn't need to prove anything to women. She was envious of him: he could probably make a go of a more permanent relationship and she didn't think she was anywhere near ready for it.

But he's so incredibly handsome, she thought. She forgot all those problems sometimes when she looked at him, especially when she could stare without interruption, when she remembered how hard it had been for her to take her eyes off him the first time Chuck brought her to the restaurant.

His long, straight nose quivered when he took a breath. His dark lashes fluttered, and she decided he was in some active part of the sleep cycle she'd read about somewhere. She wished she could know where he was, where his mind was at this moment, what he was dreaming. She didn't want him to wake up yet but she wanted to see more of him, so she curled up beside him and carefully lifted his arm to pull the covers down to the foot of the bed.

Now she could see all of him, broad shoulders, strong, corded arms, a heavier chest than his frame suggested when he was dressed. A mat of black hair there dwindled down to a thin dark line that led down past his navel and then broadened again. His cock, so white against the dark hair, lay in the same direction as her head, toward her, so she could watch them both in their sleep. It still fascinated her that he wasn't circumcised. The other men she'd slept with, the California boys and then the stockbroker she'd seen for a while when she first came to the city, had all been cut. It made Mario seem exotic, more secretive, more hidden, literally. Maybe even a little sinister, she felt, like a stranger who might share her compartment on a train between Rome and Naples.

She bent down and took it in her mouth, soft and sweet, and then she sat back and looked at all of him again, asking herself why people seemed to think women weren't turned on by visual stimulation. It was certainly exciting her to watch him, without being touched or even touching herself. She bent over him again and licked his nipples lightly with the tip of her tongue, wondering why this never seemed to be described in books. Men were sometimes as sensitive there as women; Mario was, although he wasn't responding in his sleep. Weren't they supposed to admit it? Were men and women supposed to have entirely different needs? Was it shameful for the sexes to share an erogenous zone?

She moved down to kiss the inside of his thighs, then up to his balls and the wiry hair that tickled her lips. With her nose she burrowed under them and licked the tight skin behind them, the place where his cock began. He groaned faintly and his breathing changed. She could feel him tense down there, and by the time she'd slowly kissed her way back up to his cock it had started to grow. He was just beginning to stir, his body responding before his mind was awake. Running her tongue up the length of his cock, she made it grow stiffer and bigger, fondling his balls with her hand. Now she couldn't take it all in her mouth, so she concentrated on its head, holding the rest of it in one hand, using the other to rub her own wetness. It was thick and rigid and it extended nearly to his navel; when she stopped for a moment it sprang back to his groin.

He was awake; he had to be. She looked up to his face: his mouth was open to show clenched teeth and he was breathing hard, his head rolling back and forth slowly on the pillow, his eyes squeezed shut. He began to fuck her mouth, jabbing and thrusting up with his hips. She knew when he was close because his cock grew even harder, the head became almost too big for her, his balls came up and tightened against its base. He put his hands on her now, first running his fingers through her hair and then pushing her down to take more of him. She tried to catch up with him, tried to bring herself over the edge at the moment he cried out and spurted against the back of her mouth. She came very close but she didn't make it, and she knew it was the coke, that it wouldn't quite permit her to let herself go. She felt cheated, but she promised herself a next time, soon, and she told herself this probably wouldn't have really been good for her today anyway, with everything that was on her mind.

They lay there for a while, her mouth still on him, his hands now stroking her hair gently. When she sat up, he opened one eye and then both of them, wide, and looked into hers. "You're incredible, Mag," he said quietly. "Why can't we wake up like this every day?" Pulling her face down to him, he kissed her. "I don't mean like that, necessarily, although that wouldn't be such a bad way to wake up every morning. I mean like this." He put his arms around her and drew her closer.

"I don't know," she mumbled against his chest. "Maybe if I asked you to move in, then you'd suddenly get perverse and you wouldn't want to."

"I would. I do. Why not?"

"I guess I'm too selfish," she said sadly. "Or too neurotic. Or is that the same thing?" Then she smiled at herself. She nuzzled his neck and reached down to tug his balls. "I'm really only after these. When I've added 'em to my collection, I'll throw the rest of you away like a used Kleenex."

He was silent for a moment. He'd been serious, she knew, but when he finally spoke it was in the same teasing tone as hers. "I had a suspicion that's what you were after. You must be one of those liberated women."

"You got it. But as a special, one-time-only concession, I'm going to bring breakfast in here. And let the cats in to torment you."

"Amazing," he said to the ceiling. "Her sheets smell good, she brings me breakfast in bed, and she gives great head. Who could ask for anything more? If only I could talk the cats into forming some kind of suicide pact . . ."

She yanked the pillow out from under his head, stuffed it over his face, and walked out of the room for a quick shower. She blow-dried her hair and put on her makeup while the croissants for Mario were warming — the coke had nicely taken away her appetite — and then she loaded a big silver tray with them, plus coffee, orange juice, butter, and jam. Back in the bedroom, he looked like he'd fallen asleep again, but as she leaned over to put the tray down, he dipped a finger in the jam pot and smeared raspberry preserves on her nipples. "I wanna lick the pips off your paps," he murmured.

"*Paps* is an awful word. Reminds me of babies." She shuddered. "Now, drink your coffee, baby, and don't lick Mummy. She's got to call the gallery. Really." She poured coffee for both of them and then pulled the phone onto the bed, grabbing a pad and pen, punching the buttons and stroking the big tiger tom who'd come up to sniff the jam on her.

"Sheila? It's me. Any messages?" Now Mario and the tom were both licking her, one soft tongue and one very rough one. It was a struggle to keep her voice matter-of-fact. "Jim asked you . . . oh, don't worry. He comes on to every woman under fifty like that. I know. Repulsive, isn't it? Listen, I'm going up to that meeting at the Modern and I should be in about noon. Tell Jim to wait till I get there to . . ." She ticked off orders and wrote some numbers down on her pad.

The tom was sniffing at the butter now, and Mario picked him up and threw him halfway across the room. Maggie frowned at him while she was talking, but he kicked the other cats off the bed and went back to his nursing, making goo-goo sounds. "That's just Mario, Sheila. Being silly. He thinks he's a baby and he's right. See you noonish and call me at the museum if there's anything you can't handle. 'Bye."

She replaced the receiver and lifted Mario's head up from her breast, kissing him and then holding his face in her hands. "I have to show a *little* dignity with Sheila. Poor thing, she's already hard at work and I'm wallowing around with infant sexuality and bestiality."

He kissed each hardening nipple in turn. "*These* don't have any dignity, though, do they? The most beautiful tits in the whole world."

"Mario! I don't have time." She stood up. "And don't, please don't, offer to feed the kitties. You'll put roach poison in their tuna or something."

"Fine. Just get 'em out of here. Scat, cats. Visiting hours are over. There's only . . ."

". . . one pussy around here you like." It was an old joke. "As long as you keep liking that." She was dressing quickly, pulling up panty hose, opening and slamming drawers.

"So what do you think I should do about Radnor?" he asked between mouthfuls of croissant. She looked at him blankly in the mirror. "Getting some figures together?" he prompted. "What I said last night?"

She shook her head. "Did we talk about Radnor last night?"

"Mag! You sat and listened to my whole tortured monologue. Should I approach him now or wait till he gets a little more specific? I know I didn't give you much of a chance to slip a word in edgewise, but I thought you were listening, at least." He peered at her. "Then you took that pill, but before that you were about as wired as I've ever seen you. Ever. Was Jim laying coke on you? While you were installing? Was that it?"

She turned to glare at him, her hands on her hips. "I had *plenty* of reasons to be nervous and preoccupied and insomniac yesterday, thank you very much, *without* drugs. I apologize for not remembering, but it doesn't sound like you said anything you haven't been saying for weeks." At least that wasn't a direct lie, she thought, but she hated herself for wiggling out of it so cheaply, for throwing it back in his face that way. He'd be very angry, though, if she told him the truth. They'd have a fight. She didn't have the time or energy. She'd tell him about it after the opening, she decided.

"No," he said quietly. "You didn't really miss anything. Same old dilemma."

She finished dressing and came over to give him a long, sweet kiss. "I'm sorry," she said. "I'll make it up to you."

* * *

In her dressing room at the Cornell Theater, Carole lay back on a faded pink couch. She'd spent a long time in the shower after a grueling rehearsal, letting the water pound into her and gradually feeling the muscles in her neck loosen. Now she was staring across the room at the envelope that was propped up against the big cold cream jar on her dressing table. She'd tried to will it to go away while she was in the bathroom, but of course it hadn't, and when she came out she'd looked at it closely without touching it and then retreated to the other side of the room — as far from what she knew it contained, as far from the scent of linden-blossom cologne in which it had been drenched, as she could get. It had been delivered by someone named Eddie, who worked for the Ajax Messenger Service, according to the receipt that was taped to it, and it was signed for by her dresser, a nine-by-twelve manila envelope with a typed white label and the words "By Hand" and "Personal & Confidential" typed in the corner. There was no return address.

She'd screamed at her dresser for being so stupid about describing the messenger — black and young, he repeated over and over again, paralyzed by her fury — and then she'd apologized by giving him a hundred-dollar bill and sending him out for dinner with his boyfriend. She hoped he wouldn't quit like the one a couple of weeks before: he was really very good and she ought to know by now how pointless it was to try tracing these letters. She expected it every time, every March and every September, but she always hoped it wouldn't appear. Maybe he's dead, she'd think; maybe he doesn't need the money anymore. Maybe he's found God and he's had a change of heart; and, again, always, maybe he's dead. Since she'd never seen him or even his handwriting, she had no reason to assume it was a man, but she thought of her anonymous tormentor as Him. He always found her, twice a year, on location in the south of France or in an out-of-town tryout in Philadelphia, wherever. Sometimes the letters came in the mail, sometimes by Federal Express, sometimes by hand, but they were never traceable, and there was no point in trying to find out who he was. The first message, all those years ago, had made it clear there was nothing she could do about it.

"I know about you and Terry, and I know all about that night, the twenty-first," it had read. "Just listen to the tape and you'll hear yourself talking about it. You can't afford for anyone else to listen to it, Carole, but you can surely afford, shall we say, a hundred thousand a year. Can't you, Carole? And shall we say two payments a year, in nice, tidy bundles of a thousand fifty-dollar bills? You'll probably have some trouble getting that much cash together without your accountant being suspicious, so for this first time I'll give you a month. After that, you'll have a week's notice from me, the end of every March and every September, so I suggest you put a few thousand away every so often and then you'll be sure to make my little payment schedule. This will obviously make you very angry, and you'll want to do something about it, won't you? Track me down? Destroy the evidence? Silence me without calling the police? Well, I can hardly say I blame you, but I wouldn't advise it. The evidence is very safe, you may be sure, Carole, and there's a contingency plan, a sort of life insurance policy I have, that would only mean you'd be trading me in for someone else if anything should happen to me. So don't even think about it."

He went on to tell her exactly when and where to leave the money, a park in North Hollywood that first time. After that, the letters were briefer, with greetings like "Well, it's that time of year again, Carole!" or "Here I am again, Carole, just like a bad penny!" There would be a line or two of congratulations on the success of her last play or movie, and then instructions about payment that usually involved a post office box in either New York or Los Angeles, always under a different name. Sometimes, though, she had to make the delivery herself.

The chattiness, the false solicitude, the use of her first name, all enraged her more than a simple demand for money would have done. He was right, of course — her instinct was to hunt him down, to confront him and rip the evidence from his hands — but that wouldn't be enough because the faintest whisper would ruin her.

These days, it was even more important, because these days there was Tony, and he'd be sucked into it too because his name was going to be linked with hers, very soon. Thinking about Tony gave her a burst of happiness now, and the strength to rise, move across the room, find an old pair of gloves (so the hateful cologne wouldn't come off on her hands), and open the envelope. It was exactly what she expected; he wished her good luck with her new production; told her to leave the money in a particular trash can in Central Park at a particular time; and he hoped this wouldn't interfere with her rehearsal schedule. All she wanted was to get it over with, but the instructions were explicit and she couldn't do anything for a week. She felt the same rage as the other times. Quickly memorizing the time and place, she tore both the letter and the envelope into little pieces and flushed them down the toilet. Then she peeled off the gloves, opened the window, and threw them into the alley.

* * *

While he was waiting for him to shower and change after their squash game so they could go out to lunch, Patrick knelt in front of Mario's record collection, amazed — as always — by his friend's range of taste. There was a lot of Chopin and most of Ella Fitzgerald, the complete Gilbert and Sullivan and the best Rolling Stones. He settled on the second Talking Heads album. The sound system was great, a Bang & Olufsen linear-tracking turntable, a Nakamichi amplifier, and a pair of big old Braun speakers that Mario refused to give up. There was also a B&O compact disc turntable and some discs for it, new since the last time Patrick was there, but he had no idea how to use it, so he left it alone.

He sat back in one of the two big wingback chairs, covered in cracked brown leather, that faced one another. Like the arrangement of the records, he admired the apartment without wanting to live in it. It was neat, spare, clean, light, and airy, planned for maximum efficiency and reflecting Mario to his fingertips. Patrick's was cluttered, dirty, dark, and musty. He hated housework as much as Mario did, and he could afford a cleaning woman now, too, but he didn't want anyone to touch his mounds of papers and books and clothes. He preferred to dig himself out every couple of months, and he lived happily between excavations with some goldfish and an extended family of roaches.

Mario's books, alphabetized and categorized like the records, were in built-in cases that covered two of the living-room walls. Patrick thought of his own, piled on the floor, shoved into homemade plywood-and-brick cases, stashed in closets. There was art here too, nothing priceless but certainly valuable compared to Patrick's *Penthouse* calendar and ten-dollar reproduction of David's *Death of Marat*. On a wall of this room were a small, simple David Hockney etching of tulips in a vase and two Walker Evans photographs of sharecroppers in the Depression. In the hall that led back to the bedroom, a big, wooden New Guinea shield faced a Navajo rug that was hung from a rod like a tapestry. In the bedroom, partly visible from where he sat, was a big, particularly aggressive offering of the East Village graffiti school.

Between songs on the record, he could hear — for a moment only, mercifully — that Mario had switched from "If Ever I Should Leave You" to "Some Enchanted Evening." He laughed, remembering that his shower repertoire in college was exactly the same. So was the way he lived, for that matter. The books and records in his dorm room at Princeton had been arranged exactly this way. He'd somehow managed to get a single room there even as a freshman, and Patrick had helped him drag in these same two chairs, and the same old floor lamp. Mario wasn't inhospitable, exactly — if he had someone over, there was a comfortable chair and a place to sit and eat — but he never had more than one guest at a time, and even that was rare. Patrick was always welcome, and Mario had even made an omelet for him a few times; Maggie had probably been here once in two years. That, as far as he knew, was it.

Again, Patrick realized he couldn't live this way. He was alone a lot and he had to have peace to write, but people stopped in sometimes. The old Polish lady from the next apartment would waddle in with kielbasa for him and stay for half a bottle of beer; the girl who lived with her parents downstairs would come with her boyfriend, who played in a rock band, and they'd smoke a little grass; Mario came over sometimes after work and flopped down with a big vodka on the rocks.

His eye strayed to a color snapshot, framed in silver, that sat on a bookshelf. Mario as a little boy of six or seven stood with his grandparents in front of an old building somewhere — Boston, Patrick supposed. They were all smiling happily, all dressed in their Sunday best, Mario and his grandfather in suits, carnations in their buttonholes, his grandmother in a silk dress with an orchid pinned to the bodice. Another photograph was a high-school graduation portrait of a stocky, friendly-looking boy who had the unfocused look of someone who'd taken off his glasses a second before the shutter snapped. He didn't resemble Mario very much, but Patrick knew it was his brother. There were no pictures of his parents. Patrick knew most of the story because over the years Mario had told him chapters of it, and he supposed Maggie knew too, and he was sure they were the only ones. Mario mentioned his mother sometimes, that he'd been up to Boston to visit her, maybe, or that he'd talked to her the night before, but he never spoke about his father.

By the time the Talking Heads finished their first side, Mario had shaved, dressed, and opened bottles of Rolling Rock for the two of them. He flipped the record over, turned the volume down, and threw himself into the other chair, one leg hooked over its arm.

"Every time you beat me at the club, I tell myself I'm going to give these up," he said, lighting a cigarette. "And every time I win I tell myself I'm not in such bad shape and I don't have to do it for a while."

"Do you have any idea how boring it is to listen to smokers wrestle with their consciences?"

"No, I don't have any idea. Do you have any idea?"

"Yes, I do, and screw you. What was the matter with you today, by the way?"

"When I missed those shots a ten-year-old could've made?" Mario pulled over the big standing ashtray that might have come from the same club or the same club car as the chairs. "I don't know. It was one of those days, I guess. Not that I could honestly say you were gold medal material yourself. What was *your* problem?"

"Me? Sorry. I must have been thinking about the book. It's giving me a lot of trouble, this long flashback-slash-flashforward thing I'm trying."

"That must have been it. Unless maybe you were thinking about Judith."

"If that's your way of asking me how I'm doing with her, you might as well be direct."

"You want direct? I'll give you direct. Have you been to bed yet?"

"No." Patrick frowned. "She doesn't seem to . . . want to, and I don't know what it's all about."

"Alfie," Mario finished for him. "And your social life, apart from the ice princess?"

"Shit, I get these invitations from people I've never met and then I accept them and then I get disgusted and then . . ." He paused. "Never mind. How's Maggie?"

"Busy. Tired. Edgy."

"Edgier than usual?"

Mario stared at him. They knew each other so well, they didn't need to spell things out. "Yeah. She's doing some coke. Won't admit it, but she is."

"And you hate that."

"And I really hate that." Now it was his turn to change the subject. "Let's get something to eat."

* * *

"Trouble on the ranch," Lillian hissed out of the corner of her mouth as Mario came up to her station on his way into work, earlier than usual because he'd be taking an hour or two off tonight to go down to Maggie's opening.

"Some of the ranch hands acting up, Lill? Trying to peek under your skirts out behind the old bunkhouse?"

She beamed at him. "Thanks for the compliment but, no, the boys have been pretty good about that lately. Like for the last twenty years or so." She lowered her voice. "You just missed Rudi and he won't be back and he left a list of things to ask whoosis about, the accountant, who's waiting for you. And he just fired Angel." Lillian's job really had nothing to do with the kitchen or its staff, but she had friends there and Angel was a favorite of hers, a skinny Puerto Rican boy who kept the kitchen and storerooms clean and who always worked hard and cheerfully.

"Let me guess. He was ten minutes late."

"Fifteen. But that . . ."

"But that has nothing to do with it. I know. Hell. I hope you didn't let him leave."

"No. I thought you might be able to do something. He's in the back."

Mario found the dejected Angel, fighting tears, on a bench in the changing room. He put his arm around him and told him he couldn't promise anything but he'd talk to Rudi and it would probably be okay; he should take the rest of the day off and come in tomorrow at the usual time. Then he went straight to the office and spent the next hour and a half with the accountant. He'd taken a six-week bookkeeping course at Hunter College and by now he understood the flow of money far better than Rudi did, so he and old Mr. Marx always worked well together. Today, they ignored the niggling list Rudi had left and concentrated on the most important problems. The final responsibility was Rudi's, but of course he hadn't bothered to stick around for this meeting.

After Mr. Marx left, Mario slumped in his chair and brooded. Rudi hadn't fired Angel because he was late. There were a couple of good-looking waiters who were pathologically late, but naturally Rudi wouldn't let Mario fire them. No, this was another case of simple greed: Rudi would divide Angel's chores among the dishwashers and save a tiny salary. He'd tried this once before, about a year ago, when an earlier kitchen boy was let go, and it had backfired just as Mario warned him it might. The dishwashers were too busy to get all the extra work done; the grease traps in the huge hood over the stoves weren't cleaned as often as they should have been; and a grease fire had started, which triggered the fire system, which sprayed foam over everything and everyone in the kitchen. Rudi made charming gestures that saved the day, of course, sending out for hundreds of sandwiches, pouring cases of his best champagne, picking up the check for everyone's meal the next time they came in. The whole incident had cost about as much as a kitchen boy's salary for six months.

He always told himself, when things like this happened, that it was Rudi's restaurant, Rudi's money, Rudi's prerogative to do whatever he liked, but the pettiness was wearing him down. He couldn't anticipate what the next move might be; some days Rudi would be sensible, other days he'd be on a cost-cutting warpath. If it had been that way at the beginning, the restaurant would never have become what it was. Rudi had been a perfectionist, running a very tight ship, working long hours, listening to Mario, trying new ideas. Then, as soon as Mario was made manager and immediately showed how capable he was, Rudi was less interested in anything but keeping expenses down and profits high. The wine list had been small but decent and modestly priced; Rudi chopped it down to ten reds, ten whites, and three champagnes, all overpriced. Their lamb had come from Kentucky or Colorado or California, depending on the season; Rudi switched to New Zealand cuts, perfectly good but not the very best.

Chuck had a lot to do with it, Mario knew. Rudi seemed to grow more infatuated, more obsessed, instead of less. If Chuck wanted to see a play, then Rudi wouldn't be in that night. If Chuck had some time off and wanted to go to Cozumel, Rudi took him. If they had an argument, then Rudi couldn't come to the restaurant because he had to straighten things out with Chuck. It wasn't really a matter of money. Chuck spent Rudi's money freely, but the restaurant always showed a great profit and Rudi would be in fine financial shape if it weren't for his horses.

Rudi's horses were the most insistent drain on his income. They lived in splendor in magnificent stables; they frolicked on forty acres of rolling Bucks County farmland. They were supposed to make money for Rudi by breeding with one another and with visiting mates, but so far they'd only shown a loss. Mario suspected that, although Rudi knew everything there was to know about riding and training horses, he didn't know as much about breeding them as he pretended.

Finally, Mario realized, the biggest problem of all was himself. Rudi had groomed him to become his counterpart and to take the boring jobs out of his hands and now he was jealous of him. Not surprisingly, the staff openly preferred Mario's straightforward, fair attitude to Rudi's tantrums, but it wasn't really that situation that angered Rudi so much. What did infuriate him, Mario knew, was his position with members of the loosely knit club. Initially, it was Rudi's popularity and reputation that brought them there, but they kept coming because of the place itself, because everybody else was there, and because of Mario, not because of any particular loyalty to Rudi. Worse, Mario was now invited to far more places — parties, clubs, openings — than Rudi was. Without trying, without even wanting it to happen, his name began to appear in the columns with some regularity. Mario sighed. Rudi wanted it all: he wanted all the money, all the leisure, and all the reputation without paying his dues, and now there seemed to be a form of unspoken war. More and more of the time, Mario would make a decision and Rudi would contradict it just for the sake of undermining him, just to show who was boss.

His thoughts came full circle, then, back to Chuck. Rudi wanted to have his cake and eat it too, and Chuck was the icing on that cake. Rudi was difficult sometimes and rational sometimes, but he could be depended on to be irrational about Chuck. There hadn't been, in the past couple of weeks, a repeat of the scene in the bar with Norm Epstein, but out of a given number of drunken nights it was bound to happen eventually and it could easily be uglier the next time. Mario was vaguely wondering if it would do any good to have a talk with Rudi about it again, when he glanced at the clock and realized it was time to leave for the opening.

6

MAX SILVERMAN had moved his gallery down to a Soho loft from Fifty-seventh Street because he could get twice the space for half the rent, which meant he could afford to take a few more chances and add some younger artists to his stable. With seven thousand square feet of highly polished hardwood floor, he usually mounted two shows at once, but Maggie had persuaded him that the scale of Jim Wilkins's work needed the entire area. All the temporary partitions as far back as the offices and storage rooms had been taken down to give the shimmering works the breathing room they deserved, and Maggie was thinking the gallery had never looked so beautiful.

It was only a little after six, and no one was due until seven tonight, but for her the opening party was already beginning. She'd spent the day delegating work to her assistant, to the receptionist, the secretary, and the three boys from the back room; phoning the right people to make sure they showed up tonight; holding a few final, coke-laced screaming arguments with Jim; and at last running home for a quick shower. Now, in red Norma Kamali crepe and rhinestone ear clips, she was walking thoughtfully, deferentially, around the gallery with a critic from *The New York Times*.

She stood back quietly when he wanted to study one of the big glass constructions but she was there, on the spot, if he wanted to talk. A good review in the *Times* was probably the most important boost an exhibition could have, because the serious art magazines only appeared monthly, usually too late to help stimulate sales during the standard three- or four-week run of a show. It was important for her to stay with the critic, but she was worrying about the party that was about to start, and when Mario came in she broke away for a minute to join him, kissing him quickly and whispering in his ear while the *Times* stroked its chin.

"I've got to keep close to this guy, but I was in the middle of a fight with the caterers when he showed up. It's the first time I've used them and it'll damn well be the last, but I'm stuck with them for tonight. Could you make sure they do it right? Use your talents, you know?"

"Sure. You want that table set up there or . . . never mind. I'll take it into my capable hands."

"Thanks. You're a huge lamb chop."

He had a quick talk with the caterer and then, with her permission, he organized the staff in ten minutes flat. Coatracks near the elevator, a big table spread with raw vegetables and a curry dip, two bars, three girls to circulate with little hot hors d'oeuvres. He so obviously knew what he was doing that no one resented his interference. When he looked around, the critic was gone and Maggie was coming toward him, smiling broadly and rubbing her hands together.

"It'll be in the 'Arts & Leisure' section on Sunday. He loves the work and he asked for a photograph of the big piece in the corner and it's all working and I'll bet you a case of Finlandia it's sold out in . . . eight days."

"No bet. I'd lose. Since you put me to work right away, I didn't tell you how beautiful it is, Mag, and I mean it. They're incredibly hard works to show without looking like a hall of mirrors, and you've pulled it off. It's a brilliant installation. Max should be really pleased. Have you talked to him?"

"Oh, yes, and he said to say hello. He's home from the hospital today and he called to wish us luck. Wasn't that sweet?"

"Sweet?" Mario laughed. "Jesus, Maggie, it's his gallery."

"Well . . ." She looked like a little blonde girl who'd just been told the sandbox she thought was hers belonged to the family next door after all. "Well, I think of it as mine now, even if it isn't."

"In a month he'll be lucky if you let him know which shows you've lined up for the next two seasons."

She smiled obscurely, reached up, and picked a piece of lint off his black Ferre suit, and then mussed his hair a little, pulling a lock down so it fell onto his forehead, talking as she did it. "I have another favor to ask you, and then you can come to the party just like everyone else."

He pulled away from her and ran his fingers back through his hair. "You want me to be nice to a woman, right? You know I hate this crap, but you're determined to try it anyway, aren't you? Would you like me to tug the front of your dress down and send you off to some guy who's an important client, with a pat on the butt? Of course, since I don't pull that kind of thing on you, you don't know how it feels, but you'd be the first to yell sexist if I did."

"That's not fair," she said stubbornly. "Men have been doing that to women for . . ."

"I don't care what they've been doing for five thousand years. I don't do it to you and you sure as hell won't do it to me. I dress myself; I comb my own hair; and I manage to tie my own shoelaces, thank you very much."

"I'm sorry, Mario," she said quietly. "You're right. Of course you're right. I'm such a perfectionist about openings — I guess I want to tie up every last detail. I'll try not to fuss with you anymore. I know it's insulting." She smiled crookedly.

"Okay. Okay." He put his arm around her and they kissed. "So, let's be sensible. I know you have to orchestrate things and I agree to use my famous charm even if I withhold my famous cleavage. Who's the woman I have to enthrall?"

"Mrs. Hamilton McKinnon," she said, relieved. "Do you know her?"

"Not really. We nod. At the restaurant and around at things."

"Well, she's coming here early with her brother-in-law."

"Frederick? He's a nice man, a very nice man, comes in with her sometimes. I don't think I've ever seen the husband at all, though, have I?"

"Oh, nobody does. He's older than she is and he's probably really dull and stiff. He doesn't run with her crowd very much, just makes buckets of money for her to spend and for Frederick to give away."

"So why are McKinnons coming unfashionably early?"

"Because they have to be somewhere else, I guess, or because they don't like crowds? Anyway, it's about Jim's commission piece and it's fine, because I've got more time now than I will later on. Soooo. If you could find something to talk about with her, my love, it might help. Max always handled her when she came down. She has taste and she has a mind of her own. I'd rather get Frederick off by himself. Divide and conquer."

"Calculating little bitch."

"Yes, I am. When it comes to selling, yes. It's Frederick who has the final word at the Foundation, and I do better with men alone. If he has womenfolk with him it only confuses things. All's fair in the art world. We downtrodden females have to use every —"

"Keep your voice down, downtrodden female. They're here." He and Maggie were standing at the back, so there was a great expanse of hardwood floor for Frances and Frederick to cross from the elevator that opened directly into the gallery at the front. Frederick McKinnon was like a perpetual college boy, Mario always thought, conservatively dressed except for a bright yellow bow tie, maybe a little ridiculous but likable. He probably went to all the class reunions and he'd know all the nicknames from forty years ago. He was white-haired, and Mario guessed he was in his early sixties, but he kept his tall figure pretty well. He was pink from the sun and from his own good health. Sailing, Mario decided, and probably golf, and then maybe skiing in the winter months.

It was the first time he'd seen Frances McKinnon anywhere except in a crowd — at Rudi's, at a discotheque once, he remembered, and at an opening at the Whitney. She wore a light wool coat with faintly exaggerated shoulders. It matched, in its very subtle shade of aqua, a simple dress underneath. Her jewelry was unexpected: clusters of blood-red stones at her ears. From this distance, they might have been glass or garnets, but he supposed they were rubies. They clashed with the aqua just enough to make both colors more vibrant, to accentuate the whiteness of her skin.

In the times he'd hung around here waiting for Maggie, Mario had learned to separate gallery-goers into two categories: those who actually saw what they were seeing and those who were only self-consciously watching themselves look at art. The fact that the McKinnons were the McKinnons didn't necessarily mean they understood or even liked contemporary art. There were plenty of collectors who bought because it was fashionable, because it had great investment potential, because the art scene was a fun scene (Rudi, for one, Mario thought, although he seldom actually bought anything), but the McKinnons seemed to have some respect for what was in front of their eyes. They wandered around the big glass configurations separately for a few moments. Mario was surprised to see Frederick approach the pieces seriously, methodically, the way the critic from the *Times* had. Frances was more erratic. She ignored some works and spent a long time circling others. She stalked them, he thought, a quick, slim creature, attracted by the color and the play of light, touching a surface here and there and then dropping her hand guiltily. It was fascinating to watch. He turned to Maggie to see if she noticed, but she was bent over the table, arranging some already beautifully arranged hors d'oeuvres.

"It's not time to go up to them yet, Mag?"

"It's like fishing, my dear," she said softly. "They know I know they're here and they'll come up when they're ready. Her outfit is fantastic — it's got to be Karl Lagerfeld but I've never seen it. That means a very limited edition, maybe even limited to Madame."

When they finally wandered close enough, Maggie turned to welcome them and everyone shook hands and smiled. The McKinnons immediately told her how impressed they were by both the work and the installation. They were sorry to hear about Max and sorry to be taking her time just before an opening.

"No, no, this is perfect," Maggie said. "This way you get to see it before the mob scene. And I have some photographs and sketches and a couple of maquettes of Jim's in my office. Your assistant said you'd want to see them?" She spoke to both of them, but she paid just a shade more attention to Frederick. Frances turned to him before he could answer.

"Freddie, why don't you let Maggie show them to you? I won't interfere; at least, I won't interfere till the board meeting. But, Maggie, I promised Trish Green I'd ask about any drawings for these pieces in the show. Did he do preparatory sketches for them? Are they for sale?"

"Oh, that's no problem." Everything was working out for Maggie. "They're framed; they're hanging in the little showroom; and they're — well, you'll see. They're much more interesting than drawings like that usually are. Mario can show them to you. They're fifteen hundred each. The first two on the left are reserved, but even those could have second reserves. You're her decorator, aren't you?"

Sometimes, Mario thought, Maggie opens her mouth before thinking. He didn't know much about Trish Green, but he knew she collected. If she was sophisticated enough to know Jim Wilkins's sculpture and to know there might be preparatory sketches for it, then Frances McKinnon obviously wasn't functioning as anyone who could be called a *decorator* tonight. It was a small mistake, but Maggie should have known better.

"I designed her apartment a few years ago, yes," Frances said evenly. "Trish doesn't need anyone to tell her about art, though. I'm really just doing her a favor because she wanted to come tonight but she was tied up."

If Maggie knew she'd made a slip, she let it ride. "Well, if you find any you think she might like, I can reserve them till she has a chance to come in."

"Thank you. That's very kind."

There was a small silence while they all looked at one another, smiling. For some reason, there was a strain between the two women, and Mario stepped in by suggesting they head to the bar. When everyone had a drink, Maggie carried Frederick smoothly away and Frances and Mario were left alone.

"I'm really capable of looking at things on walls by myself," she said, laughing, "unless Maggie's afraid I might slip something into my purse?"

"She didn't mention that particular fear, but maybe I'd better come with you, just in case."

"You can never be too careful."

"The Wilkins drawings, then," he said, pointing toward the back.

"The Wilkins drawings."

He led her to a small carpeted room that usually functioned as a place for clients to sit comfortably while works from the storage racks were brought in. He sank into a low leather couch and watched her walk along the line of small watercolors on the opposite wall. There were only eight of them, but she spent a long time pacing back and forth.

"Did you study art?" he asked when she seemed to be finished.

"Not as such. I did a year of art history at the Sorbonne and then I took classes at Parsons and S.V.A. and Columbia and . . . but that isn't what you asked. What made you ask?" She came over and sat at the other end of the couch, crossing long legs and opening her purse.

He fished out a lighter, and as he lit her cigarette for her he said, "You seem to really see things. Whenever I come down here I always watch people looking at art."

"And I pass the test?"

He was lighting his Winston now. As he exhaled the first smoke from it, he looked at her and said quietly, "You pass the test." It wasn't what he meant to say or the way he meant to say it. The smoke, the small, intimate act of lighting her cigarette, his voice. God, that sounded sleazy, he thought. She'll think I've been watching too many old movies. She didn't react, and after a silence that was a beat too long they both began at once.

"Do you . . ."

"I thought . . ."

He smiled. "You first."

"I was going to ask if you often help your girlfriend this way, unofficially."

"Never, as a matter of fact. I just happened to come early tonight to check on the caterers, and her second-in-command is running around with price lists and labels." The word *girlfriend* made him feel like a teenager and it would have made Maggie furious. He wondered if she knew that.

"I suspect you were told to be charming to me while she talks to Freddie."

"No one would have to tell me to be charming to you, Mrs. McKinnon."

"Thank you." She gave him a little mock bow. "That in itself was charming. And evasive. My name is Frances, by the way."

He returned the bow and nodded to her glass, which was still full. "I'm afraid the white wine is pretty terrible."

"No worse than the white wine at any opening I've ever been to. I'd really prefer Campari and soda, but they never have that and I have to hold something, so I always ask for this."

"Why do you have to hold anything at all?"

She laughed. "You're right, of course. I guess I feel naked unless I have something in my hand, because everybody else does."

He was surprised she felt obliged to do anything she didn't want to do, but Frances McKinnon — for the past few weeks, since he'd really begun to notice her — had surprised him in all kinds of ways. She was married to one of the richest men in America and he would have expected a sort of dull, gracious grandeur from her. Instead, she was sharp and quick and — at the moment, at least — a little nervous. Now she stood up suddenly.

"Do you think we could prod them a little? Freddie and I have to go on somewhere and I'm sure Maggie has plenty to do tonight."

". . . talk to Janet," Maggie was saying as they came into her office, "and I'll have to get final estimates from Jim for both proposals."

Frances put her arm through Frederick's. "If you've finished with everything here, we really have to go before we're late. Maggie, I'd like to reserve number seven for Trish, if I may. I'm sure she'll be down on Saturday."

Maggie scribbled down the number and everyone said goodnight very cordially. Mario watched them weave through the sculptures and the people who were beginning to trickle into the gallery, while Maggie went to put a red half-dot on the wall next to the new reserve. She hugged him when she came back.

"Fantastic! He liked the ones I thought he would. They do happen to be the best, and whichever one they take is going to be close to two hundred thousand. You've made a conquest too, of course."

"I don't think it was a conquest, but we got along all right. She's not stuffy; I knew that from the times she's been in the restaurant."

"I thought she seemed to like you, and I notice you're on a first-name basis. Older women like that always like good-looking younger men."

"Maggie, what the hell's the matter with you? You sound like those brittle women you always say you can't stand, the ones who think the whole world revolves around sex. God's sake, people have minds, they use them, they have conversations, they like each other or they don't like each other, and it doesn't all depend on my hair or her neckline. That's the second time tonight: it's what Rudi calls 'gratuitous bitchiness,' and Rudi ought to know."

She closed her eyes for a minute and her mouth quivered. People outside the office were talking about "surface tension" and "illusion," and she kept her voice low.

"I'm sorry again. And for the same reason again. I . . . I know I'm doing it. It's all the pressure with this place. I feel scared about the responsibility and so I think flirting is a sort of . . . leverage."

"Well, it isn't always." He hated it when she talked that way, but he accepted her explanation. He put his hand on her cheek. "And she's not an 'older woman.' She couldn't be more than maybe ten years older than we are."

She'd kept her eyes averted but now they flashed at him. "That I won't concede. Our Mrs. McKinnon is closer to fifty than forty."

"Oh, come on, Mag."

"Take my word for it. I grant you, even though you didn't say it, that she's one of the most beautiful women I've ever seen. But she's not all that short of the old half-century mark. Period."

"Okay." He wasn't convinced but it didn't seem worth arguing about and so he changed the subject. "Tell me about Frederick. What's his story? Where's his wife?"

"She died a long time ago, I think, and they had two sons. I guess he pretty much raised them, whatever that means in that world. One's in the bank, in the Tokyo office, and one's a doctor somewhere. He's really a sweet man — of course, who wouldn't be sweet, with all that money? No, that isn't fair of me. The Foundation is his life, and he runs it very well."

"And his collection?"

"Is unbelievable. Not that he buys things by the boatload, just that whatever he has is the best example of whatever it is. African masks. Pre-Columbian jewelry. Blue Period Picassos. You name it. And his apartment is perfection because *she* designed it around the art. I went with Max once. You should see . . ."

She interrupted herself to run up to Jim Wilkins, who'd just come in, and Mario decided it was time to get back to Rudi's.

* * *

"No car tonight, Mr. McKinnon?" The little old porter, holding a clipboard with a list of members' limousines, smiled up at Hamilton as he came down the steps of the Knickerbocker Club. "Would you like me to get you a taxi?"

"Thanks, Ben. It's such a nice night, I'd rather walk."

Ben, who didn't think his gentlemen should walk anywhere, especially not at night, frowned, and Hamilton could feel his disapproval as he turned up Fifth toward home. Once he was out of Ben's sight, he hailed a cab and gave an address in Chelsea, Twenty-second Street between Seventh and Eighth avenues.

He sat next to the door, out of the driver's line of vision in the mirror. As they rumbled downtown, he put on a pair of horn-rimmed glasses, which would have surprised anyone who knew him, because he only wore glasses to read and he wasn't reading anything. He pulled his hat down a little lower to shadow his face. He felt ridiculous doing this, really ridiculous, like a kid playing cops and robbers, but it was part of the routine, one of the precautions he always took. His face wasn't well known but it was always possible he'd run into someone he knew, even in Chelsea, and he didn't want that to happen.

The cab dropped him in front of an anonymous beige cinder-block building. It was only six stories high, so at least it didn't overpower the block of graceful old brownstones with its height, but it was criminally ugly and, as always, he avoided looking up at it. First, he emptied the mailbox of its Occupant mail. There wouldn't be anything addressed to Hamilton McKinnon because, as far as anyone knew, Apartment 6E was leased by a middle-aged man named Donald White. Mr. White, of course, wore glasses, kept to himself, and had quietly expensive clothes. He traveled a lot so he wasn't around much of the time.

The building had neither a doorman nor an elevator operator, and Hamilton let himself into the antiseptic lobby and took himself up in the elevator, which was lined in wood-grained plastic. Apartment 6E consisted of one big room with a kitchen against the back wall that was closed off by a soft folding screen, plus a couple of closets and a bathroom. It was furnished with a sofa, upholstered in beige fabric with strands of gold running through it, a matching chair, an enormous, hideous ceramic lamp on a small table, and, at the other end, a double bed covered only with a fitted white sheet; nothing else. The air was dead and it smelled of cork, so he turned the air conditioner on to Low. Its hum was the only sound. The room was well soundproofed: double windows, cork paneling on the walls and on the door from the corridor, thick carpeting on top of more cork on the floor.

He went straight to a closet, unlocked it, and took out a cardboard accordion file he'd left there a few days before, glancing at his watch. It was eleven and he didn't have to be . . . where he was supposed to be . . . till eleven-thirty. He sat down on the bed and emptied the file onto it. There were fifty-three bundles, each containing twenty fifty-dollar bills: fifty-three thousand dollars. He needed fifty tonight, and he wrapped them up in a newspaper, two by five by five, neatly tying string around the whole package, just as he'd been told to do. He put the file back on the closet shelf, carefully keeping his eyes from the other things that were in there, trying not to think about them right now, and locked it up again. From the other closet he pulled out a tweed cap and a cheap tan raincoat, neither of them the sort of thing he usually wore, and put them on. They looked exactly like five other caps and raincoats that were stored there. He picked up the package, turned off the air conditioner and the light, and left.

Over on Eighth Avenue, he got a cab heading uptown that took him to a small, run-down theater on Forty-second Street. Its bright red neon sign blinked *Erotique* on and off, and the marquee promised twenty-four hours of nonstop action, $2.99, three hits. The three hits tonight were *Satan's Darlings, Mademoiselle De Sade,* and *Whipped Cream.* He gave the old bleached-blonde woman in the ticket booth three dollars and patiently waited for his penny before going in.

On the screen was a dungeon of some sort, lit by a torch. A girl in high leather boots and a garter belt was saying, "Now you'll be sorry" and "You thought you'd get away with it, didn't you?" to another girl, who was tied to a stone slab, naked. Because it was such a dark scene, the film provided very little light, and Hamilton stumbled once on his way down to the fifth seat to the left of the center aisle in the fifth row from the front. He ignored the screen by concentrating on the crumbling plaster-of-Paris angels who frolicked bravely around it, but he couldn't ignore the scent that enveloped him as soon as he sat down. It was very strong and it was the same goddamn linden-blossom cologne he'd come to associate with this horror, the same smell that always told him, twice a year, another letter had arrived, even when it was at the bottom of a big stack of mail. He looked around carefully, but there was no one anywhere near him, and he realized with a spasm of rage that the seat itself — the precise seat he'd been instructed to occupy — had been doused with it, that someone had been here first and set this up. It was even possible — no, it was *probable* — that the same someone was watching him now from the back of the theater, or from up in the balcony, and was laughing at him. He stayed very still, determined not to show his fury, not to squirm, and he breathed through his mouth until it was time to take the package out from where he'd held it pressed against him inside his coat and slowly lean down to put it under his seat. He checked his watch, and at exactly eleven-thirty he stood up to leave.

Back out on Forty-second, he walked away from the theater for a block before hailing another cab to take him to 888 Fifth. Halfway there, he had the driver stop for a moment, and he left first the cap and then the neatly folded raincoat next to a trash can. By the time he was home, he looked like Hamilton McKinnon again, glasses back in his pocket. Frances wasn't home yet, and the first thing he did was to go into his bathroom. He stood for a long time in front of the sink, staring at himself in the mirror as if he weren't entirely sure who the man in the reflection was.

* * *

Frances heard water running in Hamilton's bathroom as she walked down the hallway, and she was glad he was still awake. He'd been off at a bank conference for a couple of days, and because Freddie had picked her up so early she'd just missed him tonight when he came home to change. Through the open door to the bathroom, she watched him from his dressing room. He was standing at the sink, still in evening clothes, and looking at himself in the mirror as he slowly rubbed his hands under what looked like very hot water. He jumped when she cleared her throat and he immediately turned off the tap and came out to embrace her.

"All these years, and I never knew about this narcissism problem," she said.

"Daydreaming. Not admiring the old gent in the mirror."

"No reason not to. He's looking very handsome and distinguished. I missed you. How was Seattle?"

"Pointless. Not the city, the conference."

"And how were the bulls and the bears tonight?"

"Bullish and bearish. How was the art world tonight?"

"Arty and worldly. I guess that takes care of that. Good-night."

He laughed and kissed her again. "I'm going down for a jet lag chocolate milk. Do you want anything from downstairs?"

"No, thanks. Meet you in the student union?" She couldn't remember now how it started, but they'd had a running silliness for years about their late-night chats in the little sitting room between their bedrooms, first in their wing of the old house and now here. He was in business ad and she was in art history and they were meeting for a Coke after the library closed.

She slipped out of her clothes, scrubbed her face, and wrapped herself in a blue satin robe with padded shoulders that she'd bought because it made her feel like Garbo. The windows of the sitting room, like their bedrooms, faced out to the park and while she waited for Ham she stood and followed the twinkling lights of cars winding through it. He's tired tonight, she thought, tired and strained, and she wondered if it was the trip or if he was simply working too hard in general these days. When he came in, they sat at opposite ends of facing sofas with their feet up. These were the times when Frances felt the most married. The living room downstairs was warm and comfortable, but it was too big for real intimacy; the cube on the roof was very much hers, to dream in or to work in; this little room was where she and Hamilton were really husband and wife.

He told her all about the conference and who had been there and the speech he'd given, and tonight's dinner at the Knickerbocker, but she could tell he didn't really want to talk about himself, that he was too tired, that he wanted to unwind and listen to her instead.

"One quiet evening with just me and myself and that George Sand biography," she answered when he asked her to bring him up to date, reaching over to take a sip of his chocolate milk. "I went to dinner at the Auchinclosses' one night. Last night, Trish came over and we made waffles and had too much Beaujolais and Marianne was furious this morning because I broke the dishwasher."

"The Guggenheim? That's what it was tonight, wasn't it?"

"Was hot and boring and there were too many people to really see the show. Constructivism. But I went along with Freddie first to the Wilkins opening." He looked at her blankly. "Ham, I'm ashamed of you. James Wilkins, the one who's probably doing the piece in front of headquarters. Freddie and you and I talked about it that weekend at the beach house? Freddie had a catalogue? You've really forgotten, haven't you?"

"Not entirely. Some glass thing he was ranting about." Although he considered Frances and Frederick as his guides through the jungle of contemporary art, he actually had come to surprise them both at times with what he knew, and he was only teasing her now by pretending to be more reactionary than he was. "Did you like his choice?"

"Choices, plural, I think, but I deliberately stayed out of it. The show itself was beautiful, though, and I'm sure the commission will be, too."

"Max Silverman? Is that what you told me?"

"See, you always remember dealers' names even when you forget the artists. But it wasn't Max tonight; he's been sick. It was Maggie Wetherby, his director, and he'd better watch out. She's smart and ambitious and just short of beautiful — or maybe not short of it, I can't decide — and young and she's going to be a real power before much longer."

"How young?" he prompted her.

"Mid-twenties? Late twenties? Not thirty, anyway. Her boyfriend's a little older, I think. The famous Mario, the one who runs Rudi's, you know? No, you don't know him. Anyway, they're an extraordinary couple. He's tall and dark and smooth and very handsome, but he wears glasses, so it saves him from looking like a gigolo. He even looks a little . . . literary, and he's obviously intelligent. She's shorter and blonde and built like a brick euphemism. She wrapped Freddie around her little finger, and Mario's job was to charm me, the older woman."

"You're not going to start that again, Franny."

"No, I'm not. In fact, the old bat has been getting enough compliments lately to satisfy even *her* insatiable appetite."

"Good. Then I can safely bring up the subject of your birthday again. What do you really want?"

"Oh, Ham — I don't know. Twenty yards of pearls, maybe?"

"It'd be easier if you meant that."

"Well, I don't mean it. Surprise me? Meantime, give me advice? About Steve. He's talking about that job again." Stephen Bingham, who'd gone on after this apartment building to projects that included the new headquarters, wanted her to come into partnership with him.

"But I thought you were definite? Keeping your staff there but not getting any more involved than you are now?"

"I was, but now I'm back on the fence again. I keep thinking I'm spoiled, but I shouldn't be spoiled and I'm flattered he's asked me, but I only want to do things that interest me. A full-time head of interiors for a big architectural firm? Imagine, I might actually have to do a job that was boring at some point."

"Less so with Steve's office than a lot of others, though, no?"

"It's all relative. He's probably going to do that convention center in Cleveland and I must say I'm not very enthusiastic about convention centers. And I think he won the bid for a hospital in Atlanta. Six hundred rooms, all exactly the same. I can't stand that kind of design work, and I'd have to do it if I went in with him."

"But there's still no deadline?"

"No particular time. I've been stalling so long, I can stall some more, and I have to take care of what's on my plate first. Trish's thing is going to be right down to the wire, for instance."

"You'll do it. Whatever happened with Carole Todd?"

Frances tossed her head and laughed. "You mean since the last time you asked me? Three days ago?" People who thought they knew Hamilton well would have been surprised to see what a total, adoring *fan* he could be. He seldom found time for movies, but he hadn't missed a single one of Carole's, and he saw everything she did on Broadway within the first week. He'd sulked through dinner at the White House once when she was supposed to be there and her plane couldn't land in a snowstorm. Now he was thrilled, enchanted, that he might have a chance to know her through Frances.

"I still haven't met her," she said, "but she called again yesterday to change our appointment and . . . well, I won't be able to convince you she's anything less than a saint anyway, in spite of her reputation, but as it happens we seemed to get along fine. On the phone, at least. I liked her approach. She's smart and of course I think she's a genius for asking me to do her apartment. She sounds quick and stylish and probably temperamental but not very sure of herself when it comes to her own place. My favorite kind, you know? The ones whose eyes I can open, the ones who really do have taste and who really do have strong opinions but who don't realize it until I get hold of them." She frowned and lit a cigarette before she went on. "It's another way I'm spoiled, of course. Most other designers can't afford the luxury of teaching their clients too much. If you want to make the most money, the trick is to make them feel so insecure they call you about changing a light bulb."

"Shall I say it again? You know your way around perfectly well. You don't need my advice, Franny."

"But I do. I'm not just pretending so you'll be flattered. I really need to talk things out with you." She got up and went over to him, leaning down to put her arms around his shoulders from behind.

"All right. All right." He was pleased, and when she rubbed his bald spot with her knuckles he came as close to giggling as Hamilton McKinnon ever came. "Then my advice is *not* to take the job with Steve. You can have as much work as you feel like handling, you can pick and choose — my God, what good is money if you can't do what you want?"

"But then I'm just a butterfly who flies around and lights on only the prettiest flowers."

"Listen to me." He twisted his head back to look up at her. "It's your job to make places where people live, or work, or even just walk past, and to make them beautifully. That's very important, Franny, and if the way you do it best is with work that interests you — well, then, fine. I'd hate you to compromise when it isn't necessary. There have to be people in the world who don't, so why shouldn't you be one of them?"

She sighed. "Maybe I'm having a mid-life crisis. Are women allowed to have those too? I want more of a focus, I guess is what I mean. And I really am feeling my age, you know — I don't talk about it *every* minute because it's so boring for you, always having to tell me it ain't so — but I am. So the job with Steve seems . . . oh, I don't know." She yawned. "I had a long day and I need my beauty sleep more than ever." She bent down to kiss him and then tugged on his arms to get him up. "You too. You're tired."

Alone in her bedroom, she lay for a while with the reading light on, going over things she had to do tomorrow, and then she turned it off and let her mind drift, remembering details of the evening she hadn't told Hamilton about. A man at the Guggenheim, a friend of a friend, had talked very fast about a television movie he was directing. He was fortyish and attractive, and once he realized she was with her brother-in-law and not her husband, he'd come on to her so quickly, so automatically, that it made her smile even now. Another man, younger, at the table next to theirs at Lutèce, annoyed his wife by staring at Frances all through dinner. And then of course there was the conversation with Mario. Notches in the old vanity gun belt, she told herself sharply. Stupid, meaningless little conquests that don't even count because you never act on them. She wondered what would happen if she took someone up on it, just once. She didn't think she could do it; it had to mean more than two hours in a hotel room.

Hamilton had married her knowing she couldn't have children, and she'd always wondered if a dynastic urge would have made it different, or if he was simply one of those people who weren't very sexual. It was months — four? five? — since he'd come into her bedroom, but she was sure he wasn't seeing anyone else and she knew he loved her as deeply as she loved him. They had made love more often in the early days of their marriage, tenderly, companionably, but not really very passionately. Anyway, she always told herself, they had a much closer marriage than most of the ones she'd seen, more solid, more respectful.

Just before she went to sleep, she realized where she wanted to go for her birthday dinner next week. Ham had to be out of town, and Trish wanted to know, soon, where Frances would like to have it. Rudi's, she decided.

7

T*HE DAY AFTER THE OPENING* of Jim's show, Trish Green called Mario to reserve the little south dining room for a party she was giving in a week's time. Sixteen or possibly eighteen people for Frances McKinnon's birthday. Not a surprise, a few friends, and she was hosting it because Hamilton had to be out of town. Veal, maybe? A first and second course before that, but no soup. Plain chocolate cake with just a token candle, and flowers, lots of flowers. Just champagne, no other wine, but a really great one, whatever he thought. He smiled as he pulled out the form he'd designed for special dinners like this.

Obviously something Italian, he thought. She's an Italian lady. He wondered if the fragrant, rich porcini mushrooms would still be in season in Lombardy and Emilia. September, certainly, but early October? They came dried the rest of the year, but that wasn't the same. He went to find Louis and pulled him back to the office for a conference. Yes, Louis was sure they could get them, and yes, he'd be happy to make tortelli stuffed with porcini. No sauce, just a little butter and Parmesan, they agreed.

The second course was settled, then, and the dessert was automatic, and maybe a very plain rugola salad after the entrée, but that left everything else to be decided. For the whole week, he drove everyone crazy with the arrangements, but he didn't seem to be able to stop himself. The linen rental service couldn't provide exactly the color he wanted for tablecloths and napkins, a particular shade of pale aqua, and he finally convinced their manager to have them dyed. Then the standard cream-colored Rudi's plates would look wrong on that color and he had to rent a pure white Ginori dinner service from another company. Homyak, the florist he sometimes called when money was no object (he checked with Trish first to be sure it was no object), brought by five varieties of roses, all close to the deep ruby color he had in mind but not close enough, and Mario ended up meeting him in the wholesale flower district early one morning to find what he wanted. The Chinese calligrapher for the menus nearly didn't get them done because Mario was having so much trouble making up his mind about the rest of the dinner.

"Really," Trish said, the fourth time he called her with suggestions for the first course and the entrée. "I'm so busy I haven't had time to think much about it. It's sweet of you to be so concerned, but please just do whatever you think is best. The only thing I know of that Frances doesn't like is fennel."

He and Louis finally decided on the main course: the simplest veal scaloppine cooked with lemon in butter and just a drop of walnut oil, a variation of veal piccata. Plus roast potatoes in rosemary and plain green beans. Mario was still agonizing over the first course, though. Louis had offered to make a colorful terrine that would be beautifully layered with seven vegetables and served in a wafer-thin slice. Mario wasn't sure; it wasn't strictly Italian; he just wasn't sure. Louis came closer to losing his temper with him than at any time they'd worked together. "Maybe you should send your friends to another restaurant," he'd sniffed. Mario apologized and committed to the terrine.

On the day of the party itself, it was Lillian who was exasperated. "I've got it all straight, Mario," she said. "Green, comma, Patricia. South room. Eighteen. Eight o'clock. The linen people have already delivered. The flower guy's done the arrangements. The china's here. The menus are here. The Veuve Clicquot's been delivered. Yes, it's being chilled. How complicated can it be? You'd think the Queen of England was coming to dinner."

He grunted and took the reservation book from her, working silently on the seating for about twenty minutes and handing it back. She looked at him shrewdly. "Are we preoccupied about something?"

"Why do you ask?"

"Where I come from, which isn't so far from here, that's called answering a question with a question." She was tapping idly on the desk with a pencil. "I'm asking because you're not usually so casual about the seating. You practically did it blindfolded. It's not that my little baby feelings are hurt, but you do sometimes ask me for my whatchamacallit, my input. Something's going on. How's Maggie, by the way?"

"What's Maggie got to do with it?" he snapped.

"Nothing, apparently," she said slowly.

"Anyway, she's in California."

"Uh huh. That's not what I meant, but skip it."

He had to smile. "You should have been a policeman, Lill. A policewoman. A policeperson."

"I've got eyes and ears. So does Rudi."

"What's that supposed to mean?"

"Nothing to do with what I was trying to worm out of you, only that I think you've been handling him the wrong way lately." She held up her hand when he started to protest. "Don't get me wrong. You know what I think of the prick, you should pardon my français, but there are right ways and wrong ways of getting around him. You've been ignoring him. That's the wrong way. He can't stand it."

It was true, Mario knew. There hadn't had been any showdowns with Rudi lately; there hadn't even been any little arguments about petty details. When Rudi gave an order, Mario agreed without really listening and then did precisely what he thought was best. When he found a stack of memos in his In box, he initialed them and threw them back on Rudi's desk after barely skimming them. He worked hard, the restaurant was running pretty smoothly, and Rudi was a minor annoyance to him, a fly buzzing around that he didn't feel like swatting.

"Anyway, I'd watch out for him if I were you. I'd watch out for him even if I weren't you." She stood, tucking her pencil over her ear and holding the book and seating plan to her chest like a schoolgirl. "He's coming in tonight, by the way, because those show-biz chums of his are having that do in the north room."

"Thanks, Lill. I know you're right, but I'm not so sure I give a shit."

"Well, I just don't want you to get canned, but if you do I'll meetcha in the unemployment line 'cause I sure won't stick around here if my favorite Eyetalian is gone." She threw him a kiss and walked out, leaving a faint whiff of the Jungle Gardenia she'd probably been wearing for forty years.

As the hostess, Trish was a few minutes early, and she loved the way everything looked. Moving around the table, setting out the place cards she pulled from her purse, she chattered away, so glad she hadn't tried to do this at home, so grateful to Mario, so sure Frances would be pleased. Mario was suddenly embarrassed. Maybe he'd gone too far; maybe he'd been an idiot; Frances would certainly think he was an idiot. It was Trish's party. It was Frances's party. It sure as hell wasn't *his* party. He wasn't one of the guests, even. He was a servant, a waiter, a butler. He shouldn't stay in the room; he needed to get up to the captains' station; he couldn't make himself leave.

Practically everyone arrived at once, and they all stood at the end of the room where a bar was set up. Mario knew some of them, Steve Bingham and his wife, a young fashion designer and her husband, a playwright, an Old Guard society couple who were big ballet patrons. When Frances came in, last, she was with Frederick. Mario greeted her and wished her happy birthday. He made all the right sounds, but he could barely look at her. She was in a black silk crepe suit that was loosely, classically draped, and her only jewelry was an odd, Art Nouveau necklace of opals set in loops of silver. He was jolted by her beauty, by her perfume, by her smile as she took his hand.

Then he did, finally, wander out into the main room for a few minutes. He checked in with Lillian; he stopped to talk at a table or two; he felt like a robot. By the time he came back into the south room, people were seated and a waiter named Julio was pouring champagne for them. When Julio went to the little temporary bar to open another bottle, Mario was waiting, his face dark with anger.

"Where's Don?"

"Uh, in the north room, with that other big party." Julio's voice shook. Mario was terrifying when he looked like this. "Rudi switched us around after you talked to us. I thought you must know about it. He said I should handle this crowd by myself."

"Of course I didn't know about it. It's ridiculous — they'll be here all night. We always have two waiters in here, always. Where the hell's Rudi? In with them?" Julio nodded and turned back to the champagne, working as fast as he could.

The party in the other private room was in honor of an old friend of Rudi's, a weekend neighbor in Bucks County who was designing the sets for a lavish new Broadway musical. It was a very gay crowd, all men, all dressed with carefully casual elegance, few of them under fifty. Don and another waiter were serving the first course, a caviar mousse. Rudi wasn't eating with them, but he'd pulled up a chair near the head of the table. He was laughing and waving his arms around, telling a dirty story about a dead actress. Mario went straight over, leaned down, and interrupted just before what would have been a punch line. "What the fuck's going on?" he demanded loudly.

Rudi turned and stared up at him, his face registering more disbelief than annoyance. Mario was always so discreet; Mario always whispered when he had something to say to him in public. Rising from his chair, freezing his smile, he quietly said, "I don't know what you're talking about, but I think we must keep our voices down." He tried to lead Mario away from the table, but he was shaken off.

"I'm talking about eighteen people in the other room who only have one waiter because you commandeered Don and didn't bother to tell me," Mario said, no more quietly than before.

"Oh, didn't I tell you? Sorry. Bob had an audition at the last minute and couldn't make it." Bob, chronically unreliable but handsome in a soap opera way, was always forgiven by Rudi. "So," he went on innocently, "I had to take Don off your party and use him here for my friends."

"You're full of shit. You didn't neglect to tell me: you made a goddamn point of not telling me. We've got a dozen backups we could call, and all you had to do was let me know."

Rudi's eyes narrowed, and now he too forgot to whisper. "You will not speak this way in front of these charming people."

"I'll speak any way I like in front of these charming people. There are some charming people in the other room, too, and they're spending plenty of money and getting lousy service." He stepped a foot or two back from him. "I'll fill in for Don till he's finished here, which is probably what you knew I'd do when you dreamed up this little problem. But after Frances's . . . after Mrs. Green's party has left, Rudi, after that, I'll be leaving too. For the evening. For every other evening. You can take your charming people and your charming manners and your charming restaurant and stuff them up your charming ass."

At first, coming back to Trish's party, he was tight-lipped and stiff, still so enraged he could barely speak. Silently, he kept champagne glasses full and helped Julio serve the slices of terrine. When he realized he was making them all uncomfortable, he made an effort to relax and smile, and by the time Don relieved him for dessert, coffee, and after-dinner drinks, he could make little jokes and back out gracefully before they sang "Happy Birthday." Frances's smile, as he left the room, was mysterious, unreadable.

He had a few words with Louis in the office. He called up front to the station there and informed the speechless captain that he was in charge as of this minute unless Rudi told him otherwise, and then he stuffed a big garbage bag with his things from the desk and the changing room and left quietly by the delivery door. Lillian, of course, already knew what had happened, and she followed him out in the light rain to the corner where he was trying to flag down a cab. She told him he looked like a cat burglar in his tuxedo with the shiny black bag slung over his shoulder, and then she kissed him and made him promise to call her soon. He knew she'd give notice that night and that she'd have a few well-chosen words for Rudi. He wished he could be there to hear them.

He still hadn't found a cab after fifteen minutes, and he was cursing himself for not calling a car service. His shoulders were soaked now and his hair was dripping down his neck, but he didn't have any change in his pockets and he was damned if he'd go back inside to use the phone and he was damned if he'd walk over to the front door and ask the doorman to help him. He stayed on the corner because the bag was so heavy with books and shoes and shaving cream that he didn't feel like lugging it very far, but he kept his back to the entrance and he hoped no one would notice him. When someone called his name, he ignored it at first. Then something clicked, he connected a voice with a face, and he turned and saw he was right.

Frances and Trish were under the awning, their arms linked together, staring at him, and it *was* Frances he'd heard. He made himself smile and shrug but he didn't try to shout above the swish of the traffic on the wet streets and he didn't know what he would have said anyway. Trish's car pulled up first, and she hugged Frances quickly, waved and yelled, "Thanks again" to Mario, and jumped in. The McKinnons' old Bentley was next, and the doorman was holding his big umbrella over the space between the awning and the car door, but Frances was still on the sidewalk, still staring at Mario with the same puzzled frown.

Behind her, he could see the doorman's hand come up to his mouth for what would have been a discreet cough to get her attention. She smiled, shook herself, said something to him, and then she was walking through the rain toward Mario. By the time she reached him, he'd confessed to himself that it was exactly what he'd wanted her to do, exactly the gesture he almost felt he'd *willed* her to make: to leave behind a doorman and an awning and an umbrella and a chauffeured Bentley and everything — a whole world — they implied, in order to come to him through the rain that was spotting her silk and sparkling in her hair.

She glanced at the big bag at his feet and laughed up into his face. "Are you running away from home?"

"No. Yes. I guess I am, in a way." He stumbled over the words. He was thinking he had never in his life seen anyone so beautiful.

"From Rudi's?" He nodded. "You mean you've quit? Just like that?"

"Just like that." He snapped his fingers and smiled, but the only possible way he was able to talk to her was to focus on a point between her eyebrows or the bridge of her nose, anywhere but her eyes. "It was the straw and the camel's back."

"But . . . did it . . . ?" She looked away for a moment, and then she spoke quickly. "I'd never seen you helping serve before. Did it have something to do with that? You were angry. We all noticed it. I wasn't the only one. . . ."

"I'm sorry. I know I was like a . . . a black cloud in the room for a while there. Someone had to help Julio, though, or you'd still be waiting for your main course, probably, and it was all because Rudi yanked someone and . . . but it's boring. As I said, it was one of those last-straw situations."

"Then I won't ask any more about it. It was a beautiful party, and thank you and Trish was so pleased." She looked down at her shoes. "But I have another question," she said in a voice that was very faint and oddly shy for a moment until it gained strength again. "The colors you chose for the table. That's what I want to ask about. How did you know? Trish said she had nothing to do with it." She smiled. "How did you know the birthday girl would like them?"

"I knew you liked them at least once because you wore them at least once," he said, and then he gathered up whatever courage he could find in himself at that moment and looked straight into her eyes at last. "And you were very, very beautiful in them." The colors he'd spent so much time duplicating, the pale aqua of her dress and the brilliant ruby of her earrings that night at the Wilkins opening, were his message to her, something she could either accept as a kind of secret homage or something she could laugh away as a charming bit of gallant nonsense. He held his breath until she finally spoke.

"That's what I thought," she said softly. "That's what I . . . hoped." And then she was gone, walking quickly around the puddles on the sidewalk and back to where her car was waiting.

* * *

Dorothy McKinnon Clough sat by herself in the sun at a little sidewalk table in front of a Columbus Avenue café, sipping a glass of mineral water, picking at a Caesar salad, and feeling, as she usually did these days when she found herself eating alone, that she was the only one in the world who wasn't part of a couple. It was a warm Saturday afternoon, another lovely autumn day to bring New York spilling out into the streets, and there were couples everywhere. They sat around her at the other tables; they strolled past her, holding hands; they stood and chatted with other couples up and down the street, arm in arm, digging their hands into one another's hip pockets. They all seemed so happy together, she thought, and they were all so good-looking, so healthy, so well dressed, and so young that she was positive — if they noticed her at all — they must think this old lady with the dyed curls had dropped in on them from another planet.

But *I* was young once, she wanted to scream at the crowd, and I was even pretty — a lot of people said I was — and I was half of a couple once, too. There were times when she felt she'd been alone forever, that Spence's stroke had taken place in a different lifetime instead of just over a year ago, and then at other times it seemed like he'd just left her side a little while before and he'd be waiting for her back at the apartment.

She had to tell herself, especially on days like today when she felt so lonely and when she'd had to run an unpleasant errand — *so* unpleasant she was trying to forget all about it — that she'd been lucky for nearly forty years. Her friends had always said that: she was one of the lucky ones, the ones with adoring, generous, attentive husbands who never strayed because they had everything they wanted at home. Well, it was true, even if those same friends (not to mention her family) had warned her against him at first. The Cloughs were an old, old New York family — the McKinnons were parvenus here, in comparison, although they went just as far back in Boston — and most of them were rich enough by anyone's standards. Spencer's branch didn't happen to have much money, but he went to all the right schools, and he knew all the same people she knew, and he was tall and blond and handsome and he was on everyone's list. He'd proposed to her at a friend's debut in the ballroom at the old Astor, the year after she herself came out, but then it took two years to finally wear down her family.

Spence had brought high spirits and laughter and love — so much love! — to their marriage, but never very much money. He worked, of course; he was a vice president in his uncle's brokerage house. But he never became a senior vice president or an executive vice president or whatever it was he thought he ought to become, she was never quite sure. Dorothy had plenty for both of them and for the children — for his polo ponies, too, for that matter, his only extravagance — and she couldn't see why it seemed to make so much difference to everyone, what *side* it came from, for goodness' sake.

Her family had deliberately locked up the great bulk of her money in a network of trusts so her husband could never touch anything but the income from it, and she knew — even if he never once complained — that he was hurt by that. And the wording of his will when he died had been so sad, because there just hadn't been very much he could really call his own to leave to her and the children. Of course — not that it was a figure that would have impressed the McKinnon lawyers, she thought with some bitterness — there should have been more. His estate would have been bigger, probably around a million dollars bigger, if it hadn't been for the payments he'd been making every six months for years. She wasn't positive as to exactly how long because she hadn't known anything about it at all until the week he died, when, before that terrible final stroke, he'd tried to warn her about all this and she couldn't understand more than half his slurred words. She only knew the annual amount had been a hundred thousand.

That was the reason she was over here on the West Side today, in this neighborhood she didn't think she'd visited for a long time and which she hardly recognized in all its newly gentrified shininess. She had inherited this . . . she never knew what to call it to herself . . . this *obligation* from Spence, and now she was the one who had to make these deliveries of fifty thousand dollars twice a year, to someone who would forever be faceless and nameless.

This was the second time she'd done it, and she had stupidly expected it would be a little easier, a little less painful, than the first. Instead, it was much worse, and she didn't really understand why that should be true. It must be because she was *part* of it now, she decided, because she was trapped in something that was going to go on and on. It certainly wasn't the money as such that bothered her, although it was strangely disgusting to handle so much cash at one time because she almost never handled any cash at all. She had tied it up in a neat package, just as she'd been instructed. Then she'd left it in care of the name she knew was false — different from last time, but just as false — at one of those funny private postbox businesses that seemed to be springing up all over the city. Or maybe they weren't; maybe she was only noticing them now that she'd been to two of them.

Another really *hateful* thing, something that — if she let herself dwell on it — made her angrier than any of the rest because it could never be undone, was that one of the memories she'd always cherished of her honeymoon with Spence was ruined now. They drove all over France after their June wedding, and at an inn where they were so happy (and where, she was sure, their son was conceived) was a great *allée* of linden trees with their very short-lived, very restrained sprigs of blossoms. Years later, in a little store in Paris, she bought a bottle of cologne that could bring that time back to her — not to wear, of course, because it was for men (although the salesgirl told her women used it more and more often), but just to have and to open sometimes and remember. When the second letter came, two weeks ago, when it was soaked with the same fragrance as the first, she'd burst into tears, run into the bathroom, and poured the memory down the sink.

But she wouldn't think about it. She was here now in this sweet little café, and the sun was shining, and all that was behind her, wasn't it? Blocks behind her? She had no idea how far she'd walked after leaving that place, but it was much farther than she'd walked for a long time and her back was aching terribly all of a sudden. It was an old, old injury — the diving board at the Easthampton house when she was just a teenager — but she'd stupidly done something to it again last winter. Her daughter and son-in-law had convinced her to come with them to Vail at Christmas, her first Christmas without Spence. She hadn't been on skis for twenty years, she'd fallen awkwardly and twisted it again, and now it bothered her sometimes but at least not all the time. And at least she had the right kind of medication for these moments. She waved for the waitress. She knew, *technically,* she wasn't really supposed to have alcohol with these pills — Percodan, but she always called them her little percolators — but she didn't see how a glass of white wine could hurt and it wasn't even fattening and she'd discovered that the combination did more than one or the other by itself to make her feel better. She was already taking her antidepressants, of course, and sometimes — well, more and more often, actually — a mild tranquilizer, too, and *they* certainly helped smooth things out. But at times like this, when her back was aching and when she could feel this other thing — this unfamiliar emotion that was very much like anger — trying to poke its way to the surface, she deserved some extra help in keeping it safely patted down.

* * *

Pouring himself a glass of a great old Bordeaux that he'd been saving for a special occasion, Mario sat in his apartment and toasted himself. He hadn't thought about what his next step would be. He just knew it was a beautiful Saturday afternoon and the sunlight was streaming in. He didn't have to be anywhere: he was free of Rudi as of the night before and he felt an enormous relief. He'd always imagined he'd behave responsibly — certainly give plenty of notice and probably have something else lined up when he quit — but he should have known it would end like this. It was no worse than some of the other things Rudi had pulled, really, but the timing was bad. It had something to do with the fact that Frances McKinnon was there. He corrected himself. It had *everything* to do with Frances McKinnon's being there . . . but he wouldn't think about that. It was dangerous to think about that. . . .

He stretched and splashed some more wine into his glass. The phone rang twice but he let the machine take the messages. He'd call Maggie in California a little later. He'd call Patrick too, see if he wanted to play squash or meet for dinner. Tomorrow, maybe he'd rent a car and get out into the country, let the phone messages pile up. He'd deal with Monday on Monday. He sat back in his chair and closed his eyes.

* * *

When people asked him how he'd ended up working in a restaurant after graduating magna cum laude from Princeton, Mario always mumbled something about falling into it, he guessed, but he could have truthfully answered that he'd almost literally grown up in one. Fermi's Italian Seafood occupied the ground floor of a red brick building at the corner of Hanover and Prince in Boston's North End, and Mario's family lived above it. His Nonno and Nonna Fermi lived on the second floor because they were old and they couldn't climb too many stairs. Uncle Claudio and Aunt Maria lived on the next floor with Tom and Maria Luisa, his cousins. Papa, Mama, Mario, and his big brother, Giovanni (who became Gianni, and then Johnny), were on the top. On the roof were a water tank, a maze of clotheslines, and Nonno's pigeons.

The restaurant's big kitchen at the rear of the ground floor was the center of their lives. To get down to it, they could take the front stairs to the sidewalk and then walk through the dining rooms, but mostly they used the fire escape that ran up the back of the building. It was strong, it was screened in to protect the children, and it extended all the way to the ground, so by climbing out a kitchen window on each floor they could all get down to the tiny cement courtyard and into the real kitchen. Once a year, Nonno painted it shiny black to keep it from rusting, and every spring Nonna brought out her pots of flowers and herbs and lined its steps.

Along with the trick his grandmother showed him with all his fingers (the one about the church and the steeple and the people) and the one with his toes (the one about the piggy going to market), she would sometimes hold up his thumb and tell him it was just like the North End, surrounded on three sides by the waters of the Charles River and the Inner Harbor, and now sliced off from the rest of the city by the elevated expressway. When his grandparents came to America from Naples as a young couple, there were still some Irish here — another thing Nonna never tired of telling him was that he had been baptized in the same church, Saint Stephen's, just up the street, as Rose Fitzgerald Kennedy — but it had been totally Italian for many years.

It was his father's parents who saved enough money over the years to open a restaurant in the space where their pasta shop had been. The tiny apartment in the back, where they'd raised their two boys, became the kitchen, and they moved upstairs. It was the sons who got the financing to buy the building, who then brought their wives to live there, who soon expanded into the storefront next door, and who hired the first nonfamily waiters. By the time Mario was born, it was a popular place, crowded at lunch with businessmen and at dinner with couples, but it demanded long, hard hours. Mama and Aunt Maria cooked most of the food. Papa and Uncle Claudio tended bar, waited tables, whatever was necessary to keep things running smoothly. Nonno was the official host, the head of the family, a job he took very seriously, shuffling around in his dark blue suit, smiling vaguely, charming the customers with his broken

English. Nonna rolled out and cut all the pasta; she baby-sat; and she generally interfered in the kitchen as much as her daughters-in-law would allow.

Mario's cousin Maria Luisa was the youngest grandchild and the only girl, but he was the youngest boy, he was sweet and beautiful, and he was adored and spoiled. They called him *principe,* prince, and he naturally assumed that Prince Street, where they lived, belonged to him and was named after him. Johnny was five years older, quiet and reliable, and when he pushed Mario around the neighborhood in his stroller or, later, when he walked him over to the playground on Snow Hill Street or down to the old docks on Atlantic Avenue, he took it very seriously, as if he really had been entrusted with a prince. He had to wear glasses, but he was chunky and strong, good with his fists. He could have had a successful career as a bully, but he fought only when there was no other choice. Mario pushed him to his limits, but he was devoted to him; he knew, from watching other big brothers, that he was lucky. He loved his whole family, of course, but they were all so busy, so preoccupied with their sauces and silverware and mortgages, and it was Johnny who was always there, always patient, always ready to explain all the things that needed explaining.

In the middle of the first grade, Mario had his First Communion at Saint Stephen's, and it was right after that important event that things began to change in the Fermi family. Mario wondered for a long time if it was his fault, if he'd done something wrong in the ceremony. It was very confusing because Mama and Papa were so happy about all of it and he was only happy about *some* of it. There was going to be a new Fermi's Italian Seafood, a bigger, glassier, fancier place down on the docks, just where Battery Street ran down from the North End into the water, and that was very exciting even though it meant the old place would be closed. The family was going to have a partner, a word Mario knew from the way the Sisters paired them up at recess in the schoolyard, but which didn't seem to have anything to do with the dark, unfriendly man — a Sicilian, a man Nonno hated, for some reason — who came to the restaurant all the time now for meetings.

Best of all, his parents told him (worst of all, Mario and Johnny thought), they were going to move out to a beautiful new house in a place called Belmont. Mario didn't see why they couldn't all live together the way they always had, but he and Johnny and Papa and Mama would be in one house, and his grandparents would live with his aunt and uncle and cousins in another house, only (only!) a few blocks away. They drove out to see this Belmont place one Sunday, and the boys were very quiet on the ride back. They believed there might be such a thing as too many trees and too much grass, and there was no store at the corner, only another ranch-style house that looked pretty much like theirs. He and Johnny would have separate bedrooms for the first time, and he *knew* he'd be lonesome.

They moved just in time for the children to start the year at the big modern elementary school, and he was even more skeptical then. There were no Sisters, no chapel, no prayers — that in itself was funny even if it was a relief. Stranger than that, though, not all the other kids *looked* the same as their friends in the North End: there were more blonds and redheads, more blue eyes, more freckles. Their names didn't all end in vowels; some of them went to churches that didn't have saints' names, a few of them went to a place called a synagogue. They didn't talk the same; they didn't dress the same. Johnny was in his first year of junior high school, and he had to prove himself all over again. He got into four fights in the first week, and even Mario was in two, but they'd been so well trained on the streets that they won them all, so they felt a little better.

Every day after school and all day on weekends, they went over to their cousins' house, where Nonna was now a full-time baby-sitter, keeping an eye on all of them at once. Papa and Uncle Claudio and their wives drove into town every morning and came back late every night. They were working even harder than before, the women still cooking in the original restaurant, the men everywhere at once, up and down the gentle hill between Prince Street and Battery Wharf, trying to keep one place in business and to get the new one ready for its opening. Nonno put on his dark blue suit every morning and rode into the North End with them, but he seldom went down to the water; he stayed with the women in the old place. There was something wrong, some problem with the old folks, and Johnny tried to find out what it was, passing on whatever he knew to Mario. It had something to do with the Partner, the Sicilian. Once, outside a window, he heard Nonno say to Uncle Claudio that the man's money was "dirty." Another time he was in the room when Nonna, who sometimes forgot how much Italian Johnny could understand, hissed in her husband's good ear that their sons had sold their souls to the devil. It was the kind of Old Country talk the boys were used to hearing from her, but this was the first time she'd ever said anything like that about someone in her own family. It worried them for a while and then they forgot about it.

Before the opening of the new restaurant, Nonna took all her grandchildren downtown to the big Filene's store and color-coordinated them. The boys were bought powder-blue suits and white bucks, Maria Luisa a powder-blue dress and white flats. On the day itself, the boys had miniature white carnations for their lapels and Maria Luisa had a small white orchid. Nonna herself matched her granddaughter. They were allowed to stay up very late, sitting at a big table with the old people in the best corner, glass on two sides of them. They could look across the river to the lights of Charlestown or out over the harbor to the planes landing at Logan Airport. Even when Johnny reminded him that the only restaurant he'd ever been in was the old family place on Prince Street that had just closed, Mario insisted this was the most wonderful place to eat in the world. His mama and his aunt were no longer in the kitchen; they were called hostesses now, and they both looked very beautiful, almost unrecognizable, in elaborate hairdos and bright, silky dresses, smilingly showing people to their tables. His father was handsome in a new, sober, charcoal suit, his uncle in a pale gray one, and they seemed to know everyone, to have a word or a joke for all the people who poured in. Nonna was enjoying herself; she wasn't going to let anything spoil her day, even her husband's grumpiness, even his refusal to shake the Partner's beautifully manicured hand when he came up to the table.

It was only a few months afterward that Mario and Maria Luisa, the earliest of the cousins to get out of school, found Nonna on the kitchen floor, the soup she'd been heating up for her lunch burned away on the stove. Her grandsons wore the same suits to the funeral that she'd bought for them at Filene's, with matching black ties. Almost a year to the day after that, Nonno followed his wife, but the boys had outgrown those suits by then.

The restaurant was doing phenomenally well now, and each family had a housekeeper who kept an eye on the children. Mario and Johnny were watched by a tall, middle-aged, humorless Swedish woman who lived in a little room next to the kitchen and who cooked them meals that seemed tasteless and colorless after their grandmother's. They avoided her as much as they could; there was an unspoken understanding that Johnny was in charge of Mario and that no one was in charge of Johnny.

In the next few years, as Mario went on to the third and fourth grades and then was advanced up to the sixth, he became known as the *smart* one of the four grandchildren. The cousins were . . . the cousins, clever enough but never very interested or interesting. Johnny was a good listener, always curious, good with machinery and able to fix anything, but he seemed to have more and more trouble at school. In the same year that Mario skipped the fifth grade, Johnny was held back for a second year in ninth grade, and the younger brother sometimes found himself helping the older with his homework assignments. There was never any embarrassment about it between them; they were simply made differently. Mario read everything he could get his hands on; his sports were baseball, basketball, and tennis. Johnny wasn't interested in books; he was on the wrestling team and the football team; he was stronger and, Mario thought, kinder, more honest, *better.* The family took it for granted that Mario would go on to college and that Johnny, who was already working down at Battery Wharf on weekends and in the summers, wouldn't. When he graduated from high school he'd simply go straight into the business, as his cousin Tom did two years before him.

There was plenty of room for him in the restaurant by this time. By streamlining, by creating a formula for everything, by expanding into other parts of town, Fermi's Italian Seafood had become in just a few years the kind of success that was written up in trade magazines and given awards by the Chamber of Commerce. A second place was built on the Gloucester waterfront, very much like the original one with its glass and its views, the first fishing boat of what would become a fleet of five moored to the pilings on which the restaurant stood. Then a branch was opened out on Route 9, where all the computer companies provided a steady stream of prosperous young customers. Two smaller places were tucked into corners of downtown hotels; then one in Cambridge, one in Brookline, one in Belmont itself; finally, they added three enormously popular stand-up raw bars in suburban malls.

The sisters-in-law no longer needed to be hostesses, but they'd been working all their married lives and neither of them would have been content to settle down into housewifeliness. They administrated; they helped run the empire from the headquarters on Commercial Street, just across from Battery Wharf. They redecorated their houses every year; they competed, more openly than their husbands did, for power in the company, not only for themselves but for their children. Even though Mario would be going on to college — Harvard, they all assumed — he'd obviously be coming back to join the business. The Prince was groomed very carefully, never during the sacred school year but always in the summer, all summer. He washed dishes, he shucked oysters and clams, he filed and worked with figures in the main office, he spent long days — his favorites — on the fishing boats.

Principe, they all knew by the time he was sixteen, would be fine. His cousin Tom was proving to have a tough, first-class business mind. Maria Luisa was too young to worry about yet, although privately they all hoped she'd marry a boy who'd be an asset to the company. The problem was Johnny. He didn't seem to be showing any ambition, to have even a hint of the drive the rest of the family had in such abundance. He was always willing, always pleasant, but somehow, even after three years, he'd never *excelled* at any of the jobs they gave him. His father said he just hadn't "found his feet" yet. His mother said it was because he was in love for the first time. Johnny's girlfriend, Barbara, was pretty, small and dark, quietly religious, all in all rather old-fashioned. She was a girl he'd known all his life, a North End girl, a girl who clearly thought he was wonderful. "Wait till he has a wife," they all said, "then we'll see."

He was the first of his generation to be married, and the family pulled out all the stops. Five hundred came to the wedding, a thousand to the reception. Saint Stephen's was banked with flowers, the

Battery Wharf restaurant was taken over, the parking lot was tented, and a twenty-piece orchestra was imported from New York.

That was always the point at which Mario pulled himself up, stopped himself from remembering. It was only a few weeks after Johnny and Barbara came back from their honeymoon in Hawaii that the trouble began.

8

"YOU FOLKS on the right side oughta be gettin' a real nice view of the Grand Canyon just about now," the captain announced in a southwestern accent that Maggie sourly decided was fake. She was on the right side of the plane in a window seat, but she didn't bother to look out and neither did the people around her. Everyone was crouched over paperwork or swearing at lap-top computers or sleeping. For Business Class, the flight from JFK to LAX wasn't about natural wonders.

She was trying to concentrate on the letter of agreement for the show Jim would be having with an L.A. gallery next month, arranged through her — well, through Max — as his exclusive dealer. It was all nicely complicated now by the fact that, in the week since it opened, his show in New York had sold out. Which meant he was behaving badly for a change and screaming for higher prices on the work he'd be showing out there, which meant she was taking this trip to try to smooth ruffled feathers. She'd originally planned on only three days, but she'd made so many appointments — dealers who showed other artists from the stable, a couple of museum curators, as many private collectors as she could see, a handful of artists in Venice and the downtown scene — that it was turning into a week. Just thinking about it was exhausting her.

She grabbed her purse and pushed past the man who was speed-reading a book about — she was positive that's what the title said — how to be his own best friend. On the toilet, snug but a little claustrophobic, she took out the old porcelain snuffbox, a totally unexpected present from Jim after his opening, that he'd filled with what he assured her was exactly five grams. It was half empty now, or half full, and she realized she'd been doing more than she'd promised herself. Okay, yes, shit, I know, she admitted out of the corner of her eye to the mirror. I *had* said I'd stop then, a week ago, but I tried it for a day and the crash was so terrible I barely had the energy to lift a telephone and I can't afford an entire day or two like that and I simply don't choose to stop right now, so there. I might as well be realistic about it. For a couple of months, maybe, I need it and I'll just coast along with it because, after all, they're probably the most important months of my life, and then Max will be back and I'll have lost a few more pounds and *then* I can be my own best friend again.

And Mario's best friend too, she thought, her eyes clouding over. He'd figured it out, of course, but she'd refused to admit it till a couple of days ago, when she didn't have a choice, when he grabbed her purse in a fury and found this little box. The fight that followed, in the middle of the night at her apartment, was the most vicious they'd ever had. How *dare* he snoop like that? How *dare* she lie to him? Neither of them would back down, and they didn't even come close to resolving it by making love the way they usually did. Well, after all, she asked herself now, how could we when Mario got up and went home? She'd called from the airport and left a message on his machine: she was sorry they'd fought (not the same as saying she was sorry, and he'd know it); she'd be seeing him in a week; and — a small concession — she'd miss him.

Back in her seat, next to the man who was still interfacing with his buddy, she opened her engagement book. Breakfasts, lunches, dinners, every hour in between, all filled in except for the blank space she'd left for Thursday afternoon after the meeting with the curator of prints and drawings at the Santa Barbara Museum. "Mom and Dad," she wrote in now, unnecessarily. It was etched in her mind, but maybe putting it down would make it seem like just another appointment, would loosen the knot in her stomach that always appeared when she knew she'd be seeing them soon.

She and Chuck had grown up with all the California sun and surf that Santa Barbara offered and that the rest of America envied, along with more than enough money for anything they might have wanted. Their father was a heart specialist with a big practice, and the Wetherby house was a rambling California-Spanish hacienda in the Hope Ranch enclave, with a sweeping view of the Pacific and a path that led down through eucalyptus trees and a dry gulch to their private cove. Chuck was six years older, tall, lean, and golden, the ultimate California boy with a friendly, open face, kind to and fiercely protective of the kid sister who adored him.

Dr. Wetherby always seemed tired and distracted. He spent most of his time and energy on his patients, his research, and the conferences he was constantly attending. There wasn't much left over for his children, but Maggie and Chuck and their friends decided that was true of most of the Hope Ranch daddies. He always drove this year's dark blue Volvo sedan, and when Maggie was small she could only remember him as part of his car. She ran out to say good-bye to him in the morning, before her breakfast, and she ran out to welcome him home at night if he got back before her bedtime.

She associated her mother with a car too (a station wagon with imitation wood paneling), a car that was forever roaring down the long gravel driveway on its way to the club or the stables. Mrs. Wetherby was a big, restless woman, blonde and really very pretty when she made the effort. It was her athleticism that Chuck inherited: when she wasn't on the golf course she was on the tennis court; when she wasn't on the tennis court she was off with her palomino on one of the equestrian trails that wound through Hope Ranch. Or she was in the room the club management had named The Grille. Maggie was aware, even at ten, that they didn't grill anything there and that they should have just called it The Bar, but it was only the most obvious euphemism in a long list that she and Chuck came to know by heart. When her father said, "Your mother isn't feeling too well," it meant she was hung over and they should tiptoe. When the fat Mexican housekeeper, Mercedes, said, "Señora no es for deener," they knew she was still out at the bar. When her mother's car was in the shop, it was usually the body shop.

This double way of looking at things, she realized when she was much older, was common to every family where there was a drinker, and it extended way beyond the Wetherby house. Parents of friends would say, "Your mother is just amazing, Maggie, so athletic and still so much energy left over at night . . . ," and she learned exactly how to translate, how to smile and thank them as if they'd just complimented her in some way, when all she really wanted was for her mother to be like everyone else's. Clothes, dinner parties, decorating — the things that seemed to concern other mothers — bored Mrs. Wetherby to death, and so did most of those other mothers. So did her children, for that matter, and whenever she had to spend more than an hour with them her temper was so short that Maggie would be in tears most of the time.

Both deliberately and in a hundred unconscious ways, Maggie became as much unlike her mother as possible. She'd been blessed with the same natural grace as Chuck, if not his height, but she stubbornly refused to play any sport involving winners or losers unless some P.E. teacher insisted. The only exception she made was swimming — the Pacific was her backyard, after all — but that didn't count because it was just between her and the surf. The classroom was the arena where she competed; a B upset her as much as a bad putt upset her mother. Even at ten or eleven, she considered herself *artistic* (her mother pronounced it *autistic*): writing poetry; drawing seaweed and driftwood in pen-and-ink; reading Hermann Hesse and Dylan Thomas. When she came home with solid A's, her father patted her vaguely on the head — like a dog, she finally began to think — and her mother inevitably said what made Maggie feel worse than if she said nothing at all. The little family intellectual, she called her, more or less sneeringly, depending on how much she'd been drinking.

Chuck, at least, never failed her. He arranged private celebrations, hot fudge sundaes at McConnell's or burritos at their favorite place on lower State Street, when she had a triumph in school. He framed the drawings she gave him and the poem about the sandcrab she'd written on parchment, and he hung them in his room next to the ribbons and trophies that were beginning to accumulate there. For her part, she overcame her loathing for sports when Chuck was involved, glorying in his physical brilliance, cheering louder even than her mother when he won. For a while, he tried everything and excelled at everything — swimming, diving, golf, and tennis at the club; basketball, baseball, wrestling, and track at school — but by the time he was sixteen, tennis had edged out all the others to become his passion. He kept his grades up, nearly as high as Maggie's, but every spare moment was spent on the cement court behind their house or the grass courts at the club, where Mrs. Wetherby, suddenly the mother of a local celebrity, paid for pro lessons and then proudly complained about how expensive they were.

Maggie didn't realize how much Chuck was keeping the family in one piece until he went away to Stanford. She missed him achingly, of course, but she was angry with him, too, for abandoning her to her parents. She never knew what the connection was between the fact that her mother was spending more time in The Grille and proportionately less out of doors, and that her father was now on some kind of President's Commission and suddenly had to go to conferences in places like Helsinki and Cape Town. At the same time, even though she wasn't quite officially a teenager yet and it didn't seem fair, her breasts were beginning to show and her first period arrived and that made everything else twice as confusing because she wasn't even the same person, literally, physically, as she had been and she didn't know who she was instead.

She found herself taking charge of the house because someone had to. Mercedes was lazy and stupid. Her father was either away or locked in his study or, even when he emerged, so noncommittal that she could never get a real decision out of him. Her mother grew worse when her license was suspended, because then she could rely on cabs to get her home no matter what shape she was in. Maggie became the one who undressed her and put her to bed at two in the morning and then checked on her in the morning before she went to school. She became adept at covering up and smoothing over and moderating and pretending everything was okay, not because she was so loyal to her mother but because she wanted so badly to be a family that was just like other families.

She was remembering one of the times the police brought her mother home — her father was off somewhere; Mercedes was cowering in the kitchen, forever, unnecessarily, worried about her green card — when the stewardess's voice announced "our final descent into the Los Angeles area." Maggie shook herself and began to hunt for the transparencies she needed for her first meeting.

* * *

The four secretaries in the big, expensively but coldly furnished outer office were all so sorry that Mr. Fermi had to wait a few minutes to see Mr. Radnor. Would he care for some coffee in the meantime? He would, because he'd only had time to grab a quick cup at home before jumping in a cab and getting down here to the Radnor Building at Forty-seventh and Park. It was Monday morning, and he'd finally listened to the messages on his phone machine that had been accumulating all weekend. Word got around fast: a couple of very respectable, no-fewer-than-three-star restaurants wanted to talk, and a couple of others more or less offered him — offered his recorded voice, that is — a definite job. It made him laugh, and he could see himself on an auction block, offering his body and soul to the highest bidder like a very superior slave. The only call he'd answered so far, the only call that really intrigued him, was the one that brought him here.

After half a cup of coffee, Mr. Fermi could go in now. Radnor stayed seated behind his big mahogany desk, and as Mario navigated the expanse of deep maroon carpet, he decided it was something short men with overdeveloped senses of who was in control would do. He stood up when Mario reached him, barely grunted when they shook hands, and led him through a door behind his desk into a small private dining room. Windows looked out on the glassiness of Park Avenue, but in here someone had done his or her best to simulate an eighteenth-century London town house, right down to what looked like original oak paneling. A big Chippendale table was set for two with Wedgwood and early Georgian silver.

"Figured you might not have had time for breakfast," he said, waving Mario to a chair and pushing a buzzer that produced a waiter almost instantly. "Scrambled eggs okay? Bacon? Toast? Fine." He nodded to the waiter and they were alone again. "I gotta go down to Washington this afternoon and I wanted to talk this over, maybe start the ball rolling, if you like the ball. It was Susan's idea, as a matter of fact, but that doesn't mean I won't take the credit for it." He grinned modestly. "Susan has some of my best ideas."

Mario was sitting back and, with what he hoped looked like nonchalance, sipping a big glass of fresh orange juice, but his mind was on the edge of his chair. He didn't care if the idea came from the man's wife or his mother-in-law or his gypsy fortune-teller. He just wanted to know what it was, but it was Radnor's style to keep him waiting for a while. First he had to ponderously weigh congratulations for getting away from Rudi against how much everyone who went there would miss him. Then he had to fill him in with more details than anyone who wasn't on the Planning Commission could ever need to know about the East River complex and the new tower on Fifty-eighth Street. Mario made admiring sounds, sympathetic sounds, astonished sounds, but he was beginning to wonder if there *was* a point.

"You know I'm renovating the Gramercy Plaza?" Radnor asked suddenly. Mario nodded. In terms of size, he thought, it was relatively small potatoes for Radnor Associates — a medium-sized, rather run-down hotel, dating from the early 'thirties, that was now being converted to luxury condominiums. He'd seen some of the publicity: views of exclusive little Gramercy Square Park and, by current New York standards, enormous apartments, nothing smaller than seven rooms. Prices, he remembered, ranged from a million and three-quarters to well over four.

Radnor waited till they were served and the waiter had disappeared before he said any more. "Did you ever eat there when it was a hotel? Up on the top floor, the Arthur something. The King Arthur Room?"

"Once. Once was enough. I took a date there when I was still in college. Oldy Englishy medieval swords and armor. Terrible food, terrible, and they served it on those fake pewter platters. I think we drank too much out of self-defense or sheer depression or something. There must have been a view, but I don't even know if I noticed it — just a lot of dusty velvet curtains. Oh, and I'm sure I saw a couple of roaches in the men's room."

"Exactly. Susan and I went to some kind of reception there once, and she was convinced she got food poisoning." Mario privately thought it must have been early days: Rick probably still went to the occasional unfashionable place if it was necessary for business, but Susan wouldn't be caught dead there now.

Radnor cleared his throat. "Well. All the plans have been made to turn it into a real state-of-the-art health club. We're supposed to start ripping it up this week. Pool, sun deck, running track, a whole roomful of those S&M machines, all that shit. Our ads talk about it like it was the greatest thing since the Baths of Caracalla." He paused, and Mario wondered wildly if the man was going to offer him a carrot juice concession. "Susan's idea, though," he went on, obviously enjoying this, "as of this weekend, as of the minute she heard you walked out on Rudi, actually, was to give all those health freaks a club to run around in downstairs, down in the basement. Sun lamps instead of sunlight. She thinks there oughta be a restaurant up there instead. What do you think?"

Mario's mouth was full of food. "What do I think of what?" he asked thickly.

"Of opening a restaurant. You. There. Twentieth floor. A great restaurant. Naturally." Radnor was talking between bites.

"I think it's the greatest idea since, um" — he looked down at his plate — "since bacon and eggs." He took a deep breath and decided he had to let the man know, now, right away, about the resolution he'd made the other day with the help of the bottle of Bordeaux. "I should tell you something before we go any further," he said shakily. "I want to have my own place. I mean, I've decided I won't work for someone else, as manager, as anything." There. He'd said it.

Radnor looked up from his food. "I assumed that. So did Susan. I'm sure as hell not interested in going into the restaurant business, and neither is she. I'll put a bunch of money in and maybe we'll find a few other backers, but there must be some kind of payback scheme we can work out, no? Hell, I'm not talking about a tax write-off — I don't want to lose anything on the deal. I like to introduce people to ideas and then work out all the sordid details later. We think you're the right guy for this idea. It's really pretty simple."

"It's simple if there's enough money floating around," Mario said, laughing. "I'm not sure you realize how much restaurants cost. Do you have any idea? The kind of money we're talking here? I know I was plastered the one time I was there, but I remember it was a pretty big place."

"Square feet, it's half again as big as Rudi's. Plus there's a terrace that runs along three sides of it. I know we're talking about a lot of money. I had one of my people do some fast research this morning. The renovation on '21' ran almost five million and took, what, about three months? That place, what's it called, where all the political types hang out? Aurora. It ran a million. This oughta fall somewhere in between, don't you think? But on the high side? Actually, it'll probably end up close to four or five. Christ, you haven't seen it, though. I can't even ask you for ball-park numbers when you haven't seen it yet."

Mario was, in spite of himself, impressed. This guy was talking about millions the way other people talked about tens of thousands. He managed to murmur something about being anxious to have a look at the space.

"Good." Radnor was throwing down his napkin and Mario stood up quickly with him. They hadn't finished their food, but he numbly supposed no one was supposed to finish his food at a power breakfast.

"I thought we'd at least get you interested. I had my secretary make an appointment with a guy from Kitchens Associated, Kitchens Anonymous, something like that. My people say they're the best consultants around, and I thought you'd probably want to see what they have to say. He'll meet you there at noon. Can't remember his name; Kay'll tell you on the way out. The blonde girl. By the window."

He saw the blank look in Mario's eyes and smiled. "Sorry to throw all this at you at once. Really. Not trying to railroad you into anything." Mario thought that was exactly what he was trying to do — Radnor was used to people jumping when he snapped his fingers — but he wasn't sure he minded. "Matter of timing," he was saying. "The building'll be finished the first of the year. We're shooting for New Year's and we try to bring things in when we promise. We've sold, I think, thirty percent of the apartments so far. Not worried about the rest, but this'll be a boost, once the word gets out. Make the place even more desirable, we think, sort of an anchor or something. There's nobody else I want to work with on this kind of deal, so if you decide against it, then we gotta know soon and we'll just go ahead with the original gym thing. Anyway, we need your decision and some pretty detailed cost estimates by the end of the week. We're already in early October, and I'll be out of town all week, so get in touch with Jack Halsey here if you need anything."

This time, he walked with Mario back through the office as he talked. At the door to the reception area, still dazed, Mario shook the hand that was offered him and found himself alone with the four secretaries again. The one named Kay brought him a slip of paper with something typed on it, and he was out the door, down the elevator, and bumping into people on Park Avenue before he understood what had happened to him. It wasn't very complicated, really. He was pretty sure he was being given the chance of a lifetime.

Too impatient to look for a cab or to sit in one while it crawled through midtown traffic, he walked a block east and then straight down Lexington till it dead-ended at Twenty-first Street, the northern side of Gramercy Square. He had an hour before meeting the kitchen man and he wanted to see the space for himself first, alone. The Gramercy Plaza was twenty stories high, taller and a hundred years younger than anything else on the stately old square. He could imagine how enraged the owners of the red brick town houses must have been when this was put up in the 'thirties.

He gazed across the street at what he already considered *his* building. It was a shell at the moment, with a skirt of scaffolding, a construction elevator running up its front, a crane feeding it from the side street, a fat trash chute carrying away its waste products. It didn't look like a job that could be finished by the first of the year, but he knew Radnor's reputation and he figured the new occupants would be moving in as promised. Because the building had been designed by the same firm as the Chrysler Building and was considered architecturally important, it had landmark status. That meant that, even if he'd wanted to do more, Rick could only restore the exterior and leave it alone; all the work was interior renovation, which wouldn't be stopped by bad weather.

Its lines were very clean, mostly broken by vertical strips of small coral and gold tiles that ran up thin struts between the windows. Around the high, slightly recessed entrance was a multicolored tile frieze of stylized leaves. From this angle, he could see only the top bit of the building's cap, a four-sided pyramid that, he knew, was hiding the water tower and the elevator machinery. It was stepped up in the Mayan style, echoing the shape of the band around the entrance. To really look at the building properly, to be able to see the set-back top floor, *his* floor, he should have walked around to the far side of the square, but that would have to wait. For now, he was satisfied with a quick look from the sidewalk; he was too anxious to get inside to spend any more time out here.

The inside elevators were being replaced, so the foreman fetched him in a temporary construction lift that zoomed up the building's face, its plywood sides creaking terrifyingly. It took him to the level of the parapet and he had to jump down onto the terrace. Over his shoulder, he turned down the foreman's offer of a tour but then he perversely put off his exploration of the interior for another minute, like a child hoarding a piece of candy, and wandered around outside. Paved with cracked flagstones that he immediately saw would have to be replaced, the terrace extended for about twenty-five feet out from three sides of the restaurant.

Twenty stories hadn't represented a tall building in New York for nearly a century but, because nothing came close to its height for a few blocks, these views were amazingly good — down past the Village and Soho to the mass of Wall Street on the south, west over the square to Chelsea and the Hudson, north to the towers of midtown. It would be beautiful at night, not the top of the world but certainly romantically removed from it. On the east end, at the back of the building, were solid walls that he knew must enclose the kitchens and the elevators, topped with the absurdity of the Mayan pyramid. The dining room jutted out from them like the glassed-in (but squared off) stern of a steamship.

Slowly, deferentially, he pulled open a rusty sliding door and stepped into the big, dimly lit space. The foreman had warned him the electricity was turned off up here, and faded, frayed, velvet drapes were drawn across most of the windows. The first thing he did was to circle the room and pull them open; a couple of stubborn ones that refused to slide along their fake medieval rods were yanked down in his impatience to let in daylight. Only then did he allow himself to stand in the middle of the room and look around him.

It was a much bigger space than he'd remembered, and the ceiling — far higher than he'd realized — made it seem even more vast. All the dark, heavy trestle tables and chairs and the neo-Gothic bar stools had been stacked at one end. Way up in the gloom he could barely see the fixtures that held massive chains from which hung some 'thirties decorator's version of Arthurian chandeliers — heavy, sinister, wrought-iron things with candle-shaped light bulbs, begging for Errol Flynn or Douglas Fairbanks to swing from them. The walls, except for the back one, were glass, floor to ceiling, interrupted every fifteen feet or so by columns. At the four corners were heavier pillars that probably did most of the work of supporting the roof. They were all — these thick ones and the narrower ones between the windows — faced with gray plaster, grooved with dirty white lines of imitation mortar to look like the stones of a castle.

The top halves of the windows were composed of bits of colored, leaded glass that suggested heraldic motifs, lions rampant and unicorns resting. Some of the bottom halves were small-paned windows; others were cheap sliding-glass patio doors that must have been installed in a 'fifties update. Along the east wall, between pointed arches leading to the elevator lobby and the back of the house, were panels of a mural that he could barely see from where he stood. Coming closer, he recognized very badly painted scenes from the King Arthur legends, and he laughed softly. He had only the haziest ideas about what should be done with this room, about what he wanted and didn't want, but he was already sure he wouldn't be including Lancelot or Guinevere or Merlin in his decorating scheme.

His back to the painting, he looked out over the entire space. By taking off his glasses and squinting, he could ignore the ugly, patterned carpet and the dusty drapes and the filthy stained glass. He saw surfaces that were stripped down, polished, gleaming. He saw a room filled with people, elegantly dressed, handsome people who were sitting at beautifully set tables and eating wonderfully prepared food. He heard laughter and the tinkle of crystal and the clink of silver, and, although he wasn't sure about this, he thought he heard music. Not canned music; a single piano, maybe; the room seemed to demand it.

He was hooked. If there was any conceivable way he could swing it, he was determined to make this place — in what was a terrifyingly short time — into one of the most spectacular restaurants New York had ever seen. He hadn't explored the rest of the floor yet, but he knew there had to be enough space behind the scenes to support a room of this size. After all, the King Arthur Room had fed people, however badly, for more than fifty years. He was sure the kitchens would have to be totally ripped apart, but that was a matter of time and money and he was already counting on Radnor's offer to put enough money at his disposal, and money was time. What would make this a success was the wonderful room in which he stood. He could almost believe that it had a personality, that its feelings were hurt by the cheap, false way it had been decorated, that it was waiting for someone like him to come along and make it as beautiful as it deserved to be, as important architecturally as the rest of the building was.

Wobbling across the floor, pacing it off with one foot directly in front of the other like a tightrope walker, he heard the elevator creak to a halt outside. A round, red-faced young man jumped down off the ledge, stumbling because he was carrying a bulging briefcase and rolls of blueprints and because his legs were so short. Recovering himself with a curse, he held out his hand and introduced himself as Bob Siegel. Mario already felt, coming out to welcome him, that he was receiving the first guest in his new home.

In the short time they spent in the dining room before moving on to the back of the house, Mario decided he liked Siegel's style. He asked the right questions, he seemed to have the right sense of priorities, and he didn't waste time. They stood and talked for another few minutes in the reception area and then plunged into the kitchen. It was better than Mario had feared. It would need complete renovation, and all the appliances would have to be replaced, but at least the floorplan was workable, the plumbing and wiring seemed to be in the right places, and it looked like only a couple of walls would have to be torn down or put up. As Siegel fired questions at him, as he heard himself answering, he saw that he'd known what he wanted without realizing it.

"Have you got a *chef de cuisine?*"

"Yes. Louis Comtois. He's at Rudi's now and he doesn't know about this yet — Christ, *I've* only known about it for a couple of hours — but I can count on him coming on board."

"Great. No offense, but I need his input as much as yours, more than yours. Just paint me broad pictures."

"I'm not offended." He thought for a moment. "Maybe I'd better tell you what I *don't* want, first. Noise. I want the quietest kitchen in New York."

"Okay. Expensive but possible. Sound locks between here and the dining room. Perforated metal tiles with fiberglass backing. Pirelli rubber tile floors. What else don't you want?"

"No steam tables, except for sauces. Vegetables will be partially cooked and then finished to order in serving pans. No heat lamps, except to keep the bread warm. Freshly baked bread."

"And where's this bread going to be baked?"

"There," Mario said instantly, although he hadn't thought about it until that instant. He pointed to a room that connected on the left with the main space. "I want a pastry chef and an assistant, and that seems like the obvious place. Let's say three ovens in there and a flattop and a mile or two of marble surface."

Siegel raised his brows. "We're talking *haute,* then. There can't be more than a dozen restaurants in New York with their own *patissiers.*"

"So we'll make it a baker's dozen. As it were. The woman I have in mind makes incredible ices, too, so there should be a sorbet machine in there."

Siegel made a note. "Next. Flattops. I want to hear what your chef has to say, of course, but how many do you see here?"

"Six. Seven, maybe. And three grills. One for regular charcoal and the other two for mesquite or cherrywood or whatever Louis thinks he wants to try that night. I know he's going to ask for a smoker, too, because he's always wanted one at Rudi's, but Rudi was too cheap . . . never mind. For smoking chicken in Grand Marnier, things like that. In this alcove, probably. With the coffee machines."

They stood in front of one of the walk-in refrigerators, and Siegel gave him a short lecture on conservation of energy. Plastic strips on the walk-ins' doorways, he said. Waving at where the ice-making machine would be, he explained how the heat it generated could be recycled. Mario was more and more sure that this was the right man for the job. After another hour in the kitchen and the rooms behind, they came out into the main dining room again.

"So far, so good," Siegel said thoughtfully. "It's a pretty tight time frame, though."

"I think that's called an understatement," Mario said quietly. "I would have said six months, at the very least." So far, he'd been carried along on his own euphoria, but he was suddenly scared. He didn't see how they could possibly do it before the deadline, and he had an idea Radnor would rather scratch the whole thing than back down on the date. It was New Year's or nothing, he was sure.

Siegel patted him on the back. "With anyone else but Rick Radnor on your side, I'd say it couldn't be done, but do you have any idea how much pull he has? He can move mountains — well, he probably could, literally, but there don't happen to be any in New York. He has the unions eating out of his hand, for one thing. And permits, believe me, are a snap for him 'cause he pours so much money into this town, one way or another. Besides, a lot of the stuff that takes so much time to organize and coordinate is already set up, you know — the crane and the outside elevator and a whole crew of guys who were evidently waiting to start turning this into a gym. There's just one rather important team member you haven't mentioned, though, so I figure you don't have anyone lined up yet. Who are you going to get to design the front of the house?"

Mario stared past him. "I'm going to talk to Frances McKinnon," he said slowly. Like all the other decisions he'd just made, this one seemed like something he'd known forever.

* * *

A woman stood in the bedroom of the suite she kept at the Sherry-Netherland and tried to decide what her best disguise would be. Finally, with the honesty for which she'd been known all her life (brutal frankness, it had more than once been called), she admitted to herself that no one would recognize her on this miserable little errand if she went out just as she was. No makeup, no corset, no false eyelashes, no turtleneck, no wig: just this white-haired old broad, seventy-three last month.

She sighed, rummaged in the closet for the muumuu she usually only wore for loafing around her house in Maui, and then found a belt that *really* made it hideous. The Toast of Broadway takes a walk, she thought bitterly, but they haven't called you that for about thirty years, baby, and nobody, but nobody, down there on Fifth Avenue or any other goddamn avenue is ever going to know who you are without all your props. So you're safe, and the secret (which, for all your famous fucking candidness, you're *never* going to be chatting about in some interview) is safe, too. She jammed on a pair of sunglasses just to be positive, and then she picked up the Bergdorf's shopping bag that held a newspaper-wrapped bundle and walked out of the room.

* * *

Although the man lived and worked in a nearby state, he kept a small office in Rockefeller Center for a number of reasons, some of them connected with his position, others connected with . . . certain pleasures. What he did there today would fit into neither category, this odious ritual that he performed twice a year because he had no choice. Spinning the combination lock on his desk drawer and then pulling out the bundles of bills he'd been accumulating for the past few weeks, he swore at himself for leaving the letter in with them (as if he might have forgotten the instructions!) because now the money itself smelled faintly of the peculiarly long-lasting cologne. He wrapped up the usual fifty thousand in newspaper, tied it with string, and found a plastic shopping bag under his secretary's desk. She'd been sent out to do some research for him, and his driver had been given the afternoon off: they were both very loyal, very discreet, but he couldn't trust anyone in this particular area of his life.

Hats weren't part of his image and neither were sunglasses, but he put on both today before he left the office with the bag that advertised a ladies' shoe store on its side. He thought he was lucky, making it down the elevator and out through the lobby without being recognized, but then a doorman who stood just inside the revolving doors smiled at him. "Have a nice day, Governor," he said.

* * *

Next to the pilot of a small chartered helicopter sat a man who was trying very hard not to look frightened when they tilted from side to side in a breeze that seemed to stiffen as they neared New York. He hated these rides — hated anything smaller than a 747, in fact — but this was one of those times when he didn't have any choice. If you were headlining at the newest, biggest joint on the Boardwalk and if you were collecting a quick half million for two weeks' worth of making people laugh, then you didn't dick around with the Jersey Turnpike and the Garden State Parkway and hope to get into town and back to Atlantic City in time for tonight's show.

"Hope this won't be an inconvenience for you," the cocksucker's letter had said. Well, it was, and anyone who'd picked up a paper for the past month would've known it was. At least he didn't have to fuck around with some stupid disguise: not even the pilot, who was bringing them gently down now to the Thirtieth Street helipad, recognized him without his signature mop of red curls. Sunglasses and a head that was bald as a billiard ball, he had decided, were enough. He reached around behind the seat for the alligator attaché case that held the money. Like having a second agent, he thought (it was automatic to him, sometimes, phrasing thoughts as one-liners, even when they weren't funny): ten percent of his two-week gross.

9

FRANCES PUT THE PHONE DOWN and stood next to it, looking out the living-room windows to the park. It was an overcast, damp morning, and the trees, shedding their leaves, seemed a little ragged and helpless. The apartment was warm and a fire was crackling in the fireplace, but she shivered and hugged herself. Mario Fermi had just called. He wanted to talk about some design work. It was Tuesday; her birthday party had been Friday: could he conceivably be working on his own restaurant already? She wasn't very clear about what he told her on the phone because she was so shocked to hear his voice. He obviously said the right thing to someone at Steve's office or they wouldn't have given him this unlisted number, she thought, and now I've actually invited him here instead of setting up a meeting at the office or somewhere neutral.

He's coming here, to the place where I live, in half an hour, she whispered. Thirty minutes. Mario is coming here, to my apartment. Unless I call him back and cancel, tell him to come to the office this afternoon instead. I could do that. I could tell him I forgot I had a meeting or something. Actually, there's that appointment at Scalamandre to look at fabric for the chairs in Trish's showroom . . .

She walked quickly into Hamilton's library, where there was a Rolodex that duplicated the numbers on the one in her own study. First she dialed Scalamandre and canceled her appointment. Then she dialed Hamilton's niece, Dorothy's daughter.

"Peekie? It's Frances."

"Hello, Frances. I hope you're not calling to say you and Uncle Ham can't come tonight?"

"Oh, no. We'll be there, maybe a little late because Ham's got to have drinks with someone. Do you still expect to have sixty?"

"Yes, and I'm running around wildly. I haven't had so many people to dinner since before I was pregnant."

"Well, that's why I'm calling. I don't need Marianne for anything special today and I thought she could help you."

"Oh, that's sweet, Frances, but Mother's lent me Frieda and I have Jennie, so I think it'll all fall into place by tonight."

"Peekie, I'm insisting. Can't you hear the insistent tone in my voice? And I'll have her call Danny in the car — he's taking a package out to Kennedy for me — so he can run errands or do any heavy work you need done."

"Really, Frances, I *do* appreciate it, but I think I have . . ."

"I won't take no for an answer. New mothers shouldn't exert themselves. Haven't you ever been told that? Marianne ought to be there in half an hour and Danny will be back from Kennedy by noon. And we'll see you tonight. 'Bye." She hung up before Peekie had a chance to say anything more. Then she buzzed Marianne, explained it all, sat back in Hamilton's big leather desk chair, and lit a cigarette.

She'd made the calls in a daze, a part of her doing all this arranging while another part of her stood back and watched in amazement. She tried to think about what she'd just done. After all, he was only coming by to have a sort of preliminary chat, to interview her, really. Maybe he couldn't stay more than a few minutes, just long enough to explain what it was all about or drop off some plans or something. Maybe he had to be somewhere soon. Maybe he was meeting Maggie for lunch.

She put her cigarette out fiercely in the big alabaster ashtray on the desk, buzzed Marianne again to tell her to make coffee and maybe put some pastries out on a tray but to leave it all in the kitchen, and walked firmly upstairs. Approaching the big pier glass in the hallway, she paused for a second. She wanted badly to see how she looked but she made herself walk straight past it without turning. She looked fine, she told herself, already dressed for the Scalamandre appointment in a black Kenzo tunic and skirt that she knew were good lines for her. She would *not* allow herself the luxury of mooning in front of the mirror.

Once up in her glass box, she fussed with papers and catalogues, self-consciously brisk and businesslike, but by the time the bell rang, she'd accomplished practically nothing. Walking to the stairs, she felt weak, almost nauseated with anticipation, and this time she couldn't help glancing at her reflection.

He was smiling when she opened the door to him. "Hello," she said brightly. Then, over his shoulder, she said, "Thank you, Rafael," to the elevator boy, who was waiting to be sure this man ought to be admitted to the sacred precincts of the McKinnon penthouse. When she and Mario were alone, she smiled back at him, wondering if she looked as shaky as she felt. He began to thank her for seeing him on such short notice, but she interrupted.

"It's quite all right, really." My God, Frances, she thought, did you actually say that? Maybe you should try a few other up-to-date expressions, like "Not at all," or "I beg of you, sir, don't mention it." She stumbled on. "I thought you said . . . but I didn't see how you could know, so soon, but . . . on the phone, did you say you're opening your own place?" He nodded.

"Well. Congratulations, then. Would . . . do you have time . . ." She took a deep breath. "Would you like some coffee? My housekeeper isn't here but she left some, and I think maybe some brioches or something?" She flushed. She'd just let him know they were alone. Would he realize she'd sent Marianne out for precisely that reason? No, of course he wouldn't.

"Please. That would be great."

He held on to a roll of blueprints, but she took his coat from him, hung it in the foyer closet, and waved him into the living room. "Be right back."

"It's a beautiful room," he said when she returned with a big tray, which she put on a table near the windows. He was standing in front of the Jasper Johns flag painting on the far wall. "I wouldn't have thought you'd . . . I didn't think you'd have so many modern pieces."

"Why not? I'm a modern woman, you know. Would you like cream or sugar? And would you like some pastry?"

"Just coffee, thanks, with a little cream." He came over to where she was standing and took it from her. Her hand trembled as she handed it to him, and the cup rattled.

"I've obviously had enough already." She led him to the pair of bleached-oak chairs that faced each other in front of the fire, sitting down and lighting a cigarette. He sat on the arm of the other.

"I didn't mean to sound so surprised about the room," he said. "I guess I associate old families with old furniture and old paintings, but I should know it's not necessarily true. Some of Maggie's clients are from a dozen generations of money, but I guess I still make the assumption."

"Well, *I'm* not from old money. My background is, um, rather different from my husband's."

"You seem very comfortable with it."

"I usually am, but it can get in the way. People are intimidated by *it* rather than by *me*." She laughed. "It sounds like I'm saying I want to be intimidating in my own right."

He took a sip of coffee, looking at the big Rauschenberg above the mantel. "You are."

Her eyebrows rose in surprise.

"I'm sorry." He was hoarse and he had to clear his throat. "That didn't come out the way I meant it to. It's just that you have a kind of spirit in your own right that doesn't have anything to do with being Mrs. McKinnon. And of course your talent." He gestured to the room and then, this time, looked straight at her. "And your beauty. That has nothing to do with being a McKinnon."

"Thank you," she said softly, looking back at him, then turning away, recrossing her legs in the other direction, and sitting up. She wanted to be bright and maybe slightly flirtatious, but her voice sounded grating and metallic to her. "Now. Tell me about it. You must have lined up a space already." She pointed to the blueprints.

He didn't make any attempt to unroll the plans, but he began to tell her about Rick Radnor and Gramercy Park and Bob Siegel. She tried to concentrate. This is business, she told herself. This is important to him; this could be important to me. She heard his first words but then she was adrift, completely unable to follow what he was saying. The tall buildings across the park were colorless and indistinct in the mist, and she felt lost, rudderless. They could have been anywhere. There were only the two of them in the world, in this room.

His voice was a low rumble above the sounds of morning traffic seventeen stories down on Fifth Avenue. The smell of the coffee in her cup was almost overpowering, too strong, too rich. She held it up to her face with both hands, not drinking but breathing it in deeply, willing it to clear her head. She watched his mouth, not understanding what he was saying but looking at his lips move, then at his eyes. She was free to stare at him for the first time because he was looking everywhere but at her. She remembered the word Trish had once used, that she, Frances, was *formidable*. Could he be nervous too? she wondered. He seems to be comfortable, in control of himself, but is he actually feeling like a fly in a black widow's web? Even if he's attracted to me, and I know he is, have I been too . . . obvious? Have I scared him, or am I being such a brutally gracious hostess that he thinks I'm patronizing him? Have I made him hate me without meaning to?

She shuddered. She was furious with herself, afraid she'd ruined everything, whatever "everything" was. His lips stopped moving; his eyes came back to look into hers.

"Am I boring you? Are you all right?"

"No. No, I mean you're not boring me. Nothing's wrong."

There was a moment of complete stillness, when neither of them moved or even blinked, when they both understood what would happen. Then he got up slowly and stood above her, his eyes never leaving hers. He reached down and gripped her shoulders, pulling her up to him. They kissed for a long time, very tenderly, and she felt the tension drain from her. There was no more wondering or worrying, only this melting, this feeling that it was preordained, that there was nothing they could do about it, that it was right. Or at least, maybe, not that it was right but that it would be wrong to try to ignore it. She broke away from him and put her hand on his cheek. "Upstairs," she said calmly. She turned away from him to walk across the room.

He followed her up the stairs and along the corridor to her bedroom, aware of every line of her body under the thin wool, wanting her more than he'd ever wanted a woman in his life. An image of

Maggie came into his mind just then, Maggie as she'd looked — tearful and furious — when he turned his back on her and walked out of her apartment. She's three thousand miles away, he reminded himself. She could have been in the next room, though, for all it mattered at this moment; he would still be following this woman upstairs.

In her bedroom, Frances turned around to face him with one hand behind her neck, her fingers hesitating on the first of the buttons that ran down the back of the long overblouse. The gesture was shy, tentative, even a little awkward. He moved to her, brought her arm down, and held her hands down at her side, leaning forward to kiss her. Their kiss began as gently as their first one downstairs, but then her head fell back and he began to explore her mouth with his tongue, and it became a very different kiss. His hands went to her hips, hers to his back, and they pulled closer. His erection, running up his groin, pressed against her through the layers of cloth.

They stripped each other as fast as buttons and zippers would allow, tearing, grabbing, kissing, exploring. Now that they were together like this, they couldn't move apart for a moment, couldn't stand back and carefully remove all these impediments. He had to be in her, they were saying to one another without speaking; there was no time, no need, for anything else. She stumbled, and as he caught her they fell to their knees. He pulled down her panties, the last bit of cloth between them, and she opened herself to his fingers. The bed was too far away, suddenly, miles away. His mouth still on hers, he pressed her down against the soft carpet.

Just as he was about to enter her — for only a second or two but long enough for them both to be aware of it — they froze and searched one another's eyes. They were having the same thought, that this was their last possible chance to turn back from wherever they were going, the last instant they could swerve from the center of the road and continue in their own lanes, their own lives. It was an illusion, of course — and they both saw that too. They were in love and it was impossible and they were in love. Some force, something they couldn't fight, had lifted them out of their own places in the world and brought them here and now nothing was going to be the same. Their flesh already knew this was inevitable, and a very deep part of their minds — at some point, maybe a month ago, maybe before that — had also bowed to what was happening.

He met her mouth again at the instant he pierced her, and then they had no memory of even the smallest hesitation and they had no choice and they only had to follow what their bodies told them. She arched upward, pulling him into her and squeezing him with the spasms that immediately began to course through her. Their kisses were rougher, asking for more, demanding more, and then he broke away to move his lips to her breasts. He began to thrust violently; impaling her on the carpet, trying to reach and then reaching a center, a core, triggering a long, continuous contraction that in turn brought him to the edge. His groans grew louder, his heat poured into her, and she screamed.

Wordlessly, their rasping breaths gradually slowing, they kissed, their eyes open and searching again. He stayed inside her, still hard, propping himself on the floor with his elbows so he wouldn't crush her. They couldn't bear to separate. Rocking back to his knees, his hands cupped under her and her legs wrapped around his back, he slowly stood up and carried her to the bed. Never leaving her, never softening, he pulled back the covers and gently laid her down on the sheets, just as gently smoothing her hair back against the pillows, kissing her eyes, her neck, her breasts. The first time was a leap into space together, unavoidable, mindless. But this was love they were facing, this was obsession. Because of that, what they did here, in this bed or in all the beds of the future, could be richer, subtler, more imaginative, but it could never again be simple. So when, in only a moment, they began to move again in the long, slow, luxurious rhythm that was only now possible, it was very different. This time they brought *themselves* along, and if that meant more sweetness and laughter and the most exquisite pleasure, it meant sadness and guilt as well. Reaching the same place again, it also contained something approaching anger — with circumstances, with the world, with the people they ought to be with instead of one another, with one another, even.

It was Frances who finally broke the long quiet afterward, her voice only a whisper in his ear. "I didn't . . . realize."

"I didn't either," he said softly, stroking the thick dark hair that had tumbled down around her face again. He raised his head to look at her. "We didn't have a choice, did we? Do we?"

She shook her head, frowned, and began to say more, but he put his hand over her mouth. "There has to be a way," he said. Then he took his hand away and kissed her fiercely.

She walked him downstairs when he left, an hour later, but she didn't wait with him for the elevator. They had at last been able to talk about the restaurant for a moment — yes, of course he wanted her to design it, and of course she would, and of course they would meet tomorrow at the site — but even if she managed a friendly, businesslike handshake for the elevator boy's sake, she could hardly let him see her in a dressing gown, saying good-bye to a man. Going back up the stairs, she suddenly felt — so strange to her, after the depths she had explored just now, after the passion she had felt and shown and spent — a simple happiness, almost a lightheadedness. I have a secret, she thought as she changed the sheets and picked up her clothes from the floor, delighted with herself. I'm a woman with a mysterious, other life and I must hide it from the servants. Suddenly hungry, she went down to the kitchen and stood in front of the refrigerator, eating straight from a bowl of jellied consommé, not even bothering with a spoon. Then she took some celery, some crackers, and a glass of milk up to her glass house on the roof.

Curled up in the old armchair and gazing down to the park, she couldn't believe they were the same trees, couldn't see how this could even be the same day, as two hours before. The world, her world, was a new place — unknown, frightening, extraordinary. She remembered, even though it was so long ago, the last time she'd felt anything like this. She'd been a girl, telling herself she was a woman. What does that make me now, she wondered wryly, a woman telling herself she's a girl?

* * *

It was the same chair she used to climb up in when she was very small, when it had seemed very big, to wait for her father to get home from work. Tall and thin, his hair already turning gray, he'd come into the cramped tenement apartment on Thompson Street, down in the western, smaller part of Little Italy, and stoop down to kiss his pretty wife in the kitchen. Then he'd walk slowly into the living room and over to the big armchair where Francesca was turning the pages of a picture book and trying not to giggle. He had to start to sit down and pretend he didn't notice her, almost squashing her, until she squealed with laughter and threw her arms around him. Then she had to guess what was in the brown paper bag he always had with him. It would be an eggplant and some strawberries, maybe, or zucchini and apples, because he sold fruit and vegetables in a place called Hell's Kitchen, a long way away, up in the West Forties. Anyway, it was important to know what he brought, because she'd be eating it for dinner or for lunch the next day.

The Lambettis were different in many ways from the other families in the tight little parish. For one thing, there were only three of them, and most of her friends had at least one brother or sister, all living in apartments no bigger than theirs: two tiny bedrooms, a small parlor, a kitchen with a sink that doubled as a bathtub, and a water closet. Mama had something called a heart condition, Francesca was told when she pestered her for a brother or a sister, so she wouldn't be having any more babies.

For another thing, none of the other apartments she visited had anything on their bookshelves but figurines, souvenirs of Atlantic City or Asbury Park, or prayer books, but Papa had real books, and they usually had long political or sociological titles. In the evenings, he read these books, cotton balls in his ears to keep out the sounds of first a radio and eventually a television, in front of which Francesca sprawled on the floor, as well as the sewing machine in the corner where Mama made most of her own clothes and all of her daughter's.

When he was elected to the union board, though, he was out more and more of the time at meetings. Francesca was twelve when she heard him talking softly with her mother one night while she was supposed to be asleep. Mama said he couldn't take all the world's problems on his shoulders. He said he wasn't trying to take all the world's problems on his shoulders but if something wasn't right it wasn't right.

He was killed a week later, and she knew it was connected with that conversation, that something wasn't right. A truck crushed him against a brick wall in a narrow street around the corner from the vegetable stand, but nobody saw what happened and nobody ever found the truck or the driver. After the man left, the man who came to tell them why Papa wouldn't be coming home that night, Francesca walked straight into her bedroom, tore her rosary apart and threw the ivory beads and bits of gold chain into the trash. If God was this unfair, then she'd have nothing to do with Him. Mrs. Lambetti was awed by her fury — as she was already amazed by the quickness of her mind and by the beginnings of what promised to be a finely cut beauty — but even though Francesca loved her and wanted to please her, she was very firm. The day after the funeral, the last Mass she would go to, she transferred from Our Lady of Pompeii to the public junior high school.

Her mother never tried to find out more about the "accident." Her husband was gone; she had loved him; but she had a daughter to raise. She used the entire life insurance check to buy the Bon-Ton Lingerie Shoppe up on Spring Street from old Mrs. Mattioli, who was moving to Florida and who settled for a low price. Mrs. Lambetti had worked there during the war, when she and her baby were waiting for Papa to come home from the Pacific, and she loved the beautiful silky things and the customers' chatter and the sound of the cash register. Francesca helped her paint and lay new linoleum. A neighbor modernized the front of the store at cost, with plate glass and pale pink tile that Mama would wash every morning with a scrub brush and a squeegee. By the time Francesca began high school, the Bon-Ton was providing a small but steady income. There was sometimes even enough to put a little money aside for college. Mama didn't know precisely what they taught in colleges, and she didn't understand many of the things her daughter talked about now, but her husband had wanted his only child to go to a college and that was enough for her.

The High School of Music and Art, way uptown on the City College campus, was a special school, and only a small percentage of bright students from all the five boroughs were accepted. There was a bewildering choice of classes to take and clubs to join, and Francesca wanted everything at once. She made new friends, especially a pretty Jewish girl from the Upper West Side, Trish Janis, who was going to be a fashion designer. She learned about T. S. Eliot and El Greco and eye shadow and stockings and boys.

At the beginning of her junior year, a senior named Michael Petrocelli sat down across from her in the cafeteria one day. His face was long and irregular, he was tall and skinny and he didn't know what to do with his arms and legs, but he had extraordinary eyes, dark and deeply set, that burned into her from behind horn-rimmed glasses. He talked in a low, intense voice about William Faulkner and Albert Schweitzer and John Foster Dulles. She'd noticed him before and she already thought he was oddly handsome, but now she decided he was brilliant, too. When the bell rang for the first afternoon class, she knew something had happened to her. He didn't treat her like any other boy she'd ever known. He didn't tell her she was cool or neat or pretty or cute: he told her she was beautiful; he told her she was smart. She forgot to use the flirty expressions she'd practiced in the mirror and she forgot to toss her ponytail. After school that day, they had coffee at a place in the Village where there were supposed to be beatniks, and even though she didn't see any she felt very intellectual and adult. Then he walked her home, holding her hand, and he kissed her on the steps of her building, right in front of Mrs. Castelli and Mrs. Caputo.

When she later tried to remember her junior year, she could only see Michael — running his hand through his dark, shaggy hair while he studied; loping down Thompson Street to the subway to take him home to Sheepshead Bay; kissing her in the middle of the skating rink in Central Park, ignoring the whistles and catcalls from the figures whizzing around and around them. They talked about everything and they disagreed about everything. They argued about the United Nations, and racial equality, and Eleanor Roosevelt. Like her father, Francesca had ideals, sometimes vaguely expressed but always passionately felt. Michael was more realistic; he wanted to know how things worked. He called her a dreamer and she called him a cynic. They'd fight, kiss, apologize, and find themselves in another argument within ten minutes.

Francesca's grades stayed good, to her mother's amazement, almost the highest in her class. She and Michael had the same appetite to know everything there was to know, the same determination to make something of themselves. He'd be the first one in his family to graduate from high school, and his parents didn't see why he needed any more education than that, but he wanted the best: Harvard, then Harvard Law, then an assistant district attorneyship, then either politics or, eventually, the Supreme Court. Francesca didn't know exactly what to do with her own life, but she knew it would be golden and she knew it would be linked with Michael's. When he got his Harvard scholarship for the next year, they decided she'd follow him, the year after that. Radcliffe, of course, because that was right next door to Harvard, wasn't it? It was very simple.

They both had summer jobs that year — she waited tables at a diner under the elevated West Side Highway, Michael pumped gas up on Eleventh Avenue — but they reserved one whole day a week for each other. Her Sundays were for Mama, but Saturdays were for going to the beach with Michael. All summer long, they met at the old Pennsylvania Station early in the morning, caught the Long Island Railroad to Freeport and then a bus out to the great public stretches of Jones Beach. They changed their clothes at the farthest bathhouse and walked for a mile or two until they found a hollow in the dunes that wasn't already staked out by another couple. Baking in the sun next to each other, wearing only a few bits of cotton and nylon, they were unbearably aware, much more than during the winter, of the whole delicious, painful question of sex. They came so close, sometimes, that the only thing to do was to rush into the surf to cool themselves, but Francesca was firm. It wasn't because of God and it wasn't because of what the neighbors would think if they knew, because she was still angry with Him and she didn't care about them. It was pure, claustrophobic fear of being trapped, of having a baby, of losing her wonderful independence just when her life was beginning, that made her stop on the edge of the precipice when every part of her was telling her to go on, to just *do* it.

Michael pleaded and raged. He made her admit she was as excited as he was. He guaranteed nothing could happen. He showed her the condom he kept in his wallet, filling it once with Coca-Cola to prove it wouldn't leak, but that only made her laugh. Yes, she agreed; in theory, yes. Yes, there was only a tiny chance. But, no, she wouldn't. If they didn't do it, then there was no chance at all, was there? The argument never ended, but it never really ruined the day for more than a little while.

In her senior year at Music and Art, she began to dress the way she knew the 'Cliffies would, the really avant-garde ones who sat in coffeehouses and listened to jazz. She wore loose sweaters over straight skirts over black tights. She bought horn-rimmed glasses with clear lenses. She had her hair cut very short, to her mother's horror. She stopped wearing makeup, to her mother's delight. It wasn't really a very flattering look, but Francesca had grown into her beauty in the past year and it wouldn't have been possible to hide it: it was suddenly there, a part of her. Everyone knew she'd been Michael's girl, but now he was gone and half the boys in the senior class tried to move in for the kill. Once in a while she'd accept a study date at the library and maybe a Coke afterward, but if she went to movies or dances it was either with Trish or by herself. She lived for Michael's letters, for her classes, and for the all-important scholarship, which, when it really did come, stunned her teachers and seemed perfectly natural to Francesca. That was the way things were supposed to be: she and Michael were meant to be together and of course the world would make it possible.

She wrote to him every day, even when his own letters grew shorter and didn't come so often. He was working very hard, and naturally she forgave him. When he managed longer letters, they were filled with enthusiasm for his professors and, more and more, for the people he was meeting. Of course he'd make new friends, she told herself, and of course they'd mostly be from rich families, Harvard being Harvard, but he seemed to have more to say about their backgrounds and how much their fathers were worth than what *they* were like.

When he came home at Easter, she hesitantly asked him about it. Wasn't there a gap between him and the rich kids? He shook his head. You had to make a conscious effort, of course, you had to ingratiate yourself with the right people, but they were great guys. She'd find out when she got to Radcliffe. She wasn't going to find out, she said without thinking, because she wasn't signed up for Social Climbing 1A, was she? They found themselves in the middle of a bitter, name-calling fight, different from any they'd ever had because neither of them would back down.

Their letters were very stiff for the next two months, and then he came down for a week early in June, the only time he could spare after his last final, because he'd be working in the library at school for the whole summer. They went to the beach, of course, but riding out there the first day there was a distance between them that she'd never felt before. They walked out from the bathhouse, found a spot, spread their blanket, and scattered the picnic things without saying more than a few necessary words. She knew they couldn't do this; they couldn't lie there for hour after hour, inches apart, without talking. If he wouldn't say anything, then she had to try. She had to get back the easiness, the specialness that had always been there. She began to talk, trying to make him see how it would all be fine when they were together again in the fall, but he said something cutting and dismissive, she felt a sharp jab of pain and then of anger, and they were back in the same argument before she realized it had happened.

They circled the blanket like wrestlers, throwing words at each other, anything that might hurt. She screamed that he was becoming a bourgeois little organization man, no better than the worst sharks on Wall Street or the most corrupt pigs in Washington. He said he'd take his chances, that anything was better than being a dreamer like her father, an armchair liberal, a loser. She slapped him then and scratched at his face, shouting obscene words she'd never used in her life, drawing blood with her nails. He hit her hard across her face with the back of his hand, and she recoiled. They stood apart in shock for a moment and then their arms were around each other and it was over. They sank to their knees, both of them crying, and their tears mixed with the blood from his face and ran down into the sand. They kissed fiercely and then gently and then fiercely again, holding tightly, saying how sorry they were without using words. She had to feel him close to her, as close as they could be. They'd been so far apart; they'd hurt so much; now they were together. She lay back, half on the blanket, and drew him down with her, covering her length. She felt his excitement and she responded with her own, opening to him, telling him with her body that she knew what was happening and that she wanted it to happen. The risk had always stopped her before, but now there was a bigger danger, that they wouldn't be able to repair the damage, that they couldn't do enough to make it right again.

Nothing existed for her that week but their blanket in the sand and what they'd discovered there. They'd stay till dusk and then run to catch the last bus back to the station. They spoke very little, dozing in the sun until one of them woke and began the cycle all over again. After the first time, Michael always pulled away from her at the very last minute, and she was satisfied that it was enough, that nothing could happen. He half-heartedly suggested using something, but she refused. All they had to do was to be careful, and she didn't want one of those strange, laughable, clinical things in her. She knew they'd taken a chance, once, but now they could control it. They only had to deny themselves the last moment of sharing, and that seemed like a small price to pay for so much pleasure.

The day after he left, she started at the two jobs she'd been able to line up by lying about her age and her plans for the fall. From eleven to four, she'd wear an ugly, pale blue nylon uniform to serve lunch to businessmen at a place down in the Wall Street area. From eight till midnight, she'd wear a black dress and black tights to serve espresso and pastries to students and beats in a coffeehouse on MacDougal Street. Before, after, between, and on weekends, she'd try to get through the long suggested reading list Radcliffe sent her.

There was a big letter from him, fatter than usual, waiting for her in the mailbox on the Friday afternoon before the long Fourth of July weekend, but she didn't open it right away. She wanted to savor it, and she quickly changed into a bathing suit and a wraparound skirt and walked to the open, abandoned pier over on the Hudson where she liked to lie, reading and daydreaming, in the sun. It was hot and very humid and she was damp from hurrying, but the sweat froze on her and she began to shiver after she read the first few sentences. It was very bad, but she made herself read through to the end.

He had wanted to tell her when he was home, but then they had such a wonderful week (which he'd never forget, he said in parentheses). He should have written to her as soon as he got back but he let it slide, and he was angry with himself for that. The fact was that he'd been seeing someone all spring. Her name was Ann, she was a 'Cliffie, and they were, by now, very *involved.* Not that they slept together; Ann wouldn't, and it was difficult for both of them but he had to respect her for it. She was from a very strict, very prominent Boston family. He and her father, who was a judge, had become great friends.

All the joy had been taken out of everything, all the point of her plans for the fall, but she told herself she had to go ahead with her life as if nothing had happened. She'd been given a great opportunity, she'd remind herself. She had a scholarship to one of the best women's colleges in the country and she'd be damned if she'd let Michael spoil it for her. Then she'd think about what it was going to be like, seeing him, seeing him with Ann, inevitably, and she'd begin to shake and she had to quickly think about something else, anything else, to keep the tears back. She'd try to imagine how her dorm room would be arranged, who her roommate would be. She'd concentrate on her winter coat: would it be warm enough for Boston? She'd leaf through the catalogue for the hundredth time and try to decide what classes to sign up for in the first semester. She didn't think she'd ever love anyone so much, ever again.

10

S*ITTING AT A CARD TABLE* in the kitchen of her big, empty apartment, trying to get the new coffee maker out of its box, Carole broke a nail, but she didn't even swear. She'd just bought this wonderful machine, the only appliance she'd picked out so far in New York. Frances McKinnon would be here in a little while for their first meeting, and she wanted to be able to offer her something. When it gurgled encouragingly, she sighed and sat back to leaf through the *Times.*

Toward the back of the first section was a short article that made her forget how happy she was and how good the coffee was going to be. It was the fifteenth anniversary of the death of Terence Deloit, the prominent senator from Wisconsin, and a vast stretch of national forest was being named for him. She was astonished she'd forgotten the date; not that it was ever mentioned in the papers till today, but because it had been something she'd dreaded year after year, always a hard day to get through. It was Tony, of course, who'd made her feel so happy and secure that, without realizing what he'd done, he'd pushed this to the back of her mind.

The article touched on all the facts she already knew. Terry had been the third Senator Deloit, Democrat, of Wisconsin. His grandfather, after first making a fortune from razor blades, had served for two terms. Then his father had served three. Terry himself was a congressman at twenty-eight, the youngest in Wisconsin history, and a senator at thirty-six. He was two years into his second term; he was forty-two — the dangerous age for heart attacks — and this was his first and last one, alone in his room at the Beverly Hilton a few hours after the cream of Liberal Hollywood had gathered at a fund-raising dinner downstairs for the presidential candidate Terry was supporting.

Carole had been only twenty, not exactly a star yet but close enough — after two featured parts in reasonably successful movies — to have been invited to link hands on stage with people who really were famous and sing the corny lyrics set to the tune of "That's Entertainment." Terry's wife, Martha, the beautiful and icy heiress whose face Carole had seen once or twice in *Vogue,* was only a few years older than Carole herself. Martha was at home, in Georgetown. She traveled with him only on the campaign trail in Wisconsin, never to these things where he was only helping someone else, and one of the reasons Carole's affair with him was possible was that, because of the causes he involved himself with, he found himself on the Coast so often without Martha. Another reason was the fact that Carole was ending a highly publicized fling (she and her agent had seen to that) with an actor whose favorite, only, subject of conversation was himself. He was so beautiful that she could hardly blame him, and at least he was generous with himself in bed, but she was beginning to wonder what someone with a mind might be like.

She met the senator at a dinner party in Malibu, two months before this gala. He was big and rangy, handsome in a shaggy, dark way. He was a quarter Indian: his grandmother had been pure Cheyenne, a shock that Milwaukee society had never gotten over and that had made his grandfather far more liberal politically than he would have been otherwise. Terry's hair was always just slightly mussed; his necktie was never quite perfectly knotted; he managed to give the impression that he wasn't simply another cardboard politician. He'd cultivated the image of a clear, open mind, crossing party lines in his voting record, asking painful questions about disarmament, about welfare, about pollution. He was especially involved with Indian rights — Native Americans, Carole had learned to say — and that was one of the more fashionable causes right then in Hollywood.

Seated next to him, she knew before she finished her cold zucchini soup that she had to see more of this man. The fact that he was married was irrelevant to her. She'd seduced her first married man, her biology teacher (whose wife was her home ec teacher), at fourteen. Judging by the way Terry was looking at her, she didn't think it mattered much to him either. Although none of her few political friends had ever gossiped about anything extracurricular in his marriage with the beautiful and perfect Martha, she was sure, somehow, that she wasn't imagining an attraction on his side too. In the middle of an argument about burial grounds that engaged the whole table, she quietly asked him if he was good at memorizing telephone numbers. He laughed and asked her, just as quietly, to give him an example.

When she got back to the ugly mock-Tudor house she was sharing in Mandeville Canyon, she was relieved to find her roommate's note: "Gone to the Springs, back mañana maybe." She set a fire but didn't light it till he called, because she wasn't absolutely sure he would. He did, and then he was there in twenty minutes, driving an anonymous Japanese compact and wearing a jogging suit and a dumb canvas hat that advertised Miller Beer. They sat in front of the fire with a bottle of Pinot Gris and a joint and talked about nothing and everything and she felt almost . . . intellectual. Then the sex itself was really pretty incredible, because she'd expected a kind of gentle, idealistic fuck, whatever that might be, like his politics, and instead he was really rough and she got really rough right back and they never even made it to the bedroom. Before he left, with a face she later realized was no more sincere than his convictions, he told her this wasn't the first time this had happened, but almost, in three years of marriage, and she chose to believe him. He loved his wife and he'd never leave her, but something had disappeared, something was missing. If this was going to happen again they'd have to be careful and she might end up hating him for it. He was ambitious, very ambitious, he admitted. She had to swear not to talk about it. What did she think?

She didn't really *think* about it at all; she just fell into it. He was fun, especially in but also out of bed, and he could probably teach her things about the world, but it was a shame she couldn't tell anyone about it. He had a name, and it certainly would have generated publicity if anyone knew . . . but it might have ended up backfiring for her, because he'd gotten to be such a fucking left-wing Hollywood *pet,* and a girl, an actress, who brought scandal down around his head might end up making a few enemies she really couldn't afford to make at this point.

Anyway, in the next two months she saw him as often as their complicated schedules allowed — at her house, mostly (her roommate was gone ninety percent of the time), but also in Chicago, Seattle, Phoenix, Atlanta, and Bozeman, Montana. She discovered what she'd suspected that first night, that he was wilder than any of the men she'd ever been with, maybe because when he *wasn't* with her he had to be so straight. He wanted to experience everything, he told her, all the things he'd never done with Martha, all the things his friends in the Senate Cloakroom would call perverse. She called it his Wild Injun blood.

The times they were together, they seemed to talk less and less and have sex more and more: for a while, it was an addiction for both of them. They'd try anything — a Mexican hooker who went down on both of them, a black hustler who fucked her while she blew Terry. The drugs spurred them on, of course: he found them or she found them or they bought them together — up to and including heroin, but only twice, and only snorting, never shooting up. Then it began to turn sour for her. No, more than that: it began to scare her. There had been a time or two — once when he tied her up, with her permission, another time when he handcuffed her without asking her first — when she had a glimpse of just how far he might go, when she realized it might be just a little *too* far. She decided she had to end it.

Waiting for him at her house after that big gala, wandering nervously around her patio and hacking off dead geraniums with a pair of garden shears, she tried to rehearse what she wanted to tell him tonight, wondering if she could. When he finally arrived, very late, he smiled the lopsided grin that had first charmed her and then scared her and finally disgusted her: it meant another *experiment,* she knew. Angel dust, it was this time, PCP; they'd never tried it; it would be incredible. She refused. She didn't like the sound of it and she needed a clear head if she was going to say what she'd resolved to say.

He shrugged and lit the joint that had been laced with it, the busboy at the hotel had assured him, and he sat back in one of her patio chairs to enjoy whatever sensations *this* high might bring him. She began calmly to tell him that she didn't think this was going to work out, that they'd better end it, that it wasn't fair to her because he would never get a divorce (this was disingenuous: she'd never wanted anything but a good time), that after all he was twice her age. She talked on and on, a monologue because he wasn't responding, and then, in the space of a split second, something exploded in his mind. He leaped from his chair and he was at her throat, he was roaring, he was calling her a whore, over and over, and she was grappling for the pruning scissors on the cement under her, next to the big terra-cotta pot of geraniums, and then they were in his neck and the blood was spurting onto her, blinding her, a faucet.

She backed away on all fours to the edge of the pool, gasping for the breath that he'd come so close to cutting off forever, stifling a scream that would have brought neighbors and publicity and police. She rolled into the water and washed it away, the blood but not the horror, and then she climbed out again on the far side of the pool, as far from his body as she could get, and she was able to form first one thought, then another.

Her instinct was to hide him, to hide *it,* to take him somewhere and bury him and never, never tell a soul and just pray no one would ever know. But it wouldn't work: someone knew he was here, the aide who always had to know where Terry was in case something came up, the old friend and roommate from Yale that Terry always said he'd trust with his life. All right, you bastard, she said to the figure on the other side of the pool, now you can trust him with your *death*. The longer she thought about it, the surer she was that . . . Abe? no, Al . . . would want to help her cover this up, that Terry's goddamn reputation was important to him and to the party and the fucking cause and almost certainly to his rich-bitch wife, and that old Al would help her. Besides, she hadn't done anything wrong. Well, she'd just killed a man, but only because he was trying to kill her, and there must be a way. . . .

Al had to be at the Beverly Hilton, because that was where Terry was staying, officially staying. He answered on the tenth ring, and then it was so odd because he didn't sound *at all* surprised — shocked, yes, and sad, but not surprised — and it occurred to her that a very few people who were very close to Terry must have known how really crazy he could be. After that it was out of her hands. A man, a trustworthy FBI field man, Al assured her, who wouldn't file a report but whose help they'd need, got there before Al did. Her thoughts, her feelings were confused, but she was absolutely clear about how much she hated this second man. He was cold, officious, and insulting in the way he explained to her that this hadn't happened, that he hadn't been here, and that she'd only met the senator at political functions, as if she were a child, as if she didn't already know that. He made her tell him exactly what happened, and he seemed to be as satisfied with what she said as Al was a few minutes later. It was pure self-defense; the bruises on her throat proved it. He carried Terry, wrapped in one of Carole's sheets, out to his car like a sack of potatoes, and it was over.

On television in the morning, she heard the version that became official: the senator had died, alone, in his suite at the Beverly Hilton at some time during the late night or early morning hours; his body was discovered by his aide. She had no idea how they'd done it, and she didn't want to know. Al came to see her that day, and a few times after that. He was a nice man, she decided, and it helped a little, just a little, to be able to talk about it.

It was five years later that the first letter came. There were a few seconds when she actually thought the cologne on the envelope was nice — spicy, mysterious, not too sweet — but then she opened it. "I know about you and Terry, and I know all about that night," it began. Enclosed was a tape that played back to her every single halting, tearful word she'd spoken *that night* to the FBI man. He'd either had a tape recorder in his pocket or he'd been wired. At first she was confused because she'd been so sure he'd believed her, and then she realized it didn't matter. Nothing mattered except the fact that she had committed a criminal act, that she hadn't reported it, that her words were hysterical and contradictory, and that even if she were acquitted in a court of law it would probably be ruinous for her reputation. Terry had been so popular that people had talked about his running for President a couple of elections down the line. She had killed him. Period.

She was on location in Manila, and the first thing she tried to do was call Al back in New York, at the advertising agency he'd rejoined after Terry's death. A secretary told her he'd died, only a few months before, of cancer. It was the first and last time that Carole tried to do anything about the letters. She was trapped.

* * *

The face at the door was so familiar to Frances that she felt she already knew Carole Todd, and she supposed most of America felt the same way. Actors and actresses often disappointed her after she'd seen them on film or on the stage, but Carole was stunning, radiating energy and health and every bit as beautiful as she ought to be. They agreed they were who they knew they were, shook hands, and Frances stepped into the empty apartment.

"It's a beautiful old building. I sat in the courtyard for a while and sort of soaked it up."

"I was watching you," Carole said shyly. They smiled, laughed at themselves, and the ice was broken.

"I'm *so* excited," Carole bubbled, hugging herself and spinning around in the big, echoing foyer. "It's the first time I've ever really decided to put down roots and buy something, and I wanted it as soon as I saw it. Come look out the front windows. We . . . I have the whole park for my front yard, and I'm just above tree level." She scampered down the wide corridor, a child showing off her playhouse, asking Frances what she thought of this or that.

"Is there a place we could just sit and talk for a minute?"

"Sure. Couple of folding chairs in the kitchen, and I have some coffee, if you'd like. I'm staying at a friend's place up the street, and when I have any spare time I walk over here and wander around and just dream." She led the way into the big, old-fashioned kitchen. "I'm acting really dumb about it and I'll probably get in your way all the time."

"I'm glad. I don't just come into places and *do* them. It's a kind of marriage for a while." Frances was fascinated by the mixture of naturalness and staginess in Carole, even in the clothes she was wearing, faded jeans and battered cowboy boots, but a mauve silk Valentino blouse and a pair of gold pre-Columbian cuff bracelets. She was sure Carole was difficult, probably really terrifying if someone crossed her, but she suddenly felt they could be friends. She liked her; she could imagine herself willing to make excuses for her at some point.

"I need a floorplan, including all the original structural plans. I need a copy of your contract with the building, so we'll know exactly what changes we can make without asking permission and which ones need to be cleared with a committee. I assume there's a tenants' committee?"

Carole nodded and rolled her eyes. "They had to approve me before I could finally buy in. I wore a navy blue suit and pearls and gloves, and you'd have thought I was Dina Merrill, and it worked."

"Well, we'll give them something to talk about when the apartment's done. Now, um, I know you told me 'carte blanche' on the phone, but in my experience no one ever really means that, so I need a maximum budget."

"A budget. It really doesn't matter but let's say a ceiling of . . . oh, three million? I wouldn't expect that to include any art, but I was hoping you'd be a sort of art consultant, too? When we know what we're doing?"

"My God, I think three million should do very nicely. I had no idea." It was, to say the least, a decent budget for a fourteen-room apartment that was already very well preserved.

"Look," Carole said, coming over with the coffee, "I don't know much about interiors but I know what I like, as they say. I saw what you did with your brother-in-law's apartment. We're doing a benefit preview for the Cancer Drive, y'know, and he had some of us over for drinks. Anyway, I realize a lot of his furniture is, um, family heirloom stuff and I'm sure he's forgotten more about art than I'll ever begin to know, but I thought it was the most beautiful place I'd seen in my life."

"Thank you. I don't know how much credit I can take for it, because it sort of built itself around his collection, but thank you."

"You're welcome. So, even though I'm never going to be a connoisseur, I like beautiful old things and beautiful new things and I figure if they're really the finest, then some of it'll rub off on me, don't you think?"

"Absolutely."

Carole put her hand on Frances's arm. "Can you keep a secret? You'll have to know anyway before too long, but I think we're going to be friends and I'd rather tell you now."

"Yes. Really. I'm guessing there's a man. You slipped and used the first person plural a few minutes ago."

Carole grinned and tossed her head, delighted to be caught. "Tony Vasquez." She watched Frances anxiously for her reaction, then shouted with laughter when she saw the surprise on her face.

Tony Vasquez, a darkly handsome Cuban exile, was the boy wonder of the New Hollywood, one of the few independent producers whose films never lost money. Starting out with cheap but well-made thrillers, he soon found backing for bigger budgets and he broadened his choice of subjects. Now in his late thirties, he had his pick of directors, actors, and backers. The media hated him and loved him, just as they did Carole. He was great press because of the actresses he dated and married, but he avoided personal publicity like the plague. There'd been four suits filed against him, all settled out of court, by photographers who'd lost cameras or teeth or both.

"I hadn't heard anything," Frances said when Carole stopped laughing. "I sat next to him at dinner once, and I thought he was smart and likable and far more sensible than most of that crowd, and of course he's very handsome."

"Well, *I* think so anyway. His divorce isn't final for another month and we're going to be married in Aspen in February; he won't be back from location till then. There hasn't been any press yet, no leaks at all, and we don't want any till afterwards. There's no nastiness; I mean, it isn't a messy divorce or anything. We just thought we only wanted a few friends to know. I've been through, um, several men, not as many as they say I have but quite a few, and I've been pretty wild and Tony's the only one . . . I ever wanted to just be myself with. To be *quiet* with, I guess. Maybe even have a child with?" She shook her head. "Maybe not. I won't do it if I can't spend a lot of time with him or her."

Frances looked around her. Kitchens are for confidential talks like this, she thought, and this big sunny room must have heard its share of them in sixty or seventy years. "I won't tell anyone, and I'm flattered you're trusting me."

"I could afford it myself, I guess, but I'd never want to if it weren't for Tony. Oh, I never know how much money I have or don't have." She laughed. "He saw it just before he left and he loves it too, but the decorating is up to me. Up to us, rather. Now, I want to show you everything, so bring your coffee along?"

They spent the next couple of hours wandering through the empty rooms. Frances made no suggestions; today was for absorbing what she was seeing. Carole chattered mostly about which rooms were to be used for which purposes. Tony only had three requirements: a good-sized study for himself with a desk big enough for an orgy, a small screening room that would hold fifteen or twenty comfortable chairs, and telephones everywhere. It was dark outside by the time they completed the tour, and Carole suggested a drink somewhere.

"Or food. I don't have to be at the theater for a while."

"What about Rudi's? They're very fast with light things if they know we're pressed for time. I have to be at a friend's house at nine, so it's perfect." She had told Trish she'd stop by.

"I adore Rudi's. I know the manager who used to be there."

"Damn!" Frances was trying to stuff the papers and plans into an envelope briefcase that was already filled with work for the Bloomingdale's boutique. "You mean Mario?"

"Mario. We actually had a little affairlette a couple of years ago."

"Was that . . . ? I'm sorry, it's none of my business."

"That's okay. Was that what?"

"Oh, I just wondered about the girl he apparently sees now."

"Maggie. No, I was pre-Maggie. I had to go out to the Coast for a while and he met her in the meantime. My heart wasn't broken or anything. I mean, it wasn't serious."

"Um." Frances looked around to see if she'd forgotten anything. "I'm ready if you are. My car should be downstairs."

* * *

Letting the hot, nearly scalding, water pound into him, Hamilton forgot for a moment where he was. It was always like this afterward, this sense of being in a no-man's-land, somewhere between who he'd been for the last hour and what he usually was, who he'd be again in a few minutes. He was in the anonymous Chelsea apartment; the fixtures in the prefabricated, molded plastic shower stall were cheap and badly designed, but there was plenty of hot water.

The woman had been good, very good, he was thinking; he'd ask them to send her again. The rate was always five hundred, but the tip was up to him: this time he'd slipped seven crisp hundred-dollar bills into her big, black, sensible handbag while she was tidying herself in the bathroom. She didn't acknowledge the money, of course. That would have been stepping out of character, and she hadn't done that for a minute — not even, a few minutes ago, when she left. Of course, she was only doing what she'd been instructed to do, what the agency always told them to do, but she was particularly convincing, which meant that what she did was particularly satisfying for him.

She'd knocked briskly on the door at exactly the right time, smiled, patted him on the head, and walked straight to the closet to hang up her navy blue wool coat and to change from low-heeled street shoes into the kind of slippers that are called scuffs. Then she stooped to let down the pale blue flannel nightgown, safety-pinned up so that it hadn't shown under her coat. It fell nearly to floor length. Her face — flat, broad, and shiny — was handsome, serious, and probably never pretty, he thought, even as a girl. She was big-boned, an inch or two taller than Hamilton, and he could feel the way he wanted to feel, which was smaller than she was. He guessed her age as somewhere in the late forties, and when she took out hairpins and combs and shook her hair so that it came halfway down her back, he could see the streaks of gray in it and that made him feel the other way he wanted to feel, which was younger than she was, even though that wasn't, literally, true.

Standing at the kitchen counter with her back to him, making hot chocolate, she told him sternly, her accent heavily Eastern European, to get into his pajamas. He did, of course, and then he waited on the floor next to the chair where she'd be sitting. He sighed with happiness: this was just right; this was exactly the way it was supposed to happen. She even smelled the way a nanny ought to smell: a combination of mothballs, Pond's cold cream, and Jergens lotion. After he finished his cocoa, that was when it started; that was when she noticed that he was "overexcited"; that was when she had to reach for her hairbrush and punish him. Hamilton never touched these women; that would have been wrong. It would have been almost like incest, touching Nanny. When it was really good, when *they* were really good, he didn't even need to touch himself. Tonight, down on the floor on his hands and knees, pleading with her to stop spanking him, to stop saying mean things to him, he hadn't needed to touch himself.

Drying off, he stared out the high little bathroom window. He could see the lights of, maybe, a hundred apartments; he could hear, maybe, the sounds of fifty cars swishing by on the streets down below. He wondered if everyone in those apartments and those cars would despise him for what he'd just done. After all, he hadn't hurt anybody, he told himself. Sometimes Nanny had said it was going to hurt her more than it hurt him, which was the right kind of thing to say (a nanny when he was five — no, six — used to say exactly that to him), but it always made him laugh, afterward, because the point was that he wanted to be hurt, just a little.

Years ago, he'd seen a psychiatrist for a while who'd given him a better understanding of it, but he never stopped calling the agency that supplied the string of women who came, first, to an apartment on the Upper West Side, and then to this one in Chelsea. It had to do with his mother, naturally, but although he knew that intellectually he never really felt it. The nannies were stand-ins for his mother. *She* had never touched him, except for the standard kiss before bedtime and when she came back from a trip. It had been the nannies, a succession of them because his mother had been so arrogant with servants, who gave him whatever love, whatever anger, he'd known. To use the psychiatrist's word, he had fixated on them.

There had been a period, in his teens, when he hadn't been bothered by it, when he assumed he was just like everyone else at Groton and then at Harvard, when he thought he wanted a woman in the same way as every other boy or man. The first few times he'd gone to the brothel with friends, the one just over the New Hampshire state line, he'd done exactly what he supposed his friends were doing in other rooms. Then he'd chosen an older woman one night on a dare, and she'd discovered his little secret. She'd taught him things he hadn't known about himself.

It was cheating on Frances, he couldn't deny that, but he managed to think of it as something that had nothing to do with her.

It was something she couldn't provide for him, as if he'd ever dream of asking her to provide it. He was like a man who loved soufflés, he told himself, who knew his wife couldn't cook them, who had them in restaurants instead. Their sex had always been sweet, tender, an expression of how they felt about one another, but never passionate, never fulfilling in the way this was. As he grew older, as his sexual appetite lessened, he found that when he wanted anything at all it was usually this, and he found himself staying away from Frances's bedroom for months at a time.

No, he decided for the millionth time, there was nothing wrong with what he was doing. He wasn't hurting anyone. But he'd pay a great deal of money, far more than he was already paying, to keep his secret, to keep *him* (he always thought of his tormentor as a man, although he really had no reason to think that) from doing what he threatened to do. Typed at the bottom of the first letter, like business correspondence, was the word *Enclosure*. Enclosed was a video copy of a black-and-white film taken with a camera hidden somewhere in a woman's apartment in Los Angeles — in the Valley, he thought. It was one of the few times he'd gone to a place other than his own, and it was only because he was in L.A. for a week and he didn't think he had to be as careful as he always was at home.

Several years separated his visit to that woman and the arrival of the first letter, and by then the detective he hired (as Donald White, the man with the glasses) could find nothing. Not even a laboratory report that identified the cologne as *fleurs de tilleul* helped, because it wasn't quite obscure enough. One or two shops in every city in Europe sold it, and now it was available in a few American stores too. Hamilton was helpless. The threat was to send copies of the videotapes to all the members of the board at the bank, to Frances, and to Dorothy. He was able to forget that threat for weeks on end, but every so often, when the letter was particularly insulting, when the delivery was more than usually demeaning, Hamilton swelled with a rage that was stronger than anything he'd felt since he was a child. And he was precisely as powerless as a child, but in this case there wasn't even anyone there to bite or kick or scratch. Someone was out there with power over him, power to tease him cruelly, and the way he felt was twice as intense, ten times as intense, because it existed in a complete vacuum.

11

MAGGIE ARRIVED at the Metropolitan Athletic Club at six and took an elevator to the top floor. The Metropolitan had somehow managed to keep its exclusiveness for more than fifty years; its members were wealthy, of course, but beyond that they were overwhelmingly Protestant and entirely male. Women were allowed in the lobby, in one of the three bars, one of the dining rooms, and nowhere else. Maggie was able to visit Chuck on the rooftop tennis courts only because she'd been granted a special dispensation from the elevator operator. The doors opened on several floors to let men in shorts and Lacoste shirts on and off, one carrying a squash racquet, another with a basketball, some sweaty, some still dry and immaculate, all with towels around their necks. After their initial surprise at seeing her, they ignored her completely.

When she stepped out onto the roof, thirty stories up, Chuck was raging at a paunchy middle-aged man across the net from him. "Keep your goddamn elbow down! Every fucking week I tell you the same fucking thing!" The guy probably makes life hell for his secretary, his wife and children, and every junior VP who works under him, she thought, but here he's hanging his head like the scoutmaster's telling him he's got the tent poles all wrong again. She could almost feel sorry for him, but she knew Chuck poured this kind of abuse on all his students and they came back, week after week, at $150 a lesson. It was important to be able to drop the name of the right coach. Chuck Wetherby, either in spite of his manner or because of it, had become one of the right coaches.

"Hi, Mag," he yelled to her in a completely different voice. "Be about ten more minutes and another ten to clean up."

She took one of the old-fashioned, wooden-slatted Adirondack chairs that sat on a raised area like thrones outside the hurricane-fencing enclosure, high enough to look out to Central Park over the ledge. It was cool, and she snuggled into her jacket and turned the collar up, but it was good to be here at her favorite time of day and good to be back in New York, in her own life. She'd taken a pill just before boarding the red-eye in L.A. last night and she'd slept all across the continent, but it had been a long day since then and now she was drained. She could use a little pick-me-up but she decided not to. Chuck didn't know she was doing this nowadays, and she didn't want him to know. For one thing, he hated drugs (as if alcohol weren't one! she thought) and he'd be sure to give her the kind of lecture she didn't want to hear. For another, she wouldn't have much leverage when she tried to get him to cut down on his drinking, would she?

So she couldn't tell him much about what had happened with Mario before she left for California, the fight she wasn't sure was over yet. He'd left a message for her at her hotel, almost a week ago, but she perversely didn't return it till he left a second one a couple of days later. His first rage with Rudi had worn off by the time he told her he'd quit, and his first excitement about the place on Gramercy Park was a little stale by the time she heard about it. She left a message on his machine this morning when she got to Kennedy, but he hadn't called back yet.

The sun was sinking into a cloud bank over in New Jersey, and lights were beginning to appear in the apartments on Central Park West and over on Fifth Avenue. New York seemed every bit as wonderful and sparkling as it wanted to be, and she decided that all the magical people in this magical city should be on their way to parties. In penthouses, of course, where if they weren't already in love they'd be falling in love tonight. This was just about the most valuable view in the world, and she wondered what the very rich were doing right now. Did they feel the same way she did when they looked out at the park? She could see the McKinnons' apartment building up at Fifth and Seventieth. What were Frances and

Hamilton doing right now? Sitting around and counting their money? Fighting? Screwing? No, probably not screwing.

She sighed, wishing she could sit here for the rest of the evening and make up stories about the thousands of lives behind all these thousands of windows she was seeing. Instead, Chuck — although or because he hadn't seen them for years — would want every detail of the afternoon she'd spent with their parents, and it would depress her all over again just to tell him about it. Not that it was any worse than usual, just that it was exactly, maddeningly, the same. Her mother was never *not* drunk now, sloppy and sentimental and furious and wrinkled. Her father was, if anything, smoother, calmer, more impersonal, more opaque, than ever. They asked how Chuck was doing, but it was a polite, vaguely curious inquiry, as if he were a distant cousin instead of their son. Maggie had carried messages back and forth for so long that it was hard to remember a time when it was different, but when she thought about it she knew everything had changed when Chuck was a senior at Stanford.

A tennis magazine did a profile on him that year. "There's No Stopping Chuck Wetherby," it was called, and it really did seem he had the world in his pocket. With his long hair, an erratic, dazzling style, and a temper that had already twice disqualified him from matches, he was beginning to be noticed as one of the new faces of tennis from the generation that burst into the 'seventies. He'd won more matches during amateur summer tours than anyone else his age in the country. He'd almost certainly make Phi Beta Kappa. He'd finally found time for a girl. Nancy was pretty and athletic, a Chi Omega from an old San Francisco family, and Maggie thought she was neat. They were engaged to be married in June, a week after graduation.

In March, he suddenly appeared at home, paler and quieter than Maggie had ever seen him. She'd discovered boys and they'd discovered her, so her head was filled with dates and proms and dances at the club. Chuck didn't explain why he was back in Santa Barbara in the middle of the semester, and Maggie didn't ask. He muttered something about a problem with Nancy, that he wanted to sort things out for a week or so, and she accepted that without thinking much about it. Their father was at a conference in Chicago and their mother was at a golf tournament in Palm Springs, so they were alone except for the housekeeper.

Coming in late one night from a date, she was met at the door by a tearful, enraged Mercedes. "I ask Chuck to turn down music so I sleep. He would not. He throw a bottle at me but he miss. Ha!" She shrugged.

Maggie was mystified, but she told her she'd handle it herself, to go back to bed. Following Bob Dylan's voice up the stairs and down the hall to her brother's room, she found him, cross-legged in the middle of the floor, counting and separating mounds of different colored pills, singing along with the stereo in the wrong key. There was half a bottle of Scotch next to him and an empty glass that had rolled away and evidently wasn't needed anymore. Chuck was at the stage where he was taking slugs straight from the bottle.

The first thing she did was to turn the volume on the stereo way down. She let him keep the bottle. She'd never seen him like this before, but she knew from bitter experience with her mother that he might get really nasty if she tried to take it away from him. She scooped up the pills — he must have found them in their parents' medicine cabinets — into one of his trophies and set it out in the hall. Chuck wasn't going to take them, not really, but she wasn't taking any chances. Then she shut the door, kicked her shoes off, and took a belt of Scotch for herself. She knew Chuck would tell her what was wrong. They always told each other the important things. It took a long time and a lot of prompting, but the pieces of the story finally came out.

Chuck's closest friend and his manager during the summer tours was Rob Copeland, an assistant tennis coach at the university. The day before yesterday, Rob put a revolver in his mouth and pulled the trigger. He left a note, addressed to Chuck, which the police and the dean of men read before letting Chuck see it. It was long, sad, and sometimes illegible, but the message was clear. Rob and Chuck had been lovers since the middle of Chuck's freshman year. Chuck broke it off because of Nancy. He wasn't in love with her — Maggie got him to admit that — but he was fond of her, he wanted a wife, and he eventually wanted children. Rob seemed to understand, to approve, even. Then this had happened, with no warning at all. The school wanted to avoid a scandal if it could possibly help it. Chuck was suspended indefinitely "pending an administrative decision."

Maggie was barely sixteen and she was boy-crazy. She didn't understand how he could want to go to bed with someone of the same sex, but what horrified her most was seeing him drunk, because she had the unbearable thought that he might be following in her mother's footsteps. She automatically took charge, the way she had since Chuck went off to school and left her to cope with everything here. She walked him down to the kitchen, where she made coffee, poured it into him, and spoke to him firmly. He had to tell Nancy this, all of this; it was only fair. He certainly had to break the engagement, at least for the time being. He had to see a shrink. He had to try to stay in school and finish out the year and get his degree. He had to stop blaming himself and get on with his life. People had problems, she told herself and then him; they took care of them; and then they could forget them. She was so sturdy, so sensible, so strong, that Chuck later teased her about being a throwback to one of the Wetherbys who'd come west on the Oregon Trail in the 1850s.

Stanford reinstated him for the rest of the semester, and he did all the things Maggie asked him to do. He went up to San Francisco three times a week to a therapist, a kindly older man who concentrated on the most immediate things and tried to help him sort out guilt from grief, but the problems didn't go away. Chuck was still torn: his preference for men was clearly at odds with the world he loved most. It was a time when all his friends were experimenting with drugs, but Chuck's solution was to drink.

From the time he graduated, he played on the professional circuit. Tennis had really come into its own as a big-money, spectator sport and Chuck Wetherby was one of its stars. There were wild ups and downs in his career, matches he sailed through with confidence and his own peculiar style, others when he threw tantrums or played viciously and lost. The bookmakers in Vegas didn't know what to make of him. After four years, he was seeded as one of the top half-dozen who might take Forest Hills. He'd played there twice before, but this time was the closest he was to come to the final rounds. Maggie heard the story later. He'd stayed away from liquor for two months, but on the night before the semifinals there was a big bash at the Plaza for everyone involved with the match. He met up with an old fraternity brother who made a passing reference to Rob Copeland, something that caused Chuck to order a drink, then another. He didn't show up for the match in the morning. He woke up two days later next to a strange man in an overdecorated apartment in Brooklyn Heights, and he couldn't remember what had happened.

After that, he disappeared completely from the tennis scene. Maggie had letters and late-night phone calls from him during the years she was at Smith. He moved fast; one month it was Rio, then Palm Beach, then London. The calls were drunken and self-pitying and sometimes mean. The letters were long and apologetic. She preferred the postcards, finally: they were short and affectionate, and they let her know he was alive. She realized, at some point, although he never said so and she never asked him, that he was being supported by a series of older men. It didn't shock her but it saddened her and made her cry. Chuck had been so golden and so fine and she knew this was part of a circle of self-hatred from which he couldn't seem to escape.

She'd been in New York only a month when he showed up at her apartment, overweight and out of shape. There was a despair she'd never seen in him before, something she'd only heard on the phone in those late-night calls. He stayed for three months, drying himself out and sorting himself out. Finally, he revived a few tennis friendships and managed to convince the management at the Metropolitan that it should take him on probation as a coach. He worked hard at it, meticulous about being on time, and even when he started to drink again soon after he moved in with Rudi he kept it under reasonable control. He drank only when he wasn't coaching, and even if he killed two-thirds of a bottle in an evening he showed up on the roof the next morning — white, shaky, and sarcastic but *there.* Maggie blamed Rudi. She couldn't prove it, but she was convinced Rudi subtly encouraged Chuck to drink because it kept him dependent. She hated him for it.

It was dark now, and she heard Chuck's footsteps behind her. He put his hands over her eyes and she knew she was supposed to play the guessing game they played when they were little, when it used to end in shrieks of laughter.

"Who is it?" she asked. "Is it . . . Louis Armstrong?"

"No, mayam, dis ain' no Satchmo."

"Oh, well, then, it must be Zsa Zsa Gabor?"

"No, dahlink, ziss iss not Zsa Zsa. Guess again, dahlink."

Maggie cut it short. "It's Charles Wetherby, my one and only long-lost handsome brother, isn't it?"

He took his hands away and looked down at her with affection and a little sadness. She could still glimpse the Chuck she loved so much.

"It's your long-lost brother, baby. Still lost."

"But still my brother. Sit down. It's the bewitching hour in the park. *L'heure bleu.*"

He pulled her to her feet. "I see it every day. Let's go someplace where I might be able to get a drink, just for a change of pace." She followed him silently to the elevator.

* * *

Music swelled, "The End" flashed on the screen, and Dorothy reached for another Kleenex. She hadn't seen *Waterloo Bridge* since she was a little girl and her nanny had taken her to the big Loew's down on Lexington. They'd cried their eyes out, of course, but then when they got home her mother was livid because it evidently wasn't suitable for little girls and Vivien Leigh had been something called a streetwalker and that nanny hadn't lasted very long. Tonight, though, with this marvelous machine hooked up to the television in her bedroom, with her mother long dead, Dorothy could even watch it a second time if she felt like it. Frieda, her maid, had talked her into buying the really rather ugly black box a few weeks after Spence died; she'd finally learned how to work it, and now she felt very modern — proudly carrying a membership card to that nice video club up on Eighty-sixth Street and taping "Masterpiece Theatre" segments if she had to go out on one of those nights.

While the tape was rewinding (that was one of the rules at her new club), she went into her closet for a different cassette, the one that sometimes helped her get to sleep when her little percolator pills (even when she washed them down with more white wine than she knew was good for her) weren't working as well as they should. She ought to destroy this tape, she really ought to, but she couldn't bear to do that, so she hid it in a shoebox, under a layer of tissue and a pair of brown suede pumps, way up on a top shelf.

The reason she kept it, the reason it could soothe her three or four nights a week, was that it was a way for her to be with Spence again — Spence actually moving and talking, so alive and so real that she could pretend he was here in the same room with her. There were hundreds of photographs of him from every stage of their married life, of course, and there were lots of scratchy old movies of birthday parties and anniversaries and polo matches and out on the Sound in their sailboat, but they'd never been a very high-tech couple and they never had things like video equipment around.

This had been sent to her anonymously, in one of those jiffy bags, a couple of months after Spence died. With it was a letter that brought on the worst fit of temper she could remember having since her mother tried to talk her out of the marriage that had ended up giving her so much happiness. But even though whoever sent this to her surely hadn't meant to do her a favor, and even though it was this little bit of videotape that was now forcing her to carry on with the despicable payments that enraged her and that had drained Spence for so long, she was strangely grateful at the same time.

She settled back on the chaise longue with the remote control and one last glass of wine and arranged a comforter over her legs. Her favorite parts were at the very beginning and the very end, but of course every second of it was precious and she always watched the entire fifteen minutes. It began with a younger Spence entering an extraordinarily vulgar hotel room (she knew where it was filmed because the man who opened the door to him said, "Welcome to Las Vegas") and shaking hands. Then they asked after one another's wives, and that was what fascinated her because Spence said, "Dottie's fine, just fine," and he had a particularly sweet smile on his face when he said it and of course she'd never heard him say that in forty years because no one would have asked him that with her standing right there! The part at the end that she loved was when he came right up to the mirror (behind which the camera was hidden — she'd figured that out right away) and adjusted his tie and smoothed down his hair in exactly the way she'd seen him do a million times.

The whole middle section of the film — and the letter had informed her that it had originally been *filmed,* that this slightly grainy video was only a copy — was what would be so damaging both to Spence and to the man who was very high up in the Treasury Department who was making a deal with him. She'd actually met this man a few times socially — his wife, too — and she remembered Spence whispering to her that he was a terrible gambler, a compulsive gambler, but that only a very few people knew it because he never gambled in public. So that was why he wanted the money so badly, all that money that Spence spread out on the bed for him. She always wondered how long the man was able to hold on to it, if he'd gone to some other room in that very hotel that very same day and lost it all. She'd never be able to ask him now, because he'd been about twenty years older than Spence and he'd died a few years ago.

And the reason Spence was giving him all that money was what made her sad. He'd always been so honest, always, but he had wanted so desperately to be a success on the scale of the McKinnons, and it was so unnecessary, because by that time both her parents were dead (and couldn't say mean things to him anymore) and all the rest of them loved him and respected him and it would never occur to them to call him a failure. Anyway, as she understood it — and the letter made it as clear as it could ever be and also made it clear that he would have gone to prison for what he'd done — he was buying information he had no right to have. About a company the Securities and Exchange Commission was investigating and an announcement they were going to make the very next week. Even the Treasury man wasn't supposed to know about it, but he in turn had evidently paid someone and he was planning to make lots of money on the stock market too. She remembered there had been a period when Spence was on top of the world, when he'd pulled off a deal on Wall Street that was incomprehensible to her but that involved the same company. It had made him very happy and her brothers had congratulated him on his cleverness and she had been very proud of him. But that was the last time he'd done anything like that, anything so clever or — she had to assume — anything so criminal, because the Treasury man left his job less than a month later.

She could date all this so precisely because at one end of the room in Las Vegas was a television, and it was tuned in to the Watergate hearings. They were a sort of background to what the whole conversation was about, too, because the Treasury man was saying there wasn't much time left, that Nixon was on the way out and he couldn't be sure he'd be in the next administration, that this was the first time he'd ever done anything like this (Dorothy doubted it) and that it would probably be the last.

The first letter, the one that accompanied this tape, had allowed her a couple of months to come up with the money. It might as well have been a couple of days or a couple of years, so far as she was concerned, because she didn't have the faintest idea of how to accumulate so much cash without her lawyer or her accountant asking questions. Her first instinct, after her shocking and embarrassing fury — although thank God no one actually saw her behaving so badly, weeping and screaming and tearing her clothes — had been to call Hamilton. And then she realized that Hamilton was the very last man Spence would have wanted to know about what he'd done. Not that they hadn't been awfully fond of each other, but the whole point had been to show her family he could be brilliant and make amazing deals and stand on his own two feet. She wanted him, his memory, to have that — even if it wasn't really true — and she was willing to grit her teeth and pay for it.

So she had very carefully asked Rudi if there was some way she could give him a check for something legitimate and then he could give her some cash that she needed for something secret. He was her friend and her bridge partner and he'd been so sweet to her in those first terrible weeks after she lost Spence. Of course, Spence had despised him, but then he'd despised anyone who was . . . like Rudi. Not that she had any intention of telling Rudi or anyone, not even the children — especially not the children — why she needed it. And she would never forget how kind he had been, what a gentleman — never once asking her why she was doing this, even though she knew how curious he was and how hard it was for him to keep quiet. He simply helped her figure out what to tell her accountant about the check to his horse ranch and then he gave her the cash back exactly as she'd been told to get it, in just the right denominations.

She'd asked him to do it again, of course, for the second payment a couple of weeks ago, and they'd laughed because he said her accountant must think she was keeping a gigolo or something, because there certainly hadn't been any "returns" from her "investment" in the Bucks County place. He made her laugh all the time and she *needed* to laugh, and he really was very dear, Rudi was, and she wished Spence could have realized that.

Anyway, he was being a true friend in another way too these days because her doctor was refusing to write a prescription for more than just a few of these lovely percolator pills every month and she really didn't feel that was enough. They had something addictive in them, apparently, although she certainly didn't feel *addicted,* for goodness' sake. Codeine? no, but some kind of chemical equivalent, she thought. So Rudi had managed to get some from *his* doctor and it made her much more secure to know she wouldn't have to suffer through those awful back pains and that she could have a little help getting to sleep. She decided to take another one right now, because just one obviously hadn't quite done the trick.

12

"I *WANT ELEGANCE,*" Mario said. "I don't mean Louis Quatorze or the Edwardian Room or Retro Deco. I mean . . . I don't know what I mean." He had dusted off three bar stools and he now was straddling one of them backward. On one side of him was Frances, perched properly with her legs crossed; on the other was Stephen Bingham. She'd been here once already, the day before, but that was only for reconnaissance, to wander around and absorb things in the way she told him she always did. Today, she'd brought Steve with her for what she called the heavy stuff. He was famous as the McKinnon architect, and Mario knew his advice and his draftsmen would be well worth the expense. They sat at the back of the King Arthur Room, facing out into the big, empty space.

"That's why Steve and I are here, isn't it?" Frances said, laughing. "To interpret your dreams. Like psychiatrists. To dig deep into your unconscious and tell you what you already knew if you knew you knew it."

Mario smiled faintly. His circuits were overloaded, he realized; he was feeling everything at once. This was an important moment for him, this meeting, and he was forcing his mind to concentrate on it; his body, on the other hand, was aching for Frances but he couldn't touch her because Steve was here. He'd held her arm for an instant when he helped her down from the construction elevator. When Steve's back was turned, she'd actually winked at him, very badly, her face screwed up comically.

"How many tables?" Steve asked. "Or, rather, since you've said you want this bar area to stretch out, say, forty feet, how many people could sit down to dinner at once in what's left? Three hundred?"

"It could hold that many," Mario said slowly. "But I think more like two-fifty. More breathing room. More privacy. And then what I thought would be private dining rooms, which you haven't seen yet." He waved his arm back to the narrow continuations of the room on either side of the reception area behind the bar. "They could each be split up into smaller rooms or they could each handle fifty. So that's another hundred, altogether."

Frances was frowning in concentration, biting on the pen she held. "Levels," she breathed softly.

"I was thinking that, too," Steve said.

"So was I," Mario said. It had been one of the first things he'd imagined here, and he was glad they pictured it that way too.

"The ceiling's so high, too high, really." Frances jumped down from her stool and walked toward the front. "We'd probably have to lower it, anyway. But." She stopped at about the point where they'd said the bar area would end, turning around to face them. "If the whole back of the room, the bar, were raised about ten feet? Twelve feet? And then if we had, maybe, five tiers between here and the windows? That would put each level about two feet above the next one down and everyone would have a better view." She paused. "Steps. Three? Four shallow, easy steps at each break. An aisle straight down the front, and one on each side? Of course we'd have a railing of some kind at the front of each tier, or people would be falling into each other's soup. But, Steve, the code? Would there have to be rails along the steps too?"

"Probably. Even if we sneaked under code, the insurance people would insist. If someone had too much champagne . . ."

"Well," she said, coming back to them. "We can't exactly congratulate ourselves on our brilliant, original idea. It's the obvious thing to do when you're on top of a building. Windows on the World has tiers, so does the Rainbow Room."

"Is that how you see this, Mario? Like those places?" Steve asked. "Frances hasn't filled me in on how you feel, who your customers are going to be. Do you want a real showstopper?"

Now it was Mario who climbed off his stool. "Let me give you my little speech," he said, facing them with his arms folded. "I'm going to have to explain it to backers and bankers and lawyers anyway, so I might as well try it out on the two of you. I want a spectacular place but I don't want a tourist attraction. If it works, it's going to be the kind of club Rudi's has been, bless his tiny heart, and I'm going to be taking a lot of his clientele. Plus, I hope, a younger bunch who have talent and money but who thought Rudi's was a little old-fashioned and pretentious, which it was. Minus, I hope, some of those ladies-who-lunch dinosaurs who'll be loyal to Rudi because they don't have enough imagination to go anywhere else."

"Can you talk that way to lawyers and bankers?" Frances asked with a smile. "You'll have to use words like *demographics* and *upmarket* and things, won't you? And you'll have to let them think they'd be the kind of people who'd be welcome here even if they wouldn't be."

"You're right, and maybe I'm making it sound too exclusive. What I mean is, it's not enough for the reservation book to be full every night and for me to make a bucket of money, not that I don't want that to happen. I guess what I'm saying is that if it doesn't attract the people I want to see here, if they aren't people who might conceivably be friends of mine, then I'll close it up and buy into a McDonald's franchise instead."

"Steve, if I understand what Mario said to me yesterday, it's that he really wants a sort of timeless design, like it's always existed, maybe, or at least like it always will. Not something that's absolutely so trendy and NOW that it's going to look dated in five years. Of course, that's what everybody would want, if they thought about it, but in this case we have to provide it."

"You interpret me correctly," Mario said.

"So," she said, leaving her perch again to pace around the two of them. Mario swiveled around on his stool to follow her with his eyes, remembering things they'd done in bed yesterday afternoon at an anonymous commercial hotel across from Penn Station, and of course the day before that at her apartment and . . . it seemed that he'd known her for a long, long time and it was only two days since they'd first made love. She held up a hand in a vague plea for silence, her fingers fluttering nervously, her emerald flashing. He and Steve smiled at each other and kept quiet.

To Mario she said, "I know you haven't seen much of my work, but you know something about the way I do things or you wouldn't have called me. That it's sort of eclectic, bits of different styles, different periods?"

Mario nodded. "I remember your apartment from, uh, that party you and Mr. McKinnon gave," he said slyly.

She laughed. "Of course, that party. Well, what I'm wondering is, whether we couldn't take that approach one step further." Her voice was shaking with excitement. "That could be the *point*. Oh, I'm thinking faster than I can get the words out. That place where Warhol used to go, on Sixtieth . . ."

"The fancy ice-cream parlor? Serendipity?" Mario frowned. "But, Frances, it wouldn't . . ."

"Be appropriate? Don't worry, I'm not talking about painting a lot of old chairs white and throwing them around the room. Serendipity wasn't the best example, but it was the closest I could get. I mean I'd like to use the humor that it had, the fun, but on a much higher plane and not nearly so jumbled. Table to table, maybe. Or else the tables themselves could all be the same — after all, with tablecloths they all do look the same — but at one of them there might be Eames chairs from the early 'fifties and at another there might be Second Empire and at another there might be this year's Memphis. Like a sort of museum of design with a sense of humor. A dozen colors for tablecloths and napkins. Different vases, different flowers on each one. I've obviously got to be really careful, or it'll look like a salesroom at Sotheby's and I'll fall flat on my face. Our faces. If we do it that way, we can keep away from that terrible trendiness, because it won't be identified with any single decade and you can change things around all the time, whenever you feel like it." She stood still, her hands on her hips, looking back and forth from one man to the other, waiting for their reactions.

"I think that fits," Mario said slowly. "I think that goes with what I want. I want things to *happen* here, not in a nightclubby way, but I hope people won't be coming in and finding the same scene night after night."

"And the food?" Steve asked.

"The food's going to be like that, too. I haven't talked about it, but it's sure as hell going to be more imaginative than Rudi's, and I think it's going to be like the design you're talking about, Frances, like . . . a place where everything's possible. Louis is French, so the menu will be sort of *grounded* in French, but he loves all kinds of cooking; he's not a purist. And the sous-chefs he's lining up — well, he only has definite commitments from two out of six, so far — but one of them's Chinese and one is Mexican and they'll do all kinds of special dishes, *different* dishes. But always, always, a few basic things on the menu. I mean, I know, Rudi's menu was so basic it was boring, but I don't want to go quite as far as the other extreme. I hate those places where it's impossible to get a simple, perfect steak or a plain piece of sole, where they're so insecure that everything has a sauce or it's been marinated within an inch of its life. And I want stars, I want exactly three stars from the *Times*. Two isn't enough. Four is too many — it attracts too many pretentious gourmets. Just a really good, solid stamp of approval on the food. Make the chef happy, if nothing else."

"Are you going to serve dinner only, like Rudi?" Steve asked.

"At first. This pressure, this time slot, is making me so nervous that I've got to at least keep that much simple even if nothing else is. Later, we'll see."

"Okay," Steve said, clearing his throat and looking at his watch. "I think it's a great concept, Frances. And Mario. I'd stay and tell you both for the next hour what geniuses you are, but I have to leave in a few minutes. We've got to get a team together, and with this deadline Radnor's given you we've got to do it yesterday. We'll set up a liaison from my office with your kitchen consultant for all the permits and the subcontracting for wiring and plumbing."

"And air conditioning and heating, although that obviously gets into Frances's territory," Mario said. "But they'll get along fine. He knows what he's talking about and so does she. It's just that . . ." He took his glasses off and wiped them on his shirt. "It's what you just said, Steve. That we've gotta do all this yesterday."

"Right," Frances said, taking out a notebook, startling Mario with her sudden briskness. He watched her as she became a businesswoman, tossing ideas out to Steve.

"Lighting," she said. "It's going to be a killer until it gets dark, which is fine in the winter if you aren't serving lunch yet, but come April and Daylight Saving and all that natural light pouring in . . . it means whatever you do with artificial light is twice as important."

"I'll call you about that. I'm not sure the guy I have in mind is available right now, but I'll find out."

"Okay. Acoustics. I think some nice clouds. Fluffy. Asbestos, I suppose." She laughed at Mario's horrified look. "Just kidding. With this ceiling, even when we've raised the floor, and with so much glass, we need an expert, a real genuine Carnegie Hall kind of expert. Carpeting. Everywhere, except maybe the bar? Unless you like the decibel level of those converted loft places? The ones the bridge and tunnel crowd seems to love these days? Mario?"

"Even if I wanted it, do you think I'd admit it after a loaded question like that? No, of course not. They're for people who can't believe they're in a popular place unless they can't hear themselves think. I have an exact noise level in mind, and I hope your man can come up with it. It's French, a sort of Maxim's level of loudness, I suppose, if I have to pinpoint it."

"Got it," Steve said, rising. "Now I really do have to go." It had started to rain, so he ran across the terrace to ring for the elevator and then back to them to wait for it to come up. "Frances," he said, kissing her on the cheek, "I'll call you this afternoon with a couple of names. Mario, you're very smart and very lucky to have hired this lady."

"I know." As soon as the elevator was out of sight, he drew her to him for a long, deep kiss. He wanted her, now, instantly, and he knew she would have let him take her right there on the filthy floor. He resisted. "We have an alternative," he said, smiling.

When the cabdriver cleared his throat and they had to break apart, they were in front of a town house on West Sixty-eighth, a featureless building with dark glass windows. Frances looked up and groaned. "No offense, but it looks like those sinister Mafia stretch limousines. It's a whorehouse?"

"You'll see." He showed her around the house officiously, throwing open doors, saying only "the kitchen" or "the library" as they explored the rooms on four floors. It was obviously designed for a classic swinging bachelor who had enough money to do exactly as he pleased. Huge black leather sofas cried out for seduction scenes; masses of red and blue silk pillows suggested vast orgies; a stainless steel bar folded out of a wall of fake leather-bound books. It was in breathtakingly bad taste, and Frances gasped as each new room assaulted her. Finally, in a bedroom dominated by an enormous bed that was reflected in mirrored walls and ceiling and covered with fur from an unknown animal, he turned to her.

"What do you think? Pretty incredible, huh?"

"It's certainly . . . incredible."

He burst out laughing. "I can tell you want to touch that bedspread to see what it is, but you're afraid it might bite you or give you cancer."

"I think it's the ghastliest house I've ever seen. Does it belong to a friend of yours? Is his last name Hefner, by any chance?"

"A TV producer who's in New Zealand for a few months, who's a friend of a film editor who's a friend of mine who's staying here but who's never here in the daytime. I haven't met the owner and I'm not sure I want to." He sat down on the bed and played with the dials set into the wall next to it. The lights lowered; Prokofiev's *Romeo and Juliet* began to play softly through hidden speakers; drapes were drawn. "It's all right, isn't it? Your place isn't possible and neither is mine and hotel rooms are . . . I don't know."

"It's fine. Really, it is." She came over to sit next to him, looking up at their reflections in the mirrored ceiling. "It's like the rest of the world doesn't exist."

"Does it? Do you want it to?"

"No. At the moment, no," she said, reaching for him.

He undressed her slowly, then himself, laying their clothes on a chair carefully and coming back to kiss her neck, her breasts, her belly as she lay back with her eyes closed. Twice, he brought her close with his lips and tongue.

"Please," she said, bringing his face up to hers. "Please. Now." Then they were together again, both straining and holding back to the same degree, gradually quickening until they were no longer in control, until they were racing as fast as they could.

She lay wrapped in his arms afterward, stroking the hair on his chest. "You know this is dangerous, don't you?" she asked suddenly.

"No," he said into her shoulder. "Are you a dangerous woman?"

She broke away and went to where his jacket was hanging on the back of a chair and then to the table where she'd left her purse, coming back to the bed with his Winstons and her Trues. "We have to be careful. I mean it. There's a danger we'll want to spend all our time doing . . . what we just did." She laughed at the expression on his face, his raised eyebrows. "I know, I can't imagine a nicer way to spend the day, every day. But if we keep meeting here too often in this . . ." She snapped the top of her lighter down and swept her arm to include the room. ". . . this bordello, then the weeks and the months will just roll by and suddenly you'll wake up on January first, when you're supposed to have a restaurant, and you won't have one, and you'll blame me. I thought about it this morning when we were there, that maybe I should be unbelievably noble and take myself off the most important job I've ever had. Maybe it's a . . . a conflict of interests."

"No. We won't let that happen. I saw you today, when you really got going. There wasn't any conflict: you knew exactly what I wanted, and now I won't be satisfied with any other designer."

"All right." She laughed. "Didn't take much to convince me, did it? It's going to be fun, but it's going to be a lot of work."

"Gosh. And here I thought I could get away with making a couple of phone calls."

"I'm sorry, that was a stupid thing to say. I was really only telling myself how much I have to do, and everything's happened so fast. Last week, you were still at Rudi's." She stroked his hair. "You never told me much about the night you left there, you know. Was it awful? Have you made a lifelong enemy?"

"Probably. Yes. He'll hate me even more when he hears about my plans. It's going to cut into his business and he'll know that."

"I always loved Rudi's, from the night it opened, but I never liked Rudi himself. Dorothy is a friend of his, or at least she plays bridge with him — Dorothy is Hamilton's sister — and she always talked about how sweet and wonderful he was but I always found him . . . oily."

"Oily and slippery and treacherous."

"He's gay, isn't he? I mean, I always assumed he was."

"He is, and his lover is Chuck Wetherby. The tennis pro."

She frowned. "Maggie's brother," she said slowly. "Dorothy must have mentioned it, but I never made the connection."

"Anyway," he said quickly. They hadn't talked about Maggie. "Chuck was part of the problem. He drinks and I think he makes life hell for Rudi but Rudi's obsessed." They looked at one another, wondering if they were obsessed, smiling because they knew they were having the same thought. Then she got up from the bed and headed for the bathroom. "I'll be right back and then let's get out of here. Let's prove we're serious and go back to your beautiful new place and talk about air conditioning and . . . napkins."

"Right." He laughed. "We mean business." He fiddled with buttons and dials on the wall. The lights went up, the music stopped, and the curtains opened. When she returned, her hair pulled back into a knot again, her minimal makeup reapplied, she began quickly to pull on her clothes. He was already dressed, and he sat, smoking, watching her.

"It just occurred to me," she said over her shoulder. "A name. Do you know what you're going to call it?"

"My new place? Something classy, of course. What do you think?"

"Classy? Chez Mario, then, *naturellement*. Or Mario's Hideaway. Mario's Sky Lounge."

"Top of the Mario's. The Mario Room. Windows on the Mario. Tavern-on-the-Mario."

"Seriously," she protested.

"All right, seriously. It came into my head this morning when you were painting rosy pictures for Steve and me. It's not a theme, exactly, but it sort of goes along with what you were saying about making every table different. *Tables.* That's what I decided. *Tables.*"

13

THE *LOBBY* of the Cornell Theater on West Forty-fifth Street was noisy, crowded, and smoky. Mario leaned against a pillar in the corner, waiting for Maggie, watching the glittering first-night crowd and adding to the smoke. *Rain* was one of the most-produced plays of the twentieth century, but it was a very long time since it had been done on Broadway. It was daring of Carole to revive an old piece like this, to try to breathe new life into it, and one critic had privately told Mario he was skeptical she could make it work. Its plot was dated even when Somerset Maugham wrote the story it was based on; Sadie Thompson, the prostitute, and the Reverend Mr. Davidson were wrestling with a morality that might seem laughably old-fashioned in today's climate. Mario thought she *would* pull it off, though, not only because of her talent, which everyone took for granted, but because of her amazing instinct for choosing the right vehicles. She was producing this herself, even putting some of her own money into it, he knew, and if she thought it could be done he was willing to bet it would be a great success.

Because this was a first night, the curtain was at seven instead of eight, so the critics could make deadlines for the morning papers, and the crowd looked a little overdressed for this time of the evening. What Maggie called the GQ, the glamour quotient, was very high: more celebrities than he'd seen on Broadway for the past couple of seasons. Flashguns were blinking all around him and there were television crews in front of the theater. He could see Maggie out there, her blonde hair shining above a bright green silk coat-dress, pushing through the crowd.

It felt very strange: there was Maggie, a little late, just like always, meeting him in a lobby before a play — or it could have been a movie or the ballet, exactly like a hundred other times — but now it was different. He'd only seen her once in the week she'd been back from California, and that was for a quick tour of the restaurant space and then dinner that they'd both bolted down, at a place around the corner. He had to go back to the men who were getting time-and-a-half for installing the ovens; she had to go on to a party somewhere. She'd been brittle and too talkative. He knew she was coked to the gills, but he didn't mention it, didn't even bring up the subject of their fight, and she'd stared at him with a puzzled look once or twice, as if she wondered why not. They'd caught up on the people they both knew, on her trip and her parents, on his incredible new luck. He hated himself for not telling her what was really going on, and for letting it ride and for letting her think the strain between them was only because of her drugs and the way he felt about them. Tonight was arranged before she went away, before . . . well, before a lot of things had happened.

"My God," she said when she finally made her way to him. "I'd rather battle the matinee ladies from Scarsdale on a Wednesday afternoon. Let me catch my breath and have a cigarette before we go in. How are you?" she asked, kissing him, obviously determined to be breezy. She lit one of the dark, thin Nat Shermans that she never inhaled. "You look tired and tense and maybe a little angry? Are there problems with the beanery?"

Yes, there were, as a matter of fact, but most of what he supposed was showing in his face had to do with her. And she knew it, but if that was how she wanted to play it, he thought with relief, then he'd play it the same way. "I just came from another meeting with Radnor, and Christ, he doesn't realize . . . never mind. Let's talk about something else. Anything else."

"All right. I'm always willing to talk about myself, if you insist. I just came from drinks with my personal, private albatross. Jim, His Majesty, is displeased with the deal I made with the L.A. gallery. My God, they're having a full-scale show of major works; they're paying an astronomical shipping and insurance bill for the privilege; they've guaranteed purchase of three pieces; but he thinks I wasn't tough enough with them."

She was still talking about Jim as they made their way down the aisle. Their seats were ninth row center and they were surrounded by theater and film people, friends of Carole's or at least people she thought should be there. She'd reserved a big block of seats for her crowd, he realized, and as one of the producers she probably took more than she would have as a mere star. Some of them wished her well and some of them didn't, but a Carole Todd first night wasn't an event that could be ignored.

They still had a few minutes before curtain, and they flipped through their *Playbills*, looked around to see who was there, and carried on half a conversation about Jim. Sitting behind them were Carole's agent, an immense, sweaty man, and his rather mousy wife, clients of the gallery and occasional drop-ins at Rudi's, and they had to twist around and chat for a moment. As the lights began slowly dimming, Mario was aware of two people edging their way along to the empty seats on his left, but he didn't notice who they were. It was a shock to turn and see Frances McKinnon shrugging off a fur jacket in the seat next to him. An older, gray-haired man was helping her. They had time for surprised hellos before the curtain, and Frances introduced Hamilton to them in a quick whisper. Mario was left with a confused sense of bright light (the program said "early morning"), a buzzing of insects and chirping of birds ("Pago Pago"), a white arm on the armrest beside him, and what felt like a newly formed ulcer in his stomach.

He knew Carole had sent tickets to the McKinnons too, he knew she'd be here, but this precise, nightmarish seating arrangement wasn't what he'd imagined. She probably meant for the two couples to sit together, and it just happened that he and Maggie arrived first and it had ended up this way. The audience was laughing at something on stage. He made himself smile in case Maggie was looking at him. Jesus, that was fast, he thought. I'm already covering up in case Maggie figures out what's going on. I'm sitting here in a dark theater, practically living with this woman on my right, and I'm so much in love with the woman on my left I can't even see straight. Great, Mario, and that's her husband next to her, just to make things tidier.

He couldn't concentrate on anything that was happening on stage, but he knew Carole hadn't appeared yet. He was afraid to look over at Frances but he was aware of everything about her. There was her faint perfume, something very subtle and just slightly spicy. Her fur lay back against her seat and spilled over into his, something to be grateful for, a gift to him, an overflow from her world. Her dress — he'd had a flash of something pale pink and silky just before the lights were completely gone — was sleeveless and her slender arms were exposed up to fragile shoulders.

He'd like to put his hand *there* — he kept his head up but his eyes traveled down and to the side — just below her knee, and slowly ride her dress up. He wanted to grab hold of the material at her neckline and pull it off her shoulder. He wanted to force her head toward him and kiss her, hard, the way he had a few hours ago. He didn't know how he was going to get through this.

* * *

Frances had spent too much time getting ready for Carole's opening, and Danny barely got them there through the usual rush-hour traffic and the unusually heavy crowd on Forty-fifth Street. She was concentrating on getting to their seats before the curtain went up, and she didn't notice Mario until he turned around from his conversation with the couple behind them. She was jarred but she recovered fast, made the introductions, and sat back to watch the play unfold. She almost never went to first nights on Broadway — the opera and the ballet were different — and neither did Hamilton. They'd decided long before that they could do without the glamour and see the plays they wanted to see in the first month or two, when the cast wasn't so jittery, when the production was as smooth as it was going to get. But of course this wasn't the same, because this was Carole, her new friend and client, and because Ham was a fan who would have gone to Philadelphia to see her if that was where she was opening.

So now here she was, in a darkened theater, with her husband on one side and Mario on the other. She'd had an impression of a black silk skirt and a black suit. And of course his beautiful coal-black hair, combed back and shining in the last light from the big chandelier above them, that had been so rumpled the last time she'd seen him, a few hours before at what they now just called The House, when she'd left him in bed and dashed to an appointment at Trish's Seventh Avenue space.

She'd been touched that they'd been sent tickets for this, but now she was a little irritated. Carole couldn't have known the seating would work out this way, of course, couldn't have known there would be any reason why it shouldn't, but still . . . Frances was having trouble paying much attention to the play, and she knew she'd have to think of something to say about it at intermission. She could fake it, she supposed — she'd always been quick with words when she'd been lost in a daydream — but really, she should force herself to concentrate, she should ignore the man sitting next to her. She tried that for a few minutes and then gave up.

There was a lull in the action onstage, a long speech by the minister's wife. Mario coughed, bringing his fist up to muffle it and then bringing up his other hand to enclose the fist, his elbows on the armrests. Frances bent down to put her program and her purse under the chair, crossing her right leg over her left as she sat up, embarrassed by the silky sound the movement made.

When Carole, as Sadie Thompson, made her entrance on a sailor's arm, all rouge and ruffles and ostrich feathers, there was a burst of applause and Frances jerked herself back to what was happening, clapping for her new friend. At her first line, delivered in a perfect English tart's accent — "So, I'm to be parked here, am I, dearie?" — the audience laughed delightedly. Frances took the opportunity to look around her, a fast swoop that started on the left with a smile at Hamilton, took in the ceiling and the people in rows in front and to the side, and ended up with a quick glance to the right. Beyond Mario, Maggie was leaning forward so that Frances could see both of them at once, like an imperial couple on the face of a coin, washed by light from the stage. So young, she thought, such perfect features and classic profiles, light and dark, day and night. She instinctively raised her head a fraction of an inch, tightening the muscles in her neck, before she realized she was doing it. My God, Frances, she said to herself. You're actually *competing*, you're comparing yourself to a girl who's nearly twenty years younger than you are. And, admit it, this is why you took so long to get ready. You had no idea you'd find yourself sitting next to him, but you knew Mario would be here, didn't you? And you knew Maggie would be here too.

Isn't this absurd? she thought. We're both determined to behave like adults. We're both afraid we might do something that would look foolish. So not once, in the forty-five minutes or however long this first act is going to last, will we touch or actually look at one another. And it would be so natural if we did: people do glance at their companions, to share the experience of a play, and sometimes their knees touch or their arms touch on the armrest. . . .

Offstage, Sadie Thompson was dancing with the American Marines to her wind-up gramophone while Davidson's wife fumed that the hussy was daring to dance on the Sabbath. First, the "Wabash Blues," now a tango. Frances suddenly wanted Mario to sweep her into his arms and lead her through a tango. They'd never danced. *Never,* she reminded herself, consisted of what? Ten days? There was still time. They'd done things far more intimate than tangos . . . she looked down at her hands, then stole a quick glance at his, resting on his knees now. They were long, perfectly shaped, and strong. She'd noticed his hands at the opening in Maggie's gallery; she'd been fascinated by them. Freud would have had something to say about that, she now admitted to herself.

Finally, after Sadie Thompson and the minister had their first confrontation and he announced his suspicion that she was from the famous red-light district in Honolulu, the curtain dropped. Now we can look at each other and talk, Frances thought, preparing herself to face him as she clapped but turning first to Hamilton.

"Ham, I'd like a cigarette. Shall we see if they want to come?" She still needed another minute. Mario was too close. Let Ham ask them.

He leaned across her, asked if they felt like a drink, and they nodded and followed along after them up the aisle. Frances, her jacket thrown around her shoulders, turned around twice to smile at them brightly.

When they reached the lobby, Hamilton took drink orders, turned down Mario's offer of help, and pushed off to the bar. Mario lit both Maggie's and Frances's cigarettes and started to light his own when Maggie blew out the flame.

"It's unlucky. I've always been told that, three on a match. Sorry . . ." She was embarrassed now.

Mario stared at her. "It's the lighter you gave me, Mag, not a match. You never told me you had that superstition."

"I *am* sorry. That was really silly of me. I always walk under ladders and I never knock wood, so I don't know . . ."

"Oh, I knock on wood," Frances said, "and I've never heard of 'three on a match,' but maybe people worry about it all the time and we don't realize."

"I don't know where I picked it up. It was just one of those reflexes that came out of nowhere." She dropped it. "How are you liking it?" she asked Frances.

"Very much. I think she's extraordinary." That was safe, anyway.

"Mmmm. She is *that*."

Frances heard something in her voice that made her wonder if Maggie was still jealous of whatever Mario and Carole had, even if it was before she came on the scene. Could she possibly have the faintest idea that she was facing a much more current rival?

"I just don't think it was worth bringing back from wherever old plays go," Maggie continued.

"Why, Mag?" Mario asked, at the same time Frances said, "Oh?"

"Just that it's so dated. I don't think it was ever a very important play, even if it was such a big success. It doesn't seem at all relevant to me now. I mean, Somerset Maugham is hardly one of the twentieth century's most distinguished authors, and it seems like the whole thing is incredibly middlebrow, and always was, like . . . Norman Rockwell or Ed Sullivan. A whore and a minister. Honestly."

"Oh, I disagree," Frances said slowly. "I think we can appreciate it more now. If it were a popular success from just a few years ago, then it would be yesterday's news, it would be harder to have a perspective on it. . . ." God, she thought, could I sound much more pseudointellectual?

"I think she's right, Mag. By this time they're sort of universal types, and it's such a juicy part that someone as brilliant as Carole can make it believable."

At least, Frances thought, we're getting away from the plot and the characters and the acting. "I don't think we should dismiss something just because so many people liked it at the time," she said.

"I wasn't aware that I was doing that," Maggie said edgily.

"I think you were, Mag," Mario said. "Doing that, I mean, even if you weren't aware of it."

"Oh. Now I'm not aware of what I'm saying?" Maggie was still smiling, but she was digging in, her chin thrust out stubbornly, as if there were more to this conversation than what they were saying. The triangle had changed; Maggie had stepped back a foot or two; Mario and Frances were side by side, facing her. Hamilton had come back, and he stood politely, waiting to be noticed, balancing two drinks in each hand. When Maggie saw him, she put her hand on his arm.

"Mr. McKinnon — oh, thank you — I'm outnumbered and you've come back just in time to help me out. I say it's a dated play and they say it's relevant or whatever it is they're trying to say."

Hamilton immediately sensed the tension, and even if he didn't understand it he went into action to dilute it. "Then I'll be on your side," he said as he passed out the other drinks. "I've never liked two against one. But I'm probably not the best ally because I have no idea what I think of the play. I simply think Carole Todd is so marvelous that I wouldn't mind if she recited nursery rhymes." He looked around him then, and Frances could tell he was going to change the subject without seeming to. "Is this a standard first-night crowd these days? I don't think I've been to a Broadway opening for a few years."

Darling Ham, Frances said silently. Willing to look a little unsophisticated when you're anything but, helping smooth out a conversation that's gotten rocky, for the hundred thousandth time. She took a step to stand beside him, breaking the geometry.

"No," she said, playing along as if she'd been to so many more of them than he had. "It's not usual. It's more intense than they ever seem to be. I think everyone's looking for Carole to have a flop, simply because she had such a string of successes."

"I wonder what the reviews will be like," Mario said. "Not that they'll make that much difference to the box office. Carole said there's an unbelievable advance sale."

Their conversation for the rest of the interval consisted of trying to guess what certain critics would say in the morning papers and in the weekly magazines, and they all more or less agreed. The *Times* would probably like it, or at least it was bound to respect Carole's performance; the *Post* and the *News* might damn it with lukewarm praise; *New York* magazine would certainly rip it to shreds. They ignored the first warning gong and finished their drinks leisurely before making their way back to their seats.

This time the men flanked the women — Mario saw to that by turning into their row first — so Frances sat between Maggie and Hamilton. She still had to force herself to concentrate, he was still so near, but it was a little easier than before. Carole really was extraordinary, she realized, and she was glad she'd be able to tell her so without having to lie or even to hedge. The applause, when the play ended, was clamorous, and there were eight curtain calls. The four of them walked around the corner to Sardi's afterward for the party, but then they were separated in the crowd and she didn't see Mario again that night.

14

WEAVING down the center aisle of the warm, fragrant stable, Rudi and Jimmy Bradford, the trainer, stopped at every stall to spend a few minutes with each horse and discuss him or her in detail before going on to the next.

"I don't like the look of that leg either," Rudi said about a six-year-old named Ratatouille. "Better get Smythson to look at it again, no? And she needs more of that potassium stuff, don't you think?"

Bradford nodded. "Her eyes are tired," he said, which explained everything to both of them. He was a wiry little man in his late thirties who limped along beside Rudi. He'd been a top jockey until his leg was smashed at Hialeah, but he was cheerful and he was one of the best trainers in the East. He had no idea how lucky he was that Rudi listened respectfully to his opinions, that he was spoken to in a low, polite voice, because that was the way he'd always been treated here. The staff at the restaurant wouldn't have recognized their boss from his manner: here at his horse farm, an hour and a half away in New Hope, Pennsylvania, he was a different man.

The tour of inspection over, Rudi stayed on alone, bringing an apple out of his jacket pocket for Montenegro, the two-year-old down at the end of the line of boxes. He tickled her forehead as she munched happily and watched him with her deep, intelligent eyes. She was his favorite, the fastest, the most famous, the most valuable, and he'd named her for the republic in Yugoslavia where he'd grown up. Or, rather, where he'd spent his boyhood on his family's farm, until the very end of the war, until his father was killed by Partisans, his brothers by Germans, and his mother by typhus.

* * *

His real life had begun on the rusty, old converted troopship, crammed with displaced persons, that took more than two weeks to steam out from Trieste, through the Mediterranean, and across the Atlantic to New York. Rudi kept to himself on the trip, like deposed royalty. He'd been king of the boys' barracks at the refugee camp in Eboli, and now he was nobody, thrown in with all these sentimental peasants whose pious patriotism for a country they hadn't even seen yet disgusted him. He was awed by New York in spite of himself, though. He ignored the Statue of Liberty but his eyes were glued to the skyline of Manhattan as they crept up the river to the pier. He wanted to walk off the ship the minute it docked and lose himself in these fascinating canyons, but he had to be a good refugee and do everything he was told. An organization had found foster parents for him in California, and he was taken directly from the ship to Grand Central, given a ticket, twenty-five dollars, a handshake, and a friendly "good luck."

The sponsors who were waiting for him at Union Station in Los Angeles were a short, pink couple with kind, nervous faces. They were from Yugoslavia, of course, Dalmatia, but they'd left before the war, settled in the suburb of Glendale, opened a little grocery store, and prospered. Rudi knew immediately that they were going to bore him, but he had to stay in their little stucco house and be grateful for the next two years. He went to a special high school in the days and worked in their store in the evenings. On Saturdays, he took a bus to Hollywood and strolled around. Sometimes he had sexual adventures with men who cruised him on the street — it was odd after the Eboli camp, where it had been a form of barter, to do as he pleased with whom he pleased — and sometimes he went to movies. Sundays, after church, he took a bus out to Encino in the San Fernando Valley, where he could rent a horse, ride up into the bare hills, and imagine he was exploring the farm in Montenegro again.

The day he turned eighteen, he moved into a run-down bungalow court just off Hollywood Boulevard with three boys he'd met on one of his Saturdays. They were all from the Midwest; they were all sure they were going to be movie stars; they were all, in the meantime, working as waiters and parking lot attendants and sometimes — the most money for the least work — hustlers.

Rudi fell into their lives for a while. He took the same jobs, he shared their clothes, but he didn't bother dreaming about being a movie star and he didn't waste his money on singing lessons or elocution lessons. He had no particular interest in being an actor and he didn't try to correct his thick accent or his unpredictable voice that went out of control when he was excited, exactly like Mrs. Roosevelt's. Some of his more outrageous friends, in fact, called him Eleanor. He found work as an extra whenever he could and he rode every day in Griffith Park.

It was the great period of horse operas — movies and, more and more, television. By the time he was twenty, he was getting enough work as a double for actors who could barely ride that he bought a car and moved into his own bungalow in a slightly better court. At twenty-five he was the highest-paid cowboy stuntman in town, able to do anything on or half off horses, and he was living in a small house with a small pool in the Hollywood Hills and driving a Triumph. As the studio system crumbled, independent contractors began to take over the work of their departments, and Rudi saw his chance. He found investors and he found a ranch in the Valley that he named the Bar Nothing. Within a short time, every film and television studio came to him for horses and for the cowboys and cowgirls to ride them. Actors and actresses who suddenly had a part — or who were hoping to get a part — that called for horsemanship came to his ranch for lessons.

The place was a gold mine for a few years, and he soon opened a stable in Malibu Canyon that became a club for what Hollywood considered its aristocracy. It was harder for a while to get a membership in the Bar Nothing II than in the Hillcrest Country Club. He ran a smaller branch in Palm Springs during the most social winter months. He built an enormous ranch house on Mulholland Drive that became famous for the parties he held there. Sometimes they were very gay parties; sometimes they were very "mixed" parties; always, unfailingly, they were very wild parties.

Working and playing obsessively, he drove hard bargains and

then spent every penny of what he made and more. By the end of the 'sixties, though, when he was at the end of his thirties, it began to look as if he might have to diversify. The epics that used hundreds of horses and riders were being made far more cheaply in Italy and Spain. The great wave of westerns on television had crested and was receding. Even socially, it wasn't so necessary to look good in the saddle anymore; it was more important to look good on the tennis court. The club in Malibu Canyon was reverting to what stables had always been in the past: a place for girls in their early teens to meet horses and for middle-aged women to meet riding instructors.

He began to deal in real estate, taking on a partner who seemed to know all about it. The ranches in the San Fernando Valley, in Malibu Canyon, and in Palm Springs were broken up into one-acre lots and sold off, and then he plowed most of the cash back into speculative deals. It seemed for a few years that there was no limit to the money they could make until, in the mid-'seventies, there was a recession big enough to topple the fragile house of cards his partner had built. All the profits from the Bar Nothing subdivisions vanished within a single week, and Rudi was left, halfway between forty and fifty, with not much more than he'd had at twenty-five: an Aston-Martin, a house on Mulholland with giant payments and taxes, and a closetful of labels. He sold the Aston-Martin and bought a jeep. He sold the labels and wore jeans and workshirts, half-convincing himself and his friends that he preferred the rugged look these days. Finally, he rented the big house out for twice as much as his maintenance, which at least gave him a trickle of income.

For months that stretched into a year, he lay low in a room at the Chateau Marmont on the Strip, telling himself something would turn up. At the few parties he went to, he tried to sound mysterious and excited about a deal he was working on. He helped a friend find antiques for his shop on Melrose; he gave a few private riding lessons; he had an affair with a dancer from a road show at the Music Center. Life went on, but he wasn't very pleased about it. It wasn't where he'd expected to be at this point.

At a very elegant New Year's Eve party, seeing out the worst year he'd spent since he was a teenager, Rudi found himself talking to

Larry Lengdorf, the host, an enormous old queen in a white satin caftan. Rudi was himself poured into a skintight white satin western outfit. That was the theme of the party, white satin; the room glistened. Larry was, if anyone was, the doyen of Gay Hollywood. He was already very rich from the gossip column that had reached the limit of its syndication in the 'fifties but was still going stronger than any other of its kind. Now he was pulling in even more money as the host of a weekly prime-time talk show. He was America's favorite token homosexual: fat, outrageous, jolly, and clever. He shared this big house in Bel Air, pale lavender inside and out, with a dozen lavender, neutered toy poodles that were named after the signs of the Zodiac.

Never had Larry been known to actually have sex with anyone, and most people assumed — in spite of the elaborately dirty compliments he paid to handsome men and the double entendres he squeezed past the television censors — that he was asexual, as much of a eunuch as his dogs. That wasn't precisely true, as Rudi knew from the days when he'd been a part-time hustler. Larry liked to watch, and he'd carried this voyeurism to an extreme in (or, rather, outside) a twelve-sided room on the third floor of the house, each wall hung with floor-to-ceiling mirrors on which the zodiacal symbols were etched. The mirrors, of course, acted as windows from the other side, a fact which Larry's guests in the room sometimes knew and sometimes didn't.

It was rare for Rudi to have more than a couple of drinks, but he was trying to drown his problems that night, and he remembered very little except a lot of noise at midnight, not even what he'd done with the two boys he found in his bed in the morning. When Larry called him a few days later, he was surprised. They'd known each other for years, but it was never more than a vague party friendship, with cute invitations and thank-yous sent back and forth in the mail.

"I've done your chart, my dear," Larry gasped excitedly. "You remember talking about it the other night, don't you?" Rudi didn't, of course, but he didn't admit that he didn't. Larry was famous for his fascination with astrology, and now he rattled on about rising signs while Rudi half listened.

"... so you're supposed to be in my house," Larry finished triumphantly.

"But it's too late for that, isn't it?" Rudi asked.

"No, no. I mean in my house, silly boy. Literally. Here in Bel Air."

"Well, that's very, um, flattering, but I have a house, you know. On Mulholland. I know you've been there. I'm sure I told you the other night that I'm here at the Chateau while it's being done over?"

Larry tsk-tsked. "You're fibbing to the wrong girl, sweetie. I know all about it. You're poor, which must be a terrible predicament to be in, and I'm rich. It's a marriage made in heaven. In the heavens, actually," he giggled.

He could be a powerful enemy and Rudi didn't want to cross him, so he stepped very carefully. "I hadn't really thought about marriage," he began, but he was interrupted by a squeal of laughter.

"Don't worry so, my dear! I'm not after your precious thing, although as I recall it's a not inconsiderable thing to be after." More shrieks, and then Larry began to explain, with some humor but very shrewdly, what he wanted. He'd realized lately that he wasn't getting any younger — no surprise to anyone else, he was sure, but a shock to him. He adored his estate but it was beginning to feel just too big for one old queen and a dozen poodles. Yes, he had house servants and gardeners and pool boys and four good-looking secretaries, but they were all so *servile*. Yes, of course he had tons of good friends, but they all had their own lives. No, as Rudi ought to know, he didn't want a lover. He just wanted someone who was fun and attractive and smart, who'd be around when he wanted him.

"Not a paid companion, *chéri* — that sounds just too unbearably depressing. I wouldn't pay you, but you'd have the run of the place, of course, and food, and there always seems to be an extra car or two around. Just to sort of be here and maybe smooth things out sometimes and have meals with me when I'm home? Which is very seldom, of course, because I'm such a *mariposa*. Oh, and maybe help plan parties, which I know you'd adore. And, um, of course you could use my famous star chamber whenever you wanted. I've been trying to find someone for ages, but no one had just the right chart.

It had to be a Capricorn, naturally, but I had a particular feeling about your stars the other night, and I was right."

He went back to horoscope talk, and Rudi thought very quickly. Larry was lonely; Larry was feeling old; Larry, however delicate his allusion to the room with mirrors was, would want Rudi to stage-manage scenes there sometimes but probably not all that often. In return, Rudi would have a hell of a lot more security — for a while, anyway — than he had at the moment. He moved in the next day.

It worked surprisingly well, so well that Rudi began to think there might be something in astrology after all. He really had no duties: the house was beautifully run by an exquisite Japanese butler. He could pretty much do as he pleased, but he found himself looking forward to tête-à-têtes with Larry. They became close friends, closer than any friend Rudi had ever had, during their dinners at home, cackling over the newest bit of Hollywood gossip. Although he'd assumed Larry would want him to arrange things in the twelve-sided room, he was never asked to do it. He always took tricks there — sometimes two or three at a time — rather than to his bedroom, but he never knew if they were being watched and it was never mentioned.

Larry was a surprisingly clever nuts-and-bolts businessman and he pushed Rudi to think clearly about what to do next: something that didn't need much capital, something where Rudi could use his charm and his contacts. Rod Andrews was an old friend of Larry's who'd coasted through a couple of television series on his looks but who was now discovering that no one wanted an aging, talentless beauty. He was a great cook, Larry said, but he had a paranoid, abrasive manner that turned everybody off. Rudi could barely boil water, but he was good with people, especially when he wanted something from them. Together, with Larry's encouragement and a small loan, they started Mildred Pierce Catering out of the kitchen of Rod's house down in the Flats. Just when it began to take off with a couple of big, profitable benefits and all the right publicity, Rudi had to take a leave of absence.

Always known by his custom-made lavender cigarettes and his ivory cigarette holder, Larry surprised Rudi one night by announcing that he was giving them up. Then he broke down and cried. It was a case of the horse and the barn door, he said. He had lung cancer. Rudi stayed with him through three operations, through radiation and chemotherapy and, finally, through acupuncture in Santa Monica and laetrile in Mexico. Nothing worked for long, and Larry came home to die, so thin now that an unsuspected handsomeness showed through in his face.

In one of his lucid moments, sitting up in the big canopied bed, he began to talk to Rudi about his will. There would be a big estate, but of course there was a big network of sisters and brothers-in-law, nieces and nephews, grandnieces and grandnephews. Also — in a rather touching last-minute bid for respectability, for immortality, even — he was endowing a chair of journalism at the University of Virginia, his alma mater. Anyway, none of that was the point he wanted to make, he said. It was Rudi he wanted to talk about. Rudi was a different case; Rudi was very, very special to him and he should have something really . . . *practical.*

After a short interruption by the nurse, he went on to talk — deliberately, maddeningly mysterious now — about what it might be and how it might be put to the best use. Then the dogs were brought in from a run out in the grounds, and it took a while to greet them and get them settled around him in some way so they wouldn't get tangled in the intravenous tubes or the oxygen tube or — worst of all — the catheter tube. When he began to speak again, it was only to concentrate on logistics.

There was a big Modigliani oil in the dining room: that was for Rudi; that was actually in the will. It was what was in the wall safe behind the painting, though, that was important. It was, of course, what he had just been talking about, and it certainly was *not* in the will. Rudi would have to get in there fast, soon after . . . well, soon after. He'd find the combination on Sagittarius's collar, his license number. The dog's ears went up when he heard his name and he nestled up to Larry, who stroked him absently and then fell asleep.

The day after the funeral, the four sisters and their husbands conveniently arguing out by the pool, Rudi opened the safe. Inside were dozens of photographs, a few reels of film, some videotapes, some tape recordings, photostats of letters, and a notebook in which Larry, in his meticulous writing, listed the contents. It was a cache of secrets that Larry would never have been able to use in print or on television. It was like a portfolio of very good stocks or bonds: if he could figure out how to manage it the right way, it would be worth more, year after year, than what any of the sisters — maybe more than what all of them *combined* — were inheriting. It brought tears of gratitude to his eyes.

* * *

Rudi's mind came slowly back to the stable where he was standing and to the horse in front of him, who was begging with her eyes for another apple. He turned his pockets inside out to show her he didn't have any more, and he smiled at her when she seemed to understand. He looked at his watch. The accountant who came out from the city to help launder the big chunks of cash that Rudi used for the farm's running expenses would be here soon. He wasn't his legitimate accountant, of course (and he took twenty percent for his trouble), but he managed to act like one anyway. Which meant questions and explanations, and Rudi was dreading it because his horses weren't doing as well as he'd hoped and the restaurant seemed to be covering only the town house, travel, food, and Chuck. Now that Mario had quit, he was afraid the restaurant wouldn't be doing quite so well, and then when Mario opened a new place things could get really serious. . . .

When he told friends about his adventures in Yugoslavia and Italy, Rudi always cast himself as Scarlett O'Hara in her "As God is my witness" scene. His family's rocky little farm had been nothing like a southern plantation, as it happened, but it was true that something had stayed with him from that part of his life. Reinforced in Hollywood when he lost nearly everything, and still material for his worst nightmares, was an absolute terror of losing what he already had.

After the accountant left, Rudi sat for a while in the big, open-beamed living room. It was clear he needed more money. The three hundred fifty thousand (two eighty, net, he reminded himself) that came in last month from his *patrons,* seven of them at fifty thousand each, had been committed before he even had it in his hands, and the next payment wasn't due again till March. One possibility was to tap into a few more secrets. He'd come to think of seven as a lucky number, but there was no reason it *had* to be, was there? His grandmother was born on the seventh, he himself was born on the seventh, and Larry had died on the seventh. Well, that wasn't really lucky, certainly not for poor Larry, and he shouldn't even think it because he'd genuinely loved Larry, but given that he had to die anyway . . .

The wall safe had held material that could be damaging — ruinous, in most cases — to the reputations of more than twenty people, all of them very rich, naturally, or Larry wouldn't have kept them on file. Thanks to the network of people Larry paid handsomely to find grist for his gossip mill, even if in these cases the information was so explosive he couldn't touch it, Rudi now knew the single most vulnerable spot, the precise location of the Achilles heel, of each of them. Larry had left him a surprise on top of this surprise — a life insurance policy for half a million — so he had had the leisure to approach his new life carefully. For more than a year, he researched their lives, their work, their husbands or wives or lovers or children or parents. As cautiously as a Merrill Lynch analyst, he weighed the pros and cons of each potential . . . benefactor.

At some point during that year, he made the decision to move to New York, to open a restaurant there, maybe, now that he was doing so well with the catering business again. So, even though he'd be staying in California a little longer to build up a bigger stockpile, a year or two, he thought he'd try to limit his list to people who either lived in New York or who'd be in and out of town pretty often. A wise man always watches his investments closely, he told himself, and then he began to wonder if he'd end up actually meeting any of his patrons. Until that moment, his inheritance had excited him primarily because it was a collection of such fabulous secrets (even if he couldn't share them) and because it could provide him with such a nice, steady income. But he suddenly realized what Larry had always known, which was that knowledge of this kind represented much, much more. These bits of paper and film and tape were *power*, it was as simple and as fascinating as that, and power could be a marvelous, never-ending, constantly amusing game. Purely to add to his own pleasure, he thought of little touches that would twist the knife ever so slightly: spraying every letter with the cologne Larry had always worn (that he, himself — although he rather liked it — could no longer wear); tiny references to their lives, their recent successes or failures, that told them he was watching them from somewhere; things like that.

So he chose the ones he might somehow get to know, not that any of his brood would ever learn who the enemy was, but that wouldn't make it any less interesting to see them, at close range, squirm. He was pretty lucky, too, in at the very least making their acquaintance. Dorothy was the first, because they actually met by chance at a bridge game soon after he moved to New York, and he immediately set out to amuse her and befriend her. Well, of course, Dorothy wasn't a patron per se, but her husband was, and even though he was homophobic and flatly refused to socialize with Rudi after the one time they were introduced, he found that he could sometimes keep in touch with that particular investment through her. There were occasions when Dorothy would sigh to Rudi that Spence was so tired lately, so worried, so depressed, and Rudi would know the reason, would know another payment was due just then, and it was heaven. Best of all, most delicious, were the two times since he died, when Rudi ran checks from Dorothy through his account and gave her cash that was back in his hands within twenty-four hours.

And then there was the stunning coincidence that her brother was another patron. Although, actually, why not, given Larry's concentration on the secrets of the very rich? He'd seen Hamilton a few times — at the opera, at a benefit or two — but he'd never been to the restaurant and he couldn't say he'd ever actually met him. Still, he knew his sister well. And his wife, of course, though not very well at all, and his brother Frederick very slightly, so that was a feather in his cap even if it was smallish. It would be lovely if there were something about Frederick . . . all three members of that generation of McKinnons . . . or Frances? No, he supposed not, but it was a shame. He wasn't *bound* to seven names, after all.

Because the restaurant had become so successful, because everybody who was anybody ate there eventually, he ended up meeting most of his patrons at one time or another. Carole Todd used it as her bistro whenever she was in New York, and he could certainly say to himself that he *knew* her, even though she was such a cold cunt and he'd finally realized they were never going to be friends of any kind. But she was the link with the Widow Deloit, the only one of his people he didn't at least see around from time to time — he wasn't even sure he'd recognize her — because as far as he could tell, she seldom came to New York except at payment time. Anyway, that in itself was marvelous because it was the single case — a little like a stock split, he had said to himself — in which he'd been paid by two people for keeping the same secret from the public.

As for the others, two of them were regulars at the restaurant when they were in town. One was an actress, in her seventies now, who'd sung and danced her way through a dozen Broadway musicals and half a dozen marriages, but who seemed to have preferred — for one night, anyway — the charms of her stepdaughter. Another, the Funniest Man in America, had a thing for black girls and loved what they could do to him with hot wax. Even the archconservative governor of a neighboring state, caught by a camera as he rolled around in bed with a boy who couldn't be more than ten, was an occasional drop-in with his wife.

So, really, considering the fact that he couldn't expect them all to be bosom buddies because after all they were such different types, he'd done pretty well up till now with keeping an eye on his portfolio. It was just that it wasn't yielding as much as he'd like at the moment, as much as he actually rather badly *needed* if he was going to keep this ranch going on the scale he wanted. One possibility was to go back to the original list and find a few new investments, but he was so comfortable with these particular stocks that had given him such nice, steady dividends for so many years. He decided to go with what he already had, to simply squeeze a little harder. He'd go back to the city tonight and start the ball rolling. He felt much better about things.

* * *

Standing at his window and looking down into the depths of Wall Street, Hamilton wondered if he was going to miss this office when it came time to move over to the new complex on the river. The neo-Gothic skyscraper that would be known as the McKinnon Building for only another year was built in the early 'twenties, late in his grandfather's reign. It was meant to inspire awe, and by carefully suggesting the timelessness of a French cathedral, by hinting at a special relationship between the bank and a Higher Power, it had probably been successful. The new building would be beautiful in its own way, he knew, gleaming and efficient. Frances would be designing his office and it would have elegance and dignity, space and far more sunlight, but his grandfather wouldn't have known where to lean his walking stick, his father wouldn't have known where to display his polo trophies. It would have no memory.

He shrugged and turned back to his desk. What was he regretting, after all? He'd probably miss this old pile for about an hour. He'd feel freer, he'd travel lighter, he'd carry less weight without all the reminders of his family and how things used to be when he began working here, when four percent was a good rate of interest, when railroads were still blue-chip stocks, when there were typing pools and carbon paper and water coolers. Because of him, the bank was modern, prosperous as never before; it had been brought, kicking and screaming, into the Computer Age. It lent to hydroelectric projects in Pakistan; it underwrote supertankers longer than this building was tall. He could make a sentimental speech when he retired, if he liked, if he retired. Till then, there was no time to look backward.

He flipped quickly through the interoffice memos and reports that were carefully arranged by his secretary in order of priority on his blotter, then the mail that was opened and date-stamped, and then the few pieces marked "Personal" or "Confidential" that were still sealed in their envelopes. As he slit one of them with his grandfather's ivory letter opener, something made him peer at the typed words "By Hand" again, underlined three times in a particular way, and it was a second later that the scent fully registered in his mind. Then the single sheet of cheap paper: it was from *him,* even though it couldn't be, even though it was the wrong month.

"This will certainly be something of a shock to you, coming in safe little November," it said, reading his thoughts, "but we wouldn't want to get in a rut with our payment plan, would we? We need a little extra cash. The Holiday Season is coming up, we want to have a joyous Christmas and a prosperous New Year, and we thought you'd like to help us out. We were just *sure* you'd want to contribute, Hamilton! Of course, we understand how little time you important bankers have for making insignificant arrangements like this, so let's give it a couple of months, shall we? Yes, let's. Two months from today. Fifty thousand. We'll keep you posted on all the delivery details. Bye-bye for now."

He felt such a swelling of rage that he had to get up and move around the room, clenching and unclenching his fists. His first feeling was that he'd been betrayed, that a contract — a gentlemen's agreement, at least — had been torn up without his permission. Immediately, he realized how ridiculous, how naive, it was to think of this as some sort of business arrangement. It was laughable; he'd actually managed to convince himself over the years that this parasite was reasonable, moderate in his demands, *honorable*. Because the pressure had always been so regular, because he could predict, almost to the day, when a letter would come, he'd been lulled into a false sense of security. It was always unpleasant, of course, especially the humiliation of the drop-offs — and God knew there were times when his anger had come close to boiling over — but it was predictable, a penance he paid twice a year, a kind of running expense, like property taxes on the McKinnon Building. And now this. It was only the beginning, he knew; the demands were only going to escalate from here on.

He forced himself to sit down. He lit a cigar. He tried to think clearly. Every day, he reminded himself, he and his lieutenants dealt with the cleverest traders on Wall Street, the smartest politicians in Washington, the slipperiest members of OPEC. He had to approach this problem in the same way, he had to outguess his opponent, to get into his mind even if he couldn't attach a name or an identity to it. The man had changed his pattern: that was a tiny chink in his armor, a small cause for hope. He needed more money badly enough to take a bigger risk, and that made him just slightly more vulnerable. Right?

Wrong! He slammed his fist down on the desk, neatly snapping in two the letter opener that lay there. Wrong, Hamilton. This doesn't make him even slightly more vulnerable. It only shows how utterly and completely feeble and helpless *you* are.

He made a decision. He had never rocked the boat, never once made even the smallest attempt — after that detective had been so totally unsuccessful — to find out who was doing this. It had always seemed best, safest, to make these hateful deliveries and walk away.

Anything could happen, he had told himself, if he ever waited to see who actually picked up the packages (probably a messenger of some kind, in any case, and that would tell him nothing). This had always been his policy, and it was at least partly because he wasn't sure he could rein in his own fury if he ever came face-to-face with this unspeakable man. But now the pattern was broken; now the worst *had* happened; now he had nothing to lose. The next delivery was going to be very different. And *if* he confronted his nemesis, if he felt anything like what he was feeling at this moment, he wasn't at all sure he cared whether he could control himself or not.

* * *

"Carole, we read about your big new success and it made us so happy!" the letter began. "You must be making lots and lots of lovely money, and we thought we'd get in touch with you again, even though we have to admit this is kind of irregular because it isn't when we usually write. The thing is, Carole, we're feeling a little pinched right now — what with the Holidays coming up and everything — and we were positive you'd be able to spare us a little extra. Maybe you can just think of it as a Christmas bonus! Fifty thousand would do very nicely, thank you very much. Of course, we understand it might take you a few weeks to raise that much money without involving an inquisitive old accountant or a silly old agent or somebody, so in the spirit of the Season, we'll give you till the first week of January. You can expect to hear from us a day or two into the New Year. Keep up the good work! Break a leg!"

It had been delivered here, to her dressing room, after the Saturday night performance, fastened to what must be three dozen pale lavender roses, which everyone knew were her favorites. When she first noticed them, she was sure they were from Tony, but when she saw the typewritten envelope she knew instantly, with the nausea she always felt, who sent them. The scent of the flowers had covered up the cologne. There was no point in tracing the delivery. There was no point in doing anything except to destroy the note and get the flowers out of here as fast as she could. They must have come during the last act, and her dresser had arranged them lovingly in a big clear vase. Her instinct was to toss the whole thing out the window, but they might still be there in the alley when she came in for tomorrow's matinee. Instead, she threw open the door and took the flowers down the hall to the man who guarded the stage entrance. Someone might as well have them, and she remembered he had a wife somewhere in Brooklyn who waited up for him every night. She didn't wait to hear how grateful he was or how appreciative Nadine would be.

Back in her dressing room, she still wanted to throw things, to smash mirrors, to have a real, old-fashioned, leading-lady tantrum, but she had to stay calm. It would only mean complications, explanations, afterward. Anyway, some old friends were coming soon to take her to dinner. She tossed down a stiff shot of bourbon mixed with very little water, and she tried to think. Not since the first time, the first letter, had she felt this way. She'd always been sickened and depressed and scared, of course, for days before and after the letters came and the horrible deliveries of money had to be made, but at least that was *dependable,* regular, like income taxes or her periods. This, arriving here only a month after the last one, opened up a whole new world of nightmarish possibilities. He could write to her every month, every week. Would he be too smart to ask for more money than she could afford, too clever to kill the goose who laid all these golden eggs for him? She couldn't even be sure of that, now; she couldn't be sure of anything. Every time she looked at her mail, every time a bouquet of flowers was delivered — *that* was a vicious new twist — she'd be forced to wonder if it was something from him again.

Then she did exactly what she'd been calmly telling herself she mustn't do. She hurled the bottles and jars on her dressing table, one by one, against the far wall. She overturned the chair and another chair and the chaise longue. She ripped the mirror off its brackets, held it high over her head for a moment, slammed it down, and then crushed the hundred pieces into a thousand pieces under her heels. She heard the knocking and the worried voices out in the corridor only when it was over, when her rage was spent, when she was sobbing in a heap in the middle of the floor.

She would not live like this! There had to be a way of finding a face, a name, for this formless, shapeless monster. There had to be a place to start, and there was. She could pick up the phone and make a call she had thought, in this or any other life, she would never make. She decided to do it. It would be a beginning, and the end . . . anything might happen in the end.

* * *

Knowing she was supposed to keep her cholesterol level down and realizing what Frieda had cooked for her (after quite a long argument, really) was the single worst way to do it, Dorothy was feeling guilty as she ate her cheese omelet and her bacon and her muffins drenched in butter. She couldn't help it, though: this had been a *dreadful* day, and she was going to eat what she wanted to eat, and after all she was the boss and not the other way around. When she was home by herself, she always ate with Frieda in the breakfast room or in the kitchen, but tonight she was mad at her for being so interfering, and she'd told her to set the big dining table for one. So here she was, all alone with candles and flowers and a breakfast she was calling a dinner that was bad for her anyway, at one end of an expanse of mahogany meant for twenty.

First of all, the afternoon of bridge at Millie's apartment down at River House had been, well, not very successful. She'd been dealt wonderful cards, grand slam material a couple of times, and she'd simply muffed it. The game had always been so important to her, such a source of pride, because she was really an excellent player — everyone said so, even her mother had admitted it once — and it was the one thing she could do truly well. And she'd actually reneged — twice! — today. The girls had stared at her because they'd never seen her do that, ever, and she'd known them all since Bryn Mawr days. She even caught them giving each other little glances that she positively knew were about her, and it was all so heartbreaking.

Her head had felt . . . thick, though. Millie served those pretty drinks, tequila sunrises, and she should have had just one instead of two, and they probably thought she was *drunk,* for pete's sake, instead of a little woozy from the pills she took in the bathroom between the first two rubbers. She hadn't mentioned them to the girls, the pills, because she wasn't sure they'd understand, and she supposed she shouldn't be taking her little percolators quite so often, or even the tranquilizers. But these lovely painkillers, especially, really did do just exactly that, they killed pain, and her back had been acting up again and of course sitting in a straight chair all that time didn't help.

It was a little worrying sometimes, that she couldn't seem to get to sleep without two or sometimes three, but after all she'd been very strict with herself about what she drank along with them. Two glasses of white wine, not very big glasses, was her limit at bedtime (and anything she had before then just didn't count), and that certainly never hurt anyone. Besides, she told herself firmly as she looked down at her empty plate, white wine isn't even particularly bad for my cholesterol level, not nearly as bad as those drinks today, and Millie and Puffin and Caroline should certainly be watching it themselves.

Her tiny bridge fiasco wouldn't be upsetting her quite so much, and of course it would never happen again, if it weren't for the other, the letter she found on the hall table when she came in late this afternoon. She knew as soon as she saw it — *before* she saw it, actually, because she smelled it from the door. She hadn't opened it yet. She'd put it in her purse right away and left it there while she took her nap, and then she'd brought it in here with her, and there it was now, waiting. She rang the little silver bell for coffee and some more wine — Dutch courage was what Spence always called it — and after Frieda wordlessly served her, she finally read it.

It was worse than she thought, because it was so . . . insulting. And where would it end, all this? He — she was convinced it was a he — had assured her in his first letter that it was all very simple, that these deliveries were something she would only have to make twice a year, that that was what Spence had always done. And now . . . now it could obviously go on and on and the sky's the limit. She had the most terrible thought, then. The reason she went along with it, the reason she didn't simply ignore the whole thing and let the chips fall where they may or might, was because of the children. Spence had adored them, and they'd adored him right back, and the very last thing she wanted in the whole world was for them to know that he'd . . . slipped . . . once and only once. She'd believed — stupidly, she now saw, stupidly, stupidly — that these transactions were something she could count on; that this man was some*one* she could count on to be reasonable; that those big bundles of not very clean fifty-dollar bills would keep the children from learning what their father did. And that probably wasn't true, she realized. If she walked in front of a streetcar tomorrow — her mother's expression, there weren't any streetcars in New York anymore — this *horror* would almost certainly be part of Peekie's and Gardner's inheritance.

She couldn't stand it, that thought. Her hand gripped the stem of her wineglass and would have snapped it if she hadn't reminded herself that her blood pressure was high, too high, and that she must calm down and take deep breaths and, just to be on the safe side, have another little percolator.

15

M*ARIO SAT ALONE* at the table at Four Seasons after Rick and Susan Radnor left, wondering what had been accomplished in the two hours he'd just spent with them. They'd wanted to have dinner to talk about how the work at Tables was going, and then they'd talked about everything but that. Since the most obvious place, Rudi's, was off limits to him these days, he'd thought a picnic at the site itself would be great, but Susan hadn't liked that one little bit. So they'd met here. He realized once again that neither of them was much interested in Tables itself, only in the idea of it.

Maggie had been eating here too, on the other side of the room, and now she was probably waiting for him at the bar, as they'd arranged. He knew she couldn't see him from out there and he was giving himself a few more minutes to sit and think. Earlier, when he'd passed her table and she'd introduced him gaily as "my man" to her dinner partner, a silver-haired South American client, he'd felt a sharp stab of guilt. The señor was being very attentive to her, and he'd frowned in obvious disappointment that the field was already taken. If only he knew, Mario thought. If only Maggie knew, which was more to the point.

He hadn't seen her since the opening of *Rain* (which, in just a few days, had established itself as a firm success), but they'd talked on the phone a couple of times and they'd lined up this rendezvous. The strain hadn't gone away, and there certainly hadn't been any sex to help smooth it over. She'd asked him down to her apartment after Carole's opening and party. He'd said he was exhausted and had to get up at five in the morning. She'd seemed relieved.

He had this conversation with himself about ten times a day. First he'd tell himself that at least he hadn't lied to her (he *had* been tired, he *did* have to get up that early). Then he'd say it wasn't as if he was spending the night with someone else when he should be with Maggie: he and Frances made love only in the afternoons, at the house on Sixty-eighth Street. Then he'd argue that at least he was being consistent, that he wasn't hopping from one bed to another and back again, deceiving everyone. Finally, he'd try to convince himself it was Maggie's fault, because she was being so frantic about everything right now and how could he have a relationship with someone who was having an affair with cocaine and of course he was going to be susceptible to this kind of thing. He always wound up at the same place: he was being a real prick and he knew it. It was what the nuns who taught him catechism called a sin of omission: he was lying to her by not telling her something she had a right to know.

It would be a different matter if this were one of those quick, physical affairs that fizzle out after a week or two. He'd never indulged in that sort of thing since he started seeing Maggie, but he knew it would have been easier; it wouldn't be something he'd have to tell her, except maybe long afterward, because it wouldn't matter. Whatever it was he had with Frances wasn't going to go away so easily. It would either continue or explode, he thought, but it wouldn't cool down. She was in his blood now.

He loved Maggie; there wasn't the slightest doubt about that. They were both young, healthy creatures and they'd always had wonderful, joyous, *sexy* sex. But with Frances . . . with Frances, there was an edge, a mystery, an extra ingredient, a feeling that there would always be another layer to uncover. There was something dark — not only in her, but in both of them, in the love itself — which showed up in the violence of their lovemaking sometimes. That had never been there in all the sunny times with Maggie, not once.

His mind was filled with other confusions, other contradictions. This . . . whatever it was . . . with Frances was inevitable; it was clearly impossible. They should tell everyone about it; they shouldn't allow anyone into their secret world. The whole city probably suspected it already; no one could conceivably know. When he was able to find his balance, he knew his name couldn't have been linked with Frances McKinnon's except in a perfectly legitimate business way. He'd finally talked about it with Patrick, but he knew it would go no farther. Frances had told Trish, but Trish would be fiercely discreet. Maggie had guessed nothing; he was sure of that. She had only said, the day he was showing her around the new space, that he seemed preoccupied, but then she immediately provided an excuse for him — the amazing leap his life had taken in such a short time. Then she'd apologized for her own preoccupation without mentioning the coke or the rift it caused.

He was still coasting along. He had to tell her, but he didn't know how to do it. Tonight isn't the right time, though, he said to himself.

* * *

As soon as her client left, Maggie made a trip to the ladies' room with her little vial and spoon and then came out to sit at the bar to wait for Mario. She ordered a snifter of Rémy Martin, just to balance out the coke, and she watched herself in the mirror above the bottles, trying to decide whether she looked as exhausted as she felt. Taking everything else into account, including the flattering light and the distance from her reflection, she thought she looked fine for a girl who'd spent the evening walking a tightrope. She'd been with the director of a new contemporary museum in Caracas, a courtly older man who wore too much cologne and who dropped too many hints about the view from his suite at the St. Moritz. He'd been at the gallery all afternoon, draining her and the assistant who had to bring out paintings and sculpture from the back room. Then they'd had drinks in Soho before going up to the Whitney for the opening of a big Rosenquist retrospective, and finally she'd brought him here for a late supper.

As he left, he'd committed himself to four rather major works. He had a very good eye, he knew exactly what he wanted, and it wasn't strictly necessary to spend so much time with him, but she wanted to establish a good relationship with him if she could do it without actually *having* a relationship with him. He could send her some nice, timid, newly rich Venezuelans who were just discovering the joys of collecting, who'd ask him which galleries to visit when they came to New York. Not to mention the fact that the museum itself obviously had a good budget.

"We are very well endowed," he'd said, winking. She'd wanted to laugh, but it probably would have encouraged him and she couldn't, on her high wire, do that. If it hadn't been for Mario . . . No, she said to herself firmly, apart from the fact that he was too old and too smooth, she had a strong belief that it was a bad idea to mix business with sex. She'd never really tested this belief, of course, because she started working for Max at just about the time she met Mario, but she told herself she'd always be able to stick to it. The trick was to imply without saying it that if it weren't for a whole set of circumstances she'd like nothing better than to check out the view from the St. Moritz. Along with his endowment, naturally.

She thought about her commission on the sale and she toasted her image in the mirror. She was doing very well indeed, but she hadn't stopped running for weeks. Making the most of this chance Max was giving her involved a lot more than just sitting in the gallery and waiting for buyers to come in. The trip had been bad enough, but now, looking back on it, it seemed like a vacation compared to the time since then. Every evening was spent with clients, potential clients, curators, or critics. Weekends, which were Sunday and Monday in the art world, were always taken up with paperwork, visits to as many lofts as she could manage (artists whose work she already handled and those whose work she might consider), and inevitable brunches and lunches with still more clients.

Even if there weren't this tension between them, even if she weren't doing something he so strongly didn't want her to do, there wouldn't have been much left over for Mario. This was the longest time they'd ever gone without making love, three full weeks since they'd spent the night together, but the time or two she'd felt like anything more than rolling into bed with *Vogue* and the kitties, he'd had commitments of his own or he'd been exhausted himself. In a brief, sickening flash, she wondered if he'd been making excuses, if there was something he wasn't telling her, but she dismissed the thought as soon as it occurred to her.

The brandy was relaxing her and she began dreamily planning

for Thanksgiving, only three weeks from now. For the past two years it had been a time when she and Mario could get away from everything. The first year they'd gone to Sint Maarten for sun and lovely turquoise water. Last year it was a rented house in Vermont for snow and big fires. They'd make it up to each other for this awful schedule that was keeping them apart, and she'd use the time to come off coke; she knew she could do it. She couldn't wait to tell him that Max had offered them his place in Montauk for the weekend. It was very stark, silvery bleached wood and glass cantilevered out over a cliff at the very tip of Long Island. She'd find out from someone how to roast a turkey — no, a duck, maybe — and they'd eat and walk on the beach and make love all weekend and forget there was such a place as New York.

By the time Mario got to the bar, she was on her second Rémy. She kissed him and patted the stool next to her. He ordered a double Finlandia on the rocks. "Successful dinner with your aging caballero?" he asked.

"Damn right! He's taking that big Frankenthaler and two pieces of Jim's and a Lichtenstein that Max decided to let go."

"Good for you." He kissed her on the cheek. "Did you call Max to tell him? How is Max, by the way?"

"He's better, but I'm so entrenched in that place now he doesn't need to ever get better. Or else, when he's on his feet he can just go open another gallery. In fact, he talked about that the other day. He's thinking of branching out, starting a photography gallery — master prints and some new people too. On another floor of our building or next door or wherever. It would take up most of his time, and I'd be left exactly where I want to be: running the main gallery for him."

"That's fantastic, Mag." It sounded a bit flat to her, and this time he kissed her on the forehead, as if she were his kid sister. She knew there was nothing wrong; she knew he'd been working hard all day and this dinner had probably been a strain but, dammit, she needed his praise, she needed his enthusiasm, and she needed more than a peck on the forehead.

"I guess you're tired," she said dryly.

"I guess I am. Sorry. I know it's important to you and I'm glad things might work out that way."

"Mario . . ." She stopped, not really sure of what was bothering her. "Have you been — I don't know how to say it — loath to see me lately?"

"No, of course not. We've both been so busy, I thought. *You* certainly have been." He was taking big sips from the glass of vodka, and the ice cubes rattled.

"Okay, then it's all right. I just had a twinge of the famous outdated women's intuition. It's probably no more than oversensitivity to someone I love so much, not to mention sheer horniness."

"Nope. Misdirected sensitivity. But these schedules of ours may go on for a while, you know."

"But not Thanksgiving," she said triumphantly. "Max has been a huge sweetheart and offered us his Montauk place that weekend. I'll do a duck." She laughed and quacked for him. "A Long Island duckling, of course, with kirsch and cherries. Just for us. And we can reintroduce ourselves." She put her hand on top of his.

"Shit, Mag, I can't. I'm sorry, but I can already tell I'm going to be spending twenty-five-hour days at the new joint by then."

"Mario! Surely you can sneak away? Not for the whole weekend, then, just for a couple of days? A night? I thought it was a sort of unwritten contract between the two of us."

"I . . . I didn't know you were planning anything. I guess I thought you'd be just as busy then as you are now." His voice was expressionless. She took her hand away from his and dove into her purse for a cigarette. Something was wrong. How could he be talking this way to her? He sounded like they had to make plans like casual friends. He *must* have known she'd want to spend that time with him.

"What's going on? I don't get it. It isn't like you to just decide something like that. Arbitrarily, without . . ." She paused. She wanted to be reasonable. "I mean, I don't want to sound like an old married shrew, but when you love someone you expect a kind of thoughtfulness. Are you trying to get back at me for being so unavailable or is this part of your antidrug crusade or what? I don't understand. Are you trying to tell me something?"

He was running his hand back through his hair, over and over. The bartender was close, serving the couple next to them, and Mario looked down at his drink and waited till he left. Then he took a deep breath and said, "Yes," as he exhaled. She grabbed her snifter, took a big, burning gulp of brandy, and set it down very slowly and deliberately. The rest of the room became an aquarium; faces moved in slow motion. She watched her cigarette ash grow until it fell onto the polished surface of the bar. In a small, quiet voice she asked the question, already knowing what the answer was.

"Is there someone else? Have you been seeing someone else?"

He'd taken off his glasses and he was pinching and rubbing the bridge of his nose. He wasn't looking at her. "It's something I couldn't help, Mag. I know. It's pretty lame to say that, but it happens sometimes. I really can't help it." He bit off these last few words, one by one.

"Who?" she asked, still quietly.

He waited a long time before he answered. "It's Frances McKinnon. I've only been seeing her for a couple of weeks. Three weeks, I guess, but it's . . . pretty intense and pretty serious. I'm sorry. Very, very sorry. I'll try to be as honest as I can. Now. The reason I put off telling you was because I thought it might go away. No, that's a lie. I knew it wouldn't go away and I don't want it to be over. I've been a coward about telling you, that's all there is to it, and I honestly didn't mean to tell you like this, not . . . publicly, not here."

"It's Frances McKinnon," she repeated lifelessly, carefully putting out the cigarette she hadn't smoked. "I thought it was great. That she's doing your place. I didn't even have an inkling there was more to it. No, maybe I did. . . ."

"You couldn't have," he said gently. "Nobody knows. If that's any help, nobody knows, nobody looks . . . foolish."

"Well, *now* they do, I do. Look foolish. I should have known. There was something, that night at the theater. . . ." She shook herself. "I was jealous of her because of who she was and what she had. I thought she was unbelievably beautiful for her age. Now she has you along with all the other things her husband's money buys for her. I should have realized: a girl on her way up can't expect to hold on to a man like you, not when there are women like Mrs. Hamilton McKinnon around."

"That isn't true, Mag. It's nothing like that." His head was bowed; he wasn't looking at her.

"Well, what the fuck *is* it like, then?" Her voice was high and loud and it was beginning to break. The couple sitting next to them were staring. They turned their heads away when Maggie gave them a venomous look.

"It's a . . . a love affair. I don't know what'll happen but I have to see it through."

"Like you've seen this one through," she said. "Through." He looked at her, finally, in time to see her eyes fill. Her head was tilted up and the drops began to fall, one by one, onto her dress. She stood up suddenly, wiping at her eyes with a cocktail napkin, looking in her purse for money but then snapping it shut.

"I think the drinks are on you, you son of a bitch."

He didn't try to stop her from walking away. She carried herself very stiffly as she threaded her way through the drinkers and down the stairs to the lobby. She found her coat check and she found a dollar and she found a smile for the woman behind the counter, but it didn't work. The woman took one look at her face and asked her if she was all right, if something was wrong. That was enough to make her crack, for some reason, that tiny, almost impersonal, bit of sympathy. When she got to the street, she held her arm up blindly. She couldn't see, through her tears, whether any of the cabs going by were free or whether their off-duty signs were lit.

* * *

"We've had the weekend to look at your latest estimates, and we had our people do some research," Jack Halsey said. He was Rick Radnor's executive vice president and henchman, and Mario was in the private dining room again, sitting between the two of them. This time it was lunch, basic, well-prepared lamb chops and a good Beaujolais. Radnor had talked about *our people* too, and Mario had an image of overworked, underpaid, Dickensian clerks, scurrying around in a basement, looking up figures for the boss in old reference books.

"The mortality rate for restaurants in New York is unbelievable," Halsey announced. "Something like sixty-five percent in the first year." Mario was familiar with the figure but it didn't mean anything to him because he was absolutely confident in his own success. He couldn't believe the man was throwing it out now, when they'd gone through two interim financing arrangements and they were on the verge of finalizing a permanent one. Actually, he didn't know why they were meeting at all: he thought everything was all set.

This was the first time he'd met Halsey — a perfectly groomed, middle-aged preppie who could have done commercials for a good brand of Scotch — and he'd known immediately that he didn't like him. Radnor had been saying almost nothing so far and it occurred to Mario that Halsey had been asked to look at the estimates and to sit in on this lunch because he was a brilliant real estate wheeler-dealer, because he was valuable to Radnor Associates and therefore he was someone whose pride mustn't be hurt by being excluded. Not because he knew anything about restaurants.

"You could find frightening figures about almost any business, I suppose," Mario snapped. "Those failures usually happen because there wasn't enough start-up money or because of inexperience. We don't have either of those problems." His temper was short these days and for the first time in his life he wasn't sleeping very well. He was blaming himself for what had happened with Maggie, for what *he'd done* to Maggie night before last, and he knew he was taking it out on some of the workmen at the restaurant. These aren't workmen, though, he cautioned himself. Calm down and be careful.

Halsey grunted. "Actually, I don't really have any trouble with most of the initial costs. They're even a little lower than I'd expected. It's the other. Do you mind my asking about some of the running expenses?" Without waiting to hear whether he minded or not, he began to read from the last set of figures that Mario, Frances, Stephen Bingham, and Bob Siegel had worked up. "Two hundred thousand a year for flowers, for instance. You'd be closed for all of August, so that averages out at more than four thousand a week. For *flowers*?"

"Sorry. We should have written a page or two about the concept, I guess. The decoration of the big dining room is pretty neutral, even though it's costing a lot to strip all the Arthurian crap and raise the floor and lower the ceiling and replace the windows. Where we want the emphasis is on the food, naturally, and the tables." He tried to find the right words, not so much for Halsey's sake as for Radnor's. It was all stuff he'd wanted to explain to him and Susan at the Four Seasons, but they hadn't given him a chance. "Every table is going to be . . . its own world, if that makes sense. Chairs, china, flowers, they're all going to create a different mood at each table. That estimate is just for the cost of the flowers themselves, by the way, and it's wholesale. Frances, Mrs. McKinnon, is looking for a full-time designer for us to have in-house who'd oversee everything, and a full-time assistant. Their salaries are a little farther down, on the next page. Another eighty thousand."

"I was going to ask you about that." Halsey cleared his throat. "On the other hand, advertising and PR are almost nonexistent. I was very surprised, especially since this is for the start-up year."

"I know. It would be suicidal in most restaurants, but this just isn't going to be quite like any other place. I can't really prove it because it's intangible, but you've got to believe me. It's either going to work with word of mouth or it's not going to work at all. The clientele I expect doesn't have to be told by some magazine article that they're in the right place and they don't need ads to remind them we exist." He knew what he meant but he had no idea whether he was convincing Halsey or not, and he wasn't sure if it was very important. Finally, he knew, the man would go along with whatever Radnor wanted to do. He decided to give him another few minutes. The question of the terrace was next. There was only a small provision in the budget for its renovation.

Mario smiled. "That's because we're not going to use it for anything at all. I know, everyone's going to be surprised. We've got a Manhattan penthouse and we're not rolling out the old Astroturf and jamming it with tables? It's partly because they'd interrupt the view from the dining room. Partly logistics — everything suddenly gets more complicated when you serve food outside. The distance from the kitchen, the extra staff you only need when the weather's right, awnings and heat lamps and maintenance and bugs. There aren't enough perfect evenings in the year, not too hot, not too cold, not too windy, not too wet. I know we could work all that out but it's really more of an aesthetic decision. It gives people a sense of spaciousness to leave it empty; it's as simple as that. Wasted space, just shrubs and a few chairs. If some romantic couple wants to wander out there after dinner, fine, but they'll be in full view of everyone inside and we probably won't allow drinks out there. We want the dining room to be a sort of island, I guess. Surrounded by a nice, white, deserted beach. Restful."

Halsey began to ask how many tables the terrace could accommodate when Radnor interrupted him. "I think Mario's right, Jack. For one thing, we'd have a lot of complaints from tenants, you can count on it. Might even run into some kind of zoning problem. For another, I feel like it's in keeping with the period of the building. Maybe it's because I'm in real estate, but I always thought the most impressive thing in those 'thirties movies about rich people, the thing that really proved they must be rich, was all that wasted space in their hotel suites and apartments." Mario almost laughed out loud. He hadn't realized Radnor had been listening when he'd used exactly those words to explain the idea to him. That was what made him a tycoon, he supposed.

"No, the estimates are all pretty much in line," Radnor went on. "Unless you have any major problems with the rest of it?" Halsey shook his head. "Fine, then. We've got to concentrate on the other stuff."

Mario was relieved. Halsey's pride was intact; his moment was over; the big boss was going to take control now.

"The pieces of the pie," Radnor said. "Our lawyers can work out the final details, but I want to be sure we understand each other. I think we're agreed on the lease increases? Linking them to the building's assessed value? And we're still going with forty-nine percent for us, minus whatever seed money we've already fronted. According to your last figures, our share is going to run about two million two. Better say two and a half as a safety net." Instead of ringing for the waiter, he got up and poured them all some more wine.

"So. I told you I'd find guys to put up the rest, and they're lined up now and ready to sign. Eager to sign, actually. Most of them know you, and the others all know you by reputation. They'll each throw in two fifty. Ten lucky men, or at least they damn well better consider themselves lucky if we actually let 'em in on this deal . . ." Mario didn't understand why he was putting it that way. If we *let* investors invest, backers back, angels be angelic? *If*? Radnor went on, smooth as glass, slippery as glass.

"Your problem, Mario, my friend, is that even though you're keeping your salary low, even with the extra slice of the old profit pie that's going to give you, it's going to take you a helluva long time to pay these people off. Maybe ten years before you'll have a majority interest and you can start buying me out. It's no skin off my back and I know my money's safe and out there working and all that shit, but you might like to get there quicker. Now, uh, there evidently *is* a way you could come up with a chunk of money or at least a line of credit so we could keep it clean and just between you and me and you wouldn't have to depend on the other guys." He smiled sleepily. "Isn't there?"

Mario stared at him. Fuck, he said to himself. Fuck him and fuck me for being so dumb. That was it, that was why they were having this meeting, of course. "You must have done a little checking," he said slowly, "or you wouldn't be asking that. On paper, it's pretty apparent I can't scrape up more than a few thousand."

Halsey jumped in, following his boss's lead, apologetic, kindly, almost deferential. "Any deal we're putting as much as two and a half million into, we have to work up a pretty complete profile. We explored a little further than the basic financial statement you gave us and one thing led to another. Yes, we did some checking up in Boston. But — and please believe me — we were very quiet. We certainly didn't let anyone in your family know we were poking around."

"I'm sorry, Mario," Radnor said, gentle, paternal, now that he'd shown how clever he was. "When Jack showed it to me, I figured it must be a sensitive subject because it seemed so crazy that you never mentioned it. People hide debts. No one ever hides a major asset except maybe from the old IRS." Mario ignored his wink. "I'm only bringing it up because it seems like the obvious way for you to buy us out a lot sooner than otherwise. And, to be honest, because I'd much rather deal with one or maybe two partners than this . . . minicartel we've managed to put together."

"Thanks," Mario said dully. He didn't know why he was thanking him. He still couldn't believe how incredibly stupid he'd been. "I appreciate it, that you tiptoed around the family." Oh, yes, that was why he was supposed to be grateful. "There's been some bad blood and I've ignored the whole thing for a long, long time and so I guess I never think of that money as anything that's really mine. Rightfully mine, is more like it. I should've told you, but . . . shit. It's an idea, but I can't tell you right now how I feel about it. How much longer can you stall the backers?"

"A few days?" Rick asked Jack, who nodded. "Say a week."

"Okay, I'll let you know within a week."

The cab he found down on Park was creeping along in bumper-to-bumper traffic, horns were blaring all around him, but Mario didn't notice. Goddamn Radnor and goddamn Halsey were forcing him to make a decision about something he tried never to allow in his thoughts. They'd opened the door on a room he'd avoided going near for the past thirteen years. No, he corrected himself, that wasn't quite the right image. It was a *tomb* they'd uncovered, figuratively and literally.

16

THE *LIVING ROOM* of the town house that Rudi and Chuck shared had a higher ceiling than any other room because the rear half of the first two floors had been opened up to create it. For its full height, a conservatory extended out into the garden, another thirty feet of glassed-in space that held palms, rare cycads, and masses of orchids. The room itself, like the rest of the house, was modern, stripped down and almost entirely gray. Walls were painted a glossy gunmetal color, the heavy carpets were soft charcoal, low sectional seating arrangements were upholstered in gray pin-striped suiting material. The only color, this dark afternoon, came from the bright fire Chuck had just lit, from the deep red roses in a big glass cylinder on the low coffee table, and from the emerald green of his velvet bathrobe. Two male weimaraners lay by the fireplace. They were as streamlined and as gray as everything else.

It was nearly two, but Chuck had only been up for a few minutes. Today was Sunday and he didn't have to be at the Metropolitan to give lessons. He was lounging on the pillows with the phone at his ear, mostly listening, only occasionally making sympathetic, murmuring sounds. When Rudi appeared with a pitcher of bloody marys, he ended the conversation. "Who was that?" he asked, pouring out two tall red drinks.

"My sister. She's having a bad time."

"Because of Mario?"

"No, Rudi, she's having a bad time with an ingrown toenail. Yes.

Mario, that cocksucker. Maggie shouldn't have to go through this for that greasy bastard."

"It's the way of the world. Love affairs don't always work out, haven't you heard? Here." He handed him his drink.

Chuck choked on his first sip. "Christ! There's half a bottle of Tabasco in this."

"All the better to cure your hangover, baby. You *do* have a hangover, don't you?"

"If you say so." He shrugged, drank some more, and set the glass down. "I wish to hell you'd never hired him."

"Chuck. Really. They would have met anyway, somewhere along the line. Never mind Mario. How's Maggie doing?"

"I just told you. She's miserable. It's only been a few days and I think she's still in some kind of shock. She's been really busy at the gallery and it's hit her all over again today. Sunday, bloody Sunday."

"Poor baby. Do you think we should have her up for brunch?"

Chuck stared at him. "That's your answer for everything, isn't it? Someone has spinal meningitis and you say, 'Oh, let's have him for brunch. That'll cheer him up.'" Rudi didn't reply and after a moment Chuck continued. "No, I think she just wants to be alone. That bastard!" He said it with such violence that the dogs woke up and came over to sniff at him.

"Now you've upset Pablo and Pepe. Come here, boys, come to Rudi. Don't you bother with that mean man over there."

"I can't figure out what the hell he sees in that McKinnon woman. She's about fifteen years older than Mag."

"More like twenty, I'd imagine," Rudi said slowly. "I think I can understand it, as a matter of fact, in spite of your sister's more, um, obvious charms. Frances McKinnon is beautiful and she'll be beautiful at sixty. And she's a class act. Besides," he said sulkily, "what's age got to do with it?"

Chuck had hit a sensitive nerve and he backed away. "Forget it. It's not really the point. The point is how he could be such a shit to Mag. I never trusted him, never. But of course you always defended him to the hilt. As it were."

"It seems to me we've had this conversation before." His voice softened. "Chuck. Please. You know there wasn't ever the slightest bit of truth in what you're trying to get at. I've barely looked at anyone else since I met you. Well, I've *looked* — who hasn't? — but I haven't *done*." He came over and ruffled his hair, but Chuck ignored him and he took his hand away. "I couldn't even make myself be nice to him, that last week or two before he quit, because he'd been so terrible to you."

"So it's my fault he quit? Best thing that ever happened to you."

"I didn't say that. I didn't say it was your fault." He sighed. "This new place he's working on — he must have been planning it, he must have known." Now there was bitterness in Rudi's voice too.

"You can't sue him for breach of contract or something?" It wasn't that Chuck was particularly worried about the restaurant, but he would have used whatever leverage was around to get at Mario.

"I could. It would cost a fortune in lawyers' fees. . . ."

"But you'd get that back when you won?" Chuck was interested now.

"No. I mean, yes, I would. And yes, conceivably I'd win. But it's not a good idea. It would only mean a lot of bad press and bad feelings. My customers' bad feelings."

"Oh. But you don't think he's going to be any kind of serious competition to you, do you?"

Rudi stared. "Is this the first time that idea's occurred to you?" Chuck nodded. "Yes. Hell, yes, he's going to be competition. He's spending a fortune, probably five times as much as I spent. He's got Frances McKinnon as his designer, and whatever you think of her, she's just about the best there is. And he . . ."

"And he pussied up to everyone who ever came in to *your* restaurant," Chuck finished for him. "Anyway, she's a tramp." He poured himself another big drink and took it into the kitchen, calling out to Rudi from there. "How the hell did she manage to get hold of old Hamilton, anyway?"

"Nobody quite knows," Rudi yelled back. "He doesn't look like he was ever capable of it, but he must have been pretty hot for her at some point. Dorothy says she came uptown from Little Italy somehow, but they were married in Europe and nobody knows just how she managed that. I'll bet his family fought it tooth and nail."

The dogs had followed Chuck into the kitchen, frisking around him and whining as he made toast and eggs for himself. He came out in a few minutes, set his plate down, and led them out through the greenhouse to the yard. "Go on out and take your dumps, boys, then you can come back in and I'll toast you some frozen waffles or something."

"There must be quite a story there, if anyone could find out," Rudi mused.

"What else does Dorothy say about it?"

"Dorothy usually keeps pretty quiet about that side of the family, but I happen to know she's not exactly the president of her sister-in-law's fan club."

"Uh," Chuck grunted between mouthfuls. "Jealousy. She probably hates Frances's guts for all the things she hasn't got."

"Well, they probably have about the same amount of money, but what difference does that make when it's *so* many millions? Anyway, poor Dottie just never had the style or the looks." He watched Chuck finish his second bloody mary. "Are you going to drink all afternoon?"

"I don't see why not. You got me off to a good start. This is Sunday, isn't it? I always drink on Sunday."

* * *

Maggie put down the phone and looked around at her messy living room, absently stroking one of the cats who was nesting in the pile of Sunday *Times* on the sofa beside her. The call to Chuck had only depressed her more, not because he wasn't sympathetic — he really did feel bad, she knew — but because it didn't do the least bit of good. No one close to her had ever died, but she was sure this was the way it must feel: people would murmur softly about how sorry they were that you felt so bad, and then you *still* felt bad. So you did little things — errands or phone calls you'd promised to return, whatever — that you told yourself had to be done and so they were done and . . . and then what?

This morning, as soon as she got up, she'd canceled her appointments for today — lunch with an architect who was buying art for a new hotel in Tokyo, two painters whose work she was supposed to look at in the afternoon, drinks with a woman from the Modern — and now she didn't know what to do with the sudden surplus of time. After a particularly hellish Saturday in the gallery, she thought she wanted a day completely to herself to try to sort things out. But there was nothing to sort out: she simply felt worse than she'd ever felt in her life and she should have known the only thing that would take her mind off her misery was work. But it had to be work that was already there, lined up and waiting for her. Now that she'd broken these dates, she couldn't bring herself to *create* work, to go down to the gallery and plow through papers or write letters that needed to be written.

All right, she said to herself, take a walk. It's cloudy and damp and it'll probably rain, but take a walk anyway. No, she didn't want to take a walk. She was a California girl, and the only time she ever voluntarily walked, without a specific destination and time in mind, was when Mario insisted she come with him on one of his marathon hikes around the city. Mario wasn't around to do any insisting today. Mario might never be around again.

She and the cat jumped when the phone rang, and she picked it up right away. She didn't realize she was hoping it was Mario until she heard it wasn't and felt a sharp sting of disappointment. It was Jim, wondering if she'd like to go up to the Cloisters with him. She knew he wasn't interested in anything there except a particular stained glass window that he'd want to stand in front of for an hour or so, but she was grateful. Besides, she'd run out of coke and he'd be sure to have some.

* * *

The houseboy was trying to decide whether living in one of the most beautiful houses on Maui and working for one of the most famous names in musical comedy (retired, but still famous) were worth it. Everyone told him how lucky he was — in the year he'd worked for her, they'd been in New York about half the time and he loved New York and he had relatives from the Philippines there and she'd always been kind to him, and generous, but . . . but he didn't think he could take another day like today. Not that she'd been mean to him (he'd stayed out of her way), but she'd been a crazy woman, a witch, wandering all around the house, every room, and out to the lanai and back again, muttering terrible words to herself, holding the letter that Federal Express had delivered this morning.

* * *

The governor's secretary wasn't sure if she should put the call through to him or not; she sat, vacillating, and watched the Hold button blink on and off. It was the attorney general's office about the toxic waste thing and it was important — she prided herself on knowing which calls were important — but she didn't think she should *let* him talk to anyone at the moment. He wasn't quite . . . himself . . . and he might thank her later for giving him time to calm down. She'd been sitting with him, just a little while ago, going over the details of next week's schedule while he went through his mail. Out of the corner of her eye, she'd seen him pick up a letter, one marked "Personal," and *sniff* it. Then his face had turned a frightening purplish-red color and his voice, when he asked her to leave and to shut the door behind her, had almost sounded as if he were being strangled.

* * *

The makeup girl who helped people look good for their appearances on the late-night talk show didn't think she'd ever seen the Funniest Man in America look so unfunny. All the other times he'd been on, even that three-week stint when he'd subbed as a host, he'd been so nice to her, cracking all the jokes that were too dirty for TV, getting himself charged up for the cameras. Tonight, he didn't even try to feel up the black girl who was combing out his toupee the way he usually did. He just sat and looked in the mirror while she worked on him. It was because of the letter that was delivered here a few minutes ago, she knew, but it was so strange because he hadn't even opened it. He'd just held it up to his nose, and then his whole face had fallen, like those masks of comedy and tragedy where the mouth was turned up on one and down on the other.

* * *

Floating down into Logan Airport on the Shuttle, Mario could look out across the harbor to most of downtown Boston from his window: the few buildings anyone would consider skyscrapers in New York, the green of the Common and the Public Garden, the Charles River twisting along the top, separating Boston from Cambridge. A minute before landing, he could make out the North End, the thumb, as his grandmother had so delighted in calling it. He always sat on the left side of the plane so he could have this view, just as, a few minutes later in the cab out to Belmont, he sat on the right side so he could see the old neighborhood more closely as he was swept past it, above it, on the expressway. Today, when they slowed in traffic, he caught a glimpse between buildings of the playground where he'd first learned how grass felt to roll on, to fall on, how a tree could be hidden behind or climbed. He'd spent more of his childhood, really, on suburbia's greener lawns, in and under much bigger trees, but because this had been his first knowledge of such things, his first brush with nature, it was this little patch of scruffy turf he remembered best. There was another reason for that, another way it wound itself into his dreams — into his nightmares, rather. This was where they'd found his brother that night.

It was thirteen years ago, now, that Johnny and Barbara came back from their honeymoon and settled into a small house in Arlington. The family had been surprised at their choice of neighborhood. Why not Belmont, where all the other Fermis were? Or the North End, not nearly as nice, certainly, but inexpensive, close to her parents, a short walk from headquarters? Mario understood. When he and Johnny were little, they'd cried along with Nonna on the day the family moved out to the two houses in Belmont from the one big happy house in town. After that, as the cousins grew up, the family became indistinguishable from the business, and the business seemed to take over all their lives. Barbara had signed on as a bookkeeper in the Cambridge operation; Johnny had a big office at headquarters but they still didn't know what to do with him. So the newlyweds, by living in Arlington, were carving out a little corner of privacy for themselves.

Mario was working at the raw bar in the Chestnut Hill Mall that summer — he couldn't wait tables because he was too young to serve alcohol — and cramming for the SATs he'd be taking in the fall. Any extra time he had was spent with a Brookline girl he'd met at the beach. He barely saw his parents and, shucking oysters and clams all day, he certainly wasn't aware of any change in the atmosphere at headquarters. When Johnny picked him up after work one night, a cold six-pack in the back seat, a joint in the glove compartment, Mario thought he just wanted to joyride, to blow off some steam. The big Pontiac cruised along aimlessly, and they talked about sports and movies and the girl from Brookline, passing the joint back and forth, ending up down toward the Cape, almost as far as Buzzards Bay. Johnny finally pulled over at a scenic viewpoint that would have looked down to the Cape Cod Canal if the night hadn't been so dark, and he turned off the engine. They sat for a while without saying anything while the car made all its cooling-down ticking noises. They finished the last beers, and Johnny absentmindedly crushed the can in one hand the way he always did. Mario finally asked him if something was wrong. The silence lasted for another minute and then Johnny burst out.

"Yeah. A whole fuckuva lot is wrong. I hoped maybe it'd be okay, maybe they'd be able to fix things, but they can't. This time they can't. The shit's gonna hit the old fan. Tomorrow. I thought you had a right to hear it from me instead of reading it in the *Globe,* but I waited to see if Mama or Papa would tell you. Obviously they didn't, if you've gotta ask."

"The business." It wasn't a question. It was the only thing he could possibly be talking about.

"The business. The goddamn Eggplant Parmesan Gold Mine, the goddamn Calamari Empire that supported us in style in that snotty suburb and paid for the clothes we're wearing and this car and these Buds and my goddamn circus of a wedding and everything else we've ever had."

Mario was sure he'd never, in sixteen years, heard so much frustration, so much rage, in his brother's voice. Johnny lost his temper sometimes and it could be pretty frightening for a few minutes but it always passed quickly. This was something very different. A car went past, and in the brief glare of headlights he could see the tears on his brother's face. He hadn't seen him cry since their grandfather died. It made him feel helpless; it scared him. He touched his arm lightly. "Tell me."

"Christ! I don't know where to start. I think it's something I always knew, *we* always knew, but we didn't talk about it, ever, not since we were little."

Mario had been concentrating on the hope that Johnny was going to tell him about some kind of financial problem, that the business was going into bankruptcy, maybe, or they were going to sell off part of the chain, but he knew that wasn't what it was. Johnny wouldn't be this upset about a ledger sheet; he didn't care about money, certainly not about anything as abstract as corporate money. This was much worse. When he spoke, it was barely a whisper. "It's about what Nonna said that time? When she thought you didn't understand?"

They both knew what she'd said, but Johnny repeated it anyway. "When she told Nonno that Papa and Uncle Claudio were selling their souls to the Devil. We knew what she meant but we were just kids and we just . . . forgot about it. Everyone seemed so happy. Everyone but Nonna and Nonno. It killed them. I've been thinking about it. It wasn't moving out of the North End and it wasn't that we weren't all together in that great old kitchen anymore. It was shame. They were proud of their boys, they thought they'd brought 'em up right. Do you remember, when we . . . when *they* opened the first place, and Nonno wouldn't shake that guy's hand? You were pretty little. Eight?"

"Seven, but I remember. The Partner. We always called him the Partner."

"Yeah. Well, he's got a name, a bunch of names. Watch for 'em in tomorrow's paper — no, day after tomorrow, I suppose. Salvatore Giuseppe Agnolli. Little Sal. Sunday Sally. Uncle Sally, they call him Uncle Sally now. Everybody's uncle."

"And he's still involved. With us? That's what you're saying?" Mario asked dully. "I never saw him around, so I guess I just figured they bought him out or something. That's what I wanted to think."

"You don't buy out people like Uncle Sally and his buddies unless they want to be bought out. Involved? Hell, yes. Behind the scenes. Quietly, very quietly, not just our little business but a lot of others. Dummy corporations and fake parent companies and all sorts of shit I don't understand completely. It's gonna take a long time to sort it out, but I think he and his pals own about half of our goddamn stock, maybe more. There's a task force, the New England Citizens Crime Commission, and they've had an undercover guy working in headquarters, in accounting, for the last year. He didn't show up for work a couple of days ago, and nobody can find him, and some papers — Papa calls them *sensitive* — are gone. I don't know how they heard, but it looks like we're gonna be served grand jury subpoenas tomorrow, all us big important ossifers in the corporation." He laughed for the first time. "Barbara's been trying to make me feel better. She says I shouldn't worry about a dumb old subpoena."

Mario tried to smile but he couldn't. "What do you think is going to happen? What do Papa and Uncle Claudio say?"

"What do they *say?* They don't say anything worth listening to, just a lot of huffing and puffing and self-righteous noises. Solid, upright citizens, good Rotarians, tight with the Cardinal, beautifiers of Greater Boston, all that crap. And don't think Mama and Aunt Maria aren't sweating it too. All kinds of bits and pieces are in their names. Every so often somebody clears his throat, or her throat, and maybe they admit there mighta been a few *irregularities,* or a couple of *discrepancies,* but then they all reassure themselves there's nothing *really* out of line. There's a big strategy meeting tonight, pregame huddle in the locker room."

"Shouldn't you be there? Weren't you supposed to go?"

"Sure, but why bother? So I can listen to Uncle Sally and probably one of *his* uncles remind us about how much we all owe *his* Family, with a capital fucking F? They're gonna coach everybody on how to take the Fifth. They're gonna stonewall it. They're gonna clam up like one of their goddamn cherrystones."

"What about Tom?" Their cousin was the other representative from their generation. He was only two years older than Johnny, but he'd already proved to be a much cleverer corporate team player.

Johnny snorted. "Tom! Tar-baby, he don' know nothin'. He'll be served like all the rest of us, but on paper he's clean as a whistle. He's an asshole, but so far he hasn't been a stupid asshole. Another couple of years and he would've been in the same deep shit as everyone else, but he's been able to keep out of it up till now. *I* know a lot more than Tom does," he said thoughtfully. "I made it my business to find out."

"What does that mean?" It was as shocking as anything he'd been told tonight. His brother was always so open, so straightforward. He couldn't picture him sneaking around, snooping, gathering information he wasn't supposed to gather.

"It means . . . Look, this doesn't go beyond us, but I'm telling you with Barbara's blessing. You're the only one she likes. We want out; we always did want out; we knew it when we got engaged. New Hampshire, or maybe that isn't far enough. Vermont. Maine. We've been trying to save money, and we thought we'd open a little place. Italian, of course. Fish, of course. Christ! it's the only thing I know. But *ours*. Anyway, a month or so ago I decided I'd better find out as much as I could about stuff at headquarters. Partly so I could be sure to keep my little paws clean, not sign anything I didn't understand, but mostly so I'd have something to deal with when Barbara and I leave. You know I'm not talking about money — I don't want their fucking money. I mean so they wouldn't try to get me to stay. They don't know what the hell to do with me down there, but I know they'd bring out all that heavy family pressure if I told them I was leaving. And now *this* shit." He was crying again. He shook his head and reached down to the ignition. "Let's get some more Buds."

They drove back in silence. Mario's red MG, his pride and joy, his sixteenth-birthday present a few months before, looked blue in the sodium lights of the mall's empty parking lot. Before he got out of his brother's car, he asked the obvious question, the only question. "What are you going to do?"

Johnny shrugged. "I'm not a very good liar," he said, almost regretfully. "But I'm a damn good fighter."

The subpoenas were served the next morning, all over town. A bookie in Dorchester got one, two wholesale liquor distributors in Charlestown, an olive oil importer in the North End. At headquarters, Mario's father and mother, his uncle and aunt, his cousin, and two bookkeepers were all served. It was impossible for the task force to get to Salvatore Agnolli or any of his closest business associates because they were in Barbados. It was impossible to serve

Johnny Fermi because he wasn't there. He wasn't at his house and he wasn't in his office. They found his car in the parking lot of the Dunkin Donuts in Arlington, where he always picked up an extra-light coffee and a blueberry muffin on his way in to work. That night, they found his body, dumped behind some shrubs in the North End playground where he'd first thrown a football to Mario, where he'd first learned to use his fists. His hands were tied behind him, and he'd been shot twice in the back of his head. It was a very professional, very clean killing, clearly arranged by Uncle Sally, but there wasn't much chance of tracing the killer.

At the church, Mario sat with Barbara in a pew at the back, as far from his parents and the rest of the family as they could get. They didn't take the places in the limousines that were assigned to them; he drove her to the cemetery in Johnny's car, right behind the hearse, the tapedeck blasting Johnny's favorite oldies, Nat King Cole and Johnny Mathis. They faced the family silently across the grave, but no one would meet their eyes. They refused to go to the reception back at the house. Instead, they took the big Pontiac out onto the Cape to a place in Hyannis where they ordered what Johnny used to order, dozens of steamers and pitchers of draft beer.

Mario made his message very clear to the family when he got back that night, and nobody had the courage to argue with him. He would live in their house for the next year, until he went to whatever college he chose, which sure as hell wouldn't be Harvard because he sure as hell wouldn't be staying in town. He'd eat their food; he'd be polite; he'd keep his room clean and the lawn mowed and the snow shoveled. But he was no longer part of this family. He wouldn't work at any job in any branch of the restaurant. The subject of Johnny was strictly off limits; so was anything having to do with the court case. He closed himself up. Barbara moved to San Francisco a week after the funeral, but he spoke with her on the phone sometimes, late at night. She was the only one he could talk to about Johnny, the only one he *would* talk to.

When he started his senior year, he studied even harder than before; he played better basketball than ever; he dated constantly, but never the same girl more than two or three times. He was as unapproachable as he was at home. The papers were full of the case, the postponements, the appeals, the plea bargaining, but no one at school ever said a word to him about it. Just before graduation, his father and his uncle, who, like the rest of the family, had consistently denied everything, were convicted for a grab bag of offenses that included tax evasion, perjury, contempt of court, and various forms of fraud. Because Uncle Sally was maddeningly out of reach, because what had happened to Johnny was there, in the air of the courtroom, and because first the jury and then the judge chose to ignore the defense lawyer's dramatics (about how his clients, particularly Johnny's father, had suffered enough), the brothers were given maximum sentences. Their total terms were exactly the same, twenty-three years. The wives were reprimanded, their sentences suspended. Tom, as Johnny had predicted, was never charged with anything, and he made a thoroughly convincing, absolutely innocent witness. A complicated arrangement was worked out for the business; some of the branches were sold off and the liquor licenses on the remaining ones were lifted for six months. The publicity hadn't hurt the restaurants in the least: if anything, they were more popular than ever. Tom, his mother, and his aunt took over. By the time Mario graduated from Princeton and moved into New York, it was almost as if nothing had happened.

When the cab pulled up in front of the house in Belmont, he got out his money and paid the driver very slowly. He was stalling, he knew; he always put off the moment when he had to go up the walk and ring the doorbell. Either the nurse or old Mrs. Pearson, the housekeeper he'd hated since he was a child, would answer it; he'd have the usual talk about good days and bad days. He never knew which it was going to be. His mother had a form of leukemia that was very rare for a woman of sixty; its victims were almost always teenagers. Her case fascinated the doctors at Mass. General, at Johns Hopkins, at the Mayo Clinic, but that was as far as it went: fascination, no cure. She'd been sick for a little more than a year now; it was not very likely she'd be sick for another year.

He'd never once gone to see his father in prison, never spoken to him or written to him, but he hadn't completely cut himself off from his mother. From Princeton and then from New York, he called her every two weeks; he saw her twice a year, ritualized visits that never varied. He'd arrive in the late afternoon, they'd have too many cocktails at the house, and then she'd take him to dinner at the Ritz. He'd spend the night in his old room and she'd take him to the airport in the morning before she went to headquarters. They were stiff and formal with each other; there were too many subjects to be avoided. The weather, some mild politics, the food they were eating, the wine they were drinking: these were all safe. When this illness started, he'd begun to come up more often, once a month, never spending the night. She was too sick to go into town to the Ritz now, too sick for cocktails. He always wondered what these brief visits, a few afternoon hours, meant to her. He wasn't at all sure what they meant to him.

This time, the nurse warned him, it was a bad day. There had been some pain in the night; she'd be groggy from what he suspected was morphine. She was in a housecoat, asleep on the living-room sofa in front of a big fire, her usually pale face unnaturally flushed from the heat. He sat quietly and watched her, wondering if he ought to wake her so she might at least know he'd been here, not really wanting to. When drugs made her mind wander, she tended to forget the unspoken agreement they'd always had in the past. She rambled on about things they'd avoided before, things he wanted to close his ears against because it hurt so much to hear them. She'd remember something Johnny did when he was ten, something his father said to her one night during the trial.

He got up and went to call a cab, deciding to let her sleep. He'd come back for a while after his appointment with his cousin, and maybe she'd be awake by then. If she were, then he'd be able to gossip about whatever was going on at headquarters these days. According to the nurse, her sister-in-law and her nephew seldom visited her, and she always asked Mario about the business, hungry for any news of what had been the center of her life, forgetting he'd had nothing to do with it for years and years. Today would be the first time he'd set foot in the main office since Johnny died.

Tom made him wait, as he'd expected, but he amused himself in the reception room by walking around to look closely at the pictures on the walls. Some were big, glossy color advertisements from national magazines for the products the company was marketing these days, bottles of seafood cocktail sauce, Russian and creamy Italian dressing, packages of frozen calamari and fried zucchini, boxes of oyster crackers. One wall was covered with black-and-whites of the branches themselves, more than forty. They'd begun to franchise the newer ones, so the chain was growing even faster — half a dozen on the Cape, more in Boston itself, others in Newport, Providence, Salem, Fall River, New Bedford, an artist's sketch of one that was going up in New Haven. Mario smiled: the scandal was now completely forgotten; business was booming.

The company had gone public with its stock a year before, so the requisite annual reports were stacked on the big glass table alongside the latest issues of *Restaurant Business* and *Gourmet*. Mario had a copy at home, of course, but he opened it again today to the photograph of the president on the first page. His cousin, in a three-piece suit that must have come from Brooks, was sober, unsmiling, and confident. With horn-rimmed glasses and a hairline that was receding fast, he looked older than his thirty-six years. If Mario hadn't known better, he'd say it was impossible that this man's father and his uncle were serving time in a federal prison.

When he was shown into the office, he immediately saw how false the photograph had been. In person, getting up from behind his desk and coming toward him with open arms and a dazzling smile, his cousin's image was very different — Armani suit, silk shirt open at the neck, cologne that he could smell all the way across the room, contacts instead of horn-rims, hair carefully arranged to cover the bald spot. Mario almost laughed. Tom had always been such a goody-goody; now he was the personification of early midlife crisis, a swinger who was just learning how to swing, probably a client of one five-hundred-dollar whore after another. He hadn't met the wife, but he'd seen her picture on his mother's piano; she looked like a woman to avoid — fat, dark, and overdressed, surely dissatisfied with her husband, her four fat children, and her life.

He'd have preferred a nice businesslike coolness, but Tom was determined to show how much family feeling he had, wrapping him in a big hug and then keeping his arm around him as he led the way to a pair of black leather armchairs. The first thing he did was to put a little worried frown on his face and ask how Mario's mother was doing.

"She's dying, is how she's doing." He knew he was supposed to have a good heart-to-heart talk about ups and downs, remissions and treatments, but he didn't have the patience for it. He wanted to get to the point and get out.

"I came to see you because I wanted to tell you I'm going to open a restaurant. My own restaurant. In New York."

"Hey! Fantastic! That's super!"

"Yeah. Well. Thanks, but there's more to it, and you're not going to think it's either fantastic *or* super, cuz. I've got to borrow a big bunch of money. About two and a half million, if I want to have a controlling interest within a couple of years. My shares in the company are worth twice that much, but I can't find a bank that'll lend me more than fifty percent of the market value."

Tom had stopped smiling. "You can't do that."

"Beg pardon?"

"I said, you can't do that, you little shit. You can't walk in here and tell me you're pulling a number like that. No one in the whole family has been good enough for you for a fuckuva long time except your mom, and that's amounted to a few token visits. You've just let your interest in the company sit there and get more and more valuable while we've all worked our asses off to make it happen, and all of a sudden the money isn't filthy anymore because there's something you want to do with it. You can't do it."

"I just did. I don't see why it's any skin off your nose. If I go under, the bank simply sells enough of my stock to pay itself off. You've all been trying to buy me out ever since I turned twenty-one. And don't, please, give me that crap about how you've worked your fat asses off. You've all voted yourself big enough salaries, I notice. If I go under, then I have that much less power in the company, not that I've ever done anything except give Mama my proxy." He smiled. "I still think the money's filthy and bloody and I'm still not touching it. That might seem like an arbitrary distinction to you, but it isn't to me, and I've been thinking about it solidly for the last few days. I'm not *using* it. I haven't spent a penny of it since I left Princeton and I never will. I'm borrowing against it. That's all. When I pay off the loan, I'll give the company the chance to buy me out and then I'll set up a scholarship fund in Johnny's name."

"Brings tears to my eyes," Tom sneered. "But if you go under, then the bank puts your stock on the open market and one of the big chains that've been sniffing around has a helluva good chance for a takeover."

"Oh. That's what this is all about. Then you'd better hope I make a big success of my new enterprise, hadn't you?" He stood up. "I didn't need to bother, coming in and telling you about this personally, you know. I just thought it might be good manners, but I guess it was a mistake. I think you should wish me good luck, cuz." He held out his hand, but Tom stayed in his chair and refused to look at him. Mario shrugged and walked out.

17

FRANCES STAYED ON alone in the student union for a while after Hamilton went off to bed. She was worried about him, he looked so pale and strained, and she wondered if she could convince him to take some time away from the bank in January or February. She was feeling very tender toward him lately. It was partly because he was traveling so much and she missed him; partly, she knew, because she was feeling so much guilt and she wanted to make it up to him. He really was such a good man. . . . She lay back against the cushions of the sofa, half dozing, remembering how genuinely loving and kind he'd been when she'd needed his help so badly.

* * *

In the weeks after the letter from Michael came, when she felt as if her life had ended at seventeen, she knew her unhappiness was obvious to everyone who saw her. If her regular lunch customers at the place in Wall Street tried to joke with her, she could barely oblige them with a smile, and there was only one, a heavyset, well-dressed banker in his late twenties, who seemed to know how she was feeling, to sympathize with her silently. He came in alone two or three times a week, after the big rush, when she had more leisure to wonder about him. He asked for the same table each time, the same well-done steak, salad with oil and vinegar, and iced tea, and he usually read all the way through his meal. He'd lift his clever, sensitive, and — she thought — rather sad face up from a book to ask her how she was today, and she found herself looking forward to seeing him. They began to have brief, interrupted conversations about what he was reading or what she was trying to get through on her Radcliffe suggested reading list (she told him her secret, that she'd be leaving this job the last week in August). Finally, smiling at his own cliché, he asked her when she got off work, and he was waiting for her out in front of the restaurant that day. He walked her home, up Broadway, pushing through the crowds in the July heat, and she told him how much she was liking Flaubert and how disappointed she was in Henry Miller. He listened closely, he spoke carefully, and she was more and more sure of what she had suspected, that he was an immensely cultured man, that he read omnivorously, that he had something to say about everything that interested her. But even though he was so much older, he was never for a moment patronizing: if he didn't agree with an opinion of hers, he said so, but he was very respectful of her mind and she found herself opening up to his intelligence and his knowledge and his dry, self-deprecating humor.

His name was Hamilton McKinnon and he was twenty-nine, which seemed an enormous age to her. He worked at an investment bank, whatever that was, and there was some connection with his family. He lived with his widowed mother, just as she did, somewhere uptown, but the mother, a brother, a sister, and their families were all out at a beach somewhere right now. For four nights in a row he walked her home, and then on Friday he asked her if he could take her out to dinner the next night. When she accepted, he amazed her by saying he should meet her mother first, that it would be more proper, and that, after all, she was underage. It was the first time he made her really laugh, the first time she teased him. Did that make her *jailbait?* she asked. Was he what was known as a *cradle-robber?* He took it well, he laughed along with her, but he insisted.

At the Bon-Ton, after he got past his embarrassment with the displays of corsets and brassieres, he charmed her mother with his manners, with his respectful questions about her business, and he even managed a few polite Italian phrases. After the past weeks, she would have been happy to see her daughter take an interest in almost anyone or anything, but she seemed to approve of this man particularly. When he'd gone, Mama, who knew about these things, told her in an awed whisper that his suit, his shirt, even his shoes, were custom-made. He was a gentleman, she said, and Francesca agreed with her although not necessarily for the same reasons.

She knew this had nothing to do with the way she'd felt with Michael. That, she said to herself, was passion; this was something else, this really very strong affection she'd begun to feel for him in such a short time. She told him about Michael, and he said he'd imagined there was something like that and it would probably be hard for any man to replace him. Then she kissed him because he was good to her and understood her and allowed her to be herself. She decided if he wanted to make love to her she would let him. It might give him pleasure, this man who was so tender with her, who treated her with such care, but she was just as happy when he didn't try anything like that. She didn't think it was only a question of her age; she sensed that it wasn't quite what he wanted.

They went for a few Sunday drives, Hamilton double-parking his white Chevrolet convertible in the narrow, noisy street and coming in to chat with her mother for a minute when he picked her up. She'd make sandwiches and they'd go as far as Asbury Park, or Bear Mountain, or West Point. They kissed softly and held hands, and she sat next to him in the car and put her head on his shoulder. They seemed to have an unspoken understanding: they were very fond of each other.

One Sunday in the middle of August, he picked her up earlier than usual to take her out to his family's beach house in Easthampton. Except for Mama, they'd avoided friends and families and found it enough to be quietly companionable together, but now Hamilton said he wanted her to know more about him. None of the McKinnons would be there, he assured her — they migrated to the Adirondacks in August. All the way out, he talked quietly about his background. He was preparing her, she later realized, for a shock. She'd always known he was from what her mother called a "well-to-do" family, but the McKinnon name never appeared in the newspaper except in the business section and the society columns, and neither she nor her mother read those.

First, he said, history. There had been McKinnons in Boston, shipbuilders, since the late sixteen hundreds, and they became one of the most important families in the colony. Then, in the Revolution, they made the mistake of siding with the Crown, and there was a low period in the family's fortunes that, he laughed, was still never mentioned. Luckily, in the next crop of children were two brothers who brought the business aggressively into the nineteenth century, and by the 1840s the family had done so well that it was able to leave "trade" behind for what had become a more socially acceptable business. They opened a banking house.

Three generations later, in 1905, Hamilton's grandfather moved the center of operations from Boston to New York and built a house on Fifth Avenue. In the mid-'twenties, his only son, Frederick McKinnon III, married the daughter of a New York doctor. Sarah was handsome, well mannered, and well educated; there was nothing his parents could really object to; but she didn't come from one of the families the McKinnons *knew,* and they worried quietly about her. They needn't have: she became, in spite of her background and because of her married name, a tireless leader of New York society. She dominated committees, friends, servants, and, to a large extent, her husband. Her children — Frederick IV, followed by Dorothy and then by Hamilton — were all terrified of her when they were growing up.

Frederick was the heir apparent, of course, but as it turned out he was completely uninterested in finance, and there was nothing anyone — not even Sarah — could do about that. It automatically fell to Hamilton to carry on the leadership of the McKinnon Bank, gradually taking the power out of the hands of uncles and older cousins who had run it since his father died in the early 'fifties, when Hamilton was still at Harvard. Now, although his title was senior vice president, he was actually running the bank. Both Frederick and Dorothy married and had children, although Frederick's wife had died, tragically, a year before in a sailboat accident on Narragansett Bay. So old Sarah, satisfied that the dynasty would continue, could now devote all her energy to her favorite charities and to her unmarried son. It was a constant battle, Hamilton admitted to Frances. He was almost always able to resist her will, but there were still times when she could wear him down and drag him along as an escort to parties and charity balls that bored him and infuriated him.

He had tried to prepare Frances. By the time they got to Easthampton, she knew he was more than well-to-do, he was rich, but she couldn't help gasping when they pulled up in front of a stone French chateau that was the biggest house she'd ever seen, and as they came into the entrance hall, she gasped again. She thought places like this existed only in movies, and she said so, to Hamilton's amusement. The year-round servants, Dieter and Hannah, seemed very nice, but Frances was nervous with them — should she shake their hands, should she really call them by their first names? Wandering through the enormous rooms on the ground floor where the furniture and even the chandeliers were draped with dustcovers, she tried and failed to imagine how anyone could actually *live* here. There was a vast ballroom, which Hamilton said was built for his sister's coming out, and that amazed her more than anything else — an entire room, twenty times the size of the apartment she'd grown up in, built for one single party.

His own two rooms were different, and she suddenly felt comfortable again. In the whole rest of the house there were only family portraits and dreary, overvarnished, nineteenth-century Salon paintings on the walls. Here there were things to *look* at, fascinating clues to Hamilton: a series of wonderful Hogarth prints, a couple of group school photographs, equipment for sports she'd never seen played, some rather messy watercolor seascapes that Hamilton laughingly admitted were his own, a little Mannerist bronze of Mercury, a collection of seashells. There was a piano that took up a corner of his sitting room, and he sat down and ran through a Chopin étude for her, without music, just like that, and she hadn't even known he played at all.

She was very quiet on the way back to the city, and he didn't try to keep a conversation going because he knew she needed time to digest what he'd shown her. The house had awed her and — she had to admit — intimidated her, but she hadn't coveted it, she hadn't envied the people who used it for one or two months out of the year. It was cold, impersonal, unimaginative, the way a big pile of money would be, and she wasn't *impressed* by it. Hamilton's rooms, what he had allowed her to see of himself, were what she was thinking about. Now that she knew so much more about his background, now that she saw what it meant, what he must always have quietly fought to carve out a life of his own — to become the gentle, honest, kind man she knew him to be — she found herself loving him and respecting him, in a strange new way, even more.

It was that week, just a few days after the trip to Easthampton, that she finally had to face up to what had been at the back of her mind for a while now. She had missed her period a month before, and of course that worried her, but she told herself it happened sometimes, that it might be just a coincidence and, after all, she'd been through a trauma when Michael's letter came and that kind of experience could affect her physically, couldn't it? Now, a month later, when her second period failed to appear, she couldn't ignore it any longer and she went to a clinic in the Village that advertised in the *Voice*.

Three days later, when she found out for sure, she walked slowly home through Washington Square and tried to fight off the blinding panic. Whom could she tell? Not her poor mama, who was so proud of her daughter, so sure of her rosy future. Not Trish, who was in Paris, unless she waited two weeks for a reply to a letter she wrote today. The people at the clinic asked her for the father's name, of course, but she'd shaken her head, and she watched as the nurse wrote "Unknown." She stopped for a moment by the fountain when the thought of Michael came to her. He and she had made this baby together. He was the proud father, but before she'd ever, *ever* ask him for help, she decided, she'd jump off a building. Or she'd throw herself in front of a train like Anna Karenina.

She spent the next few days in a kind of limbo, able to forget what was happening to her only by willing herself to think of nothing at all. When Hamilton returned from a trip to Brazil, when she heard his voice on the phone, she knew she'd been waiting for him, knew she'd been pinning her hopes on him without realizing it. He sounded, for him, almost effervescent, and she had to make her voice match the excitement in his. He wanted to take her somewhere special to celebrate his homecoming. The Rainbow Room, maybe? Would she like that? Had she ever been there? He'd pick her up at eight, the next night she was free. Saturday.

She was planning to talk to him about it right away, but she was so dazzled by finding herself in such a glamorous place, sixty stories above midtown Manhattan, that she put it off till after dinner. She was wearing a little black cocktail dress that her mother, excited for her when Frances told her where she was going, had run up on her machine the night before. They danced a foxtrot and then a cha-cha and then, when they came back to their table, he pulled out a tiny box. It was a big emerald, more than five carats, set in platinum as a solitaire. Frances could only stare at it dumbly. She had no idea how much it might have cost, but she knew it represented a fortune to her or to her mother or to anyone she'd ever known. It terrified her. It somehow made Hamilton, her sweet, dryly humorous, wonderfully knowledgeable friend, seem like someone she didn't really know very well after all.

"Try it on." He was so eager, he pulled it out of the box for her. "I bought the stone in São Paolo and I carried it in my pocket all the way back. I hope it fits — I had to guess, and I got the people at Cartier to set it in twenty-four hours." She slowly put it on the ring finger of her right hand. It was tight, but her fingers were a little swollen lately.

"I hoped," he began shyly, looking out over the dance floor, "I . . . it's a gift, and you can do whatever you like with it, but I hoped you might wear it on the other hand. I mean, on the same finger but on the other hand. I'm proposing to you, Frances."

"No, Ham. I have to say no," she said dully, gracelessly. "It's not a good idea." Her hand lay in front of her, limp, the ring sparkling with a life of its own. He put his own hand over hers, peering across the table at her, trying to read her face.

"There's something wrong, isn't there? Are you unhappy to see me? Have I insulted you just now, in some way I didn't intend?" Looking down at her hands, half mesmerized by the emerald, she gave him all the facts, reciting them in a low voice with very little expression.

"In that case, we're certainly going to get married," he said hoarsely.

"It's a terrible basis for a marriage, even if it were *your* baby."

"I don't need a good reason to marry you, Frances. I love you. I realized it this last week, how much I depend on you, how much I trust you. This doesn't have to be a tragedy. I'll simply accept the child as mine. Any baby of yours is bound to be wonderful. I'd . . . try to make you happy."

She shook her head. "I'm not even eighteen years old, for God's sake." Her voice was cold, colder than she meant it to be. "I love you too, in a funny way that I can't really explain, but my life . . ." She started over. She wanted to be absolutely clear, but she owed it to him to be kind, too. "The whole mess with Michael was only two months ago, and up till this week I thought I'd be at Radcliffe in September, in a dormitory, cramming for midterms and going to poetry readings. I *cannot* suddenly turn my whole life around and marry you and raise this baby and settle down and run a house with servants and a castle out on Long Island with a . . . a ballroom. I'm not going to leave one world where I don't really belong and move straight into another. I won't do it!" She stopped, horrified that she was hurting him so much but feeling incapable of telling him anything but the truth.

"Are you thinking . . . ? If you want to, um, have an operation, I'm sure we could . . ."

"I want to have the baby. I mean, I don't *want* to. I *have* to. I won't . . . get rid of it." She sighed. "I know you're thinking it's because I was Catholic. I don't think that has anything to do with it but it might, I guess. Mostly it's because of a girl I knew. She had that kind of operation and something went wrong and now she can't have children." Her eyes filled with tears, and she looked up from the emerald. "I want children. Eventually. Not now. But I won't keep this baby. I can't stay in New York. I'll have to go away somewhere. I can't tell my mother. It would hurt her and she'd worry, and her heart . . ."

"Then you'd put it up for adoption as soon as it's born?" She nodded. He was staring past her shoulder, thinking. "I'll do whatever I can to help, you know that, and you know you can have as much money as you need. But I won't stop asking you to marry me. All right, now. Let's think."

She should go to Boston anyway, he said after a moment or two. It was a beautiful city, it was far enough from here but close enough so he could see her easily. The McKinnon Foundation would probably be moving down to New York in another year or so but it was still based up there, and Hamilton's brother, Frederick, could keep an eye on her. She could tell her mother she couldn't face seeing Michael everywhere on the Harvard and Radcliffe campuses — that would be the hardest part of the story — and that she wanted to take it easy for a semester or two. She'd say she had a part-time job and that she'd still be taking a few classes somewhere. Her mother didn't know very much about colleges, and Frances thought it would work.

Hamilton's brother found a comfortable one-bedroom apartment in an old brick house in the Back Bay, and every month Hamilton deposited far too much money in a checking account for her. The brothers had settled everything for her: a good obstetrician saw her once a month, a private hospital had a bed reserved for her when the time came. She was strangely happy to be alone most of the time, but of course she didn't really consider herself alone because she had her constant companion, the child who was growing inside her. She talked to it, often, on the long walks she took. When no one could hear her, she described, in a low voice, the pictures she stood in front of in the museums. She wore a gold-plated wedding ring now, and her official story for neighbors or anyone else who wondered was that her husband was off in Korea in the Air Force and that she was staying here to have the baby. She took two art history classes, one in pre-Columbian and one in early Flemish, at the Museum School, and she sometimes had coffee with one or two of the other students. Once, walking through Harvard Square on her way to the Fogg, she saw Michael from a distance and her heart stopped. She hid, trembling, behind the newspaper kiosk, and she avoided Cambridge after that. Frederick, livelier and more puppyish than Hamilton, became a new friend, not only because she could relax and drop her role of Air Force wife, but because he knew all about art and architecture, music and dance, and he would talk to her for hours about them. And he was lonely: his wife had died the year before and he had loved her very much.

As the time grew nearer, Hamilton came up every weekend, staying at the Beacon Hill house where Frederick was raising his sons with the help of a housekeeper, but spending all his time with Frances. She was proudly serving him a grilled cheese sandwich on the little walnut drop-leaf table she'd lovingly refinished when Hamilton asked her if she thought the baby was going to be a boy or a girl.

"Oh, I'm convinced it's a boy. I can feel him kicking, and they're very masculine, soccer-player little kicks."

"And you'd prefer a boy?" he asked quietly.

"I guess I would," she said, her voice suddenly sad. "I . . . I've gotten to love him. He's my friend, and I talk to him and tell him he's got to be noble and smart and handsome. I think it would be easier, giving my friend away, if it's a boy, because they can take care of themselves better, can't they? The idea of a little girl — she'd seem so much more vulnerable."

"Well, it isn't as if your baby is going to be sent to some gloomy Horatio Alger orphanage, you know. I'm not sure what Freddie's arranged, but he told me he's found a good family, and they're bound to love a little girl as much as a little boy."

"That's all he's told you about it?" She was very surprised.

"Yes. I think it's better if I don't know all the details, because you might try to get it out of me once we're married and I might tell you."

Hamilton had proposed at least once on every visit. She patted her stomach and changed the subject. "Did I tell you I've gone to the Gardner almost every day this week? For a paper in my Flemish class."

"Given that you aren't going to marry me right away," he said, ignoring her, "are you positive about what you want to do afterwards?" She nodded. Trish, the only other friend who knew the truth, had asked Frances to join with her in Paris, where she'd gone the day after graduation to work for Balenciaga. There was a one-year course for foreigners at the Sorbonne she could take. It seemed crazy, impossible, but Trish assured her she'd arrange it, that it could be done.

"Well, then, don't worry about money. We can . . ."

"No!" He was startled, and she apologized. "I can't take any more money from you when this is over, Ham. I made a mistake and thank God you've been here to help me, but anything more would be . . . wrong. Unfair."

"But you'll have to eat, you'll have to have a roof over your head."

"Trish thinks she knows a couple who need someone to help with their children. To live in. So they're bound to have a roof, aren't they?" He sighed and gave up, for the moment.

A month later, while she was walking through the Common on a cold, blustery day, it started, a few days earlier than the doctor had predicted. She calmly called Frederick from a phone booth on Tremont Street, and he picked her up within ten minutes in a cab. Hamilton was in San Francisco, and they decided not to call him till it was over. He'd rush out of an important meeting and charter a plane and snap at everyone and then feel terrible for snapping at everyone, and he wouldn't get there in time anyway. Her room at the private hospital, which seemed like an elegant hotel to her, was overheated and she was drenched with sweat as the pains clutched her. Frederick patted her face with a cool washcloth and sweated alongside. After six hours, when the respites from the blinding pain could be counted in seconds, she was gently slipped onto a gurney and wheeled into the delivery room.

They kept asking her to push and then to breathe and then to push again. She tried very hard to do what they wanted, but she knew, somewhere in her mind — somewhere in her *soul,* she thought — she didn't want this to happen and she was resisting. She wanted to keep her baby, she wanted to have her friend safely inside her. Once he was gone, once he left her body, she'd never see him again. She heard the concern in their voices, she heard the words *nitrous oxide* and then *spinal,* and then something was at her nose for a moment and then she was being rolled halfway over, on her side. She was grateful to them, then, because she didn't feel anything at all, suddenly, and because they were making it easier for her to give him up. As soon as her friend was out in the world, as soon as he'd deserted her, she passed out.

When she awoke, back in her room, she felt emptier, more alone, than she'd ever felt in her life, more than when her father died, more, even, than when Michael betrayed her. Frederick was there, of course, and he'd filled the room with white roses. With the heat, the scent was so overwhelmingly sweet that she almost threw up.

"You have a healthy baby boy," he told her.

"No, I don't," she said furiously. "I did, but now I don't." She began to cry and she cried, weakly, helplessly, for the next three days. She gave away her child, she signed all the documents that had to be signed, in a blur of tears, never looking to see what was printed on them, not wanting to know.

Until this inevitable misery at the end, the time she spent in Boston had been a long, calm, bittersweet period in her life — more sweet than bitter, really, much happier than she imagined it would be. The year in Paris, where the worst was supposed to be behind her, where her real life was supposed to be starting, was uniformly dark, and she'd hated the city ever since. Paris was where she mourned for the son she'd never really had, where she had to take care of a two-year-old and a three-year-old who didn't understand her high-school French and didn't know why the mere sight of them made her cry. It was where she was told, after days of painful bleeding and more days of tests, that she would never have more children. It was where she'd been when the news came that her mother had died in her sleep. After that last blow, Frances stayed in her room for a solid week, refusing to come down even to mind the children, and Trish finally called Hamilton. He took the next plane, and when she fell into his arms, he didn't ask her, he informed her that they were going to be married.

After their wedding at the embassy, with Trish as the only witness, they honeymooned for a week in Egypt. That was where she found Hamilton to be very gentle, very generous, and not at all passionate in bed. She was grateful for that.

18

T*HE DRIVER* appeared to be lost, and Maggie couldn't help him. They were on a two-lane road in New Jersey, somewhere near Montclair, and they were trying to find the little airport where Jim and his plane were waiting for her. Now she wished she'd pinned him down for more exact instructions. "The driver'll know, for Christ's sake! I always use that car service." Well, this driver *didn't* know, as it turned out, and it was costing her a fortune. He had turned on the overhead light to study a map, and now he was talking to himself. She tried to make herself relax. After all, the point of taking a private plane was that if you were late it wouldn't leave without you, wasn't it? Jim had said they were locked into a takeoff time that was reserved with the controllers, but she didn't believe him.

She'd been late leaving the gallery — everything that could have gone wrong had gone wrong — and she hadn't really had time till now to think about what she was doing. She was suddenly nervous. Four or five hours with Jim in a tiny plane, an entire Thanksgiving weekend with him somewhere in North Carolina, four or five hours back — I must be out of my mind, she thought. How the hell did he ever get me to agree? You know perfectly well why you're going, a voice told her then. Because you're lonely and unhappy and at least Jim's a warm body, and he can actually be what's known as an agreeable companion every so often. He's not stupid, he sometimes has a pointed, cruel sense of humor that fits in with the way you're feeling these days, he's sexier than you used to think he was . . . but shit! Why can't he be Mario? Why can't I be looking forward to a long, lazy weekend with Mario?

With the light on, she noticed the bags on the seat beside her. Wherever it was they were going, Jim said there'd be no one to cook for them and no stores or restaurants for miles around, so she'd stopped at Balducci's, the gourmet deli in the Village, and loaded up with smoked turkey, smoked ham, smoked salmon, pasta salads, fruit, cheeses, and breads. She'd usually gone there to buy provisions when she and Mario went away, and it suddenly made her horribly sad to see the big white shopping bags with their dark green lettering that said *Buon Appetito* over and over. When the driver made confident noises and turned the light out, she dug into her purse for her coke bottle, frowning when she saw how little there was left. Anyway, she was sure Jim would have plenty, and she needed just a little bit right now. She rattled bags, ducked down, and sniffed as quietly as she could, just in case the driver minded.

When they found the airport, they drove slowly around the periphery of what looked like acres of parked planes until she finally spotted Jim standing in front of the strange-looking Staggerwing. He was mad, of course, but they evidently still had a few minutes till their flight time. She looked at the plane skeptically. The only time she could remember being up in anything this small was a twenty-minute hop somewhere in the Yucatán, but that plane had had two engines, she was sure, and this had only one. She felt a little better once she was settled inside. It's like a nice, substantial, old sedan, she thought when she saw the two soft leather seats in front, the leather sofa behind them, and the pleated fabric on the walls. There was even a window at her side that cranked up and down like a car's.

Once they'd taken off smoothly into the stiff breeze, once they'd circled out to the east and then begun to head south, she relaxed. Jim seemed to be at his best when he was playing with his toy; he was even polite to whoever was giving him instructions on the radio. She looked over at him, his face lit by the three-quarter moon and the lights on the dashboard — no, it was called an instrument panel — and she felt a small stirring of desire. Their sex, a few nights ago — the first and, so far, only time — hadn't been very successful. He was too fast, too excited, and she was somewhere else, not there with Jim Wilkins, not there at all. For more than two years, she'd slept with the same man, a man she now fully realized she loved very much, and even though *he* was the one who'd broken it off with *her,* she couldn't help feeling unfaithful. She'd wept for a long time afterward and Jim had held her close, silently puffing on one of his awful cigars. She didn't suppose he was thinking about her, but at least he was there, he was smart enough to say nothing, and he was letting her lean on him.

Tonight, once they were set on their course, they shared the last of what was in her vial. It was enough for her — for a while, at least — but Jim wanted more. After showing her exactly how to keep the yoke steady, he shifted the throw-over control to her while he searched his pockets, and she was suddenly flying the plane, terrified but — in the first high from the coke — exhilarated. Even after she passed the control back to him, she was chatty and animated for a few minutes. The glass in front of her sloped back so she could look up to the sky, and she began to identify constellations.

"This was the only biplane where you could look up like that," he said proudly. "Because the top wing's set back."

"So they could see the Red Baron coming down out of a cloud?"

He rolled his eyes. "In the first place, this was built about twenty years later. In the second, it wasn't meant to be a fighter. It's a workhorse. Farmers, oilmen, that kind of thing." She thought he was being, for Jim, amazingly patient.

"A Rotarian plane," she murmured. "How far will it go?"

"Range. It's called its range. About a thousand miles."

"And how far are we ranging?"

"About eight hundred, because we have to swing way out around D.C. They adapted them sometimes, though. Chiang Kai-shek had one with extra fuel tanks that could do about sixteen hundred."

They talked very little after that. Jim seemed to be content, lazily keeping in touch with the controllers in the zones they passed through, more relaxed than she'd ever seen him. She was so tired that the coke didn't keep her speeding for very long. They followed the coastline most of the way and Jim pointed out cities off to their right — Wilmington, Norfolk — clusters of light that were beautiful from two thousand feet up, but that she thought might just as easily have been Fort Lauderdale or Palm Beach. As they got closer, Maggie began to squirm in her seat. She should have peed before they left New Jersey, she realized, and the coke made it worse.

"How far is the airport from the Collinses' place?"

"It's *on* their place. They have a private landing strip. I told you that when we were talking about it the other night."

"Oh. Sorry. I was having a hard time deciding whether I'd actually do this, so I probably wasn't listening very closely. Tell me about it again. Does it have big white columns?"

"Hell, no. Is that your only picture of the South? These tobacco plantations, the ones on this part of the coast, are real working farms, not the same style at all. People in North Carolina have a saying, that it's a valley of humility between two mountains of conceit, between all that antebellum shit in Virginia and South Carolina. Not that they're *really* humble; you notice they always tell you how many generations back their families go and how many ancestors they had who fought the Yankees. Anyway, maybe it's the crop that makes a difference, tobacco instead of King Cotton."

"The Collinses won't be there at all this weekend?" She already knew the answer to that one, but she was trying to distract herself.

"I also told you . . . Jesus! No, they won't be there. We'll have it all to ourselves, except for the housekeeper, but she doesn't live in the main house. I hope to hell she remembered to turn on the runway lights. And the hot tub, for that matter."

"My God! That doesn't sound like the Old South."

"They're a funny mixture, George and Eileen. Their families both go back to before the Revolution in this part of the state, but they're determined to be modern. They're in Utah now, I think. They backed some asshole who's doing an earthwork thing out there." He snorted, and she sighed. Why couldn't Jim ever appreciate the work of any other living artist? "Anyway, it's a little weird. This big old house with all this modern sculpture scattered around it."

"So when is your piece going to be joining them? You're about two years behind schedule, aren't you?"

"Yeah, more like three, but George doesn't mind. They like me and they know I'll do it eventually."

She laughed. "Where have I heard that before?"

She was afraid they'd have to land on dirt, but it turned out to be a strip of asphalt, lined with orange lights. They taxied to a little shack at the end of the runway, and Jim told her to carry the things out to the jeep that stood there while he shut up the Staggerwing. It took more than half an hour for him to go over the whole plane, to check the motor, to tie it to rings set into a patch of cement, and, finally, to turn off the runway lights. She went into the bushes to pee and then she sat in the open jeep with her coat wrapped tightly around her. She'd imagined balmy southern nights. It was certainly warmer than the weather they'd left behind, but there was a clamminess that made her shiver.

"How far are we from the coast?" she yelled to him.

"About thirty miles, but it's damp like this for a long ways inland." He climbed in beside her and drove for a couple of miles along a dirt road, brushing low pine trees that gave way occasionally to tobacco fields stretching as far as she could see in the moonlight.

"Drying sheds," Jim said, pointing to some long buildings on one side. "We'll go look at them tomorrow. The house is in those big pines up ahead."

"They certainly have a lot of land, if this is all theirs."

"It is, you may be sure. I think it's the biggest spread in this part of the state."

The house was big and — Jim was right — nothing like Tara. It had grown awkwardly in two hundred years, rising to two stories at one end, a long, rambling hodgepodge of weatherbeaten boards. Tin roofs covered its wide verandas. The housekeeper who opened the door to them was a fat, smiling black woman, and Maggie was glad to see that at least part of her fantasy was intact. Yes, to answer Jim's first question, she'd turned on the hot tub. She helped them carry their bags up to a room on the second floor that was furnished with what must have been family pieces, and then she left them to go on home. She'd be just a mile down the road if they needed anything.

Jim laid out a couple of big lines as soon as they were alone, and then he stripped off his clothes, wrapped a towel around his waist, and ran out of the room without bothering to unpack. Maggie came down a few minutes later, wearing a raincoat because she hadn't thought of bringing a robe. She wandered through the spacious, friendly ground-floor rooms, deciding after a few minutes that she'd probably like George and Eileen. She found her way to the porch that ran along the back of the house, and from there she could look out to a stretch of bare grass that was dotted with sculpture. Beyond that, in a dark mass of pines, she could see a faint glow, and she picked her way along a gravel path that led to a clearing. The big cedar tub sat there in its own mist, gurgling like the witches' cauldron in *Macbeth,* she thought. Jim's head, just above the surface, lit by the underwater light beneath him, could have been disembodied.

"I've already got a hard-on thinking about you," he said pleasantly.

It was exactly the kind of thing that would have infuriated her a few weeks before, but now she giggled. "Mah goodness, suh, ah shuhly hope y'all don't think ah'm jus' another ol' rotten magnolia blossom, jus' sittin' 'round an' waitin' to be plucked." She threw her coat down, kicked her shoes off, ran up the steps along the side, and jumped in.

"Ow! Jesus! It's a lot hotter than I thought it'd be."

"Hence the expression. I thought you grew up in the land of hot tubs." He came toward her, grabbed her hand, and made her feel him underwater.

"Jim!" She squealed. "Ah declayuh ah think theah's a big ol' watah moccasin in heah, ah do."

"Take a deep breath," he said, pushing her head down, guiding her mouth to him, making her take him as far down her throat as she could. When he let her up she was gasping for breath.

Then he disappeared and she felt his fingers, his tongue, in her. She leaned back against the smooth wooden planks, giving herself up to the bubbles that swirled around her, the heat of the water, and the other heat that was centered where Jim's tongue was probing. When he came up he pushed her under again, this time guiding her tongue to his balls, hanging low in the hot water.

He entered her, at last, standing with his legs apart, his hands supporting her, her legs wrapped around his back. Then he took her hands, and her head fell back so that her face barely cleared the water. She shoved toward him, moaning, hearing herself though the sound-chamber of the water in her ears. She came very soon, clutching him with her entwined ankles, bringing him as far into her as she could. He didn't come. When he released her she looked at him, sweat streaming down her face, her eyes glazed.

"I'm saving it," he said, his hand underwater, stroking himself. "You want more, don't you?" She nodded. "Dry off, then, and go upstairs."

She did as she was told, without speaking. Jim was a bastard, Jim always had to have his own way, but there was something very powerful in him, there was a force that excited her in spite of herself. She'd known it would be like this, this weekend, and she came down here wanting it, wanting him to tell her what to do, to order her, to exhaust her. She dried herself, shivering, unable to take her eyes off him as he sat on the edge of the tub, his cock springing up from the wet red hair around it.

"Go in and lie down. Wait for me."

When he came up to her, after a few minutes, she was still in a trance, her hips lifting up off the bed in anticipation.

"Play with yourself," he said roughly, dropping the towel he'd had around him, still hard. "Make yourself wet. I want to watch you. I want you to get ready to take this." He held his cock, pointed it at her.

A part of Maggie — of Jim, too, she supposed — believed in what they were playing out, the harsh words, his dominance and her submission. It was certainly there in Jim, and whatever corresponded to it was there in her, but they both knew, and each knew the other knew, that it was partly a game. Only partly, though, because it was real too, and the excitement came from not knowing how far they would go. She felt bad about herself, these days, unlovable, *low,* and she entered into this with a very real need to be dominated. Tomorrow, in the daylight, she might laugh about it, but tonight it was serious.

She masturbated slowly, her eyes never leaving him, bringing herself closer and closer again. Finally he knelt on the bed at her feet, groaning, still holding himself.

"You really want it, don't you?" he asked her softly.

"Yes! Fuck me, Jim! Fuck me!"

He fell on her, ramming into her in one stroke, jabbing brutally, hurting her but driving her on to her climax, her eyes shut and her teeth bared and her head straining up off the pillow. When she came he pulled out and sat up, straddling her, his knees pinning her arms. His cock throbbed in front of her and he came, jerking himself off, his semen spurting into her hair, running down her face, stinging her eyes.

They didn't say a word then. He rolled off her and they fell asleep almost immediately. In the morning, she woke before he did and, looking over, she silently thanked him. It had been pure, sexual, animal coupling, and it had been the release she needed, the drug she'd wanted it to be. She hoped there would be a lot more of it, all weekend long.

* * *

Because she wouldn't be spending the night, Carole had no luggage to claim, and she walked straight through the Milwaukee airport, practically deserted today, to the cab stand. The flight had been almost empty too: it was Thanksgiving morning. She was glad no one recognized her, but she would have been very surprised if anyone had. She'd paid cash for her ticket, using the first name that came into her head. She was Ms. S. Thompson, the name of her character in *Rain*. The three men who'd shared First Class with her had barely glanced her way, but she could tell they thought she belonged in Economy. She was in the outfit she'd worn a few times for secret meetings with Tony, a shoulder-length wig of tight black curls, brown contact lenses, heavy pancake makeup with much too much eye shadow, and pale pink lipstick. She wore a shapeless, bright orange pantsuit, white sneakers, and a nondescript trench coat. Ordinarily, she would have loved the deception and she probably would have expanded on it with an exaggerated accent of some kind and a story to match, but today she was only relieved. Today, she told herself, the consequences are much more serious than being spotted by a reporter or one of those fucking autograph freaks.

She'd been in Milwaukee years before, two weeks in an out-of-town tryout of an unfunny English farce that never made it to Broadway, but that had been a matter of shuttling between a downtown theater and a downtown hotel. The scenery the cab was taking her through today, she thought, could be Connecticut or Cincinnati or almost anywhere: a freeway, another freeway, a highway, finally a narrow road that wound through big estates. Houses that would be hidden in the summer could be clearly seen now through the leafless trees. The cab turned into a long driveway through gates that were swung back from brick pillars. She checked her watch and saw she was only a few minutes late. She'd been very calm until now but she was suddenly nervous. At any other time, she'd have fixed her makeup but there was no point in touching up the ghastliness and she didn't want to see herself in a mirror. It was possible she was making a terrible mistake. She was coming to see a woman she'd never met, a woman whose picture she'd gazed at in the newspaper years before. She had an appointment with Martha, the woman who had been the wife of Senator Terence Deloit, the woman *she* — although, goddammit, she refused to feel guilty — had widowed.

The house was huge and stately and impressive, everybody's idea of a mansion: red brick, shaggy vines, white pillars. It was not, she saw with her newly developing eye for this kind of thing, very interesting architecturally. It had been built by the grandfather, the first senator, the razor-blade king, and Terry had grown up here. She wanted to stay outside. His grave was here somewhere on the estate and she had a longing to find it and have a little chat with him, tell him how much she hated him — more, even, than that moment when his hands were at her throat — because of what she'd been going through for the past ten years. But there was someone inside who had to be met; there were children inside (she could hardly hate *them*) who mustn't suspect who she was or why she was here. Shoving some money at the driver and asking him to wait, she slowly climbed the steps up to the porch and rang the bell.

A very pretty, very young Spanish maid came to the door. It occurred to Carole that this girl wasn't old enough to have worked here when Terry was alive, and for some reason that made her feel more confident. She had a moment of panic because she didn't know how to identify herself, certainly not with her own name, so she simply said that Mrs. Deloit was expecting her. That seemed to be enough and she was allowed in and led down a broad hall. She could hear the excited chatter of teenage girls in a room off to the right, Terry's daughters, of course, and she could smell the Thanksgiving turkey.

She was shown into a small room that was furnished tastefully but institutionally with a few modern pieces and some reproduction Hepplewhite. It looked as if it might have been used by three generations of Deloits for interviews with the press, or maybe it was a convenient place for giving orders to secretaries and servants. She wondered if it had ever been the scene of the kind of talk it was about to witness.

She was alone only for a minute before Martha came in, locking the door carefully behind her. They stared at one another across the room, neither of them saying a word at first. Carole had always pictured her in black, probably because the last photograph she'd seen of her was at the funeral. She had thought of her only as a widow, and it was true she had never remarried, so it was jolting to see her in a simple forest-green wool dress today. She was about forty, she knew, but with ash blonde hair tied back from her face and very little makeup she looked a few years younger. Carole was reminded of her own absurd appearance by the expression on Martha's face, her raised eyebrows. She wished, fiercely, that this costume weren't necessary, that she could have met this woman who must loathe her — not that she cared — as herself, Carole Todd, actress, fiancée, whatever, anything but this tastelessly dressed bimbo.

"We didn't decide who I'm supposed to be."

"I know. I realized that after your phone call, but I didn't think I should call you back. I was sure you'd use your imagination. As far as the children are concerned, you were a secretary in one of Terry's campaigns and now you're down on your luck and you need a reference." She spoke in a universal finishing-school drawl, cool, poised, as correct and as impersonal as the room where they stood.

Carole opened her plastic purse, found a cigarette, and lit it. "Sorry, again, that this had to be Thanksgiving," she said without sounding at all sorry. "The theater's dark, and it's the only completely free day I've had for a couple of weeks."

Martha shrugged. "You explained. It doesn't matter. I don't think this ought to take very long, but we might as well be sitting down."

"All right." Carole fell into the nearest chair, took a deep drag of smoke, and began. "I assumed you knew . . . something or you would have been much more curious about why I wanted to come here."

"I didn't know anything until about ten years ago. Anything. Then I suddenly had to find out as much as I could. I had to rearrange all my thinking, everything I thought I knew about Terry, everything I felt about our marriage."

"About ten years ago," Carole echoed. She wouldn't touch the subject of Terry's marriage, but she was tempted to say something like: Terry always talked about how much he loved you while he was screwing me.

"I had a letter, a filthy letter, with a tape of your . . . performance. I wanted to ignore it, I wanted to give it to the police, but I thought I should check with Al Mueller, just in case. Al was Terry's friend, his assistant. But of course you knew Al. Of course. He was *there*." Her eyes blazed with hatred. "He was on heavy medication for pain, he was dying, but I had to see him alone. I had to throw my weight around, I had to push his family out of his hospital room so I could talk to him."

Carole was damned if she felt like taking all the responsibility for everything that had happened, for all the distasteful things Martha had been forced to do. Terry had something to do with it, for God's sake, she wanted to yell. Blame *him*. Blame the kid who sold him that crap that made him psychotic. Blame the Great American Public. Blame the son of a bitch who's bleeding you, bleeding both of us. She was trying to keep her temper. "And Al said —" she prompted icily.

"He was so drugged he could barely put two words together. He . . . cried. He said it was true, that I had better pay, that I didn't have a choice. He said he, the FBI man, must have been — what do you call it? — wired. Obviously, a certain number of other people had to know Terry didn't . . . have a heart attack, but Al swore none of them knew it was *you*. And he paid them all off, and it's only the one man who could *prove* it, isn't it? Because you only told that story to one man? Right?" Carole nodded. "Anyway," Martha went on, "Al wasn't lying. He couldn't have lied to me at that moment."

"Of course, *I* knew it was the agent. I never suspected Al because

I knew he wasn't there yet when I told him what happened. And his voice is on it, naturally, the agent's. I never even knew his name."

"Al told me. It doesn't matter now," Martha said wearily. "*He's* been dead for four or five years, the FBI man. I had him followed, I especially had him watched at the times of the year when I knew I'd be contacted, when I knew I'd be getting another of those little scented billets-doux. I did what you're doing today, I dressed up in the worst clothes I could find and I went to a detective agency with a lot of cash. They sent reports to a post office box. He wasn't the one. Well, obviously he wasn't, because they didn't stop coming when he died."

"How did he die?" She didn't know why she asked.

"He gassed himself, in his garage. No." She kept Carole from interrupting. "No, you're thinking it was guilt, and then maybe someone picked up where he left off? In the first place, if he felt so guilty, he would have made sure no one else could use the information, wouldn't he? In the second place, he didn't have a dime, he never did. In the third place." She paused, and Carole saw that she was, perversely, enjoying this now. "In the third place, the reason he didn't want to live any longer was because he was sick. I don't know how sick but the point was what the disease was. It was AIDS."

It's getting too complicated, Carole thought. Tragedies within tragedies. She tried to remember what the man looked like, for some reason, but she couldn't. "But, then, was he . . ."

"He wasn't Haitian, as *you* know because you saw him that night. He wasn't a junkie, my detective was sure of that. He'd never had a blood transfusion. That leaves one probability, unless he was a vampire, and I think we can safely rule that out. Homosexuality is not a . . . recommended orientation . . . if you're in the FBI, J. Edgar Hoover aside." She allowed herself, for the first time, a thin, bitter smile.

"So it's someone else. You think he sold the tape to someone? Or maybe someone knew about him and put pressure on him?" Carole asked slowly. She was forgetting to be as cold as this woman was.

"Yes, but not for money, not on his salary," Martha said with the contempt of a woman who'd never depended on a salary. "As I said, he never had any money. What he had was a secret — probably others, too, but at least this one — and we both know how valuable it turned out to be."

"Is that as far as you got? Did your detective . . ."

"Get any closer? No. The only reason he found out so much was because the report — of his death — was filed before the FBI stepped in and took over from the local police. They put federal seals on his house and they did their own housecleaning. Any evidence there might have been, any clue about lovers or friends or enemies — it's all in a file in Washington if it even exists at this point. There's no private detective in America who has that kind of access, and I gave up. Until a few weeks ago."

"When the cocksucker got even more demanding." She used the word deliberately, but Martha didn't flinch. "The last straw, or at least that's the way it was with me."

"Yes. I don't know whether the money matters all that much to you, but I can spare it. It was that I realized all of a sudden that it would never end, that now it isn't even going to be nice and dependable, twice a year. We keep hoping he'll drop dead tomorrow, at least I do, but it probably wouldn't make any difference because someone would just take his place. If I died tomorrow, I'm sure the children would start getting letters a few days after the funeral. *That* is what I'll do anything to prevent."

And for me, Carole thought, there's Tony, there's my career, my life. And now, if we had children . . . Jesus, then I'd have even more people to protect. "But now you're looking for him again? You think there's something that can be done?"

Martha nodded slowly. "You may or may not know that my brother is a congressman." Carole didn't know. "He's been on the Hill for seven years now and he's on a couple of important committees. I told him the whole story three weeks ago, and I know he'd rather die than tell anyone, because Terry was his hero. He thinks he might be able to do something, trade a favor with someone at the FBI, get a look at the file, but he has to approach it slowly. Very, very cautiously. It may take a while."

"I've waited this long. The problem is, then what do we do?"

"I don't know. There are times when I think I could murder him, if it's a him, if I thought it would do any good." She stood up abruptly. "That's it. That's everything. I'll let you know when I hear, if there's anything to hear." The interview was over. Martha walked her to the front door, they said good-bye, they even shook hands. Carole, in spite of herself, had to admire the way this woman had handled her.

19

"IS THAT FABERGÉ?" Rudi asked Dorothy as she opened an exquisite gold and lapis lazuli pillbox that was shaped like a tiny hand. They were sitting in the big living room in Rudi's town house. Chuck was at the other end, mixing a pitcher of vodka martinis. The dogs were hard at work being decorative in front of the fire.

"Mmmm." She was preoccupied, making soft clicking sounds with her fingernails as she rummaged for what she wanted. When she found it she looked up, snapped the box shut, and answered him properly. "Yes. It's beautiful, isn't it? It was made for a cousin of Prince Yussoupov. You know, Yussoupov was the one who killed whatsisname."

"Rasputin," Chuck said, coming over to bend down and look at it when he brought her the drink tray. She hurriedly put it in her purse and took her drink. She doesn't want me to look too closely, he thought. I might want to handle it. I might even open it. She washed down the pill with a gulp of her martini. Chuck glanced over at Rudi, who was rolling his eyes upward. Neither of them said anything about the danger in what she was doing.

Once it was safely out of sight, Dorothy evidently felt free to talk about it again. "Spence gave it to me years ago," she said to her drink. "Poor Spence! Poor Spence had such perfect taste. He was always saying to me that I didn't know a Degas from a Vargas — y'know, those cartoons that used to be in *Esquire*?" Her eyes filled with tears. "I know what he'd think about this afternoon; he never understood how I could play so much bridge. 'Bridge again, Dot?' he'd say. 'Going off to play cards with a bunch of . . .'" She stopped herself. "Silly fairies" was probably what Spence had always said, Chuck thought, and he silently agreed with him. He didn't like bridge and he certainly didn't like the two rich old queens who'd be completing this foursome.

"Chuck, can you help me in the kitchen for a minute?" Rudi asked suddenly, getting up. "I don't know if Claire left enough sandwiches."

When the door swung shut behind them, Rudi faced him. "Jesus, it's not even noon and Dorothy's on her way already. You know more about substance abuse than I do, God knows. Isn't there anything we can do to pull her into shape before the others get here?"

"Thanks. We're all the same, right? I may know a lot about drinking, but I keep it simple. Never mix, never worry. I don't think black coffee and a quick run around the block are quite the ticket, if that's what you mean. All you can do is hope for the best, but don't count on anything. You're the one who got her more of these fucking pills, though, so I don't want to hear about it."

"You make it sound like I handcuffed her and stuffed them down her throat . . . hell. She was a little wobbly a few nights ago, but we didn't play cards then. She doesn't even know she showed up half an hour too soon. It's going to be a rocky afternoon."

Dorothy was making an effort to pull herself together when they came back into the living room. She'd taken out a mirror and was brushing her curls furiously. "How are things at the restaurant?" she asked Rudi thickly, her manners asserting themselves.

"Difficult, Dorothy. I'm having a hard time finding someone to replace Mario."

"Mario? That sweet boy I met at your party here? I always thought you were so pleased with him. Surely you're not thinking of letting him go?"

"I was pleased with him, but of course he hasn't been there lately." Rudi was trying to be patient. "I'm sure I told you he quit? That he's going to be having his own place?"

"Oh? Oh, of course you did. But, now, Chuck." She turned to him. "I know I've met that clever girl . . . your sister. I'm sorry, I can't remember her name, but she was at that muscular dystrophy auction at Christie's and your Mario was there with her, Rudi. And I'm sure I remember that they were seeing each other?" She knew all these facts perfectly well, but they were muddled in her head these days.

"They were. He's dumped her now."

"Oh, I'm sorry to hear that," she said automatically. "But of course it's always so hard to know what really happens with couples, isn't it? From the outside?"

I'll bet you trot out that little speech whenever you hear about some couple being separated or divorced, Chuck thought. He hated obvious, meaningless platitudes like that. AA was full of them: "One day at a time" and "Turn it over." Shit, hadn't this silly woman heard him?

"He dumped her," he repeated stubbornly. "If you don't know what that means —"

Rudi interrupted him. "I guess you haven't heard about your sister-in-law?" His face had lit up, a slow smile spreading across it. More and more people seemed to know about Frances and Mario — not a few of them told by him or by Chuck, of course — but it was possible Dorothy hadn't heard. She didn't really move in the same set, after all.

"My . . . Mario and Berry? Spence's baby sister, Berry? I can't believe it. Berry hasn't even been in town for the past . . . Well, you know she lives in Philadelphia and people from Philadelphia think there's no good reason to ever come to New York, although it always seemed to me . . ."

Rudi let her ramble on about Philadelphia, and what an unattractive woman Berry was, although awfully nice, of course, and however did rumors like that get started? She just didn't know. He sat back against the pin-striped pillows and Chuck saw him lick his lips like a cat. When she'd finally run down, he said, "Not that side of the family, Dorothy."

She stared at him, her eyes going in and out of focus, trying to grasp what he'd just said. "Frances? Your maître d' and . . ."

"Manager," Rudi corrected her. "Former manager. She's doing his restaurant for him, decorating it. That's how it started, we think."

"Manager, then. And Frances." She shook her head, trying to

clear it, trying to sort the knowledge out. It was a complete surprise, and Rudi was smiling triumphantly. Chuck was still frowning into the fire.

"But he's years younger. Years," she said at last.

"He's a year older than Maggie, actually," Chuck said nastily. "Twenty-nine. How old *is* Mrs. Hamilton McKinnon, anyway?"

She looked at him blankly. It's not that she's avoiding the point, Chuck thought, it's that her mind isn't doing a very good job right now. She had a long conversation with herself about Frances's age that included the year she'd come out, the year Frances was married, her daughter's age, and the current year. When she finally produced an answer, she beamed.

"She's forty-seven. She just turned forty-seven. I'm sure of it." She held up her glass. "Could I have just a teensy bit more, please?"

Rudi reached for the pitcher. "Say when," he sighed.

She's going to be out of control at the bridge table, completely useless, Chuck thought with some pleasure. He almost wished he could stay around to watch it, but he had to give a lesson in an hour.

"When!" she giggled, after Rudi filled her glass to the top. She took a long sip and her face clouded over.

"I wonder if Hamilton knows." She looked helplessly from Rudi to Chuck and back again.

Rudi examined his nails. "My dear, you'd have a much better idea of that than I would. Our concern," he said solemnly, giving Chuck a quick look, "our only concern is how terrible it's been for Maggie."

"But who *is* he?" she asked abruptly, ignoring the question of Maggie. "Where's he from? What's his background?"

It made Rudi laugh. "Dorothy! What difference could that possibly make? We're not talking about a royal marriage. Would you approve if he were from a good family?"

"No. Oh no, of course not. I was just wondering who he *is*." She sat up straight and set her drink down on the coffee table, spilling some of it. "I simply thought he might be taking advantage of her. She has a great deal of money. Well, Hamilton obviously does, but I know Frances has some of her own. Not that she came to the marriage with a penny, but I'm positive Hamilton settled some on her. I would hate to think he's after her money."

And that's really the point, isn't it, Dorothy? Chuck thought. Bad enough that a piece of the McKinnon fortune was already turned over to the sister-in-law you can't stand, someone who didn't grow up in the East Seventies or Eighties, but then if any of that dough should find its way into that lady's lover's pocket . . .

Chuck smiled sourly. "Dorothy, I'm sure he's not after *your* money. Only as much as he can get from Frances McKinnon. He's a climber. He used Maggie till she couldn't do any more for him, and then he found someone who was in a position to help him."

"But where's he *from?*" she asked desperately.

Do I do this when I'm smashed? Chuck wondered suddenly. If someone tells me something, do I get hold of a tiny, unimportant corner of it and chew on it relentlessly like this? He didn't know, just as Dorothy wouldn't know whenever her head was clear again. He felt some sympathy — empathy, he supposed — for her, and he answered gently.

"Boston, originally," he said. "A middle-class Boston Italian family, I think, before they made a lotta dough with some restaurants. But no *real* money, not like your money, not enough for someone like Mario. Obviously."

"Boston . . . ," she mused. "How odd. How very strange, really." She forgot all about Mario's background and went off into a long, rambling monologue that was impossible to follow. Boston and Frances. A baby. An adoption. Twenty-nine years. Chuck was confused but fascinated. He wanted to keep her talking, but she snapped back to the present when Rudi, greedy for facts, interrupted and made the mistake of trying to pin her down.

"Sorry," she said. She made yet another effort to get a grip on herself, tossing her head impatiently. "Just silly old family myths." She focused on Rudi, recrossed her legs, and firmly changed the subject.

"I saw Emily Williams the other day at a little tea. She wanted to know if you were going to the tournament in Scottsdale and *I* said . . ." The conversation turned to bridge then — Masters' points, duplicate tournaments, a new convention in bidding.

Nothing was more boring to Chuck than bridge talk, and he sat and tried not to listen. When the doorbell rang, he went to let the other two players in and to quietly warn them about Dorothy's condition, and then he went up to the bedroom to get ready for work. On his way out, passing the study, he was surprised to see Rudi sitting at his desk with his back to the door. Downstairs, everyone was laughing loudly at something, and Rudi hadn't heard him coming down the thickly carpeted hallway. Rudi had deserted his guests for a few minutes, which was strange in itself, and he was concentrating on writing something. Chuck was suddenly curious, and he approached him as quietly as possible, covered by more gales of laughter from the living room. By the time Rudi was aware of him, before he could slap it shut, before he could compose his face into a big good-bye smile, Chuck had seen the small purple — lavender, really — notebook. He was sure he'd never noticed it anywhere in the house before. At the top of the page on which Rudi was writing was the word *McKinnon*. Neither of them mentioned it.

* * *

The crowd at the opening of the Patricia Green space on the fourth floor of Bloomingdale's had overflowed to the aisle and on into other designers' areas, and it was near a rack of Ungaro skirts that Maggie saw Frances and Hamilton McKinnon talking with Trish and some people from *Women's Wear.* This is what I came for, she reminded herself, to show my face to Trish because she's always been such a good client of Max's. And of course I knew I'd see *her* or I wouldn't have dragged both Jim and Chuck along as moral support, so I wouldn't have to face her alone. Although God knows Jim's no help and Chuck's so drunk and if Mario's here somewhere . . . the hell with it, of course I can do it, she thought. I'm a big girl and we're all adults and all that shit. She squared her shoulders, took Chuck's hand in hers, and forced a big smile.

"Mrs. Green," she said brightly, "it's a wonderful collection. I may have to come back tomorrow and see if I can afford that linen jacket, the apricot one? With the silk piping? Hello, Mrs. McKinnon. Congratulations to *you,* too, of course. The space is really elegant."

"Hello, Maggie. Thank you. You're Charles, aren't you? My husband, Hamilton McKinnon. Charles Wetherby." Maggie was wishing the others weren't wandering off — a bigger circle of people would have helped. Face-to-face with Frances, who looked so beautiful, so thin, so — really, she had to admit — so young, she was losing her nerve.

"Chuck," Chuck said sullenly, putting out his hand to Hamilton.

Trish began to talk about art, asking Maggie about next week's Post-Impressionist auction at Sotheby's. Hamilton tried to carry on a conversation about tennis, but he got only monosyllables for his trouble. Chuck was staring at Frances, and after a minute he interrupted Hamilton in the middle of a question about clay courts. His voice was loud enough to stop Maggie and Trish's chatter, too. "How's Mario these days, Mrs. McKinnon? We haven't seen much of him lately, have we, Maggie?" Maggie felt herself flush. It was exactly what she'd dreaded: even though he didn't seem to be here, his name was suddenly here, in front of them, in the air.

"He's well, I think," Frances said neutrally. "I was at the space this afternoon to check on some things and he seemed pleased with how it was going."

"Tables," Chuck sneered.

"Yes. It's a wonderful name, don't you think?"

Chuck's a walking time bomb, Maggie was thinking. She wouldn't have minded getting in a few punches herself, maybe make Frances a little uncomfortable, make her squirm a little, but Chuck was going too far. Trish, bless her, tried to cover up.

"Maggie, if you're really interested in that jacket, call me at my office tomorrow. You've lost some weight, my dear — it's very becoming — and I think there might be one at the showroom that would fit you."

She said all the right appreciative things, and then she quickly drained her glass and turned to her brother. "Could you bring me another glass of champagne, Chuckles?" She didn't really want him near the bar again after she'd spent so much time prying him away from it, but she obviously had to separate him from Frances.

He grunted and did as she asked, turning away without another word. She spun around then to include Jim in the circle, anything to keep things moving along, knowing he was far too self-centered to pay attention to anything but art world gossip. He surprised her by being amazingly polite to Hamilton and Frances and they all enthused about the commission for the bank until she saw Chuck heading back toward them. Then she elaborately checked her watch.

"We've got to go soon, Jim. Middle America awaits." She gave a mock sigh. "We have to eat dinner with the *most* boring man and his little wifelet who may want a piece of Jim's for their new place in Great Neck. Nice to have seen you, congratulations again to both of you . . ." She was able to intercept Chuck before he got all the way back to them.

In the past few minutes, he'd gone over the line. He seemed to have forgotten the trouble he'd just caused, or tried to cause, and he was happy enough to be led away.

"God's sake," Maggie hissed in his ear. "I may *be* your little sister but I don't need you to fight my fights for me anymore."

"Wasn't fighting, Mag. Just didn't want that McKinnon bitch to think she's getting away with anything." She shushed him and his voice dropped to a conspiratorial whisper. "Think her husband knows about it? 'Bout her screwing Mario?"

"I don't know, but it certainly isn't our business to tell him. If good manners won't keep you from bringing it up like that, just try to remember that the McKinnons are clients of mine now."

"Aw, c'mon, Mag. You've got lots of clients."

"And you've had lots of drinks," she snapped. "Jim and I have got to go. It's really too early but I said we were going, so now we can't hang around. Come on, we'll drop you at the house."

"Not going back to the house."

"Then we'll drop you wherever you want." Sometimes, when Chuck was drunk, he talked like a little boy, leaving off the subjects of sentences. Trying to appeal to the fact that she was his baby sister had only worked to get her some champagne she didn't want. Beyond that, at times like this, she might as well have been his mother.

"Staying here for a while," he said stubbornly. "Rudi's gone off to New Hope. Hopefully gone off with hope to New Hope. Don't wanna go home yet."

"Oh." If it had been Mario with her tonight, he would have tried to help. Jim only glared at him, impatient to go.

"Christ's sake, Maggie, your brother's old enough to take care of himself."

"Of course he is. I just thought . . ."

"Mag," Chuck said plaintively. "Can I stay with you and the cats tonight? Don't wanna go home. Rudi's off with his fucking ponies. C'n I stay there, like when I first came to New York, like when I lived there and it was just you and me and the kitties?"

"Oh, Chuck." He made her want to cry sometimes. She wanted so much to help him, and the few times when he actually admitted he needed her, all she could really do was just be there. "You know you can stay whenever you want. Do you have keys with you?"

"Course." He pulled out the little Dunhill keycase she'd given him years before, snapping it open and jingling the keys.

"Well, I'll see you later, then. Are you sure you don't want to go straight down to my place? I know I've got eggs in the fridge, and probably some lettuce, and some cheese. . . ."

"Nope. Gonna hang out here for a little bit. See you later." He lurched toward her to kiss and their heads bumped painfully.

"Better have another drink," Jim said nastily. "Might be a concussion."

"S'okay. Don't worry." Chuck turned away from them and began to make his way back to the bar. By the time he got there, he realized he already had a full drink in his hand, but he asked for another one anyway. He stayed there, draining first one drink and then the second, munching on cheese puffs that were warm and flaky, smiling vaguely at people. He focused for a long time on the Christmas tree, a tall silver fir that was decorated with a thousand rosettes of pastel silks and linens that matched the clothes on the mannequins. He wondered how Christmas had sneaked up on him so fast, and then he remembered he was in a department store and it was more than three weeks away and he hadn't lost complete track of what day it was after all.

A couple of people waved to him from the safety of groups, but no one approached him. They can tell I'm drunk, he thought. They're afraid if they come up to me I might say something that's true. While he was pondering this, feeling powerful because only he knew the truth about things, Frances McKinnon appeared next to him and asked the bartender for a Campari and soda. Stupid, self-righteous bitch, he said to himself. Doesn't even have a real drink. It might make her fat, or she might lose control for a minute. She saw him staring at her and she smiled briefly, nervously.

She knows I can see right through her, he thought. She must be thinking she doesn't have to worry about Maggie anymore because by now everyone knows Maggie's been seeing Jim. That's not the point, he wanted to tell her. You're not so safe. It's just one of those love on the rebound things. It's not important to her. Maggie isn't even going to get hurt by it because she basically doesn't give a shit about Jim. At least, he didn't think she did, he didn't see how she could. He himself thought Jim was an even bigger prick than Mario, but he didn't worry about her feelings getting hurt and he didn't care who Maggie saw if it helped her get over the way she felt.

Anyway, I know more about this cunt than she realizes. Like about her baby. She gave her baby away. . . . His mind grew cloudy and he couldn't remember what there was about it . . . something Dorothy had said. Right! That Frances was old enough to be Mario's mother, which everybody knew. He wondered again what it was that Rudi was writing about the McKinnons, that day when Dorothy had spilled the beans or lost her marbles or whatever she'd done. He knew Rudi wouldn't tell him, he knew by the expression on his face when he surprised him, the way he'd covered up what he was doing, but he decided he might try to snoop around the house, see what he could find out. You have a good mind, he told himself, you can figure it out — it's just a little unclear at the moment. You can think about it tomorrow.

Everybody seemed to be leaving in couples, probably all going on to parties or going out to dinner together or going home together. Well, he and Rudi were a couple, he wanted to say to them, it was just that Rudi was off with his horses for a day or two. Watching them couple, he giggled. All right, so maybe they weren't a nice, old-fashioned, loving pair — maybe love didn't have much to do with whatever he and Rudi had — but they had Christmas cards printed with both their names on them, didn't they? He'd promised to go home and address some of those cards tonight, he suddenly remembered, but he didn't feel like it now. I can't deal with it, he said to himself. I'm too drunk and I'd screw up all the zip codes.

Besides, Rudi wants to have this fucking New Year's Eve party at the house and I don't know which cards are supposed to get enclosures because we never got around to talking about who to invite. Rudi just waved his hands and grandly said to invite everybody, but I know he doesn't mean it. It's not one of his usual little get-togethers, because he wants to upstage Mario's opening that same night and he wants the crème de la crème de la crème.

Privately, although it would have given him great pleasure, Chuck didn't think Rudi would be putting much of a damper on Mario's big party. He thought they were going to get stuck with the leftovers, the second-raters, the — what did they call them in 'seventies novels about Hollywood? — the B Group. Everybody who was anybody was trying to get on Mario's guest list, if he could believe the gossip he heard and the columns he read: the hottest ticket in town, they called it. He wondered briefly if Maggie was going, if she was on the list. He'd meant to ask her tonight but then he'd forgotten when he saw Frances McKinnon. Anyway, Rudi had actually been invited. Chuck had seen the invitation with Mario's handwritten note on it — "Bury the hatchet?" it had asked — before Rudi threw it into the fire. He thought Rudi would have been smarter to accept: send a big, ostentatious bunch of flowers, show up there and smile like an uncle and pretend he was proud of his young protégé. But that wasn't Rudi's style, and so they were going to have this party for a bunch of people who'd rather be somewhere else. He dreaded it.

20

MARIO THOUGHT the big closed van, sparkling white with discreet black lettering that simply said *Tables* on the driver's door, was beautiful. The paint job had just been finished the day before, and now he was driving it for the first time. The signals on Second Avenue were synchronized, there was very little traffic, and he cruised along without taking his foot off the gas pedal. It was four in the morning and he'd only slept a couple of hours, but he was refreshed and excited. The city was exactly the same as it was at four o'clock when he approached it from the night before, rolling in from a party or a club, but it *seemed* different, and he had the smug, self-righteous feeling he always had when he got the jump on the day.

Louis was in the seat next to him, sipping a container of coffee and trying to wake up. He was on salary as of today, and this was the first thing he'd wanted to do, this trip out to the Hunt's Point Food Distribution Center, the vast wholesale produce market in the Bronx that serviced the whole city. Nearly every restaurant in New York had its fruits and vegetables delivered, but Louis had worked for years in a French town where such middlemen were unheard of, where chefs automatically went to the market themselves early every morning. He'd always been frustrated by his dependence on whatever the suppliers brought to the back door, and Mario had made him very happy by agreeing to buy a van so Louis and his sous-chefs could shop personally. They'd rotate, each of them taking a week at a time, so they could have the pick of whatever was available, the freshest of the fresh. It wasn't really necessary for Mario to make this reconnaissance trip with him, but he always found Hunt's Point fascinating and he wanted to be involved with every detail of his dream.

Patrick, when Mario mentioned his plans to him, had immediately begged to come along, and they were on their way to pick him up now. He'd argued against it for a minute — this was business, after all, and Louis might think it was insultingly unprofessional for him to bring a friend — but Patrick had seemed so lost lately, so depressed, that he relented. As it turned out, Louis didn't mind at all.

"I won't distract the big boys, really I won't," Patrick had said. "I won't badger you with dumb questions, I pwomise. It's just that I love While The City Sleeps places, and I want to see where my rutabagas come from."

"Have you ever actually had a rutabaga in your possession?"

"No, and I don't even know what they look like, but I always liked the sound of the word. I'm a writer."

After they collected him, they got on the FDR Drive to follow the East River up to the Triborough Bridge and on into the Bronx. Patrick, sitting on the floor in the back, was quiet the whole way, but when they left the highway he crawled up to squat in the space between the two seats so he could see out. To get to the market, they had to bump along over potholes and railroad tracks, through dark streets that were cluttered with abandoned cars and sprinkled with broken glass. Half the buildings were burned out, and the only businesses seemed to be salvage yards and ironworks. As they got closer to the market, there was a heavy garbage smell and, overlying it, a stench from the water beyond that Louis said was the corpse of the river itself. Patrick looked at him with respect, but then his head was turned by the hookers who were lounging against parked cars and under the few lampposts that still had bulbs, pursing their lips in kisses, calling out to the truckdrivers. Most of them were women, but a few were transvestites or — it was an expression that always made Mario shudder — preoperative transsexuals. At an intersection, while they waited for a big diesel to lumber past, one of the genuine women poked her head in the window and suggested a group rate. She was fortyish and beer-bellied, with breath that made the river smell sweet. Mario shook his head sadly.

Patrick spoke for the first time. "Irma La Douce she wasn't." A minute later, they came to the gatehouse and they could see the big, ugly cinder-block buildings of the market. "And Les Halles it ain't," he added.

"Les Halles is not Les Halles anymore, anyway," Louis said. "It was moved to a *banlieu,* a suburb."

"And this? Did this all used to happen in Manhattan?" Patrick asked.

"Washington Market, it was called," Mario answered, because Louis didn't seem to know. "Over on the West Side. Till they built this in the late 'sixties." It was hard to imagine how anything this big could have been jammed into a few narrow city streets. The buildings here were arranged like the four tines of a fork, stretching a quarter of a mile out from a block of offices at the far end. On both sides of them were hundreds of trucks and vans — nuzzling up to them like nursing piglets, Patrick said.

There were a few suppliers Louis wanted to make a point of seeing, but they decided to make a complete tour of all four wings. The buildings were composed of a series of high-ceilinged storerooms that opened onto broad covered porches running along their entire lengths, where sample crates were set out and where all the action was. Bosses — almost all of them Jewish or Italian — sat in glassed-in booths with their cashiers. Louis led the way along a floor that was slippery with flattened fruits and vegetables, stooping to pinch and sniff. Mario was close behind him, and Patrick wandered along in their wake. By now it was five o'clock, and the market was at the height of its frenzy. Everybody seemed to be yelling at once, trucks roared in and out of spaces, forklifts and hand dollies created constant traffic jams along the aisles. Reading the lettering on the trucks and vans, Mario was struck, once again, by the obvious fact that — even though he always thought of Hunt's Point as the ultimate source — only half of them were taking food away from here, and the other half were bringing it in. There were trucks unloading tomatoes from California and apples from Washington, others pulling containers lifted off ships and trains, still others with smaller containers from what seemed like every airline in the world.

He could hear Patrick behind him, excusing himself every time he bumped into someone, which seemed to average about twice a minute, happily chanting the messages he read on the sides of crates. "Belgian endive and New Zealand kiwis," Mario heard him say, as if it were a line of poetry. "Nova Scotian blueberries. English shallots. Haitian mangoes. Italian radicchio from Verona." Every so often, Mario would turn to find him standing at the entrance to one of the refrigerated storerooms where tons of potatoes were stacked on shelves that ran two stories high, their red mesh bags creating a shimmer of color under the naked light bulbs. In other rooms were turnips in purple mesh or cabbages in green mesh.

Louis stopped for a long time at a specialty wholesaler's that displayed exotic mushrooms from a California hothouse. "Lobster," he said, holding up a bright orange-red clump to show Mario. "Tastes a little like that when it's cooked in butter." Then he held up a bright yellow one. "Canary, tastes like eggs."

He was most excited, farther along, by a sign for Heirloom Seeds. Under his breath, Patrick said to Mario that it sounded like a sperm bank, but he listened politely to Louis's lecture, which was really for his sake because Mario already know about them. "It means these are old-fashioned varieties," he said. "They are not so — what is the word? — durable, so they are much more expensive. And not so pretty, but the *taste*." He kissed his fingers in a classic French gesture that made Patrick laugh. "Sweet dumpling squash," he crowed, holding up something with green stripes that looked like a miniature pumpkin. "Yellow pear tomatoes. Golden raspberries — they are sweeter. And this." He cradled an oval melon lovingly in his hands like a baby. "This is the Stutz Supreme Melon, which has — oh, an *incroyable* taste, like flowers."

They took a break halfway along, just as the sun came up and the planes from La Guardia began to take off above them. Louis was so happy he didn't seem to notice the dishwater coffee or the depressing canteen where they drank it.

"I repeat," Patrick said.

"I know," Louis said sympathetically. "It is not Les Halles. No *soupe à l'oignon*. But this place, this market." He turned to Mario. "There is so much more than a year ago. The hair-looms."

"There's a meat market out here too? I saw signs," Patrick said.

"There is, but the one in Manhattan is bigger," Mario explained. "The Gansevoort Market, over on West Fourteenth."

"And someone has to shop there every day, too?"

"No," Louis said. "It is not necessary. We know — I know — the best for pork or veal or beef. And the same for fish. They deliver, but maybe once a week I or a sous-chef or the *rôtisseur* will visit them."

Patrick had more questions, intelligent questions that Louis didn't mind answering, and Mario sat back, sipped his dishwater, and relaxed. He'd been spending so much time interviewing waiters, worrying about the air-conditioning ducts and the decoration of the elevators, that he'd had moments of panic in the past few days. It wouldn't do much good to have the most beautiful place in New York if there was no food coming out of the kitchen. Now that his chef was on board, smiling, happy and confident, Mario knew he was going to be opening a restaurant.

Back in the city, after they dropped off Louis, Mario and Patrick went for breakfast at a diner where they could park the van. Patrick was full of questions — so full that Mario knew he didn't want to talk about himself. How were things with Frances? How was the kitchen at Tables shaping up? How did his last trip to Boston go? Did his mother know him this time? And, finally, a question that fascinated Patrick, was she still fixated on the same subject?

Yes, she was. The last few times he'd been there, she'd told the same story to him, almost gleefully, proud because it had been such a good trick, because the secret had been kept so closely, because no one in the neighborhood ever guessed. She'd gone for a few months to visit a great-aunt in Italy and she'd come back with Mario. So far as the North End knew, she was pregnant before she left, and then she'd been so sick, so fragile, that she'd decided to stay on in Naples and have the child there. In fact, she told Mario, laughing — as if she weren't talking about *him* — he'd been born right here in Boston just before she returned. A deal had been worked out, the people involved were very powerful, papers were forged, money passed hands, money that they'd used to expand the little storefront restaurant. At this point in the story, she always looked directly into his eyes and he couldn't pretend she wasn't aware of him. She would say, very earnestly and, he supposed, truthfully, that they had *wanted* him, that he should never, ever, think they hadn't wanted him and loved him. Johnny hadn't been born until she was thirty, he'd been a very difficult birth, she was told she shouldn't try to have more children. And then they'd been given their beautiful Principe, and wasn't it lucky? Even though Johnny was gone, they still had a son. That was the point at which Mario couldn't listen to any more, and he'd get up to pour a glass of water for her or find a reason to call the nurse.

He'd been shocked when she first told him, two or three months ago, but he was used to the idea now and he never thought about it until his mother forced him to listen to the story again. This was the family he'd been dealt, whether he was literally born into it or not. It made it easier, in a way: he had never felt very guilty about ignoring them but now he had an even cleaner conscience. They should have told him before, he supposed, but he knew he hadn't given them any openings for that kind of talk, not since he was sixteen. He'd confided only in Maggie and Patrick — well, in Frances now, too. Maggie had laughed and said it sounded like a plot twist in a badly written soap opera; Patrick thought it was like something out of Thackeray or Dickens. They were both far more interested than he was about who his *real* parents were. If his mother had told him when he was younger, he might have tried to find them, even though she said it wouldn't be possible. Now he simply didn't care; it didn't have anything to do with who he was; and he found himself getting a little irritated with Patrick as he went on and on, spinning elaborate theories. He finally told him to shut the fuck up about it.

* * *

Frances yawned, stretched luxuriously, awake but still sleepy, and leaned over to the phone to ask Marianne to bring up her breakfast. She'd given herself the present of this rare morning off but now she'd slept much later than she'd intended — it was almost ten — and she was ashamed because she'd meant to spend a couple of hours poring through catalogues from auction houses and antique dealers before her exercise man came at ten-thirty. Then the masseuse would be here at eleven, and she'd have to rush to bathe and dress and meet Dorothy for lunch at twelve-thirty. She decided not to regret the extra sleep; she decided she needed it.

She'd been foolish, she now realized, to think that finishing Trish's boutique was going to give her more breathing room. The combination of the restaurant and Carole's apartment and Trish's Seventh Avenue showroom had kept her on the run, day after long day and on into the evening. Tables had priority, naturally, because there was an absolute deadline — just a little over two weeks, she reminded herself. If there were no problems — no major ones, that is; there were bound to be thousands of minor ones — she thought they'd squeak by, barely, and then she could devote all her time to Carole and Trish after New Year's. Her schedule on top of Mario's — *squared* with Mario's, really — had allowed for only a few extra hours to spend together at the house since Thanksgiving. That wasn't enough, not nearly enough, and from now on it was going to be even harder, if not impossible, to arrange more time. They'd been planning to meet there yesterday, and then at the last minute she ended up having to cancel because of a disaster with Carole's floors.

Marianne always brought her a minimal breakfast — dry toast, coffee, and fresh orange juice — on the three mornings a week she exercised, and because she was eating so much closer to the time than usual today, she didn't even bother with the toast as she went through her mail. It seemed to be the height of the Christmas card deluge, and she remembered once again that she was going to have to find time — but when? — to sit down with Ham's secretary and send out theirs. She glanced quickly at what seemed to be an incredible number of invitations and announcements of openings of one kind or another, requests for donations to charities or political campaigns, and she put them all aside to stuff in her briefcase and look at later in the day.

The stack of Christmas cards made her wonder, once again, what she could possibly give Mario, assuming she found time to shop for anything at all. The problem was that this affair, this whatever it was, had a very short history. Yes, of course, she felt she'd always known him, that she understood him in a way no one else ever had, but actually they'd only been seeing each other for two months. She wanted to buy him something lavish and beautiful — sapphire cuff links and studs, maybe, or a fur-lined overcoat — but she knew it would be wrong. He couldn't afford that kind of extravagance and it would only end up embarrassing both of them. But what, then? Art of some kind would be the best idea. For Hamilton, for his dressing room, she'd already found a little pen-and-ink caricature, a man being fitted for shoes (unsigned, but she was positive it was Daumier and that he never would have seen it). But she wasn't at all sure about Mario's taste. She knew he *had* taste, but they couldn't go to galleries or museums together because they'd be recognized, and so she couldn't really see things through his eyes, the way she could with Ham or Trish or Frederick. And dammit, she wasn't even allowed to visit his apartment, so she couldn't pick up any clues that way.

It was a strange, upsetting idea to her, somehow, the thought of Christmas and Mario. Christmas was family: Hamilton's family, of course, since there were no Lambettis anymore except Frances, but family nonetheless. Even this lunch today had become one of the McKinnon traditions, an event Dorothy decided years ago was a sweet thing to do, just the two sisters-in-law for their own little celebration in the middle of the holiday whirl. She didn't know where a lover fit in. She'd almost taken a little tree over to the house, set it up in the bedroom, and decorated it, but then she thought there might be something sad about that. She only knew she had to have some time with him at some point soon. She'd hang some mistletoe over the door to their bedroom, she decided, something they could call their own Christmas.

How hard it's been lately to concentrate, she thought. Even when you're working on *his* project, worrying about all the details for *his* restaurant, all you really want to do is sit around and moon about him like a lovesick teenager. She asked herself, for the hundredth time, how it looked to people, what the world she knew so well, in which she moved so easily, was saying. When she was with Mario alone, physically next to him or entwined with him, it seemed *right*. They belonged together, they deserved each other in every sense, and there was — well, almost — no doubt in her mind. And, even though they were discreet, she didn't really concern herself much with what contractors or cabbies or plumbers might be thinking. But friends, friends of friends, everyone who knew her as Mrs.

Hamilton McKinnon — it mattered to her, in spite of herself, what their opinion of her was, if they whispered to each other that she was robbing the cradle, that he was using her, that she was using him. There hadn't been any awkwardness yet because she never went anywhere with Mario where they'd be likely to run into any of that crowd, but she knew there must be gossip by now.

Eighteen years younger — you couldn't get around it. There were certain events everybody her age remembered. Mario hadn't even been born yet when Kennedy was elected . . . probably ran around with machine guns that squirted water when Vietnam was happening . . . wouldn't have understood all the fuss about Watergate. . . . She was only torturing herself, she knew, playing variations on the same theme over and over again, like calculating how old she'd be when he was her age and trying to imagine herself at sixty-five — and starting to collect Social Security checks! She always ended up resolving to try to forget it. It certainly isn't going to go away, she told herself. I'm always going to be eighteen years older than this man I'm so much in love with.

Of course, Ham was twelve years older than she, but that didn't seem to matter as much as this other. Yes, everyone thought it was *okay* for men to be older but not for women to be older, and that was part of it, but her marriage, what she had with Hamilton, had nothing to do with age because . . . Well, because what she felt for him wasn't so physical. Now she was getting into the waters she tried to avoid. Hamilton. Hamilton and Mario. Hamilton *or* Mario? No. Mostly, when she was with one or the other or when she was simply working hard, she managed to keep them in separate, watertight compartments. They were different people; she could tell herself they represented different parts of her life. They even complemented one another, she could say. She loved Hamilton dearly. She loved Mario . . . what? Desperately. That's a lovely couple of adjectives to play around with, Francesca, she said to herself now. Dear and desperate. Like the title of a really terrible book, like . . .

The truth was, she was determined to have them both. Hamilton was the very foundation of everything important to her. Well, no, she had to admit, obviously not *everything* important to her. Mario, when she was in his arms, was as essential as all the world she shared with Hamilton. There were moments when she was totally lost in him, when *he* was everything and there was nothing else. And — now that the word had come into her mind, she couldn't get rid of it — Mario was "dear" too. He was someone; he was an intelligent, sensitive, imaginative man and there was nothing embarrassing about falling in love with him.

Except. She was being unfaithful to Hamilton, of course. There was no getting past that. She was an unfaithful wife and that was shameful. She wasn't Lady Chatterley; Hamilton wasn't paralyzed, in a wheelchair; she didn't, in the eyes of the world, have a whisper of an excuse. She could rationalize and rearrange and adjust and compromise to her heart's delight, but the fact remained. She was doing something that would hurt Hamilton horribly and that was the last thing she ever, ever wanted to do, and she absolutely couldn't stop this, now that she'd begun. That was all she was ever able to tell herself, at these times when she couldn't keep it all nice and tidy in her mind, that she couldn't help herself.

She heard the doorbell, heard Marianne go to answer it, and knew it must be Lou, her exercise coach, or dance teacher or physical guru or whatever she was supposed to call him — in fifteen years, she'd never known. She jumped out of bed, quickly pulled on a sweatshirt and sweat pants, and ran down the hall to meet him in the room she'd converted from a guest bedroom by laying down rubber matting and lining the walls with mirrors. In all the time he'd been coming here, they'd never spoken about anything but muscles and tendons and fat, but she was always glad to see him and she had to assume he liked her because he had a reputation for being very choosy with his clients. Most of the women she knew tried new disciplines every few months, the latest machines in the latest gyms or the most fashionable private coach or the newest videocassettes, but she'd always been loyal to this stony-faced black man whose body reminded her of athletes on early Greek vases, the same exaggerated shoulders and tiny waist and high buttocks. Lou never bored her; he brought a different tape cassette every time — it might be Gershwin or Donna Summer or David Byrne — and he put her through totally different combinations of dance and calisthenics. Today it was rap songs, and she felt like a sassy black chick as she followed the movements that were so carefully calculated to exhaust her by the end of the half-hour session.

She staggered back down the hall to her dressing room, where her masseuse was waiting with the table already set up. She'd had a man for this at one point, but he'd begun to linger a little too long on her inner thighs and she'd found this nice, middle-aged Cuban woman, Rita, instead. Today, for the tenth time in the past couple of months, Rita exclaimed at how wonderful her skin tone seemed to be, how glowing! such health! Frances, for the tenth time, blushed and said she couldn't imagine what was causing it. She knew perfectly well it was because of Mario — because of what she *did* with Mario — and she suspected that Rita guessed something like that.

Afterward, every part of her stretched and oiled and pounded back into place, feeling like a gladiator, she relaxed in a hot bath. Then, wrapped in a towel and back in the dressing room again, she had the moment of doubt she always had when she was seeing the family — never with Freddie, of course, but with any of the other in-laws — about what to wear. Frances had feared and hated her mother-in-law for so many years when she was alive, and Dorothy still had a little power, as Sarah's daughter, to make Frances feel gauche or tasteless when in fact she knew — and *Women's Wear* seemed to bear her out, for what that was worth — that she had an odd, original taste of her own. She decided on a ruthlessly simple navy blue A-line skirt, a plain white silk blouse, and the little frogged Adolfo jacket she couldn't even remember buying — which she'd never liked, in fact — but which Dorothy had openly admired once. And pearls.

When she found her sister-in-law in the crowded dining room of her club, she knew immediately that she didn't need to worry about what she was wearing. She was only five minutes late, but Dorothy was well into a glass of white wine and it was obvious there was some other substance — or more than one? — in her system already. Dorothy rattled on and on about her bridge, her new little granddaughter, her plans for the holidays, and Frances had no trouble keeping up her end of the conversation with smiles and interested murmurs. She'd never seen Dorothy so . . . fuzzy. Garrulous, but fuzzy. She realized things must have gotten out of hand, and she decided on the spot to talk with Hamilton about it, but there was certainly nothing she could do in the meantime. She picked at a shrimp salad and stared out at the other women lunching in the big, noisy room. This club on Madison Avenue in the Sixties, for which Dorothy's mother had probably signed her up the minute she was born, was originally open only to *Social Register* ladies, but the membership committee was marginally more liberal now. Dorothy told her they expected at any minute to be invaded by men claiming their equal rights, just as women had stormed the walls of some of the more exclusive men's clubs, but Frances privately couldn't imagine why any man would bother. She knew some of these women today, McKinnon family friends, other patrons of the Modern, patrons of the American Ballet Theatre, patrons of the Metropolitan Opera: patrons, patrons, patrons. Almost none of them worked; it wasn't that kind of club and they weren't that kind of women.

How many of them had heard she was seeing Mario? She knew it would at least be a juicy bit of gossip for them to chew on. She looked younger than most of them, even the ones who had a few years on her, and it occurred to her that any spite they might have would be flavored with envy, even if they'd sooner die than admit it. There was a table near her, four matronly Republican ladies, and she knew them all. They were in the set that old Sarah had tried to force her into when she was first married, postdebs, young wives of lawyers, bankers, heirs. My God! Frances thought, they're only five years older than I am, ten at the most, and I'll bet they're all grandmothers by now.

Dorothy had strayed onto the subject of bridge, about which Frances knew next to nothing and cared less, but she brought herself sharply back to attention when she heard her mention Rudi Kranovic. ". . . so hard on him," Dorothy was saying. "He's such a brilliant man, and he can't seem to keep his mind on his cards these days." I wonder, Dorothy, Frances thought, if you're even able to arrange the suits in your hand, *these days*. ". . . and he says he's having such trouble at the restaurant because that young man who used to work for him — what's his name? Mario Something, Italian — anyway, he left poor Rudi completely in the lurch. Walked out without any explanation one night."

"Mario Fermi. And that isn't the way I heard it, actually." Frances speared a fat shrimp and washed it down with the mediocre white Bordeaux. "I'm sure I've told you I know Mario, that I'm designing his new place. Haven't I?"

Dorothy's eyes were crafty now. "Oh, of course you have. Well, I could so easily be wrong. Maybe it's just Rudi's silly old sour grapes. I'm sure you have the — whatchamacallit — the inside story. . . ."

Frances didn't blink. "I think it's so sweet, Dorothy," she said carefully, "that you've made such good friends through your bridge playing. They must be a comfort, all those nice men you play with, aren't they? And so few of them are married or even have girlfriends, so they must have lots of time for cards and I'm sure they adore you. But not in any way that would have made Spence jealous, of course."

Dorothy abruptly raised her hand to signal for more wine. When she began her monologue again, she changed the subject to her daughter's problems with breast-feeding the new baby.

That was unnecessarily bitchy of you, Frances said to herself. Dorothy would never have come out and said it, but you just didn't want to listen to any more dripping innuendos, did you? You know you couldn't care less if Dorothy makes herself an absolutely permanent *pillar* of gay society, but you know all those men she sees are a sensitive point for her because Spence hasn't been dead so very long, and he would have hated it and all you had to do was remind her. Anyway, I was just wondering this morning if people were beginning to gossip, and now I know she knows, and it was obviously Rudi who told her — with great relish, no doubt.

Frances was nearly positive, though — as positive, she had suddenly seen today, as anyone could be about what Dorothy might do nowadays — that she'd keep quiet about it. She'd wanted to make her sister-in-law uncomfortable and she'd wanted to see if it was true, but she wouldn't talk about it with any of her friends — either these ladies who were lunching here today or her gay bridge partners — because she was a McKinnon and if there was a scandal in the offing, then McKinnons must close their ranks and protect the family name. Most important, she wouldn't tell Hamilton. Partly because she couldn't be sure, partly because she'd be afraid of his anger, but mostly (and Frances had to force herself to admit this) because she was fundamentally a decent woman and even if she had never liked her younger sister-in-law, she'd think it was wrong to tell tales about her. That, at least, was what Frances hoped.

21

UNTIL THE WORKMEN finished his office, which ought to be only another three or four days, Mario was using a table in one of the private dining rooms. The hinged walls, cleverly designed by Frances to divide it into smaller rooms, were flattened against the side today, and down at the other end all his captains, waiters, waitresses, and bartenders were in their second day of a week-long course that the wine steward was conducting.

Wine stewardess, actually, but that sounded like a flight attendant, so everyone just called her the *sommelière*. Priscilla Del Bosque was young, enthusiastic, and knowledgeable, and now, listening to the way she was patiently taking her class through the ropes, he knew he'd been right to take a chance on her. Her parents had a small but prestigious winery in the Napa Valley, so she'd grown up knowing how different soils affected Pinot Noir grapes, how oak casks were better for Cabernet Sauvignon than redwood. In a very short time, using his hope chest in Brooklyn as a basis for it, she'd put together a brilliant, imaginative collection that combined obvious classics with fascinating unknowns. There were going to be two lists. One would be printed on the back of every day's menu, and it would have about a hundred choices that could be kept in a small room behind the kitchen and replenished every day. The complete list had more than five hundred selections; requesting it would automatically bring Priscilla or her assistant to the table to advise; and those bottles could be brought up in the freight elevator from the storerooms in the basement. The entire inventory was already down there, a quarter of a million dollars' worth. The bottles were resting, she'd said tenderly, settling in after their travels.

The top kitchen people, the captains, and the head bartender had all been on salary as soon as he could get them. As of yesterday, the whole rest of the staff was here. Even the busboys and the dishwashers, who didn't have that much to do right now, could run errands and help move supplies. He wanted a team in which they all knew each other and understood precisely what had to be done, and this wine course was part of that. They'd taste everything on the short list, and she'd see to it that their pronunciation of Gewürztraminer and Hermitage was correct, that they brought the right glasses, that their opening and pouring were impeccable, that they could make suggestions but that they would never insist. She didn't expect them to know much about vintages or *grands crus* or *climats* — that was her job. Next week, Louis would be doing the same thing with the menu.

At the moment, Mario was listening to her field questions, some of them intelligent and some of them amazingly ignorant. No, most champagne was at its best in six to ten years, and only a few aged well after that. Beaujolais was sometimes better after the first year, but never more than two years. Rhône wines should be chilled, never iced. Johannisberg Riesling had nothing to do with South Africa. Again and again, she reminded them that the customers were always right, that if they asked for a heavy Burgundy with a delicate fish, it wasn't the waiter's job to correct them.

Another example of things being taken out of my hands, Mario thought. He'd made the basic decisions; laid the ground rules; hired the best people he could find and set them in motion; delegated authority the way he was supposed to be doing; and now they were all beginning to function on their own. For a moment, he could pretend he wasn't necessary anymore, like a midwife after the baby was born, but he knew it was an illusion: the baby wasn't born yet. Maybe this is the calm before the storm, he thought, or the eye of the hurricane or something. He reminded himself that it was D-Day minus twelve, his stomach turned over, and he started to move.

He got up and walked back to Lillian's office. He'd made sure her space came before his own in the construction schedule — it was partly a way of thanking her for her loyalty, but it was also important for her to have a calm refuge. A bookkeeper, a full-time secretary, and two temps to help during the final push were working outside her door, but it was this office, of which she was touchingly proud, that was the nerve center of the whole operation. Frances had become very fond of Lillian, and she'd spent extra time helping her furnish it with a graceful fruitwood desk, soft blue drapes and carpeting, Audubon reproductions, and violets growing on the windowsill in Victorian pots.

She was at the keyboard of the computer terminal that sat on the end of her desk, peering at the screen and talking gently to it. Mario had sent her to the New School for a crash computer course. She'd resisted; she'd talked about old dogs and new tricks; now she was as fanatic as a born-again Christian. She'd worked up programs for payroll, for inventory, for credit card billings, for the wine list, for reservations; everything that could possibly be run through what she called Baby had been fed into it. Her conversation was peppered with rams and megabytes, soft disks and hard drives, most of which was beyond Mario. He couldn't resist teasing her about it sometimes.

"I'd like the latest printout on the toilet paper consumption in the employees' bathrooms, please," he said today. "And make it snappy. On both a weekly and a daily basis. And projections for the fiscal year."

"Nobody likes a smart aleck." She glared up at him from over the half-glasses she'd taken to wearing. "What Baby and I *will* give you, if you talk nice, is the final guest list."

That was what he'd come in to see. The invitations had respectfully asked for a reply by December fifteenth, four days ago, and now the list was complete; now they had to arrange the seating. Mario had decided to throw a sit-down dinner party for two hundred and fifty, with a shortened menu and wine list that would give a good idea of Tables' range. A lavish buffet would have been much easier, far less expensive, and perfectly acceptable, but he wanted it this way. Cocktails would be served at the bar, in the foyer, and in the private rooms, then dinner at tables for four, six, or eight — no deuces that night. People could dance to the little quartet he was having for the evening; they could table-hop; they could sit wherever they liked after dessert; but they'd have to eat where he put them. He wasn't going to make any exceptions, he wouldn't allow any last-minute place card switching, so he had to be sure in advance that he had the right mixture for every table. On extra-wide paper, Lillian had programmed a seating chart with numbers that referred to names on the list, and he sat down across from her to look it over while she continued her conversation with Baby. Because his back was to the door, he knew someone had appeared behind him only by Lillian's little gasp, by the surprise on her face. He turned around and there was Maggie, standing hesitantly.

"Don't you look swell!" Lillian said. "And you've lost weight." She stood up, recovering faster than Mario, coming around her desk and drawing her into the room.

He hadn't seen her for six weeks, not since that last, ugly scene at the Four Seasons; there hadn't even been a phone call. Ordinarily, he'd be certain to run into her at an opening or a party or a club, but he hadn't been on any of those circuits because he'd either been here or with Frances. He didn't think she looked great at all. She must have lost twenty pounds and she hadn't needed to lose any. Her eyes were too bright, and under them, not quite covered over by more makeup than she used to apply, were the dark smudges that coke always painted in.

"Thanks. You look great, too." Maggie held her at arm's length and looked her up and down. "Your hairdo's very becoming, and so's the new corporate look." At about the same time she became computer-savvy, Lillian had cropped her hair short and bought some simple, tailored suits, plain white blouses, and sensible shoes. The contrast — her hair was still hennaed, her lips and nails were still cherry-red, her scent was still Jungle Gardenia — was startling.

"I was literally in the neighborhood," Maggie explained, kissing Mario on the cheek and talking very fast in a voice that was as shaky as the hand that had settled on his arm for an instant. "Across the square at the Arts Club and I thought maybe I could have a quick sneak preview 'cause I won't be able to come to the party."

"I saw your note," he said haltingly. "And I was sorry." He was sorry for more than that, of course. Sorry for what he'd done to her. Sorry she was lying — he'd walked past the Arts Club this morning and noticed it was closed for renovation. Sorry she must have felt she could come only when Frances was gone — the board of the Foundation was announcing McKinnon Grant recipients at a luncheon today and Maggie would have known about it, would have assumed Frances had to be there. Now, he suddenly wanted to take her in his arms and tell her how glad he was to see her, how everything was going to be all right even if it wasn't. He wanted to sit down and talk, but he didn't know what he'd say and he was afraid he'd end up trying to excuse himself again for something that was inexcusable.

"Listen," Lillian said. "This is the only quiet spot in the whole place these days. You kids stay here and talk while I go check on the booze in the cellar." She grabbed some papers — the guest list, Mario noticed, which wasn't going to do her much good in the cellar. They stared at her for a moment, neither of them willing to say yes or no. It was Maggie who decided.

"That's sweet, Lillian, thanks, but I can't stay long and I thought I'd just ask the boss man to give me a whirlwind tour. Mario?"

"Sure. Sure thing." If that was the way she wanted it, then he'd go along. She seemed so close to a breakdown, an explosion, that he'd try to do whatever he could to make this easier. He took her arm and led her back through the kitchen and out onto the bar level, where they stood and looked down on the big main space. The workmen, about twenty of them, were taking a break, munching on the ham sandwiches the kitchen provided. It wasn't really up to him to feed them, but he didn't want them going out for lunch and getting back late or stopping for a beer or a joint.

"Everything depends on everything else," he said. "They can't put up the glass dividers till the carpet's laid. They can't lay the carpet till the false ceiling's finished. They can't hang the ceiling till the air purifying system is up and running. The air purifiers got here late because there was a strike at the factory in Ohio."

"But you'll make it?"

"Yeah, by paying a fortune in double time and triple time, but I allowed for most of it in the budget. The kitchen's completely done except for my office — well, you saw."

"It's very beautiful. Already. It's elegant and witty and I loved it as soon as I got in the elevator — Japanese scrolls and an Op Art carpet. Your . . . Frances has done a brilliant job, and I should be the last person to admit it."

"Maggie, don't . . ."

"I won't. I'm not." She shook her head and started to ask questions, one after another, hardly waiting for his answer before coming up with the next. He found himself talking faster just to keep up with her, to get a word or two in. "Those things over there, they're for the ceiling? The false ceiling, rather?" She pointed to the big panels that leaned against the wall like canvases in an artist's studio, ranging in size from four feet across to about six by nine.

He explained that they were pieces of acoustical material, over which heavy flannel had been stretched. They were all geometric forms: three of each form but each a different size: squares and circles and rectangles and triangles and diamonds and rhombuses and some others Mario couldn't name. At the moment, down here, they looked a little silly, a little arbitrary, but Frances's mock-up of their arrangement had convinced him that it was going to be fascinating. Each was a different color, but all the shades were in the same depth of tone — not pastel, not muddy, but slightly muted.

"To absorb sound?" she asked.

"Yes. And to look pretty. They'll be suspended about six feet down — far enough so none of the ducts along the ceiling will show — in a kind of geometric jigsaw, about five inches apart. And the air conditioning and heating will shoot out from between them."

"And then everything else is pale? If those guys would get their fat asses off the rolls of carpet I could peek at it. What color is it? Same as the drapes?"

"No, not so gray. A kind of pale taupe with a little green. And then the glass panels on the edge of each level, they've got a touch of green too — tempered, like windshields." He wanted to tell her to keep her voice lower, that he badly needed to keep these men happy, that they worked hard, that their lunch hour was well deserved, but he was afraid that might lead her to another comment, maybe louder. He'd seen her edgy, of course, even before she started doing this fucking coke — at openings, for instance. But he'd never, ever, heard her make cracks, audibly, crudely, about people she'd never met, people who'd done nothing to her. It was as if he didn't know her anymore.

"Well. It's inspired. It really is — this coat-of-many-colors ceiling, then about six shades of neutral, and then . . ."

"Then the *coup de résistance,* of course. The things from whence we've taken our name. The tables. I'm afraid all the different sets of chairs are being collected in a warehouse, and the tables themselves — well, they're just tables. But the cloths and the napkins are *exactly* those colors up there in heaven, except they're the next tone or two *up*. Up? Anyway, more intense. Dazzling, I hope, when the whole room's scattered with them."

She spun around and waved to the stepped-up pyramid that echoed the one on top of the building itself, surrounded on all four sides by the bartenders' workspace and then by the counter. "I love that thing too, whatever it is."

"It's from a ship, the *Ansonia,* from the 'thirties. It was a sort of centerpiece in the first-class dining room — you know, for displaying desserts and flowers and things. Frances found it. . . ."

She broke in. "But now you have to tell me how to find the john."

"Off the lobby, on the right. Etched glass door. Mermaid. Also from the *Ansonia,* as a matter of fact."

She was gone only for a minute. When she came back to him, she was prepared with another question, something about the pyramid. He didn't listen. He'd realized again, when she crossed the room, how much weight she'd lost. Now her eyes were even brighter than before, which didn't seem possible. She was sniffling slightly.

"Lillian's right, Mag, you're a lot thinner," he said carefully.

"Oh . . . willpower, thanks. Hard work. Maybe just a soupçon of unhappiness." She brought a Blistik tube out of her purse and applied it.

He registered another classic sign, chronically dry lips. "You're doing a lot of coke, aren't you? A whole lot more than before?"

"And? If I am?" She backed away a couple of feet but she looked straight at him, her hands on her hips.

"Then . . . shit!" His voice was sad. "We always said it was for people who were bored with themselves."

"*We* said a lot of things. *We've* had to rethink some of them."

"But I hate to see you . . ."

"Excuse me!" she interrupted. Her voice was carrying across the room now and he could sense the workmen listening. "I'm not sure you *ever* had the right to tell me what I ought to do, but I'm pretty goddamn positive you've got no right at all now. None. Whatsoever."

"I care about you. I care about what happens to you," he said simply.

It was as if he'd slapped her. Her face crumbled and when she spoke, he could barely hear the words. All the anger was gone, replaced by weariness and sadness. "I'm sorry. I shouldn't have come here. Itchin' for a fight." She gave a low laugh and came and took his arm. "Show me the way to get out of here?"

He walked her to the elevator and they were silent until it came. Then she kissed him — on the mouth, this time, but just for an instant — and she wished him good luck. He stood there for a minute after the doors slid soundlessly together. He wondered when he'd see her again. He wondered if she'd ever forgive him. He wondered if he'd ever forgive himself.

* * *

I'm not doing anything wrong, Chuck was thinking, although he jumped guiltily whenever a car went by in the nighttime streets or when he heard footsteps on the sidewalk. He was up in Rudi's study, and he was searching very thoroughly through everything in the bookcases, in the desk, and in the file cabinets, careful to leave things exactly as he found them. For the past three weeks, since the day he'd found him up here making a note of what Dorothy had been telling them, he'd wanted to see what had become of it, see if there might even be more of the same. He'd thought about this the night of the thing at Bloomingdale's — Rudi had been gone that night, too — but he'd been lonely, he'd gotten drunk, and he'd stayed at Maggie's. This was the first time he'd been both sober and positive of having the house to himself, sure that Rudi wouldn't come back from the restaurant unexpectedly. He was out in Bucks County for the night again with his precious horses. Those ponies better pay off, Rudi, he thought, because you sure as shit aren't paying much attention to the restaurant lately. Rudi had wanted him to come along, but he'd begged off with a nonexistent early morning lesson as his excuse.

It took him a long time to go through all the papers and books. He didn't really expect to find anything in them but he had to eliminate all the easy, accessible places first. It was mostly his instinct that told him there must be something to be found, but it was his memory of the way Rudi sometimes locked himself up here, the way he looked when he came out again, that told him it must be here, in this room, if it was anywhere.

He sat in the big leather chair behind the desk and swiveled around slowly, letting images from mystery novels and television shows float through his mind. Every so often, he got up and tested another idea. The drawers of the desk and the cabinets seemed to fit exactly, with no extra space left over for anything like a hidden compartment. There was no wall safe behind any of the paintings or prints. The built-in bookcases all seemed firmly attached and perfectly matched up, none of them liable to swing out and expose a tidy little niche in the wall. There was no wooden flooring with a subtle break in the pattern, only wall-to-wall carpeting that was firmly tacked down along every inch of its perimeter, with no patches or seams that could conceivably be pulled up. The bleached-oak paneling sounded exactly the same, wherever he tapped it. The fireplace would have been a good place — it was never used because there was a rather valuable Stubbs equestrian scene hanging over it — but he couldn't get any of the inside bricks to move. The mantel was a solid chunk of marble, the hearth a single slab of slate.

All right, he said to himself, so much for overworked plot devices. He'd have to rely on his own intelligence; he'd have to use what he knew about the man whose house he'd shared for two years. He fidgeted; he was getting stale. He badly wanted a drink, and he moved around the room restlessly. He'd been home from work for a couple of hours and he'd ordinarily have had three or four by now, but he wanted to keep his mind clear. Amazing what a powerful thing curiosity can be, he thought.

He decided to go down to the kitchen for a Perrier with lime and bitters, nonalcoholic but something to sip on. Coming out of the study, he startled both himself and the dogs, who were waiting outside when he opened the door. It was built to keep out even the loudest noises from the rest of the house and he hadn't heard them out there. When he came back, he stood in the doorway for a moment, trying to see the room with a fresh mind, trying to see it, to move into it, as Rudi would. Directly across from him, on the wall between the two windows, was the Modigliani oil that had been left to him. It was by far the most important painting, the most valuable, in the house, and Chuck had always been amazed that Rudi hadn't sold it. Maggie estimated once that it would fetch at least a million and a half at auction, and he knew that kind of money would come in very handy in Rudi's stables. He must have had stronger feelings for the old gossip queen than he ever admitted.

Gossip, he said to himself, turning the word over and over in his mind. That's really what we're dealing with here, isn't it? Larry Lengdorf built a career on it, made a fortune on it, enough to buy paintings like this one. By collecting information, by writing down little snippets on bits of paper, he supposed Rudi was carrying on a kind of family tradition. He gazed across the room to the woman in the portrait, a classic Modigliani figure with an impossibly long body and neck. She stared back vacantly, her eyes solid black ellipses, looking at him and through him, everywhere and nowhere.

Suddenly, he turned and put his hand on the door behind him. It must have something to do with the door, he was thinking. It must! The portrait was lined up with it so precisely that it seemed to be sightlessly directing him to it. Maybe there was no elaborate code, then, nothing worthy of a great thriller, just a small joke, a little bit of visual *à propos*. Maybe Rudi was playing a game, not only with himself but with Larry's ghost too. He held on to the edge of the door as he stood there. It was nearly four inches thick, painted glossy white on the outside but tufted with green leather, like the swinging door to the kitchen in an old-fashioned restaurant, on the inside. He prodded the dogs back into the hall and slammed it. He didn't think there would be any kind of mechanism along its edge; if there was some trick to it, it must be worked from the inside, once Rudi was safely locked in the room.

Shiny brass studs, nickel-sized, were sunk into the soft leather like belly buttons, six across, twenty or so down. He pushed at them methodically, starting at the upper left. By the time he came to the lower right, seven of them had made a small clicking sound, sinking in a little farther, but nothing happened. He sat back on his heels and thought. A maid who was cleaning them could have done this much by rubbing hard with brass polish, so there must be more to it. Beginning at the top again, holding his breath, he pulled instead of pushed, choosing only the studs that hadn't yielded the first time around. Six of them came out a quarter of an inch; the seventh one pulled out even farther. By tugging on it, he caused the whole panel to swing open.

Facing him, cut into the door itself, were rows of shallow racks, about an inch deep. They held loose-leaf manila file folders; videocassettes; rolls of sound tape and Super-8 film; and a small notebook, the one he'd seen Rudi writing in. He had imagined he might find some notes, some diaries, maybe a little pornography Rudi was too ashamed to leave around the house, but this, he told himself, laughing quietly, was a different kettle of fish, a whole 'nother ball game. He didn't touch anything until he'd poured himself a very tall vodka on the rocks and slowly brought it back upstairs, and then he sat down on the thick carpet and opened the lavender notebook.

It was the key to everything. The first half — twenty-three pages of tiny handwriting in lavender ink — was written by Larry Lengdorf, he was sure. Each page had a number at the top that referred to a tape or a film or a file of letters or photographs — glancing at the door, Chuck could see that everything was clearly labeled — and below that were brief notes. A name, some dates, the way it had come into his hands, a matter-of-fact account of whatever it was that would have shattered that particular one of twenty-three reputations, and that was it; that was as far as Larry seemed to have been willing to go. He'd either collected this dirt for its own sake, like the owner of a stolen Rembrandt who could never show it to anyone, or he'd applied it as leverage to find out things he could use legitimately in his column or on his TV show.

It was the second part of the book, written in Rudi's hand, that showed what the next step had been. It was immediately clear from the rows of figures that he'd chosen seven of those names and that, over the past few years, he'd been bleeding them regularly for significant chunks of money. At the very back of the book were other, newer pages (potential clients?), gossip he'd heard, notes to himself on how he might follow up, names of people who could be pressured or paid to furnish proof. He was beginning to realize that the man he lived with loved this crap *for its own sake.* These dirty little secrets, even the ones he wasn't parlaying into money, must thrill him when he pored over them. Or else . . . or else Rudi was planning to add to his clientele? He obviously preferred people who either lived in New York or came to town often, and maybe the rest of Larry's list couldn't provide that many appropriate names?

Anyway, it was that part of the book in which he found the page on Frances McKinnon. It simply consisted of everything Dorothy had said, with a lot of question marks scattered around, and a reminder to himself to check Boston birth records. Chuck didn't pay much attention to that; it was too vague, too minor, compared with everything else.

He shuttled back and forth to the den, where the tape recorder and VCR were, taking only one videocassette or reel of sound tape at a time so he could be sure of getting it back in the right place. The few reels of Super-8 film all seemed to be older, before the days of home video cameras. He couldn't find a projector, although he was sure there must be one, but by holding these up to the light he could see exactly what was going on.

When he'd seen and heard and replaced everything, he came back to the study to look through the individual files. Rudi had scrupulously kept copies of all the letters he'd typed up and, reading them, Chuck was now thoroughly sickened. He'd been so fascinated by these glimpses into the private lives of famous names that he'd forgotten to make himself another drink; after reading some of the cruel demands, the unnecessarily vicious little twists of Rudi's knife, he quickly went down for a stiff refill. He felt dirty. He looked at the gold Patek Philippe watch he was wearing, a present from Rudi that must have cost close to ten thousand dollars, and he wondered which payment from which victim had paid for it. He remembered the lavishness of their trips — the houseboat in Kashmir with a staff of fifteen, the chartered jets for weekends in Acapulco or Aruba, the palazzo outside Rome they'd rattled around in for a few weeks last summer. Of course, he could tell himself that those had been paid for with nice, clean restaurant money, that this cache of secrets had only been supporting a bunch of horses in Bucks County, but . . . money was money. A big part of Rudi's income came from what was in this door, and Chuck had to admit he'd never minded helping him spend it.

The last file, behind all the others, was simply labeled "Chuck." It held a single typed sheet of paper, a carefully worded, signed, totally true version of everything he knew about the night in Marrakesh when Chuck had run into him, fresh from the scene of a murder, hysterical. It was worthless now, of course. The boy with the knife had never been found, but the man in the Moroccan consulate in New York had been extremely polite, terribly grateful for Mr. Kranovic's deposition, which said Chuck had been with him for the entire evening, and Rudi could hardly go back on that now. Chuck had been totally innocent, however bad it had looked, but Rudi, in his love of secrets, his mania for cataloguing them and squirreling them away for the future, had included something that at one time could have been very harmful to the man who was supposed to be his lover. Rudi could never use it, it was really only a kind of memorandum to himself, but its very existence added something extra to what Chuck was already feeling.

He stayed sober for long enough that night to find the plain, cheap envelopes and typing paper that were so unlike anything Rudi would ordinarily use; as well as the ball for the IBM that was the same all-capital font as the flimsy carbons of the nauseating sheaf of letters. On the front of each envelope, he typed the name and address (and the message, "By Hand," because he was planning to take these to a messenger service tomorrow) of each of the lucky seven people, the ones who helped Rudi buy the wristwatch Chuck now took off and carefully smashed with a big bronze Art Nouveau paperweight. Inside each, he inserted a single sheet of paper on which he typed the identical five words: "You might find this interesting." He didn't sign the notes. Instead, he enclosed the thick, engraved cards from Tiffany which began with the message, "Messrs. Rudolf Kranovic and Charles Wetherby request the pleasure of your attendance on the evening of December thirty-first. . . ."

He was sure they'd understand. Imagining himself in their shoes, he thought their hearts — or their stomachs — would almost certainly turn over the minute they saw what must be a familiar envelope, a familiar type font, a familiar absence of a return address. He cleaned up the office carefully, and then he brought the envelopes down to his bedroom and put them in his gym bag for the morning. Just as he was settling in front of the fire downstairs for some steady drinking, he had a sudden thought, and he sighed, climbed back up to his bedroom, and returned with one of the envelopes. He held it for a moment, and then he threw it in the fire. There was no reason he should do Frances McKinnon's husband any favors, no reason he shouldn't twist in the wind for a little longer.

22

THE MAIN DINING ROOM at Rudi's was filled to capacity, and Maggie could see that the smaller ones on either side of it were jammed too. Her guests, Mr. and Mrs. Harold Anderson, president and first lady of the Anderson Staple Corporation, were delighted to be part of this crowd, she knew. It was such an *exclusive* place, she could hear them telling their friends. So much *fun,* having dinner with that zippy blonde girl who ran such an important art gallery (and so young) and that artist, the Wilkins man, the one who did the sculpture that might be just perfect for the atrium of their new place in Palm Beach.

Maggie thought she was hiding it well, but she was as tired as she'd ever been in her life and she was thoroughly bored. The Andersons, as connoisseurs, were at the opposite end of the scale from, say, Frederick McKinnon. They were the bread-and-butter collectors, though, the kind who kept the art world humming along from day to day. That is, they weren't really collectors, they were "acquirers" or "acquisitors" — she used both words to herself at times. They really didn't know the first thing about art and they never would, but they were very rich and they always seemed to be building a new house in Aspen or Palm Beach or La Jolla, or a new corporate headquarters or a new regional headquarters. They knew art gave them a cachet that nothing else would, and they were learning all the right names to throw around and the right things to say, but in their heart of hearts, Maggie was sure, they thought all it amounted to was a slightly superior form of interior decoration. By donating generously to the contemporary museum in the midwestern city where they'd made their fortune, they both had places on its board of directors and that, in turn, opened doors to them that would have otherwise been closed.

Even so, they never could have gotten a reservation at Rudi's on the strength of their own names, and it was Maggie who had booked, even though the woman who replaced Lillian gave her such a hard time she had to take deep breaths not to slam the phone down on her. Maggie's name wasn't on a list of any kind because it had never been necessary — everyone there used to know who she was, not only someone who should automatically be given a table in her own right but, of course, Mario's girl. Well, that's ancient history now, she said to herself.

Looking around the room tonight, she wondered if the restaurant itself wasn't about to become part of the history of New York watering holes, yet another scene that had a few years of glory and then sank into mediocrity. She couldn't put her finger on the change in the atmosphere. It wasn't only that nothing was running quite as smoothly as it used to, although that certainly was the case. She'd had to ask a rather languid waiter — someone she'd never seen before — to take her steak back because it was underdone, and she didn't remember ever having to do that in the past. She'd noticed a few small incidents at adjoining tables, too — the wrong wine had been brought to one, an entrée was served too soon after the first course at another. She didn't think those things would have happened when Mario was in charge. Everyone was carefully reserving judgment right now, of course, but it was beginning to look like there'd be a mass exodus to Tables as soon as it opened.

She excused herself to go to the ladies' for a little toot, so tired that this was the third time tonight she'd powdered her nose and she wasn't even sure it was going to carry her safely through coffee and dessert. Just one more day, she thought. One more heavy day at the gallery, and then North Carolina, and I can fall completely apart, wear a flour sack if I feel like it, eat peanut butter sandwiches and contemplate the pinecones or the tobacco plants. She asked an unfamiliar captain (Hell, she thought, Mario must have hired two-thirds of the staff away — no wonder none of these guys seem to know what's going on) if Rudi was in tonight. No, ma'am, he wasn't. He looked as relieved as Maggie felt. She'd been afraid she'd run into him, she'd been positive he'd take her aside and tearfully ask her to carry a message to Chuck, and she didn't want to get involved in whatever the trouble was between them. Chuck was spending almost every night at her apartment lately, which meant there was trouble in paradise, a problem of some kind at the town house. She wanted to get away from everybody's problems, including her own, especially her own.

Back at the table, Mrs. Anderson asked her in a whisper if everything was all right. Maggie nearly burst out laughing, but she forced a little embarrassed frown to her face and mumbled something about the time of the month. Mrs. Anderson nodded wisely, and Maggie had an almost uncontrollable urge to do something unbelievably shocking, to offer her some cocaine right here at the table, maybe, to shake her capped teeth and her complaisance right out of her. Calm down, bitch, she said to herself sternly. They're not really that bad. They're no worse than a lot of other people whose money you've gladly taken. They're nouveau riche and gauche and naive — why is it the French have all the right words for that kind of thing? — but they do spread art around. They do contribute to museums, they do help artists, even though they're usually artists who are already so well established they don't need help. You were even rather touched today at the gallery, when he picked up the stapler on a desk — an Anderson stapler, luckily — and said, "Now, that's my kinda art."

It's just that this man has such horrible jowls — awful, stubbled Nixon dewlaps — and his wife's clothes are in such perfect taste they make you want to barf. Some other time, another night when you're not so tired and so wired, you'll be able to see them for what they are. They're a little pathetic, really, trying too hard, uncomfortable with their old lives and friends back there in Staple City, but certainly not very relaxed with all the glamorous new people they think they want to know. It's because it's so close to Christmas, she thought sadly, that's why you're feeling so mean.

She had the leisure to think about all this, to look around the big room and daydream, because Jim had completely taken over the conversation. They were feeding him all the right lines ("We saw your big piece in front of the Federal Building in . . . ," "We thought your piece in the group show at the museum in . . .") and he was sitting back, puffing on an after-dinner cigar, pouring forth complaints about how little he'd been paid for that, how badly that show was installed — a difficult, conceited, creative man, a real artist. Well, Maggie thought, he really *is* an artist. He's a damned fine one, and these people are absolutely right to think they're rubbing shoulders with the genuine article. It's just that they have no idea how much he despises them.

She wondered if they had the faintest clue that she and Jim were an item. They could hardly have known by the way he was treating her — by the way she was treating him, for that matter — but they might have heard rumors from some other dealer or artist. God knows they were dropping names liberally enough and it was obvious she and Jim weren't the only ones who were wooing them these days. It was funny, she thought, the way she felt about people knowing she was seeing a lot of Jim. With Mario, she'd been so proud of what they had that she'd been happy for the whole world to know. With Jim — with Jim, she realized, it didn't much matter one way or another. He simply didn't touch her in any way except physically.

He was talking about his piece for the plaza in front of the bank building now, and they were asking him if he knew the famous Frances McKinnon. Frances, she thought. Seeing her that night at Bloomingdale's had temporarily given her the illusion that she could *do* something about it — scratch the woman's eyes out, tear her dress off, wipe the smile of secret happiness off her face — one of those melodramatic things that no one ever really does. After the adrenaline drained from her, when she realized Chuck was about to turn it into a really nasty situation, she was left feeling just as dull and numb as before.

She was forced back into the conversation for a few minutes when the Andersons wanted to know what she thought about the traveling Lichtenstein retrospective that had just come to their fair city, but she drifted back into herself when Jim began his long, predictable harangue about how Pop Art was dead, how it always had been dead, never an important movement, and so forth. Hell, she thought, everything reminds me of Mario. She'd gone with him to the opening of that show at the Whitney, the first stop on its tour, just about this time of year, only a year ago. And then, right after Christmas, they'd flown down to Puerto Plata together for a few heavenly days of laziness in the sun before New Year's. This year . . . she sighed. This year she'd take lots of books she'd been meaning to read. Jim would work on his plans for the McKinnon commission — she'd see to that — and play with his plane. And they'd go to bed a lot, or wherever Jim wanted to do it. And so what?

There isn't anyone I can talk to about it, she thought. Chuck is impossible, and my friends . . . what friends? Mario could always talk to Patrick. Frances McKinnon seemed to be close enough to Trish Green to confide all sorts of things to her. She, Maggie, hadn't thought she needed any friends for a long time now, she realized. Her mother used to tell her she was a man's woman, like herself, and she supposed it was true. Not that she gave a damn about the Super Bowl, not that she could clean a carburetor in ten minutes flat, just that she'd always preferred the company of men. *A* man, she corrected herself. There were some girls she'd known at Smith — a lawyer, a stock analyst — who called her for lunch every so often, but she had absolutely nothing in common with them anymore. There were a lot of art world friends, but no one she felt particularly close to, no one she trusted very much, really. Face it, Maggie, she said to herself, there's nobody. Mario had been her best friend. She'd had her work and a hundred people to gossip with, and Mario. Now she had her work, and a hundred people to gossip with, and . . . Jim.

She wanted to go home, suddenly, to crawl into bed and feel the warmth of the cats all around her, to pull the covers over her face. She made what she called her International Excuse (expecting a call from Hong Kong about a sale — that always impressed people and confused them because of the time difference). She turned down the offer of a ride home in the Andersons' stretch, insisting they all stay and keep talking. She refused Jim's half-hearted suggestion of going with her, made sure the waiter knew this was to be billed to the gallery, and grabbed a cab outside. Chuck will be there, she said to herself as they wove in and out of the heavy holiday traffic on Second. He'll be drinking, one can assume, because he doesn't have to work for a few days, but even if he's drunk he'll *be* there.

When she got to the apartment, she could tell immediately that he was going to be more trouble than comfort. He was somewhere short of passing out, but not far short. It was just him and the bottle and a glass — no ice, no mixer, no vermouth. At least, she thought sourly, he hasn't chugged it straight from the bottle since that time in Santa Barbara, when he was just an amateur, but that wasn't very much consolation. She sighed; she almost wished he *had* passed out. She had only wanted her bed. She had only wanted oblivion and maybe the sense that someone was there in the apartment, conscious or not, sober or not, who loved her. He was sprawled on the couch, singing along to a Christmas carol that some awful, saccharine station was playing on the radio. He was concentrating on the lyrics, and he only waved vaguely to her when she said, "Hi."

In the bedroom, she shrugged off her clothes and threw them on a chair. She knew the cats would nest in them and probably claw them if they were feeling perverse enough or bored enough, but she didn't have the energy to put them away. She pulled an old flannel nightgown over her head and went to the kitchen to pour herself a glass of milk.

"Milk is for sissies, Mag," Chuck yelled from the couch.

"And vodka is for nonsissies? Is that it?" She usually tried to keep from sounding quite so mean about Chuck's intake, but tonight she didn't bother. Tonight, like the act of hanging up her clothes, it was too much effort.

"Macho butch studs like me, o'course." He stared at her as she came into the room. "Mom used to wear nightgowns like that."

"That's why I usually wouldn't be caught dead in one." She flopped into a chair, spilling a little milk, which a cat promptly licked off the carpet.

"Mag!" His voice was hurt, shocked. This was one of his personalities when he was drunk, she knew, the best little boy in the world, ready to stand up for God and America and Motherhood. It was like walking on eggs when he was like this. Or, rather, it was like trying to avoid the pendulum inside a huge clock. He could swing to nasty in a split second.

"Mom always loved us very much," he said, singsong, sitting up straight on the couch, reminding her of the little Cub Scout he no longer was.

"She always loved us when she had spare time," she said softly. "We've talked about it. You agree with me when you're not . . . when you haven't had so much to drink."

He snorted. "I'm drunk. You can say it." His face turned dark and brooding. "You think she didn't even want us, Mag?" It was a question he asked her sometimes when he was like this, and it always made her furious. A fully grown man, feeling sorry for himself because his parents might not have planned his birth. It was a cliché and a cop-out. Besides, who ever really knew what went on in women's minds when they got pregnant? She'd had an abortion once — the stockbroker, and Chuck didn't know about it — and her feelings had been anything but simple.

"I think — oh, hell, you know what I think. I think the decision to have a child is unbelievably complex. I think our mother, even if she seems like someone who only cares about golf and horses and booze, is a complicated woman. I think it's society, and the way marriage used to be, and . . . shit! I can't talk rationally with you when you're so drunk and I'm so tired. We're *here,* aren't we? Isn't that the point? That we're supposed to . . . ?" She stopped when she realized he wasn't listening. He was talking to himself in a monotone.

"I think she didn't want us but she didn't know what else to do. Some women just don't want children. I mean . . ." He spoke very slowly, very low, putting on a great, conscious show of thinking clearly, making sense to himself, seeing himself as very subtle and wise and cutting. "*Some* women, some cold bitches, some women have children and then . . . they give them away, Mag." He stared at her. He was having trouble focusing but he was obviously trying to give her a meaningful look.

"You must be tired," she pleaded. "Let me make the bed for you. Get up. Let's fold the couch out and I'll bring you some blankets."

"It's called adoption," he whispered, in awe of his reasoning.

"Well, *that's* a ridiculous new twist. It's crazy, we're not adopted. I can only humor you so far: we're our parents' children."

"Didn't say *us,*" he roared. The cat who'd been curled on her lap jumped up and ran out of the room. "Not talking 'bout us . . . it's that cunt, that . . . where's the phone book?" He was on his feet now, unsteady, looking around the room with wild eyes.

"Over there. Bottom shelf." She was puzzled.

He pulled it out, still standing but swaying on his feet, riffling through the book and tearing some of the pages. "Jesus!" he said, throwing it down. "Of course they're too important, just too fucking important, to have their number listed."

He grabbed his jacket from the chair, dug a red morocco appointment book out of the pocket, and reached for the phone.

"Who on earth are you calling? It's after one." She softened her voice, coming over to him and taking his arm as he punched the buttons. He had the exaggerated craftiness of a drunk. His eyes were slits.

"Dorothy? Chuck Wetherby. Sorry it's so late, but Rudi asked me to call. Yeah. Yeah, I know, I'm really sorry, but listen. Rudi wants your sister-in-law's number, something about a lunch she's having . . . uh, tomorrow? Oh, sorry, well, I s'pose you have lunches and don't always invite her? Anyway, he can't find her number, must've left it at work, and there's some problem . . . I dunno. What, Rudi? Oh, Rudi says it's something about, uh, smoked salmon. Anyway, do you mind? Great, thanks, and Rudi thanks you. Sorry again. See you soon." He hung up and sat down. The performance had exhausted him, but he held tightly to the phone, his eyes still narrowed.

Maggie stared at him, trying to think fast, wondering how she could talk him out of it. Gentleness, she decided. "Chuckles, now, come on. There's no good reason to call the McKinnons. It's late, really, way too late. Let's talk about it in the morning."

"Nope." He shook his head, holding the slip of paper over his head in case she tried to grab it from him. "Someone's gotta tell him. Not a nice job . . ." He shook his head sadly. "Not a nice thing to do but someone's gotta do it. He's gotta know what's going on. He's gotta right to know."

"Chuck!" Her voice was harsh now. "If you mean Mr. McKinnon, if you mean you have to tell him about Mario and, um, his wife, then you cannot . . ." She grabbed for the phone, but he was too quick. He pushed her away roughly and she lost her balance, fell against a table, and slid down to the floor, stunned. She couldn't believe he'd shoved her, couldn't remember that he'd ever done anything like that to her before, even when they were little, even when she'd deliberately bent the spokes on his bicycle, even when she'd drawn trees and houses in one of his favorite books with her crayons. She wasn't hurt but her feelings were badly bruised and she was panicked. She knew he was going to do it and he wouldn't let her near the phone. She was helpless, and she began to cry quietly. All she'd wanted was a hug from her big brother, maybe a sympathetic word or two, a glass of milk, and bed.

He wasn't looking at her. It was taking all his concentration to deal with the number and the buttons on the phone. "Mr. McKinnon? Chuck Wetherby here," he said precisely.

* * *

Half an hour, Frances said to herself. I'm going to give myself exactly half an hour to go through this damned Christmas card list and cross out the names of people I've decided I don't like and never did, plus the ones who've died and gone to heaven since last year. And then I'm going to spend another half hour spinning the Rolodex and pulling the cards for new people. Then Ham can take the whole mess to the office with him in the morning and throw it on his secretary's desk and let her sort it out and address the envelopes in that schoolmarm handwriting of hers. It was only two days till Christmas, it was after midnight, and she was sitting up in bed with the list on one side of her and the Rolodex on the other, feeling bad for almost totally ignoring Christmas this year but telling herself, truthfully, that because of Tables she'd really had very little extra time this month or even last month.

She worked quickly, ruthlessly, and she finished the whole thing before her self-imposed deadline. Then she leaned back against the pillows, lit a cigarette, and made a few notes in her daybook about the last-minute presents she and Ham had decided on in one of their student union talks tonight. Without ever discussing it in advance, with no duplication of energy, they'd independently come up with exactly the right ideas for the family, just as they miraculously did every year.

In a gallery a few days before, she'd reserved a wonderful, witty Ruscha lithograph of a teacup flying through space for Frederick's son Billy, who was in the Tokyo office. Billy collected California artists, and Ham thought it sounded perfect. She could have them deliver it to his office and he could sign a card for both of them and send it in the bank pouch, all in the same day.

Ham had seen a Georgian silver epergne in the window of James Robinson with simple, classic lines that he said had screamed Dorothy to him. She had seen it too, and she agreed.

Finding herself with five extra minutes on Fifty-eighth Street between appointments last week, she'd wedged her way into the mob in F.A.O. Schwarz, spotted a stuffed giraffe that was nearly as tall as she was, and had them figure out how to wrap it and send it to Peekie's new baby.

Peekie herself and her husband were now fancying themselves as wine connoisseurs, and since Ham knew far more about it than she did, he could call Sherry-Lehmann tomorrow and order a few cases of something amazing. He could also have Abercrombie & Fitch send Dorothy's son, a lawyer in Pittsburgh whose central passion seemed to be fishing, a rod and reel that Ham happened to know he wanted. Frances could phone the Sierra Club and donate some money in the name of Freddie's younger son. He'd been such a serious, religious child that everyone used to think he'd become a priest, but he'd turned into a doctor and a rabid environmentalist instead. And Freddie was off skiing in the Dolomites, so Sotheby's could hold the beautiful little Shaker table she'd picked up at auction and deliver it after Christmas.

And that's that, family-wise, present-wise, Frances said to herself, mentally dusting off her hands. She and Ham were having Trish, Dorothy, Peekie, and Peekie's husband to Christmas Eve supper, but she was letting Marianne plan everything down to the menu. Then Peekie was having dinner for a whole assortment of relatives and in-laws — probably exactly the same people who were at the christening, Frances thought dispiritedly — on the day itself. Dorothy had wanted to do it, but her daughter managed to head her off at the pass. The family was beginning to whisper about her, beginning to wonder if nowadays Dorothy was capable of getting so much as a tuna casserole on the table, let alone an elaborate dinner for thirty. Anyway, Frances thought, I don't have to think about anything except what to wear.

She'd had Trish's present for months, a pair of simple coral-and-diamond earrings that had been in the Duchess of Windsor's estate and then in someone else's. If they'd been in a third estate sale in such a short time, she'd have hesitated — there was such a thing as jinxed jewelry — but this seemed safe enough. And then there was Mario. She'd finally decided, just yesterday, to buy the four empty frames she'd reserved a week ago. They'd come out of a house Frank Lloyd Wright designed in the late 'forties, and they were very stark and very beautiful: burled walnut with a thin ebony inlay running along the borders. The price had been outrageous because almost everything Wright did was in museums by now, but at least they didn't *look* like a ludicrously expensive present. She was going to frame four of her most complete renderings for Tables in them, maybe even make collages of them with other scraps of paper, receipts from delicatessens when they'd called out for pastrami sandwiches, even bits of fabrics they'd used, but that would have to wait till after New Year's. In the meantime, tomorrow, she'd give him the frames and a promise to fill them. She was happy with her idea: it was something a designer could justifiably do, it was personal without being romantic, as such — although she was determined to work a few private references into the collages, the label from a bottle of champagne they'd shared at the house, for instance — and he could hang them in his office as a sort of four-panel scrapbook of their joint effort. No one would have to know they were a history of their love as well.

She yawned, finished her cigarette, and switched off the bedside lamp. It had been a long day, spent mostly at Tables but punctuated with a couple of other things she couldn't avoid. She'd chafed at a Foundation board meeting that lasted forever because Freddie wasn't there to keep things rolling. Then she'd fretted in the heavy traffic that caused her to come close to missing Lot 110 at the Christie's sale, the pair of Louis XV jardinières she'd seen at the viewing with Carole earlier in the week, prizes she was determined to get. She smiled with satisfaction at the memory of her entrance into the auction room, the disappointment on the faces of the dealers who knew her. Word was out: she was buying for a client who seemed to have an unlimited budget, and the dealers knew she'd outbid them for these if she really wanted them. As it happened, they decided to be gentlemen, dropping out of the bidding when she first raised her catalogue, and she got them for Carole for only forty-three thousand for the pair. She would put some wonderful shrubs or small trees in them — Carole had wanted ficus but she suggested something fuller and rarer — and they'd be stunning on either side of the big double doors that led into the dining room.

There had been no time for even a brief rendezvous at the house, of course; there hadn't been for nearly a week. She had to be content with hurried conferences and quick kisses in one of the storerooms or in the elevator, which fortunately didn't have its TV camera installed yet. She looked forward, these days, to moments like this, just before she fell asleep, because they were the only times she could give herself up to the pure luxury of Mario. It was a poor second best to having him next to her, but it was something. She began to drift, to remember his smell, his feel. It was always this way. She'd begin by thinking of something specific, the way he'd looked today, something he'd said, and she'd end up, just before sleep, with a sense of him that was close to being abstract, a distillation of who he was and how much he meant to her.

When the phone rang, she resented it not only because it brought her fully awake but because it took her away from Mario. Then, since it was such a nice thought, she wondered if it might even *be* Mario. Maybe he knew she was thinking about him and he wanted her to know he was thinking about her. It was out of the question, she realized in the next split second; he'd never, never call when he knew Ham was in town. She picked it up after the second ring, holding her hand over the receiver while she cleared her throat, and she heard Ham pick up a second later. She was on the verge of letting him know she was on, when he said, "Hello," in his brisk banker's voice.

"Mr. McKinnon? Chuck Wetherby here," the voice at the other end said in an equally businesslike tone. It was like other calls Ham got late at night sometimes, someone from the bank, clipped and apologetic, with an urgent message. But those always came in on Ham's private number and this was on one of their two personal lines or it wouldn't be ringing in her room. And it was Maggie's brother. She froze, her hand still over the mouthpiece.

"Something I've gotta talk to you about. Something . . ." His voice seemed to catch in a rush of sentiment before he could continue. "Something really bad, and I hate to be the one to tell you, hate it . . ."

Ham was puzzled. "Mr. Wetherby, it's awfully late, and you've awakened me and probably my wife as well. Are you on, Frances?"

She couldn't open her mouth, couldn't take her hand off the receiver. He's going to tell him, she thought. There's nothing I can do, nothing I can say to prevent it. It was this feeling of inevitability that paralyzed her. For some reason — some misguided sense of chivalry, it must be — this man had decided he hated her. She remembered how strongly she'd felt his cold resentment at Trish's Bloomingdale's party. He was about to tell Ham that night, she was sure, already dropping his drunken, heavy-handed innuendos when Maggie managed to send him away. And I felt an incredible sense of relief, she reminded herself. I keep saying Ham's bound to find out sooner or later and it's better for him to know and it would be kindest if he heard it from me instead of from someone else, but I don't *want* him to know, not really, not at all, because nothing can be the same after this. So she listened, she eavesdropped, she pretended she hadn't picked up the phone a split second before her husband.

"'S probably out fucking him somewhere," Chuck's control of his voice came in waves, alternating between sloppy and precise.

"Mr. Wetherby, if you have something to say to me, please call me at the bank in the morning," Hamilton said evenly. "Otherwise . . ."

"No!" Chuck screamed. "*Vino veritas* and all that shit. I won't be drunk in the morning. Gotta say this *now.* Your wife is cheating on you, Mr. McKinnon. She's been fucking Mario Fermi for weeks — months, I guess. She saw something she wanted, she saw *someone* she wanted, and she took him away from my sister and . . . you probably don't even know what I'm talking about, do you?"

"Mr. Wetherby," Hamilton began. Frances was once again astonished by his self-control. He'd just been told his wife was having an affair, and he was capable of sounding as cool as if there were some problem at the bank, a run on gold in Singapore, maybe, or the Prime Rate dropping four basis points.

"You call me *Chuck,* for crissake," he barked. "I don't like this, don't like doing it, and if it was only that, only the little fact that she's . . ." He belched. "'Scuse me. If it was just her screwing up Maggie's life so much, then I prob'ly wouldn' be doing this . . ." He repeated it quietly, sadly, even. "I don't like doing this."

"All right, then," Hamilton said. "You prefer to be called Chuck. Chuck, you don't like saying whatever you're saying and you may be very sure I don't like listening. I don't think you have anything to tell me that I want to hear or that I need to hear. I'm going to say good-night."

"Not *yet*. 'Snot all. Reason you gotta know, reason you gotta know is 'cause it's her son, for Jesus Christ's sake. *She's screwing her own son,* you poor old man. Her own flesh and blood. Her son. Your son?"

Frances sat absolutely still. She didn't take in a breath or let one out. She was terrified they'd discover she was listening. If they didn't know she was on the other line, if she kept perfectly quiet, then she could make it go away. If she wasn't really there and if she didn't move or breathe, then this couldn't really be happening, could it? From far away, she heard Hamilton say, "I don't have a son."

"Ah." Chuck was crafty again. "So she's always been a whore, so maybe 'snot your son. *I* dunno. I dunno who the fuck's son she is, I mean *he* is, I mean I don't know who the fuck the father is. Dorothy said she left a son in Boston. You gotta brother, right? Frank? Fred? Christ, all these goddamn brothers and sisters and mothers. Anyway, maybe he told Dorothy all about this crap. So Mario's from Boston but his mother wasn't his mother. Maggie told me all about it the other day. She wasn't s'posed to but why the hell should she worry about Mario's fucking secrets *now?* I mean, he was adopted and . . . hell, you can ask whoosis. Fred. Or Rudi. Rudi's got it all figured out, too, 'cept when Rudi knows things about people he gets money out of 'em but I'm not like that, and I'm just telling you because . . ."

Hamilton stopped him by speaking a little louder and very much faster. "I think you've said more than enough, Mr. Wetherby. Chuck. I don't like to hang up on people, but that's exactly what I'm going to do. This is the end of our conversation. You can apologize when you're sober, if you want. It doesn't concern me one way or another, but I would imagine you'll feel like apologizing if you remember in the morning what you've just said. I'll tell you one thing, though, young man. If you so much as whisper any of this filth to anyone again, you're going to find yourself in the middle of the biggest slander suit this city has ever seen. Now I *am* saying good-night."

He replaced the phone firmly. Frances hung up an instant later, and that was the only movement she made for a very long time.

23

HAMILTON SAT on the edge of his bed and tried to think. It was warm in the room, but he'd been awakened from a deep sleep and he was chilled. His body temperature was down, he supposed, and he padded quietly across to his dressing room for a robe. I mustn't wake Frances. That was his first clear thought. I can't talk to her tonight. She'll know something's wrong and I can't possibly discuss it with her until I understand better, until I have some facts.

Goddamn that drunken bastard, he raged. Why, in God's name, does someone named Chuck Wetherby think *he* has a responsibility to tell *me* about what my own wife is or isn't doing? He's a complete stranger, almost — I met him briefly, exactly once, I think, and only very recently, at that opening of Trish's.

He tied the sash of the soft cashmere dressing gown tightly around his waist, drew open the curtains, and sat down heavily in a chair by the window. He made an effort to assess his feelings objectively, the way he'd run his eye down a company's financial statement, the way he'd review the performance of a junior officer at the bank. Yes, Hamilton, old boy, you are far more jealous than you would have imagined you'd be, far more than — really, considering your own little peccadillos — you have any right to be. And, yes, it does make you feel horribly old and inadequate and unnecessary and unloved. And, dammit, yes — you wondered if maybe there was something. . . .

But it was wonderful, seeing Frances so happy. She *has* been happy, too, she's positively glowing with health and confidence lately. She's still fretting about her age, of course. That won't go away if — *if* — she's seeing a younger man. On the contrary, I should imagine, but she's so much freer, so much more affectionate, to you, to everyone. The part of you that loves her in the most generous sense, the best part of you, has been pleased, for her sake, without letting yourself dwell on why it might be so. You know she won't make a fool of herself. You know she'd never want to make a fool of you. You assume — dear God, you *hope* — she'd never think of leaving you.

He groaned. He couldn't bear that thought; he simply would not allow himself to consider it. Life without Frances . . . but it would never come to that. If this had happened — and he knew it had and it wasn't really necessary for anyone to tell him — then it must have been some extraordinary attraction that pulled her into it. He was very sure she'd never done this before. But if she had, he would have borne it, he would have waited it out and hoped it would end soon. Which is what he would do now. He would do anything to keep Frances, even if it meant he had to look steadily in the other direction for . . . for a while? A few months? A year? If this was something powerful enough to break through her reserve, her will, then where would it end? Would it end at all?

So, captain, he said to himself, you've inspected that part of the old battleship and it's all very neat and shipshape. No, it isn't. It's a mess, it's taken on water, it's been hit — but it's afloat. But this other thing, this . . . he couldn't find words for it. It would have to be the most unbelievable coincidence, wouldn't it? Mario seemed to be about the right age, and Hamilton thought he'd detected the remnants of a Boston accent. Frances might have mentioned something about his background, but he couldn't remember. Anyway, that was all he really could say he knew. He *may* have been adopted, but Chuck Wetherby didn't seem to be the most reliable source of information and he was evidently out to hurt someone — to hurt Frances, presumably — in any way he could find.

Twenty-nine, he calculated. The boy, Frances's son, is twenty-nine now, and he could be anywhere or anyone, he could have any name in the phone book. He might have died a crib death, he might have grown into a wild teenager and killed himself on a motorcycle, or sniffing glue, anything. Hamilton had never even set eyes on him — not, of course, that he'd be able to match up a baby's unformed, wrinkled little face with a fully grown man's if he had. He didn't think Frances had seen him or had asked to see him, even if the hospital had permitted such a thing. Freddie had arranged everything. Only Freddie — and an agency of some kind? he wondered — knew where the child had been sent, knew who had reserved him in advance, like someone buying a theater ticket for a show that hadn't yet opened.

And Dorothy — dammit, damn her — how *could* she have talked about this? He'd been much closer to his sister when they were in their teens and twenties. Even after she was with Spence, up until his own marriage to Frances, they'd been loyal allies in their resistance to their mother. It wasn't Frederick who'd told Frances's story to Dorothy — he'd have cut out his own tongue before he'd do that. He himself had. It had been a mistake, but how could he have known that, all those years ago? She'd been his confidante, and who'd ever have guessed she'd betray him, and Frances, this way? He tried not to blame her. Frances had told him tonight about how Dorothy behaved at their lunch a couple of days ago, and now he could only assume that, if she'd told Chuck such a thing, she must not be quite in control of herself. So maybe, probably, it was her goddamn painkillers or her goddamn tranquilizers that had spoken, but he'd still have to ask her if she remembered doing it. The damage was done, and she'd feel ghastly when he confronted her, but he had to make her understand that she'd done something very, very wrong and that she *could not* repeat this kind of slip. He knew, however much he denied it to Frances, that Dorothy didn't like her. But he also knew how much the family meant to her, and that would be his approach.

No, he reminded himself. It's Chuck Wetherby who's the loose cannon on the deck. He calmly considered all the ways a rich and powerful man could buy silence, cataloguing them neatly, up to and including . . . whatever was finally necessary. He'd do anything he had to do; he'd forget the values he'd always tried to live by if there were only one, unavoidable way to save his wife from the most terrible pain. Nothing could be public. Frances would be crushed as surely as if he'd deliberately set out to hurt her. It was absurd for him to threaten a slander suit, but it was the only thing he could think of at that moment on the phone, the great impartial, comforting force of the law and the best lawyers money could buy. He wasn't even sure if cases like that ever made it to court these days, but what would be the point? It wasn't slander. Frances *did* bear a child twenty-nine years ago, the child was illegitimate, and she did give it up for adoption. As for the other, the unthinkable, it almost didn't matter if it was true if people thought it was. It wasn't the kind of thing that would ever be *published,* for God's sake. It would simply be the meatiest little bit of gossip anyone had heard for years.

That was the point, of course. That was why he'd have to stop it before Frances could be hurt. Frances is brilliant, beautiful, and capable, he thought, but she still needs protection at times. She's never quite realized what wealth means, never understood the special vulnerabilities and strengths it carries with it. Because most people are delighted by her, she doesn't always recognize the ones who want to know her because of what she has rather than who she is, and there must be people out there who resent her, who hate her, people who would gleefully pass on any kind of filth . . . any kind of filth. . . .

He had decided to go back to bed, and he was halfway across the room when he thought of it. Someone else knew about this. He'd just remembered Chuck's drunken words that didn't seem to have anything to do with all the other things he was saying. Rudy, he said. Rudy knew about it. But that wasn't all. Rudy asks people for money when he knows things . . . Rudy. Who the hell did he know with that name? No one, was the answer, but didn't Dorothy have a bridge chum named Rudy? Of course. A few pieces fell into place. Dorothy's friend was Rudi, with an *i,* the man who had the restaurant. And that was the place Mario used to run, wasn't it? And Chuck must be another friend of Rudi's? He was a tennis pro, he remembered, but could he be one of those bridge addicts, too?

Standing perfectly still in the middle of the room, his robe unbelted, Hamilton struggled to make connections. Could this Rudi be *my* man? he asked himself, *my* retailer — wholesaler — of filth? *Vino veritas,* Chuck had said, and he'd believed he was telling the truth. If Rudi was a blackmailer . . . whatever he was, Chuck seemed to consider himself above that sort of thing. So. Is this a coincidence? Another one? Or is there a link?

He had to *know* more. He'd try to find out whatever he could from Frances about this man — Rudi's used to be her favorite restaurant, didn't it? And Chuck was the brother of Mario's girlfriend, was that it? Former girlfriend? Concurrent girlfriend? But it was Freddie he needed to talk to most. Freddie was his big brother, Freddie was the only one who knew what had happened up in Boston, Freddie was the man he trusted more than anyone in the world except Frances, and Freddie was off in the Italian Alps on one of his skiing retreats. He would talk to him as soon as he came back. New Year's Eve? He thought that was what he had said.

He didn't go to sleep for a long while, but he was gradually able to calm himself. At least he knew where to begin now.

* * *

Frances's mind was refusing to settle on any one thought, so it jumped from one question to another. Could Hamilton have known she was on the line? And then: Mario's birthday was April first, wasn't it? She'd had to tease it out of him, but didn't he finally say it was April first? April Fool's Day? Did that mean he was kidding? Should she slide back down into bed and pretend to be asleep? She couldn't, she knew she couldn't, face Ham if he came in to talk.

Mario was twenty-nine. Twenty-nine? The number spun around in her mind until she stopped it by facing what simply had to be a complete coincidence. Her baby, her boy, would be twenty-nine. Twenty-nine last March. March tenth, it had been — she always remembered it, that day, year after year, as if someone had died but there was no grave to visit. Mario had told her, one afternoon when he'd come straight to the house from the Boston shuttle, that he was adopted, that he hadn't known long, that he had no intention of trying to find his real parents, and that it really didn't matter very much. But that didn't mean anything, did it? Why should that have anything to do with her? It couldn't. It was ridiculous. She used the word again: it was a *coincidence*.

Her thoughts flew back to Hamilton. Would he come in to have a talk with her? She was almost positive he wouldn't. She was sure he'd want time to think it all over, in his deliberate, practical way, before he'd say anything to her, if he ever mentioned it at all. She wanted a cigarette badly, but she was afraid to light one. He *might* come in, and she *must* be asleep. She wanted to turn on the lamp — it all was so much worse in the dark, so much more unreal — but she mustn't.

She tried to imagine what he'd do, not just tonight, but tomorrow and the day after. Would they just go on as they always had? Would he try to talk to her about it? No, of course not. This had never happened in their marriage, there was no precedent, but she knew . . . no, she didn't *know* anything! She was sleeping with a man other than her husband, and her husband would feel as terrible as *she* would feel if he were seeing another woman. . . .

He would certainly check on Mario, find out if he was decent or if he had a criminal background or a reputation for breaking older ladies' hearts or for hunting fortunes, or . . . she suddenly wished he *would* fly into a murderous rage and confront her and threaten to shoot Mario and make it all simple, but she couldn't imagine that. Ham wasn't built like that, he never was and he never would be, and of course that was one of the thousands of reasons she loved him in the way she did. He was terribly, terribly hurt, she was positive — or he would be when he somehow made sure she was sleeping with Mario — and she ached for him. But he would always try to protect her. He would put her first, and that was a terrible burden on her, in a way, because she knew she had no *right* to so much consideration. She was in the wrong; she had broken her marriage vows.

A wave of fear swept her. In spite of everything her mind was doing to shield her, a picture had come into her thoughts that she'd been fighting to keep back. It was Michael, of course, the way he'd looked the last time she'd seen him. No, not the very last time, she corrected herself, because that was just a glimpse of him in Harvard Square. She meant the last time she'd actually been with him, the day in June he'd gone back to Boston on the bus, leaving her pregnant — even if neither of them knew it — and already planning how he was going to slough her off. And next to his face, in her mind's eye, in spite of everything she could do to prevent it, was a picture of Mario. When the tears started to come, the faces swam in front of her until they became one face.

* * *

Maggie was still on the floor against the table, exactly where she'd fallen when Chuck lashed out at her. He'd long since hung up — or was hung up on, it sounded like from her end. He'd looked at her sadly, guiltily, and then he'd lain down on the sofa and quietly passed out.

The cats came and rubbed against her, looking puzzled that she should be on the floor, and then apparently deciding, with the absolute egocentricity of all cats, that she was on the floor to be with them. Maggie stroked them absently, her mind far away. She was trying to remember everything Mario had ever told her about his birth and his parents. They had celebrated his birthday on April first, she knew that, but then, when he found his mother wasn't his mother — as Chuck put it — it became a kind of joke. She teased him about being a foundling, a rootless bastard. They'd made up pseudopsychological theories, in fake Viennese accents, about Oedipal Conflicts and Breast Fixations. He laughed along with her, but she sometimes wondered if she'd gone too far, if it was really a sensitive spot, buried beneath his pride and his sophistication and his humor. She decided, dreamily, that she wouldn't tease him about it again.

She shook herself and sat up. It was a habit she still had, thinking about things she'd do with Mario, making resolutions about how she'd try to change for Mario. There isn't any Mario, you stupid bitch. So far as you're concerned, there simply isn't any Mario. He's with that woman who's old enough . . .

She almost laughed out loud. Some joke, Maggie. For a moment, she was obscurely pleased with this new twist. Secretly, so deeply she could barely admit it to herself, she hoped it might bring the most excruciating pain to the both of them. She had a quick flash of memory, a play on a bare stage in Paris — the scene where Jocasta, Oedipus's mother, kills herself when she knows what she's done. Then she recoiled from that. Your mind is working a little too fast, baby. This was that bottle of Finlandia from your icebox talking, not the anchorman on the eleven o'clock news. She only knew Mario's side of it, the fact that he didn't know who his real parents were. If Frances McKinnon, or whatever her name was then, *had* had a child, born in that year, what were the odds? A million to one? Two million? As for Dorothy Clough, she'd only met her once or twice at Rudi's house, but she'd had the impression that anything she said would have to be taken with a few grains of salt.

Still . . . just the possibility made her feel better, in a way she knew was sour and mean-spirited, than she had for a long time. It was easier to see the whole thing as a perversion, a compulsion. Mario couldn't help himself. She, Maggie, wasn't competing with another girl, she'd been dumped for Mother. She was positive it wasn't literally true, but it somehow made her see Mario in a different light. If she could only *wait,* only keep herself from hating him for what he'd done to her, only try to feel sorry for him for being caught in this mess. If she could only wait.

* * *

At first she simply felt a great sense of relief. The white room, the nuns, the little baby boy, the blood — only a dream. She was here, safe, in the sunlight. Ham must have drawn open the drapes. Sweet, dependable Ham, dressed except for his jacket, ready for the bank. He was holding her breakfast tray, and the smell of coffee reminded her of the time Mario had come here. She closed her eyes again, holding on to first that memory and then others from the same day — the way he'd looked, the light in the room, this room, afterward, when he'd stood naked over by the window. She remembered the phone call, then, and she was suddenly, sharply, awake. In the same instant, she remembered she didn't want Hamilton to know what she was thinking.

"Nightmare, Franny?" he asked quietly, the same concern in his voice that was always there when she'd had a bad dream.

"Mmmmm." If she told him about it — the hospital, her baby — it would be too transparent. He'd realize she'd been listening. She knew she must have screamed, although it might have come out as a low moan, and she prayed she hadn't actually *said* anything just now, while he was standing here. Good for you, Frances, she thought drearily. You're starting your day, from the minute you wake up, with lies. But there's no time right now to despise yourself; you don't have that luxury.

"Tarantula," she said, opening her eyes again and smiling crookedly at him, wondering how on earth that image had popped into her head. "This horrible, huge, hairy tarantula, and my father was there but . . . oh, damn, they always just fade away. I don't remember it all. Thank you, darling."

She sat up and took the tray, pouring out his coffee first and handing it to him, then hers. He sat down on the edge of her bed, balancing his cup and blowing across the surface to cool it before taking a sip. She flipped through her mail to give herself time to gather herself together, glancing up at him from lowered eyes. He looked even tireder this morning, old and wrung out, as if some of his spirit had been drained away in the night. She felt so bad for him she wanted to take him in her arms and hug it away. Tell him it would be all right, tell him she knew all about it and, yes, she was having an affair with Mario Fermi but that didn't mean she loved him, Hamilton, any less. And no, the rest of it was a ghastly, sick fantasy that existed only in Chuck Wetherby's mind. She couldn't do that. If Ham preferred not to talk about it, then the very, very least she could do was to respect his feelings.

"Do we know when Freddie's coming back?" she asked casually. "I need to tell Sotheby's when they can deliver his present. They get so worried about holding things, and we have to pay extra insurance and storage."

"The day before New Year's, I think." He was skimming the front page of the *Times* he'd brought in with him. As if this were just another morning, she thought. "I know he was planning to come to your party."

"My . . . oh, the Tables party. But do we know exactly where he is?"

"Somewhere in the Dolomites. Why?"

"Oh. I just thought we could send him a Christmas cable."

"You could call the Foundation, I guess, but I doubt they'll know."

"You mean he's playing Happy Wanderer again?" She frowned. "*You* couldn't get away with that. You have to let someone at the bank know if you're taking a walk for an hour."

"Franny! Freddie and I have different kinds of pressures. You've always encouraged him to get away from it all."

"Well, I do, but I think it's really inconsiderate of him, that we can't get in touch with him at Christmas." She was whining. She couldn't help it.

"We could try, but I think he checks into little inns in whatever village has good snow that day. My brother, the sixty-three-year-old ski bum." He laughed. "Actually, since he goes two or three times every winter and no one ever seems to know where he is, I've wondered if he isn't visiting a little pink-cheeked fräulein."

"A little olive-skinned signorina, I should think, since it's Italy," she said, irritated. Do I have to wait till New Year's to talk to Freddie? she wondered. She felt a black, engulfing panic, but she managed to keep chattering. "What's your schedule today?" she asked. "Oh, be sure to call Abercrombie's and Sherry's." Was it only last night we were talking about those presents?

"I will. Nothing special. Things ought to be all quiet on the banking front. And then I'm taking Dorothy to dinner — at the Carlyle, probably. I just called her, and she wasn't doing anything tonight and I thought it would be a nice brotherly thing to do. I was sure you said you'd be tied up all day and on into the evening. Didn't you?"

"But she's coming here tomorrow night, Ham. Christmas Eve." You're sounding like a fishwife, she told herself. He obviously wants to ask her what she's been saying, he obviously wants to shut her up. God knows you should encourage it.

"I know, but I think she's feeling blue. Anyway, you're not free, are you? Shouldn't I have assumed you'd be working late?"

"No, no. I'm sorry, darling. I may be at the restaurant till midnight, and it's sweet of you to take Dorothy out." She began to sort through the mail again, and he went back to his paper.

"Had you planned to invite Dorothy to the party? When your restaurant opens?" His face was still buried in the business section.

She made herself smile. "Ham, I know when I talk about it, it must sound like *I'm* the one who's opening it, but it's not really my restaurant. I don't have anything to do with the guest list, and I shouldn't. You're coming with me, of course, and Mario automatically put Freddie and Trish on it, but they'd be invited whether they knew me or not. I doubt Dorothy's been asked, though. It's not really her crowd, and anyway, she's in a different camp."

"You mean because she's a friend of that Rudi person?"

Here it comes, she thought. Keep that nice, casual lilt in your voice, Frances. Hamilton is trying to do a little detecting, and you've got to do your best to help him. "Rudi Kranovic. Yes. Not that she was ever a regular customer at his restaurant, but she's certainly a friend of Rudi's and Chuck's." She brought in the name very carefully.

"Chuck?"

"Wetherby. Remember? That tennis man we met the other night?"

"Of course. But I don't remember Dorothy ever mentioning him."

"Oh, she's much more a friend of Rudi's, really. But Chuck is his friend. His lover. They share a house. I think Dorothy's gotten in rather tight with their . . . set. Since Spence died." There! You've made the connection for him. He can get straight to the point when he sees her tonight, if she's not too addled to understand what he's saying.

She suddenly couldn't stand any more of her own posturing. Please, please, Ham, she thought, don't stay too long. I have to be at Tables in an hour. I have to face Mario, all day long, and I've got to have a little time before that to fall apart, to pull myself together, to try to *think*. Just get out of here, Ham-whom-I-love-dearly, before I really do scream.

He may have sensed her desperation, because he got up from the bed and reached for his jacket. "So I'll see you later tonight sometime?" He stooped down to kiss her. She was unbearably relieved that he was going, but she held him to her for an extra minute before letting him go. She wasn't pretending. She wanted him to go, but at the same time she needed his strength. Ham had always been there to help her when anything happened, ever since Mama died, since . . . before that. And now he was the last person in the world she could ask for help.

24

CAROLE WANDERED slowly around her new apartment with her cigarettes and a mug of coffee, looking for a place to land that wasn't covered in plaster dust, finally carrying a folding chair over to the living-room windows. Her driver would be here soon to take her up to her director's house in Connecticut for dinner, but it was Christmas Day and she'd wanted to have a little while here alone — the first time in weeks without any workmen around. She was amazed — a little intimidated, even — by what Frances had set in motion, the number of people who'd been contracted to do all the ripping up and fixing and installing. She knew they'd probably work harder if she didn't hang around, because they tended to drop whatever they were doing and stare at her whenever she passed through a room, but she hadn't been able to make herself stay away.

She was hoping for a call, and she'd told her service to give out this number today only if it was a particular call. She was waiting for Martha Deloit to phone her back. She'd left a message with a maid the night before to please call Sadie Thompson, which meant absolutely nothing to the maid and might mean nothing to Martha herself because they hadn't thought to arrange any sort of code when they talked in Milwaukee that day. She was simply hoping it would click, that Martha would remember the name of *Rain*'s heroine and put two and two together. She was trying to decide what kind of message to leave if she couldn't get through directly to Martha a second time, when the only phone installed so far, back in the kitchen, did, in fact, ring.

"Merry Christmas," she said automatically when she answered.

"Thank you," Martha said dryly, not returning the sentiment. "I'd like to speak with Ms. Thompson, please."

"This is she and thank God you figured it out. I was just going to try again. I've had something in the mail. Well, messengered, actually, but . . ."

Martha interrupted her. "I can't talk long because I'm at a pay phone and I'll run out of change. My cook thought I was crazy when I insisted on going out for more butter we didn't need, and I'm in a Seven-Eleven parking lot."

"You've had the same letter? The same invitation, rather?" Impatient as she was, she couldn't help but smile at the idea of the coolly elegant Widow Deloit in a convenience store.

"No," Martha said, puzzled. "I don't know what you mean, but let me talk first. I would have phoned you anyway today, but then you . . . I don't understand, but let me tell you what I know." Carole wondered if Martha's envelope with the note and the invitation was sitting in a pile of Christmas cards somewhere, the way hers had been for three or four days before her secretary sorted out her mail. She couldn't wait to tell her about it, but she had to, because Martha was simply not going to let her talk until she was finished.

"It's not very concrete. My brother, you know, the —"

"Right. I know. The congressman." Her driver appeared at the door and she signaled for him to go back out to the car and wait.

"Well, he's had this, um, information for a couple of weeks, but he's even more careful than *we* are. He wouldn't tell me on the phone and today was the first day since the beginning of the Christmas recess he's had a chance to see me."

"Please," Carole begged. She didn't need to have the scene set for her. She wanted a name. She wanted the *same* name as the one in her mind.

"Well. I don't know if this will mean anything to you, but our man, our gay FBI man, used to be chummy with someone called Larry Lengdorf. There were a couple of invitations to parties in with his things. There was a ticket for drunk driving, and someone in the department wrote a memo on it, and it seems he'd been at this Lengdorf person's house, and there was another memo about Lengdorf's, um, proclivities. They must have been trying to decide whether this agent was a security risk. Before he killed himself."

"But he's dead! Larry, I mean. I knew him — my God, everyone in Hollywood knew him and loathed him. He was exactly the kind of monster who'd collect dirt like this, except he was so rich I can't imagine why he'd ever need to use it. Anyway, he's been dead for years. But . . ."

"Exactly. But. My brother has this theory that Lengdorf passed this on to someone. Maybe other things, too, about other people. We worked out the dates: I started getting these damn letters about a year after this Lengdorf died and so did you, from what you said."

"You might be right, but he knew *everybody*. He used to give parties for three hundred of his closest friends, he . . ."

"But apparently there was one man who was with him during the time he was dying. My brother had someone check on the probate. He left most of his money to his sisters and his college, and then some small bequests to friends and his gardener and his chauffeur, but the biggest thing was a Modigliani. To his dear companion, the will said. Someone named Kranovic. Rudolf Kranovic."

It took Carole an instant to translate Rudolf into Rudi, and then she gasped with relief. "I know him." There was a recording that asked for more money, and she could hear coins tinkling in a machine a thousand miles away. "I *know* Rudi, and what I was just going to tell you . . ."

"Does that mean he can't be the one?"

"No!" She wanted to scream with frustration. "It doesn't mean that at all. I didn't say I *liked* him. He's an odious man. But that isn't the point . . . shit, what's the number there? I'll call you right back. You've got to hear what I was going to say, the reason I phoned you in the first place, goddammit!"

Carole finally had a chance to explain, once she got Milwaukee on the line again, and this time Martha listened very carefully. She gave her only the barest outline first, that she was positive it was the same as the other letters, that Rudi and Chuck lived together, that of the two of them she had thought their ghoul almost certainly wasn't Chuck, that now of course they knew it wasn't, that for some unknown reason Chuck was giving them this incredible Christmas present, that it *couldn't* have come from Rudi himself, because there was no cologne. At least on hers, and she was convinced there wouldn't be any on Martha's either.

"But it might be someone else," Martha said. "I mean, *our* bastard has to be this man, but someone else in his house could have sent you that invitation. Maybe he has a snoopy valet or butler or something, whose wages we've been paying for years. It isn't necessarily this Chuck person."

"That hadn't occurred to me," Carole admitted. She had looked at the two names on the top of the invitation, she had been ninety-nine percent sure one couldn't be her monster, and she had assumed the other was the one who'd anonymously sent her the message that was enclosed with it.

"Does he *do* anything?" was Martha's next question. "I mean, does he earn a living of some kind when he isn't sitting around sucking blood?"

"He owns a restaurant. It's called Rudi's, it's very . . . well, it's been my favorite place in New York for years."

"So has he gone bankrupt lately or something? Is there any reason he'd be breaking his own pattern? That he'd suddenly get so much greedier?" Martha's voice had real excitement in it now.

"Yes. His manager — he's a friend of mine, a *real* friend — anyway, he quit a couple of months ago, and he's about to . . . look, can you come here? For New Year's Eve? First, go home and go through your letters and I'll bet —"

"There hasn't been anything."

"Well, then, it's the Christmas rush. Mine was hand-delivered. Yours was probably sent in the mail. You'll get it soon, don't you think? Anyway, I can't get away easily because of the play, and we need to sit down and talk about this. You're welcome to stay with me."

"Thanks, but I think I can swing a hotel."

She thought fast. "We'll go to his fucking party. That's what Chuck means for us to do. I was already invited, actually, and I'd already sent regrets because I'm going to another . . . well, I'll explain. But I'll unregret, and you'll come with me and we can — I don't know — we can at least *see* him. We can watch his face when we come in together, or we can try to get Chuck alone and . . . and get him to admit it somehow without telling him what it is we're trying to find out? But it's Rudi I want to concentrate on. There's no reason you and I *shouldn't* be friends, no reason he should be surprised, unless he knows what we think he knows."

"Couldn't we just meet for dinner at his restaurant?"

"No," Carole said slowly. "That's not good enough. He might not be there. He might spot us across the room first and have time to avoid us or put on one of his disgusting restaurateur smiles or something. And we wouldn't know any more than before."

"Okay. I don't know what good it's going to do, but we'll beard him in his own den. I'll be at the Westbury from, say, two in the afternoon, New Year's Eve. Will you be performing that night?"

She made it sound faintly like a trained seal act, but Carole ignored that. "Yes. We can talk in the afternoon and then, please, come as my guest to the show and we'll leave from there. Bring something really dressy, and we'll go to Rudi's party first and then this other one, if you like." The gracious lady of the theater, she thought. And now I'm giving fashion advice to this bitch. Pretty soon we'll be borrowing nail polish from each other.

Martha said something then, just before hanging up, that brought her back to the reality of what they were doing. "I wonder if I'll be able to see him without wanting to kill him," she mused in a perfectly neutral voice.

I wonder the same thing, Carole whispered to herself. She had no idea whether he was even in town this week, but she knew she couldn't take the chance of running into the man she now knew was her tormentor till she and Martha had decided what to do when they confronted him. She'd have to duck out of that dinner at the restaurant on the twenty-seventh for precisely that reason. She'd be hurting her costar's feelings — it was a celebration of a great movie part he'd landed — but, for once in her life, she wasn't totally confident that she could handle the role.

* * *

As soon as she was alone in her bedroom, Frances quietly locked the door to the hall behind her, and then the one that connected to the sitting room. It was Christmas night, and this was the first chance she'd had all day to be by herself. She'd gone through the last three days on sheer nerves, and she didn't think she could have come up with one more smile, one more polite word, for anyone.

The twenty-third, all day and on till nearly midnight, she'd been at Tables. There was so much to do that she would have been frantic anyway, but the phone call from Chuck the night before, fresh in her mind, gave everything an extra hellish touch. She was glad Mario was so preoccupied he'd barely talked to her, even when she'd badly needed his decisions on things. She didn't think he sensed anything different about the way she was acting, but if he did she hoped he'd chalk it up to the strain everyone was feeling. He's never seen me work under pressure, she reasoned.

The next day was just as terrible — worse, because she'd slept so badly — but at least, as far as seeing Mario was concerned, it ended earlier. He was staying late again with some of the staff and workmen, but she had to rush home for the little Christmas Eve dinner she and Ham were giving. Dorothy had been surprisingly clear-eyed all evening, but so jumpy that Frances was sure the minute she left (and she excused herself before dessert), she'd run for this drug, whatever it was, that she seemed to need so desperately. Ham's talk with her must have been mortifying, must have made her resolve to be good that night if she possibly could. She was positive Dorothy would never mention it, what she had done, but she wished she wouldn't look so sorrowful, so apologetic, every time their eyes met across the table. Trish, of course, knew something was wrong and took her aside to ask about it, but Frances shrugged it off as exhaustion. When that didn't seem to convince her, Frances laughingly added that it must be sexual frustration because she hadn't had time to be alone with Mario.

Then today had been awful in an entirely different way. Marianne had served a late breakfast for Ham and herself in the dining room, they'd exchanged presents, and she'd felt as miserable as she could remember feeling on any Christmas since her mother died. All the lovely, warm, generous feelings she usually had about the holidays were simply not there. Breakfast was bad enough, but the big mid-afternoon dinner at Peekie's was far worse. The very last thing she wanted to see right now was a baby, but of course little Sarah was passed around and she really was very lovable, but Frances had been just barely able to keep from crying.

It all contributed to the feeling she had now, a kind of suffocation, a claustrophobic sense that everything in her entire world was closing in on her. She tore off her clothes, ripping her blouse and then her slip. She didn't care. She threw herself on the bed and gave in to the tears she'd felt springing to her eyes all day. That night, the night of the phone call, she'd wept quietly, but these were loud, racking sobs that came so fast she gagged and had to run to the bathroom to throw up into the toilet. She stayed on the floor for a long while, and when the tears finally subsided, when there was nothing left in her, she was so weak she needed to hold onto the sink to pull herself up.

She threw cold water in her face and then she almost choked again on a swig of strong mouthwash. She was shivering, and she grabbed a terry-cloth robe from the back of the door before she stumbled into the bedroom, where she walked up to the full-length glass and confronted her reflection as if it might tell her something she needed to know. Her face was streaked, her eyes red, her hair a rat's nest, but she straightened, she held her hands down, she made an attempt to carry her head proudly. For an instant, staring at the woman in the mirror, she saw, in her long, white robe, a character in a Greek tragedy. She laughed, once, and she had to dig her nails into her palms to stop the hysteria she could feel welling up, but she couldn't make the thought go away.

Oedipus Rex, of course. I could be — what was her name? Jocasta, she remembered, his mother, the one who stabbed herself when she knew the truth. She used a pin of some kind, an elaborate brooch, and then her son — her husband — used the same pin to blind himself. Those plays were all about fate, of course, tricks of fate. This terrible idea, if it could conceivably be true, was like that: a trick, a cruel joke that she didn't deserve to have played on her.

Or do I deserve it? she wondered. Maybe I deserve everything that's happening to me. I didn't abort my baby, that's true, but it wasn't really religion or morality that stopped me, it was the danger and the dirty feeling that the word *abortion* carried with it all those years ago. But then I gave my child away to a stranger, to an abstraction, to no one at all. They took him away, and for all I know they let him die somewhere. So even though I didn't kill my baby, maybe I've committed a monstrous, unnatural sin by not raising him. At the very least, I should have made sure he was safe and well fed and loved, and I didn't even do that.

Her mind veered again. I ought to be calmly considering this whole thing for what it is, she said to her reflection. It's a nasty, mean joke, is what it is. It grew out of the mind of a drunken, crazy man. It's no truer than a rumor someone could start about me being a compulsive gambler, or an opium addict, or a kleptomaniac. It's a coincidence, she told herself once again. But maybe when these things happen they aren't only coincidences? Maybe Mario and I were so strongly attracted to each other because we actually have the same — what? — the same genetic makeup? It did seem like we'd always known each other, like there were so many things we didn't have to explain, but that could just be because we're both Italian — Italian-American — couldn't it? And of course, that's what people always think when they fall in love, that there's an unspoken communication, that they've always known each other. . . .

Is that the way it was with Michael? she asked herself. It was strange, but she couldn't really remember anymore what being with Michael was like. It was so long ago, they were so young, it was almost as if what she had with Mario had *erased* it. Without being completely conscious of what she was doing, she left the mirror and went to the little Second Empire lady's desk on the other side of the room. She opened the bottom drawer, pulled out an old stationery box that was filled with snapshots, and dug down to the only picture she'd kept of him. He was standing on the deck of the Staten Island Ferry, the skyline of Lower Manhattan as it had been then looming behind him. In the same box, on top, was a picture of Mario that she'd taken on the Brooklyn Bridge the day they walked over to have lunch at the River Cafe. Both men were squinting into the sun, so it was hard to see what they really looked like, but she held them together under the desk lamp and tried to find a resemblance.

They're certainly the same type, she thought. If I were casting a movie that called for dark, thin, Italian types, than either Mario or

Michael would get the part. Michael had a wider nose, a slightly smaller mouth, and fuller lips, but his build was the same as Mario's, the same as mine, really, if I were a man. Tall and thin, with wide shoulders, slender legs, rather narrow hips. And the eyes — we all three have the same dark, deeply set eyes. But, my God, that could mean anything. Maybe our ancestors all came from the same dusty little town outside of Naples, or the same quarter in Palermo. I admit I've always seen something of Michael in Mario, but that still doesn't prove anything. Maybe I can only fall in love with men who look like Michael because he was the first and I learned about love from him?

She put the pictures away, took her robe off, found her jightgown, and went to the medicine cabinet to look for the sleeping pills she'd stupidly refused to take for the past two nights. I can't do any more about it tonight, she thought. She had tried to track down Freddie but nobody could tell her where he might be. She couldn't ask Mario anything more about his past because he'd already told her everything he knew, which was next to nothing. I have to wait, she told herself, and I have to work very hard in the next few days. I'm Frances McKinnon. I'm Mrs. Hamilton McKinnon. I have things to do and places to go and people to see.

25

"YOU ALL LOOK GREAT," Mario said to his entire front-of-the-house staff. He'd hiked himself up onto the bar, and they sat below him, scattered around at the little café tables. They were wearing their uniforms for the first time, so it was a kind of dress rehearsal for the next night. He'd commissioned a young Japanese girl who did costumes for dance companies and off-Broadway shows, and she'd designed beautifully tailored black suits that suggested tuxedos without using any satin trim. With them, waiters and waitresses wore simple, rather full white shirts and black bow ties; the captains had the same shirts in black. Busboys looked like captains who'd taken off their coats and ties but who'd left the top button fastened. The bartenders looked like busboys who'd been bleached — medium gray shirts and pants. Everyone had the same classic, comfortable lace-up shoes, even the same black socks. It was exactly the effect he'd wanted — stylish without being trendy, just formal enough.

"Consider this a bull session or a rap session or an interface or whatever the hell you want to call it," he said to them. "Or a pop quiz. We've got less than twenty-four hours till showtime and I want to be sure you've been listening to me and all your other professors for the last couple of weeks." He pointed to a tall black waiter. "Leroy, what the heck's this here Pullet Chicken on the menu?"

"Um, it's natural. Sir. It's tender and firm and juicy." He rolled his tongue around his lips and everyone laughed. "No chemicals. No additives. From a farm in northern California."

"Jenny, what's an Oreo Dory?"

"Fish." Mario had hired this pretty, middle-aged Irish widow straight from a diner in his neighborhood where he used to talk with her over breakfast sometimes. She'd been overwhelmed by all this and intimidated by the others, but she'd done her homework and now she sounded as professional as the best of them. "From New Zealand, and it's very delicate, sort of like sole. And we grill it on coconut wood."

At the far end of the room, he could see Frances and the flower man pulling something out of a crate and holding it up for him to see. The custom underpads for the tables, which would help muffle sound a little more, had finally arrived. Another problem he could cross off his list. "Bob, how's the partridge prepared?"

"It's stuffed, but not in its, um, interior cavity." Bob told everyone who'd listen that he'd just found himself. His passion for the restaurant had replaced the faint interest he'd shown for pre-med at Columbia. Mario was already grooming him for a captain's job. "There's ricotta cheese and Mexican marigold mint between the skin and the meat and then it's roasted. Sir."

"Frank, what's wrong with Julio's uniform?" Julio was a Dominican busboy who was finishing the food course at Park West High School. At the moment, he looked like he might cry.

"He's . . . uh, he's wearing an ID bracelet," Frank said, "but I'm sure he wouldn't . . ."

"I know he wouldn't, and I'm not trying to set up some kind of Stalinist informer network. I'm just making the point again. No jewelry, no nail polish unless it's clear and . . . what's the third dress code no-no, Julio?"

"No heavy cologne."

"Right. Or perfume. Now, I'm . . ." Louis, in the running shoes he always wore, padded up behind him on the other side of the bar and shoved a plate under his nose.

"Canaillon melon," Louis whispered with awe. "They had it at Hunt's Point and on top — *alors,* you guess."

He tasted the chilled slices, dressed with a few drops of a golden dessert wine but meant to be served as a first course. "Muscat de

Beaumes-de-Venise," he pronounced. "And now you want it on the party menu." Louis nodded solemnly.

Mario smiled. "I think it's nectar. I think you're right. I think I'm glad I'm not the one who has to convince Lillian to call the printer again."

Louis shrugged and Mario turned back to his staff. "Cheryl, I'm Barbra Streisand and I'm sitting at that table over there. What do you call me?"

"Superstar," someone at the back of the crowd said. "Babs," one of the busboys yelled. The look on Mario's face stopped their laughter. "Ma'am," Cheryl said. "I call you ma'am."

"Exactly." He looked at them for a moment while they fidgeted. "I know I've said this about seventeen times, but I'm saying it again and you won't have to hear it after tonight. The people who eat here are Sir and Ma'am, unless they're royalty or heads of state, and then you can assume someone'll tell you what to say." He took a breath. "I know some of you think this is elitist or that I'm trying to keep you in your place or something, but actually I think it's pretty democratic. Mostly, it's because I think people with famous faces deserve a break. We can't stop someone from another table fawning over them — although I don't think there's going to be much of that with this crowd — but we sure as hell *won't* be doing it ourselves. Besides, there might be some guy — at Streisand's table, say, or the next one over — whose name you *don't* know and his sensitive feelings might get hurt. After a while, everyone'll figure out that this is the way they're going to be treated here. And if I hear anyone, *anyone* — except conceivably one of the captains — saying 'Loved your show' or 'Great new album,' then that anyone is no longer a waitperson at this restaurant."

An older Irish waiter named Michael spoke up. "But it's okay to ask 'em to autograph a menu as long as we say 'Sir' or 'Ma'am' first?" Mario grinned and shook his head. His class decided it was all right to smile again.

For two hours — between interruptions from Lillian, Louis, Frances, Priscilla, and a half-dozen others — he tossed out questions as fast as he could think of them. What wines would they recommend for a simple veal *escalope?* For swordfish? For roast pork? How do you tactfully tell a customer he/she has had too much to drink? That his/her credit card is N.G.? Are the gooseneck barnacles from Portugal or British Columbia? Why are we serving farm-raised catfish rather than Channel catfish? What's the least awkward way to crumb the table and take the salt away before dessert? When he was satisfied, he stopped and got them to throw questions at him for another hour. It was past midnight by the time he jumped down off the bar. He was very tired and his voice was hoarse, but he was pleased with all of them and he told them so.

The flower man, his assistant, and some busboys were still pulling the underpads out of cartons, checking them, and plopping them down on tables. A crew of workmen were up on tall ladders, hanging the last few elements of the patchwork false ceiling. Frances was slumped in a chair over by the window that the glaziers, at her insistence, had just reinstalled because she'd discovered a slight draft. From across the room, he wiggled his eyebrows, jerked his head toward the back of the house, and she nodded and held up five fingers. He walked slowly down the corridor to the kitchen. It was silent and empty for the first time today, but someone had made fresh coffee in one of the big urns, and he poured himself half a cup. There was a lot of noise from back in the locker rooms, where everyone was changing out of uniforms, but his office was blissfully quiet. He found a bottle of Courvoisier at the little wet bar, splashed some into his coffee, and sat back to wait for her.

The room was surrounded on three sides by glass, and he got up suddenly to let down the pale wood venetian blinds that made it cozy and private. He lowered the lights; he switched on a tape of Ella Fitzgerald singing Rodgers and Hart; if there'd been a fireplace, he'd have lit a fire. He badly wanted, he *needed,* to hold Frances close, to be alone with her for a while, but this wasn't really a seduction scene he was setting up. Even if he had the energy — which, he said to himself, was debatable at the moment — this was the wrong time and place for making love. Afterward, he thought, after tomorrow night. Maybe they'd even be able to go away somewhere for a night? A weekend? They hadn't met at the house for a couple of weeks, and in the few private moments they'd had since then, their embraces had been hurried and nervous. This last push, since Christmas, had been the worst, a blur of constant motion. He hadn't been home for days, grabbing two or three hours of sleep on the reproduction Empire daybed (a *lit de repos,* he'd learned to call it) that Frances had put in his office, showering and shaving in the locker room. He couldn't have said what he'd had for dinner the night before, or if he'd eaten anything today since breakfast. Thinking about it now, he was amazed to realize he couldn't even remember when he'd last kissed Frances.

Without knocking, she came in, threw herself in the chair on the other side of the desk, and smiled weakly. He gazed at her for a minute without speaking. Her hair was tied back with a ribbon, but some of it had escaped. She wore almost no makeup. She was obviously very tired, but he thought she was very beautiful. Her skin was pale to the point of transparency, and he saw a tiny blue vein at her temple that he'd never noticed before. Without asking if she wanted any, he got up, poured a snifter of brandy, and brought it to her from behind, leaning down to kiss the back of her neck as he reached around to hand it to her. She jerked so abruptly that a few drops were spilled on the carpet. She held on to his hand for a moment, long enough for him to feel her trembling, and then she released it and reached across the desk for his pack of cigarettes. He straightened, put his hands on her shoulders, and rubbed them gently. They usually seemed so delicate, so fragile, to him. Now he could feel hard cables of tension.

"We're a bundle of nerves?" he asked, leaning down to take the lighter from her, flicking it for her cigarette and then his own.

She closed her eyes as she inhaled. "We're a bundle of nerve *endings*. I'm sorry. My mind's still racing. This'll help." She raised the snifter and tilted her head back to smile up at him. "Thank you. Chin-chin!"

"Let's be somewhere else. Let's be in . . ." He looked around him. "Venice? Is that where they invented venetian blinds?" He moved against the round bolster at one end of the daybed, leaving space for her. "No Tables talk?"

She snapped her fingers. "Just like that? It ain't so easy." She dug into the pocket of the loose silk jacket she was wearing and pulled out some crumpled papers. "My list. My life at this moment is reduced to what hasn't been crossed off this list. First thing in the morning, I have to get the marble replaced in . . ."

"Details." He could hear the petulance in his voice. He was

disappointed. He'd been so sure she'd follow him over here but she was still in that damned chair, gripping the snifter with one hand and the armrest with the other. He told himself to calm down. "Those are details. All the major stuff is done, all the heavy problems are solved. It's incredible, you know it is. Now you can let go for just a little bit, just a few minutes. The last big deal was the ceiling, and they must have finished that by now."

"Shall we go see?" She set her drink down and jumped up. Her hand was on the doorknob before he found his voice.

"Frances!" She froze, moving neither out the door nor back from it. "You just got here. You've only had a . . . a sip of brandy and half a cigarette."

She slowly turned around to face him. Her skin was flushed now. Her eyes glittered, and he was shocked by what he found in them. He told himself he must be wrong, that what he was seeing wasn't panic, the look of a woman running away from . . . from what? A rapist? A murderer? When she spoke, her words tumbled out feverishly.

"I can't. It's not possible. I have to keep moving or I'll . . . I don't know what. I've got to get out of here and go home and take one of those sleeping pills and fall into bed and then get up unbelievably early in the morning and get through the day, and then tomorrow night I'll *know*." She stopped herself, but she was talking again before he could get a word in. "I'll know if I'm a real designer, if I can cut the mustard. All the money you've spent, all the faith you've put in me . . ."

"Have been worth it," he finished for her gently. "Every penny, every bit of faith. I can't believe you have any doubt about it — it's the most beautiful restaurant I've ever seen and everyone else is going to feel the same way." He paused. He didn't know how to ask her. "Is there something else? Are you afraid? Of something? Of me?"

"No. No, it's just . . . I'm sorry, Mario." She tried to laugh. "This job is so important to me because of you, because it's your future I'm playing around with here, and I've sort of whipped myself into a frenzy, I guess, and I have to keep myself intact. I can't let myself go, I can't let you hold me. I'll shatter, I'll break into a million pieces and . . . and then you'll have to find a broom in the janitor's closet."

He was standing, but he didn't dare move toward her. He closed his eyes and nodded slowly. "Then we should say good-night? And sleep tight?"

"And don't let the bedbugs bite, yes. It's going to be all right. After tomorrow. I *know* it's going to be all right." She turned and left.

We're both exhausted, we're running on empty, he told himself as he switched off Ella, undressed, and took a blanket and pillow out of the closet. Everything's going to be distorted, with this kind of pressure. Everyone's bound to overreact. He wished he could forget the look on her face, though, the fear, the feeling that it had something to do with him.

* * *

This hasn't been such a good idea, Maggie was thinking for the hundredth time. She was sitting in the hot tub, and the steam that rose around her frizzed her hair and made the sweat pour down her face. The point of coming to North Carolina for this holiday week with Jim was meant to be relaxation and a little work. Looking back, she saw that all she'd gotten out of it was too much coke, too much sex, and not even enough sleep. She'd brought some papers from the office down with her — the introduction to a catalogue she was supposed to edit, the schedule for next season, some letters — but she hadn't touched them. She'd intended to catch up on some reading — a new monograph on Man Ray, maybe the last Joseph Heller, even a little Proust — but the books were still there, unopened, on the table next to the bed. Jim was over at the airstrip tinkering with his plane, and she'd been here alone all morning. The weather was cloudy and depressing, almost raining but never quite getting around to it. She was bored and miserable.

The last day of the year, she said to herself. Some year. The last day of *last* year, I was worrying about whether Mario could get away from Rudi's early enough to join up with me at a party. I was wondering if I could squeeze into the new Norma Kamali I bought myself at an after-Christmas sale. I was hoping Max was going to let me curate a group show in the spring. Now I'm running Max's gallery, my dresses fit me fine, thank you very much, and God knows I don't have to worry about what Mario's doing. I know exactly what he's doing: he's running around his new eatery with Frances McKinnon on his arm and they're checking on all those oh-so-important last-minute details so the opening tonight can be a fucking *succès fou*.

It was one of the reasons she'd come down here with Jim — she'd even begged him to stay longer than he wanted to — so she wouldn't be able to change her mind at the last minute and go to the party. Of course, she could have gone to Chuck and Rudi's thing. It would be second string, junior varsity, all the people who hadn't managed to get on Mario's list, but it would be crowded and noisy and, she was sure, lavish. She'd be so tempted to make it clear that she *had* been invited to Tables, though. She tried to imagine it. Chuck would be truly, genuinely sympathetic if he weren't too drunk. Rudi would muster up some false solicitude. Some of their nastier gay friends might be the worst of all. She could hear them. Thought you'd be at Tables tonight, my dear. Sorry to hear about you and Mario. She couldn't have taken it. She would have drunk too much and snorted too much. She would have ended up *throwing* something, she was sure of it: a glass or a dog or some little creep who'd manage to say just exactly the wrong thing at the wrong time.

So. There was less than half a day left in the old year, and here she was, poaching herself like an egg or a salmon, feeling, as a babysitter used to say about her, as mean as a snake. When Jim came back for lunch, he'd probably have scored another few grams from his buddy down the road. He'd be ready for another round of stupid, role-playing, meaningless sex, and naturally he'd assume she'd be ready for the same thing. She was suddenly thoroughly disgusted with herself. She stood up quickly, and the water poured off her and sloshed down the cedar boards onto the pine needles.

She knew where she wanted to be, and that was with Mario. "All right," she said aloud, drying off, "I can't exactly be *with* him but I can at least go to this goddamn party." She thought about what it would be like if she opened her own gallery, really her own, with her name on the door, and she knew how Mario must feel about this. Like it's the most important thing that's ever happened to him, she thought, maybe even more important than that bitch is, even now. I ought to be there. I ought to show my pretty face. I have a *right* to be there. It's as simple as that, even if it's so embarrassing and painful I can only stand ten minutes of it.

She ran back to the house and began to pack, first her things and then Jim's. She'd go over to the housekeeper's place, she was thinking, and let her know they were leaving, give her some money for all the extra work they'd caused her. She had too much to carry, though; she couldn't walk to the airstrip and she couldn't wait for Jim to get back with the jeep. She'd call a cab to take her from one end of the farm to the other. She'd convince him to fly her back, now, this afternoon. He'd be enraged because she was changing her mind, when he was the one who'd wanted to go back yesterday. He'd find a dozen reasons not to go, he'd call her every filthy name in his vocabulary, but he'd end up doing it. She'd discovered something about Jim Wilkins that had first intrigued her and then bored her, like everything else about him: when it really came down to it, when she was totally immovable, absolutely insistent on having her way, he gave in. More than that: he actually *liked* to be told what to do, he liked to be given orders. Scratch a sadist, she'd said to herself when she understood it, and you'll find . . . well, you'll find Jim. They still played the same sexual games, but once or twice he'd hinted that he'd like the shoe to be on the other foot. She hadn't taken up the challenge, not there, not in bed, and she'd never sorted out whether that was meaner and therefore kinder and therefore meaner, or vice versa. Anyway, today she knew she'd get what she wanted.

She found him next to the plane. Parts of it lay on a piece of plastic he'd spread on the ground, and he was fiddling with one of them. Once she told him what they were doing, once he said it was impossible, which was what she knew he'd say, she barely listened to him. All that mattered to her was the weather, which seemed to be okay even if it was a little dreary, and the permission from the traffic controllers, which she knew he could arrange. After that, everything he said about electric struts and ailerons and moisture in the gear wells went straight past her. She sat patiently in the jeep, knowing she'd won. She opened a book for the first time that week.

It took most of the afternoon for him to get the plane in shape, and he was still swearing about some problem when she climbed aboard and strapped herself in. They taxied slowly down the runway so they could take off into the wind, and he threw his coke bottle in her lap and told her to give him a couple of spoonfuls. Since he could have done it himself without much trouble, she knew he was getting some of his pride back by making her serve him, but she didn't care. She'd be late, she might not make it till after midnight, but she'd *be* there, she'd be where she belonged. She snorted only a little — after all, she didn't want to get totally wired tonight — but it was enough to give her a lift that came at the same moment as their takeoff.

She thought they were climbing at a steeper pitch than she remembered from the other time she'd left from this strip, but she didn't pay much attention. She was trying to decide what to wear — too elaborate would be just as pathetic as too plain. Black, she thought dreamily. Makes me look even thinner. And maybe the silver Manolo Blahnik sandals? She was only vaguely aware that her head was thrust back against the seat for a longer time than before, that they were still climbing at the same dizzying angle, that they'd easily cleared the trees by now, that they should be starting a more gradual ascent. She looked over at Jim, and she saw the veins that were standing out in his neck. He was gripping the yoke, trying with all his strength to fight against whatever it was that had jammed. His lips were pulled back; his clenched teeth were bared; for an instant, the way his face contorted when he had an orgasm flashed through her mind.

Then she could only see a skull, the terrible grin that skulls always seemed to have, and she screamed. The plane began to climb more sharply, as if steps in the sky were growing steeper until they were a ladder. For a moment they were heading straight up and then they went into a perfect backward somersault, just one, as neat as any amusement park ride. Somewhere in the great circle they made, the engine coughed and then it stopped.

In the silence, as they fell, as he tried to restart it in the few seconds they had left, she could hear every word Jim was whispering. He wasn't talking to her or to his mother or to God. He was talking to his plane, he was pleading with it, but it wasn't responding. As for her, she'd stopped screaming; she'd left her fear behind, somewhere on the carnival loop-the-loop. Now she felt only rage.

She said, "No," over and over again, very clearly, because she was going to die, because this wasn't fair. The last thought she had, as the plane came down into the highest pine, as the first branch slashed through the windscreen and cut into her throat, was that she would never see Mario again.

26

MARIO WAS REMEMBERING what he'd said when he was a little boy at the opening of Fermi's Italian Seafood down on Battery Wharf, that it was the most beautiful restaurant in the world, at which point Johnny had reminded him that he'd only been in one restaurant in his short life. Now, freshly showered, shaved, and dressed, he stood with his back to the elevator lobby at the top of the three wide, shallow steps leading down into the bar, and repeated the same words quietly to himself. And then, to Johnny, he added that this time he *knew* he was right and he wished more than anything that Johnny were there so he, Mario, could prove it. He was all grown up, he'd eaten in most of the world's best restaurants, and he had a thousand points of comparison.

His guests would start to arrive at nine, half an hour from now. He had double- and triple-checked everything he could possibly worry about, and he was claiming this moment as his own. Tables was complete, they'd done it, they'd made it, and he was deciding it was worth every cent, every drop of sweat. From where he stood, he couldn't see beyond the big stepped-up pyramid, banked with masses of white peonies, that was the centerpiece of the bar. He walked slowly down the steps and around it to the edge of the bar level, cleared of all its miniature Knoll pedestal tables and its witty little gilt fin-de-siècle chairs for now because it was one of the areas (along with the private dining rooms, one on each side of this space) where stand-up cocktails were going to be served from nine to ten. After that, during and after dinner, there would be dancing on its parquet. The quartet, which would start with soft background music at nine, was warming up at one end, and their plunks and tweets and honks accompanied him as he approached the simple, pale-green-lacquered half-moon that was the captains' station and gazed out over the enormous room.

It was probably never again going to look quite like this, he said to himself, never so perfect, never so still, never so empty of even a single waiter or busboy. They were back in the locker rooms, changing into their uniforms from the jeans they'd worn all day. He hoped they were relaxing for a few minutes, because they had turned over their minds and their muscles and, he felt, their hearts to him today and all the past few days, and he wished he could find something other than a bonus that might conceivably show how grateful he was to them for becoming the team he'd asked for.

The lighting consultant had only just now found exactly the right settings everywhere, because it was only tonight that it could be done, only tonight that every last element was here. The jigsaw of the ceiling was finally in place; the last yards of drapery were finally hung; the busboys and the waiters and the flower man and his assistant had set the tables; the sun had set itself. It was, Mario thought, so perfect that it seemed a shame to ruin it with people.

Frances had planned the juxtaposition of forms and colors for the ceiling like a hard-edge abstract artist, twenty-seven pieces, three sizes each of nine different geometric forms. He had known how it would look from the maquette she made out of cardboard for him, but he hadn't realized how wonderfully the lighting fixtures she designed would complement it. There were nine of them, lined up three by three and suspended on the thinnest possible wire so that they floated a few feet below the ceiling, which in turn floated above them. They were about four feet across and a couple of inches thick — like pizza boxes made of frosted glass, Frances had explained to him when she first had the idea, except that each of them represented one of the ceiling's nine textbook shapes. Attached vertically, flat against the ivory-colored pillars that lined the room, were the same shapes again, also Frances's design. They were much smaller, fabricated of tempered pale green glass that was sandblasted to exactly the right degree so the bulbs they held wouldn't glare.

The only other lights in the room glowed at the tables themselves. Depending on their size, they were allotted from one to four little silver butane lamps, flat round bases supporting simple cylinders that were topped with parchment shades. And the city itself, of course — outside the floor-to-ceiling windows that surrounded the dining room of Tables on three sides — blessed (that was the word Mario used to himself now) his restaurant with its own light. Frances had hung three layers of pale gray draperies at the windows — one diaphanous, one a little less so, one a little less than that — to work together or separately in handling all the different degrees and angles of sunlight. She had reminded him that her living room used this same idea, and he had reminded her that the very last thing he would have noticed, the one time he was there, was what her curtains looked like. Tonight, the most transparent of these three softened the lights of Chelsea and downtown and midtown and made them dreamy and unreal and very much like a stage set, which was precisely the effect he'd wanted.

And it really was a kind of theater, he thought. From where he stood, the four tiers dropped gracefully down to the very bottom row of tables, at the base of the windows — the proscenium, beyond which the city was the show itself. Straight down the center from where he stood ran a broad aisle, broken along the way by gracefully proportioned steps leading from one level to the next. Along each side of the room ran another aisle, which was where the ushers — the waiters and waitresses, rather — would do most of their running back and forth to the kitchen. The low partitions of pale green glass that had originally been meant to line the steps and the edge of each tier of tables had been vetoed at practically the very last minute. Less than two weeks ago, Frances announced (and Mario now agreed with her) that they were wrong, that she was sorry but, with the hanging fixtures and the sconces and the windows themselves, it would be too much glass, that simple rails would be better, that she would absorb the cost because it was her fault. A foundry in Connecticut, working day and night for a week — the only major item that went over budget — had produced these simple steel bars plated with nickel (which he hadn't seen in any building younger than Radio City Music Hall) that added a kind of softly burnished warmth to the room.

Walking along each level, touching every table (for good luck? he didn't know, but he had to do it), he decided that, in another sense, every table was its *own* theater. The colors of their cloths, mirroring those of the ceiling but heightened, brightened to a more brilliant tone, were sprinkled like jewels around the room and repeated once or twice. The suites of chairs, though, were never duplicated. Each table had been bestowed with a different style, along with the appropriate underplates and vase — all reproductions except the most modern — and so each table became a world. Frances had thought they might be able to carry the themes farther, down to the last salad plate and fork, but Mario had to talk her out of it: the kitchen and dishwashing logistics would have been overwhelming, and so (except for the underplates) they settled on the plainest white Rosenthal china, the simplest Christofle silver plate, and classically shaped crystal.

Tonight, each little stage set was very pure. On the table surrounded by Second Empire chairs was a Limoges vase filled with old-fashioned pale yellow roses, and the correct underplates. At another, black-and-white speckled Memphis chairs accompanied a jagged Neo-Egyptian vase out of which papyrus spilled, and bright green faux-malachite underplates. In the future, though, the in-house designer intended to play with periods, and Frances had agreed that he should do exactly that. So there might be an Art Nouveau vase with calla lilies at the table of Saarinen chairs, and the underplates might be Louis XVI. Or the Charles Rennie Mackintosh chairs might be living for a night with a Finnish vase from the 'fifties and Wedgwood underplates. Nothing would ever be static. On no two nights would Tables ever be precisely the same.

By the time he'd gone back and forth across the room on each tier, the captains and waiters and busboys had begun to emerge from the back of the house and these moments alone with his first-born were over. He toured the kitchen again quickly, finding a way of touching everyone in it in the way he'd made contact with every single table, to appease the same superstition he'd suddenly discovered in himself. He was back out in the elevator lobby, paneled in alternating stripes of rosewood and Philippine mahogany, just as the first people arrived.

He had asked Frances and Steve to stand here with him tonight in what he had imagined would be a kind of receiving line that everyone stepping out of the elevators would pass by, but they had both refused. This was *his* restaurant, *his* night, they said; their jobs were over; his was only beginning. So, except when the Radnors joined him (and soon grew bored because no one paid enough attention to them), he stood alone, his captains a few feet behind him, and welcomed two hundred and fifty guests in a kind of daze. Their names were ticked off the list down in the ground-floor foyer; their coats were checked in the ground-floor cloakroom. There was nothing for them to do, once they were up here on the twentieth floor, other than be handsome and beautiful and admiring and congratulatory — and that was what they were — and to be pointed toward a drink or two before the captains led them to their tables.

Everyone was seated by ten, just as they were meant to be, and Mario could find a moment once again to look out over his domain. Now it's complete, he thought, now it's as I imagined it when I first stood in the middle of a dusty, depressing, fake medieval room and heard voices and laughter and the tinkle of crystal and silver and china. And music, of course. After tonight, it would be a piano and one of several Juilliard students. Tonight, the quartet was beginning to play danceable tunes and in another minute couples would be leaving their first courses to climb up here for "Begin the Béguine" or "Stardust" (he'd specified what he wanted: old tunes, nothing wilder than a cha-cha, nothing that needed as much space as a waltz).

For the second time, he thought, never again will the room look quite like this, although this time he laughed at himself, at the way he seemed to be prone right now to sweeping historical pronouncements. Anyway, never again would every man in the room be in black tie and never again would nearly every woman in the room be in an evening gown. Of course, it would have been the perfect setting for charity parties. He'd already been approached by a dozen ladies on a dozen letterheads topheavy with sponsors, and it could be filled two or three times a month with tuxedos and gowns and jewels again, even if they were worn by a very different crowd. But he had decided there would never be a benefit here, that Tables would never rent itself out, that it would be open to the people who used it as their club and that those people would never be greeted downstairs by a sign that read "Closed for Private Party."

He was allowing himself to relax a little now. Everything was happening that should be: waiters were taking orders from the short menu for the first course, others were already serving it, wine was being poured. The room was excited and happy and — from their faces as they looked around, he was sure of it even from here — as much in love with the place as he was. He smiled at the notion he'd had for an instant an hour ago, that it was so perfect it was a shame to fill it up with people. His clientele, his club, his friends — they were the point. All the rest was meant to bring out all the beauty or charm or grace they possessed. He would give them the best food and drink, he would provide them with the most beautiful setting in which to eat and drink it, and they would write and rewrite and act in their own dramas and comedies, night after night after night.

* * *

"May I have this dance, miss?" Mario put his arm around Lillian. The band was making a segue from "Lady, Be Good" to "The Lady Is a Tramp."

"If there's an extra square foot, I'd be chahmed, I'm shuah." Most of the tables were at a point somewhere between the second course and the entrée now, and this bar level was jammed with happy fox-trotters. He and Lillian had to wedge their way in.

"Have I told you how lovely you look?" He smiled down at her.

"No, you haven't." She shrugged. "But everyone else has and I'm getting a little blasé about my great loveliness. Wait'll you see the bill, though." He'd told her to get herself a sensational dress for this party, his treat, and she'd invested in pea-green chiffon, miles of it, sprinkled with rhinestones in strange places. It wasn't that it was ugly, exactly, or unflattering, he thought, it was just . . . perfect for Lillian.

"Hates California, it's cold and it's damp," she sang softly to the music, and he was glad she was having fun, that the captains had found time to dance with her, that the gallant Hamilton McKinnon had claimed her for a surprisingly graceful cha-cha, that everything was going so smoothly.

He could see Hamilton now, dancing with Trish Green, but it

looked as if they were having a very serious conversation and they were hardly moving. Mario guided Lillian over to the edge of the crowd so he could look down to the McKinnons' table on the lowest tier, over at the windows. Trish's escort, the handbag manufacturer, was concentrating on his food. Frances, big pear-shaped diamond pendants flashing at her ears — the only jewelry she wore — was leaning across to say something to Rick Radnor and his wife. Her hair was pulled back in a loose knot, and her pale gray watered-silk dress left one shoulder bare and then fell to the floor in loose folds. Givenchy, she'd said when he asked her, early 'seventies. She'd worn it because it was timeless, because it blended with the taupes and ivories and grays she'd chosen for the walls and carpet and drapes.

There were other beautiful, brilliantly dressed, lavishly jeweled women here, but Frances commanded the room tonight without trying, without, he thought, even being conscious of her power or wanting it. He didn't know where her mind was, but it certainly wasn't here at the party. From this distance, she seemed very still, very serene, a figure from a Greek frieze. Closer, he knew, her face showed all the exhaustion and tension and — he was sure of it — *fear* that he'd seen yesterday. Whatever it was that had made her so tense and miserable was still there, just under the surface. When he'd stopped by her table a few minutes before, he'd noticed how often she was glancing up to the entrance, and now he wondered if this might have something to do with the empty place next to her. Frederick McKinnon was getting back from somewhere tonight and he'd apparently be coming straight here from Kennedy. . . .

He felt Lillian tugging his sleeve, and he shook himself and looked down at her. "I said your name twice just now and I was about to stomp on your foot," she said. "Some gals don't *like* dancing with zombies, you know."

"I'm sorry. Really. I was thinking about something."

"You were thinking about some*one*." She arched a severely plucked eyebrow. "What's the matter with her tonight? What's been going on for the last week, now that I'm asking?"

"Has it been that long?"

She nodded. "You've been bouncing off walls so maybe you

haven't noticed a lot of things but, trust me, something's been wrong since before Christmas. And it's a crime — she ought to be happy as a clam right now. Every single person here is just . . . just *entranced* with the way this place looks and it's all thanks to her. She should be relaxing and patting herself on the back, and instead of that she's wound up like a top and she looks like she expects the ceiling to cave in any minute."

The band was swinging into another number and Mario led her off the floor to a quieter corner of the bar. "The worst thing," she went on, "the thing that makes me mad — and I know it's not her fault and you know how much I like her — is that it's ruining *your* night, and you should be feeling like the king of the world or something right now. You've been working your butt off for months, excuse my French, and now it's all come together and you've got yourself a *smash*." She spread her arms to include the whole room. "Look at 'em. Or don't. Walk around with a blindfold on and just *listen* to 'em and what you're gonna hear is nothing but solid raves, Mario. They're crazy about the food and the design and the service and the whole whatchamacallit. Ambiance." She stood up on her tiptoes and gave him a kiss. "I'm proud of you, and for you, and I hate anything that could make you even one percent unhappy tonight," she said.

He smiled and hugged her and thanked her, but she wasn't finished yet. "And if you want to know what else I think — well, even if you *don't* want to know — I think there's something else that's sorta dragging you down. Maggie should be here, that's all there is to it. I'm disappointed in her. I thought she had bigger b—— I thought she had more guts."

"You can't blame her, though, Lill, and Christ knows I don't have a right to expect anything from her. But, no, it doesn't feel right and it makes me sad. All that time she spent listening to me squawk about Rudi."

"And now she's up at *his* little soiree?"

"No, she was going down south with Jim Wilkins."

"*That* schmuck. Well, maybe she'll call. If . . ." He tuned out. A captain was leading Frederick down toward Frances's table, and Mario watched to see what she would do. Even from this distance, he could see her freeze for an instant when she noticed. Then she rose quickly and flew up the steps toward him, intercepting him halfway. She whispered in his ear, took his hand, and they climbed back up to the bar level and straight through the dancers. She led him into one of the empty private dining rooms.

Just as you thought, Mario said to himself. She *was* waiting for him and she obviously wants to talk with him alone. So, now that you know that, you know . . . exactly nothing.

* * *

"Hamilton. Listen to me. You must have *some* idea of what's going on with her," Trish was saying to him. They were on the dance floor, locked in a box step that was barely acknowledging the music. "I'm sorry. I shouldn't be asking you, but she's been like this for days and she won't tell me what it is. She won't even admit anything's the matter. Pressure, she says. Stress, she says. And if you won't tell me, then I can't even *try* to help."

He frowned, he shook his head slowly, he screwed up his face to give it what he hoped was a puzzled look, but his mind was racing. Of course, something was very, very wrong with Frances — anyone who spoke to her for two minutes, anyone who so much as glanced at her, could see that. He had thought there was some sort of trouble with Mario. A lovers' quarrel, he'd told himself, deliberately using those precise words, however much pain they gave him. Now that he realized she wasn't even confiding in Trish — and she would have, he knew, if it was something like that — then . . . then he could think of only one thing that could be doing this to her. For some reason, now that he forced his mind to concentrate on the way she'd been, he was sure she didn't *know* anything, one way or another, that the possibility was there but not the certainty. There was something in her that was waiting, suspended. Like him, she had to hold on until she knew, and the way she'd find out, once and for all, the one she'd go to . . . was Freddie.

Of course. He suddenly remembered how many times in the past week she'd mentioned Freddie, how often tonight she'd asked what time it was and said she hoped Freddie's flight wasn't delayed. Because he'd been so distracted himself, because he'd been waiting for the same plane to land, meaning to take his brother aside the minute he arrived here, Hamilton hadn't been paying as much attention to her tonight as he usually would have done. He was so angry at his own blindness, for a moment, that he forgot where he was, forgot to shuffle his feet. Trish waited patiently.

Frances had been so busy that he'd seen very little of her since the night of Chuck Wetherby's call, but whenever they were together he was so wrapped up in behaving normally, in not letting anything slip out, that he hadn't seen *her* fear. Not till tonight and, even then, not till just now. It was clear, suddenly, everything except how she could have known. He'd gone to the office late every morning so he could be the first one to see the mail at home, and there had been nothing — no envelope without a return address, nothing with the familiar typewriter script. He'd even asked Marianne to let him know immediately at the office if something came for Mrs. McKinnon by messenger, but please not to mention it to Mrs. McKinnon because it was something that might upset her and he would handle it. There must have been a phone call, he decided. That was the only way Chuck — no, *Rudi,* he always had to remind himself, although it was Chuck's voice he could still hear — could have done it.

Of course, Trish had no idea of what she'd just told him. He hadn't answered her, they were still moving slowly around the same box, and she was still trying to convince him that something was seriously the matter with Frances. ". . . fifty people," she was saying. "At least. And I watched her say *exactly* the same thing, word for word, to each of them. 'Thank-you-that's-so-kind-I-have-to-admit-I'm-pleased-with-it-myself.' Like a princess at a garden party who's been coached by her governess, Hamilton, or a . . . a *robot.*" Her voice caught and he saw the tears in her eyes. He felt so bad for her, he was so tired of holding it all in, that he came very close to letting her know what was happening. But it's Frances's secret, he said to himself, Frances's and — if it's true and, please God, it mustn't be because it will destroy her — Mario's. I have no right to tell anyone, not even her oldest, dearest friend.

The band finished playing around with "Luck, Be a Lady Tonight," the last number of the medley, and paused. Hamilton and Trish stood apart, clapping politely with the other couples, and it was then that he saw Frederick. Frances had him by the hand and he was following her into a private dining room. "I think, I hope," he said quietly to Trish, "we'll have Frances back again very soon."

* * *

"Should we wait a few minutes?" Carole asked Martha Deloit. Their limousine was pulling up in front of Rudi's house, and Carole was suddenly as scared as she'd been since her first first night. "It must be almost exactly midnight, and if it's any kind of party at all it'll be pandemonium for a little while."

"And our entrance will be ruined?" Martha had been practically *nice* all day — gracious over tea in her suite at the Westbury, almost embarrassingly enthusiastic about Carole's performance, patient with the maddening traffic jam in the theater district after the show — but now the strain was showing.

"You may not believe it, but that wasn't what I meant," Carole snapped.

Martha switched on the dome light and looked at her closely. "I'm sorry," she said simply. "I just want this to be over and done with."

"No, you're right. He'll never recognize you anyway, so it doesn't really matter when we go in 'cause we don't have to worry about getting the jump on him." It was true: Martha looked nothing at all like that graveside photograph. Her makeup was heavy, her hair — partly hers, partly someone else's — was even heavier. Her taffeta Ungaro concoction of black-and-white polka dots billowed around her in stiffened poufs that rustled noisily when she made the slightest move. A little youngish for her, Carole thought, and definitely wearing her instead of the other way around, but understandable and even touching. It wasn't meant to be a disguise; it was *armor.* She'd been conscious of it herself, when she was dressing, except that she'd chosen the stripped-down-for-battle look: a simple white satin Krizia, slit up the side, no jewelry, her hair scraped back, and severe makeup. They checked their faces and hair once more, snapped their compacts shut, and smiled tightly at one another. "Now," Carole said to the driver, and he jumped out to run around and hold the door for them.

Once inside, they were swallowed up in the frenzy of a big marble foyer that, with a dining room off to one side, was doubling as a discotheque. To reach what they decided must be the living room, they slowly pushed through dancers, balloons, Happy New Yearses, and sloppy kisses from people Carole barely knew. Martha, of course, didn't know them at all and certainly didn't want to, but she was the daughter-in-law and sister and widow of politicians and she managed to smile. It was a very fixed smile and it didn't travel beyond her mouth. Her eyes, clearly announcing that this wasn't her kind of party, were glacial.

Everyone seemed either to be dancing or watching the dancing, and when they finally reached the big gray room, it was sprinkled with only a few people. Couples of one sex or the other lolled on sections of a couch that seemed to go on forever. She had asked someone on the dance floor where she could find Rudi and he'd flopped a hand in this direction, but he wasn't here now.

The holiday decorations — a white Christmas tree that must have been fifteen feet high, garlands of flocked pine boughs swooping along the walls from room to room and then up the stairs — reminded Carole of the lobby of a Sixth Avenue corporate headquarters. And the people they'd pushed past — talking and dancing and laughing, positively *gleaming* with good looks and beautiful clothes and beautiful teeth — were trying too hard, she thought. They were like models in an ad for cologne or a new imported liqueur made from something unlikely — mulberries, maybe — a two-page spread in a slick magazine. "Homey," she said to Martha out of the corner of her mouth.

"Mmmm. Like a furniture showroom," Martha replied.

One of the horde of circulating cater waiters approached them, and she and Martha accepted champagne and then stood by the fireplace, sipping it. Near them, on one of the gray-flannel sections, an older woman who looked wildly out of place, dressed in what Carole guessed was vintage Mollie Parnis, sat between two men who'd had a lift or two but who were probably about her age. They were having an animated, rather fluttery conversation across her, but she didn't seem to be aware of what they were saying. She didn't seem to be aware of anything at all. Carole was almost positive she was Frances's sister-in-law, the lady who'd been so gushy to her at that charity kickoff at Frederick McKinnon's apartment, and she thought she'd never seen anyone enjoying herself *less* at a party.

She noticed Chuck, then, leaning against the other end of the long mantelpiece and smiling vaguely at some point in the middle distance. His face was very red with what could have been heat from the fire but was more likely from the champagne bottle he held loosely in one hand. She nudged Martha. "That's Chuck, the host who might be our . . . savior," she whispered.

Martha turned carefully to look. "I don't think he's going to be much help to us or anyone else in his condition."

Just at that moment, through the wall of glass that separated this room from the greenhouse or whatever it was — a conservatory, she was sure Rudi would call it — she saw him. He was half turned away, explaining an orchid to a handsome young man who didn't seem to be paying much attention. She set her glass down carefully, her hand shaking, and linked her arm through Martha's. "Our other host is out there with his Venus flytraps and I think we should go pay him our respects," she said under her breath.

They moved slowly around the edge of the room, through the glass door, and into the tropics, never taking their eyes off him. He didn't notice until they were only a few feet away, and his face lit up when he saw Carole. I'm a coup, she thought. I may be the only one here who could have gone to Mario's party but who chose to come here instead.

"My dear!" he crowed. "Happy New Year!" He folded her in a big hug and kissed her noisily on the cheek. The knot in her stomach tightened and for an instant — breathing in this humid, rotten air and the overwhelming sweetness of Rudi's cologne, feeling the horror of his touch — she thought she was going to be sick. She stepped back, she recovered. You have one more line to deliver, she told herself.

"This is my friend . . ."

Rudi stepped on her line, though, by turning to Martha and holding out his hand. "I'm so glad you came," he said to her, still smiling broadly. "I'm Rudi Kranovic." Then he frowned slightly, puzzled, flipping through files in his mind. "I'm sorry, but I think maybe we've met? And I'm not remembering?"

Martha didn't take his hand. She looked at him calmly for a moment and then, in a very low voice, she said, "Not exactly. I'm Martha Deloit . . ."

He registered first the name alone and then what the name implied. He looked from one silent, perfectly still woman to the other and then back again and then straight ahead, into the house where he was giving a party. A little twitch appeared, down at the corner of his mouth, and then the fear showed in his eyes, almost immediately replaced by fury. He *knew,* and because of that so did they. One, two, three, Carole counted silently. You've just indicted, convicted, and hanged yourself, Rudi.

The pretty boy had been staring at them while this was going on, confused but fascinated. Carole turned to him now and gave him a dazzling party smile. "Us grown-up folks have some things to talk about," she said. His face fell into a pout and he disappeared.

"Not here," Martha said to her, ignoring Rudi. "We'll stay for a little while, don't you think, and have another glass of that delicious champagne? And *when* Mr. Kranovic has a spare moment, and *if* Mr. Kranovic can think of a quieter place, *then* we'll have a little meeting?"

Carole nodded. They turned and walked away, but she could feel his eyes boring into her back. So far, so good, she thought. Now we wait for a while, I guess.

They found places on one of the pieces of the sofa and let their glasses be filled. Casually, as if it were Tylenol she'd remembered to bring along just in case one of them had a headache, Martha murmured, "Might as well mention it, I suppose. I'm packing a little pistol in my purse."

"So am I," Carole said softly but not at all casually.

* * *

"I won't dance. Don't ask me," Patrick sang as Mario came up to his table. "I may look available, but I'm not really."

"I wouldn't dream of asking you. You look far too happy, sitting here by yourself." Everyone else from Patrick's table was on the dance floor. He smiled as Mario brushed off a Biedermeier chair and sat down. Other than the band's "Auld Lang Syne," the single concession to New Year's had been white confetti, concealed above the false ceiling and let loose at midnight. Now it blanketed every surface, it floated in every glass, and it was caught in everyone's hair.

"I've been hoping to get drunk but, y'know, it's just not working," Patrick said sadly.

"I wouldn't say it's been a complete failure."

"No, maybe not . . ." He filled a glass for Mario and raised his own to toast him. "Sorry. I'm a little bluish tonight but that doesn't mean I can't be happy for your sake, does it? I congratulate you without qualification. You've pulled this together and it's a complete goddamn hit, isn't it? I can tell you confidentially that I myself plan to come here all the time, which of course positively guarantees and cements the success of any establishment east of the Rockies."

"Thanks. But it's really Frances Mc—— never mind. I was about to say approximately the same thing I've been saying all night, that false-genuine-false modesty shit. I *know* it's a great place and I'm glad you think so too because you're my friend and I depend on you to be honest."

"That's better. I'm not sure if I can stand so much sincerity at . . ." He broke off, squinting across Mario's shoulder to the far side of the room. Two men, the only men here who weren't in black tie, were following a captain up to where Lillian was talking with a waiter. "Who are those guys?"

Mario turned in his seat. "Don't know. They look like cops, don't they? You think there've been some complaints about your behavior?"

First Lillian, her hands on her hips, looked like she was demanding something, and then the men pulled out wallets and flipped them open, obviously showing badges. "They *are* cops," Patrick said. Her reaction to whatever they told her was to step back a foot, as if they'd insulted her or slapped her. She turned away from them and looked out around the room.

When Mario stood up, she spotted him immediately and motioned for him to join her. "I guess it's me they want after all. Get Louis to bake me a Sachertorte with a file in it, will you?" he said over his shoulder.

Patrick followed him with his eyes for a moment, wondering what the police could conceivably be doing here — too much noise for the tenants in the building? or were they even moved in yet? Maybe some kitchen worker was an illegal alien? — and then he forgot about it and sank back into himself. I'm somewhere between the old year and the new year, he thought. I'm somewhere between drunk and not drunk. I'm nowhere at all, and I haven't been able to get a single decent sentence down on paper for more than a month. . . .

A man near him was loudly telling his table that he really meant it this time. This is it, he was saying. Sure, yes, he was still smoking tonight, but after tonight, no more, and he depended on them, his best friends, to remind him if he slipped. New Year's resolutions, Patrick thought. Maybe that's what I should be doing. Okay, I resolve . . . he couldn't come up with anything to resolve. All he wanted, all he could think about, was to see Judith again, and that didn't really count as a resolution, did it? No, he told himself, not unless you're planning to do something about it. He was back at the same place he'd been for weeks. He was bored with it; he was bored with himself; he couldn't let it go.

He sighed; he pulled the bottle out of the ice bucket, emptied it into his glass, and looked around guiltily for a waiter to bring another. That was when he noticed that the two policemen were heading back to the elevator. He saw Lillian, her hand on Mario's arm, say something to him and he saw him shake his head and walk away from her, fast, toward one of the doors that opened out onto the terrace. He watched him bump into someone and he was sure, even from here, that he hadn't apologized. A tableful of smiling people saluted him with their glasses and he brushed past as if they didn't exist. Even if Mario was drunk — and he knew he wasn't — he wouldn't be acting like that. It didn't take him very long to decide he should go after him.

Standing up made him a little dizzy, but his head cleared when he came out into the cold air. The terrace was icy, he was wearing new, slippery shoes — the ridiculous, embarrassing evening pumps he'd bought today — and he had to pick his way along carefully to the far corner of the terrace. Mario looked around when he heard Patrick's approach, but then he quickly turned his back to him again. In the light that poured out from the restaurant, he'd seen that Mario's face was wet with tears. Mario had never cried in front of him, and it was a strange, almost surreal, contrast to the party that glowed in the background.

"What's happened?" he asked quietly when he got up to him. Mario shook his head, but Patrick didn't think he was being shut out. He thought that, whatever it was, it must be very hard to say. He started over, carefully, with smaller, easier, yes-or-no questions. "They were cops?" Mario nodded. "New York City cops?" No. "Federal?" Yes. "Immigration?" No.

"Narcotics." Mario got the whole word out.

"But . . . you're about as drug-free as anyone I know . . . that's really dumb."

"Not me. They . . . found a lot of coke, on Mag . . ." His voice broke.

"Maggie? You told me she was doing, uh, more than was good for her, but I can't believe she was *dealing* it. And even if she was, then someone must know a great lawyer who . . ."

"*No.*" He turned slowly around to face Patrick. "No. I didn't finish." He was fighting to contain himself and he took a couple of deep breaths. "They found a lot of coke on Maggie's *body*. On Maggie's and Jim's bodies. That fucking cokehead plowed his fucking antique fucking plane into the side of a hill. Down south." He jerked his head in that direction, as if they could see it from where they stood. "North Carolina."

Patrick stared at him, and it was a few seconds before he found anything to say. He was a writer — a good writer, he believed most of the time — but he had to use the same inadequate words that everyone else used. "I'm so sorry," he said. He put his arm around Mario's shoulders and they stood there like that for a little while, shivering in the cold. The details didn't matter, but he got Mario to tell him as much as he knew anyway. It had happened at about five o'clock, just before dark, but they didn't find the bodies till seven and then, because of the coke, the federal agents were called in because the local police had thought: small plane plus private airstrip plus big-city types equals drug smugglers. The two men who came here were from the New York office; they'd already gone through her apartment. When they didn't find anything, they finally asked the super who should be notified.

"But why not Chuck?"

"Because the super couldn't remember his name. And if he was in her address book, he was probably just under 'Chuck.' So he doesn't know. I got them to agree. That I'd be the one to tell him." He shook himself. "So I'd better go. I should have gone right away but I had to sort of . . . absorb it, I guess. Anyway, our teeth are chattering."

"Then . . . look, a guy at my table just offered me his car and driver. He's leaving with someone else's wife or something," Patrick said, following along to a side door, grateful that at least they wouldn't have to walk back through the party. "I'll come with you."

Mario nodded. They made it to his office without seeing anyone but kitchen staff. Lillian was waiting there. There was no point in telling anyone about it, he told her, and she nodded. She should say he'd be back soon, even though he probably wouldn't.

Going down in the freight elevator, Mario suddenly said, "She shouldn't have been in that plane, not tonight. She wasn't going to come back to the city till this was over. She was deliberately staying away." His voice started to crack again. "I think she changed her mind. I think she wanted to be here after all."

27

N*O ONE HAD FOUND TIME YET* to clear the private dining rooms after the cocktail hour, so the room where Frances stood was still messy with dirty glasses and trays of hardening hors d'oeuvres. She was at the window, smoking, looking up to the lights of midtown without really seeing them. Frederick had just left her. She'd promised to join him back at the table soon, but she had to have a few minutes alone first.

It's over, she repeated to herself. It's all right. It isn't true. She wanted to feel a great sense of relief; she waited for an overwhelming wave of joy to wash over her, but it wasn't going to be like that. The strain was gone, the fear, the terrible feeling that she was going to break apart, and what remained was only numbness and exhaustion. I've got to — what's the word? — *decompress,* she told herself. I've been in deep water. I can't just shoot up to the surface, up to the light, all at once. I have to be patient, I have to learn how to inhale and exhale normally again.

Poor Frederick, she thought. Rushing here from Kennedy, probably changing into a tux on the plane or in his car, all ready to appreciate what I've done and to have a good time, and I grab him and pull him in here and hit him with this. She hadn't led up to it, hadn't tried to explain why it was so vital that she know. She had simply asked, the minute the door was closed, if there was the slightest, faintest chance that Mario Fermi could be her son. His face had registered shock, but he'd answered immediately, with no hesitation, and she was very sure he was telling the truth.

"No. It's not possible. It is literally not possible. Mario isn't your son. He's not your baby." He looked at her closely. "You must have been going through hell. I've heard talk and I can imagine why it might matter so much, if you suddenly found out he was . . . but, good lord, Frances, I can't conceive of how a thing like this could even occur to you."

She told him the whole story, leaving nothing out: how it started, how crazy she'd been, how hard she'd tried to track him down. She believed him but she couldn't help it, she had to hear it again and she asked him twice more if he was sure, if there was any doubt in his mind. At last, he said, "If you want proof, if you want me to tell you *why* I can be so positive, then . . . then I might be telling you more than you want to know." He smiled at her sadly. "I thought it was very brave of you, very sensible, not to ask me, not once in all these years. You know I'd have told you and you know I still would. You have the right to know what happened to your own child, but . . ." Of course, he was right. Anything beyond the simple No he'd given her was playing with fire. Maybe sometime in the future, she thought, or maybe never, but certainly not tonight.

That was when she had said she needed to be by herself for a little bit. Finishing her cigarette, carefully drowning it in a half-empty glass and listening to the little hiss it made, she realized Hamilton would be asking his brother the same question just about now. Freddie had agreed with her, of course: Ham should never be told she'd overheard that phone call. He'd blame himself, he'd torture himself in some way, if he knew she knew, and she had to make it as easy for him as she could so that . . . so that *what?* she asked herself. So I can go on seeing Mario, so Ham and I never have to face one another about it, so we can both pretend it isn't happening?

Yes, that's exactly what I mean, she admitted. I still want to have my cake and eat it, too. I want all the comfort and security and warmth Ham can give me, just as he's always done, and I want — all the rest, everything Mario and I have shared. And I think, I *know,* I can have them both. She raised her head, felt to see if her hair was tucked into place, and turned away from the window. She felt a part of herself begin to relax a little; she was just beginning to believe it was over. She'd never be able to tell Mario the truth about the past week, but she'd try to make it up to him. She'd start *now,* this minute.

When she didn't find him in the elevator lobby or on the dance floor, she stood at the edge of the bar level and scanned the tiers below her. Only Trish and the Radnors were sitting at her own table, and she realized Ham and Freddie must have gone somewhere private to talk. Because every man in the room was in black tie, it made it harder to pick out Mario, but after a few minutes she was sure he wasn't in the dining room and she decided he must be in his office.

Making her way there, coming into the sound-lock corridor, she suddenly felt she was intruding, that she was out of place in the way she was when she went backstage to see someone. She'd been in and out of here hundreds of times in the past months, but now her job was done, the staff had taken over, and she didn't belong. That part of my life with Mario is finished, she thought, and now it will be different. Better, she hoped. Just as she was about to sweep through the swinging door into the kitchen, Lillian came through the other one. There was a moment when it looked like she might not stop, like she wanted to pretend she hadn't seen her, but then she gave her a tired smile. Have I been *such* a bitch lately? Frances wondered. I must have been. Everyone's tiptoeing around me, afraid to get too close.

Lillian looked at her oddly, and she didn't answer right away when she asked her where Mario was. Frances wanted to throw her arms around her. I'm back, she nearly said aloud. This is my smile — it's a *real* smile, see? — and everything's all right now. Just tell me where I can find him.

"He . . . had to go out for a while," she said. "Something came up." Her voice was drained, and Frances thought she must be very, very tired.

"But he's coming back? Where on earth did he go?"

"Oh, he'll be back in a little bit, I'm sure." She didn't sound sure.

"Lillian?" She was hiding something, covering for him, it was obvious. Maybe he hadn't felt well . . . all the tension . . . and he didn't want anyone to know? But, surely, she can tell *me.* "It's important," she said. "Please. Where's he gone?"

"To . . . another party," she finally said, dragging the words out. "At Rudi's house."

Frances stared at her back as she turned slowly and walked away. It was the last thing she'd expected to hear, and it was a moment or two before she understood that it must be some kind of peace offering and that Lillian was upset by it, didn't approve of it. It may not work, so he doesn't want anyone here to know he's trying, she thought, but he wants to hold out an olive branch to Rudi, maybe even bring him back here with him for a glass of champagne. She was delighted; it was fair and noble and gentlemanly, exactly the kind of gesture Mario would make. But . . . Rudi?

She shuddered. It was a generous idea — in the abstract, for someone else, maybe — but she didn't think she herself could ever look at Rudi again without wanting to do something unspeakable to him. Then she was struck with a horrible new thought. Was it possible that somehow Mario had discovered what had been tormenting her, that he was going to Rudi's to have it out with him? He certainly hadn't known yesterday or he wouldn't have wanted her so badly in that awful moment in his office, but what if Rudi had deliberately tried to ruin tonight for him? Or Chuck? What if there had been a phone call, for instance . . .

She'd already happily decided to follow after Mario because she wanted so badly to see him, to start making everything right again. Now, wondering if the waters were closing in once more, if something terrible was about to happen, it was even more important to find him. Asking the captain to call down to the doorman to whistle for Danny, and then thanking the girl downstairs for finding her coat, she could hear the desperation in her voice, as if it had never really gone away.

* * *

"I'm going up to that bastard's house," Hamilton said to Frederick, his voice bouncing off the metal steps and cinder-block walls of the fire stairwell where they'd been talking. "He's apparently hosting a big do, so he must be there."

"Tonight? Now? Can't it wait?" Frederick chuckled. "You've never crashed a party in your life."

"I'm not in the mood for jokes, Freddie." His great relief had been immediately replaced with a sharp new anger. It had all been so unnecessary, then, all Frances's misery, all his watchfulness. He hadn't taken his eyes off the door to the room where she'd led Frederick, and he'd pulled him in,here as soon as he came out. He knew his brother's face so well that he immediately saw it was all right, that it had all been a terrible lie, but he needed to hear the details and, since he couldn't ask her himself, to hear what her reaction had been.

"But . . . hell, I hate all these secrets within secrets." Frederick took a deep breath. "Look, I promised her not to tell you this, but the point was that you weren't supposed to know *she* knew about this filth, and somehow you figured it out anyway, so you may as well know the truth. Which is that there was no letter, there was no communication of any kind from Rudi. She was on the other extension when Wetherby called you. Smelly as I've always thought Rudi was, it's entirely possible the man has nothing to do with all this."

Hamilton was momentarily stunned, but he shoved it aside. He didn't see how it made any difference. He was *positive* Rudi was involved. "I wouldn't really be crashing a party," he said slowly. "As if it matters. Dorothy's there. I can legitimately collect my sister and take her home."

"Oh. I assumed she was around here somewhere."

"She was invited but . . ." Hamilton smiled for the first time. "Poor old Freddie. You haven't really been to this party yet, so how could you know who's here and who isn't?" He squeezed his arm. "You flew thousands of miles to get here tonight and Franny and I jumped on you so fast, one after the other, that you haven't even had time for a drink. I didn't even wish you a Happy New Year."

Frederick glared at him. "I won't make any jokes if you won't insult me with diversionary bull like that. You've obviously made up your mind to go calling on Rudi tonight and maybe you're right, maybe he's at the bottom of it. But I don't see how we can make him admit anything without telling him more than . . ." He shook his head. "I think it's pointless."

"It's not pointless." Hamilton had the odd feeling they were sinking into one of their endless childhood arguments. Is so. Is not.

"For one thing, now that I'm sure Mario isn't . . . who he might have been, I want to talk to Dorothy again. She's done enough damage, and I don't want that man . . ."

"Ham, we have to have a real family conference, soon, about Dorothy, but in the meantime: do you have any idea what sort of condition she might be in right now? You want to have a good, serious talk with her? You want to set her straight, be sure she's crystal clear about this mess? She may not even recognize you."

"Then that's all the more reason to get her out of there."

Frederick shrugged. "All right. It's not going to do any good, but I'm not going to convince you. Let's go. Sam's downstairs with the car."

"Then I hope you don't mind if I borrow him for a while. I'll leave our car in case Franny decides to go home, and I think you should stay and . . ." Frederick started to interrupt, but he held his hand up. "Please. I'm depending on you to be here for her. She and I have worked ourselves into these absurd corners, and now we can't talk about it. Secrets within secrets, as you said, and it's all because we love each other. We may or may not untangle it all, she and I, but not now. Tonight, she's had a ghastly time and you're the only one who understands why and she may still need you."

Gliding uptown on Third Avenue in the back of Freddie's big Rolls, Hamilton was able to tell himself he hadn't lied to his brother. He really *did* want to get Dorothy out of there and he truly *did* rely on him to help Frances. There was no need to tell him he'd planned it days ago, when Dorothy first mentioned this party. No need to tell him he had other reasons for wanting to talk to Rudi Kranovic.

* * *

Chuck wasn't sure he could move. My body's confused, he said to himself. *I* feel pain, so it thinks it's obligated to react to that by paralyzing me, but it's got the whole thing mixed up with the way it's supposed to behave when I'm in *physical* pain. He'd been holding himself, doubled over; he'd slowly slid down from the cast-iron bench onto the cold cement floor of the empty greenhouse; and now he didn't think he could get up again, not ever.

"Sit down," Mario had said — half an hour ago? — taking the seat across from him after insisting he leave his nice perch by the fireplace and come out here with them.

"What is this? A fuckin' soap opera?" he'd asked. But he'd done it, because he'd been a little wobbly from all the champagne, and then Mario had told him about Maggie. He'd made him go away, after the first wave of grief had passed over him. Patrick, who'd been hovering over there under that palm tree, had gone with him, but maybe they were still inside somewhere. He hadn't said a word except to ask them not to tell anyone here, not even Rudi, especially not Rudi. They'd all leave him alone, as long as they thought he was drunk — just smashed again, that old Chuck Wetherby — but they'd be out here with their sympathy if they knew. They might even try to touch him, and he wouldn't be able to stand that. There was another reason: as long as no one heard, as long as the party kept bubbling along, as long as the deejay kept pulling the crowd with him up long slopes of disco, reggae, old rock, new rock, and rap, then maybe it hadn't happened.

He knew he was drunk but he wanted to be much, much drunker. He didn't want to feel anything at all, but this pain was refusing to leave him alone. When he tried to focus on something, the way he could when he was happily plastered — a leaf, nearby; an ornament on the Christmas tree, far away in the living room; anything — it would only work for a minute or two. Then *it,* what Mario had said, would come back. The problem was that if he wanted another bottle he was going to have to get up and go back into the house. The waiters weren't coming out here because there was only himself, and himself, he was sure they were saying to each other, had already had enough. "Not enough," he said aloud.

For now, for the past few minutes, for what had become a lifetime to him, his world consisted of this little bit of tropical jungle, and it was almost impossible to imagine getting up from here and making it to the other side of the enormous windows. It would be like passing through a movie screen, he thought. No, it was more like a bigger version of one of Lord and Taylor's Christmas windows, partly framed with the scallops of pine boughs, twinkling with the lights on the tree and all the little votive candles that were so artfully clustered on the coffee tables. Shiny people moved through it soundlessly, and he could only just hear the faint beat of music in the rooms beyond it.

The memory, the pain, slammed into him again viciously, furious with him for trying to lose himself in cheap, department store dreams. It was such a terrible, living thing this time that his body gave in and loosened its grip on him. By holding on to the bench, he managed to stand up and, once he'd accomplished that, to take a few steps. The world seemed just slightly larger to him now that he was moving, and he realized that he had a bedroom. He tried to remember: it had doors, he was sure — two doors? — and he'd be able to lock them. He could keep everyone away with two simple little buttons. It was on the third floor, miles from here, but — with a little help from Messrs. Moët and Chandon, he said to himself — he'd make it and then he'd be safe.

What he really wanted was vodka — nice, clean potatoes instead of all those sugary, fizzy grapes — but that meant a trip to the kitchen and that was way too complicated. In the living room, he simply found the cater waiter with the fullest champagne bottle and grabbed it from him. By edging along the wall of the foyer, he squeezed past the dancers without colliding with any of them, and he congratulated himself. He kept to the wall when he went up the stairs, too, because the banisters were wound with more of those damn flocked pine garlands with which Rudi seemed to have draped the entire house.

He slammed the bedroom door behind him, he locked it, and he was halfway across the room to lock the other door, the one that led to Rudi's room, before he saw the two men and the woman who were sitting on one side of his bed. He froze, staring at them in the faint light from the bedside fixture. One of them, the woman — a girl, really — smiled dreamily and held up a little opium pipe, offering it to him. There was a moment when he thought, Sure, why not? He even took a half-step toward them before everything came back, all the horror he'd kept at bay while he was concentrating on making his way up here.

Still heading in their direction in what felt like slow motion, he saw their faces begin to respond to whatever they saw in his, and by the time he reached them and stood over them they were clearly terrified. His words left him, one by one, very softly. "Get. The.

Fuck. Out." To their backs, when they were at the door and fumbling with the lock, he made it clearer. "Out of the house," he said, not at all softly.

His fury was very pure and very simple: he hated them because they were alive and because Maggie wasn't. He stood by the bed and felt it grow in him until there was no space left for anything else, not even grief. It cut through all the champagne and it gave him the energy to walk out of his bedroom, into Rudi's suite and down the hall, weaving in and out of the other rooms on the third floor and then on the second floor. He threw out a man in one of the guest rooms who had his pants down around his ankles, and he threw out the girl who was kneeling in front of him. He threw out the three giggling boys who were snorting coke in one of the bathrooms. The only door he didn't open was the one to Rudi's study, the one that was stuffed with secrets. He hadn't seen Rudi for a long time, he suddenly realized, and it occurred to him that he might be in there. Fine, he thought. I can get rid of these vermin without any interference, and I'll see him sooner or later.

Coming down into the foyer, he stood up on the riser behind the deejay for a minute and watched him as he worked the two turntables and the volume knobs, carefully mixing the last bars of one song with the opening beat of another. Then Chuck reached down, lifted the arm from the new record, tilted it all the way back, and ripped it off at its base. In the absolute silence that followed, a hundred bodies froze, a hundred stunned faces looked up to him. "The party's over," he roared. All his fury, all the very real violence he was capable of committing, was there in those three words, and not a single murmur of complaint was heard from the entire floor. When he stepped down and strode through the foyer and on into the dining room, the crowd made way for him as they would have if he had blood on his hands. He had committed a kind of murder, and the arm he'd torn from the stereo and was still holding, its brightly colored cords sticking out of one end, seemed very human.

He made a conscious effort to speak nicely to the caterers in the kitchen — they were just doing their jobs, after all, he told himself; they were nothing like the parasites he'd just thrown out — but the silence in the next room and the rage that had spun through the swinging door with him was enough for them to back away from him in fear. When he unlatched the door to the cellar and the two big ghostly dogs leaped out joyously, one of the women gasped and dropped a glass, as if the animals themselves were extensions of what she sensed in him, weapons he was unleashing on her.

As he passed through the foyer, all the people who could have danced all night were now pushing to get into the den where they'd checked their coats. They fell silent again when they saw him, and none of them met his eyes. At the entrance to the living room, he turned the knobs of every rheostat, flooding the room with light, but it was already empty. He wandered back out to the conservatory, and he wound up on the iron bench, the one where Mario had been, that faced away from the house. The white heat of his anger drained away as soon as he sat down. The hurt was back, and it brought tears with it this time.

He put his face in his hands and let the great sobs go through him, a thousand pictures of Maggie flashing in front of him. He saw her little golden head appearing over the edge of the platform he'd built high up in a eucalyptus tree, delighted with herself for making the climb. He saw her from far out in the water, waiting for him impatiently on the beach as the late afternoon sun caught her blondness while he paddled to meet just one more wave on his board. He tried to imagine her without movement, in the stillness of death, and he couldn't.

The weimaraners found him and came up to lick his face. He'd never had much of a relationship with these snobbish, rather stupid, designer pets of Rudi's; he knew they were only after the salt in his tears; but he found it strangely comforting that they were doing this and he sat passively for a while until they finished. Then he remembered that he was very thirsty, that he was far more sober than he'd been all night, and that this time he could get to the vodka without fighting through a mob. The dogs, sniffing at all the interesting scents the crowd had left and nibbling at the bits of food that had been dropped, followed him out to the kitchen through the silent rooms.

His impulse was to drink straight from the bottle, but he made himself perform the ritual of getting down the kind of oversize old-fashioned glass he liked, filling an ice bucket with cubes and hunting for tongs in a drawer, cutting wedges of lime, and then carefully arranging it all on a silver tray with a new liter of Stolichnaya. He noticed a plate of water biscuits and steak tartare that the caterers had been about to pass, and he put it down for the dogs. Then he carried the tray into the living room, turned down the lights, and set it on the table in front of the fireplace. He sprawled on a piece of the sofa and began to drink very fast.

The Stoli kicked in quickly, and he imagined a whole battalion of French grapes inside him who'd been paralyzed in shock for a while along with his mind, but who must have been biding their time and waiting for these sturdy Russian troops to arrive and join forces against his enemy. There was a wonderful, numb cease-fire for a few minutes, a Mexican standoff in which all the forces inside him were perfectly balanced, and he looked down on the scene from far above. He watched himself turn slowly around, he saw his hand hurl his glass at the far wall, and he watched it shatter there. Then he turned exactly ninety degrees and hurled the ice bucket through the glass and out into the greenhouse, watching it roll along to the bench where he'd been sitting earlier. The détente was over; it was suddenly urgent for him to break everything in the room that could be broken — the one exception being the vodka bottle, of course, which he placed reverently on the mantelpiece. He lurched from table to credenza to table for more ammunition. All the crystal obelisks and black onyx cubes, all the decorator objets d'art that were scattered around, became his victims. His eyes were wet with tears, but he was feeling weirdly playful. He thought this was a highly satisfactory activity, as soothing as banging tennis balls against a wall or skimming rocks across a pond. It was precisely what he'd have liked to do with all the pretty people who'd been here earlier.

The dogs, who had eyed him sleepily from the hearth while he was drinking, were now barking happily and racing around him. He paid no attention to them; he bent down to pick up a big formation of quartz crystals with both hands. Run along now and join your friends out there in Rudi's fucking *conservatory,* he said to it. It was very heavy and it fell short and crashed through a small glass table that held some holly and a cluster of stubby votive candles.

He stood in the same spot, looking around vaguely for something else to smash but not really caring very much. The chunk of quartz was the last big breakable thing that could give him any satisfaction, and now the behavior of the candles interested him much more. They'd mostly suffocated in their own liquid wax as they fell, but one of them had landed upright on the carpet and was still flickering gamely. He was fascinated by it, pleased for it, and he wondered what odds it had overcome. It was only a few seconds later that he realized another candle — on its side, this one, but still a survivor — had ended up a few inches away, over by the windows that were half shattered now. It lay up against the end of a pine garland that had fallen down sadly to the floor, and it was the smoke from the smoldering needles that had caught his eye. He sighed. He should do something about it, but he was so tired and all he wanted was to climb slowly upstairs with his Russian friends and pass out.

There were usually hoses out in the greenhouse, but they were always relegated to the cellar when there was a party, like the dogs, because someone might trip over them. There were faucets out there too but, looking around, he couldn't see anything in one piece that would hold more than an ounce of water. He was suddenly mad: he'd already been a one-man pest control service tonight, and now he was expected to be a one-man fire brigade too? It's not fair, he thought; I'm not the only one who lives here.

Stumbling once or twice on his way through the foyer and then the dining room, he yelled up the stairs for Rudi. There was no reply, so on his way out of the kitchen, after he'd cleared the dirty glasses out of the sink and filled a big pitcher, he went to the intercom by the door and began stabbing buttons.

Rudi answered from the study with a curt "Yes."

"Where the hell are you?" Chuck roared.

"I'm obviously here."

"Well, get the hell down obviously *here,* you bastard. There's been a little accident and there's a little fire in the living —"

"I'm in the middle of something important," Rudi explained with elaborate patience, his accent very thick, "or I would certainly be down there with our friends. Get some of the caterers to help you. Promise them a nice tip."

Chuck stared at the speaker that was built into the wall and tried to understand what he'd just heard. Rudi thinks there's still a party going on down here, he said to himself. How long has he been up there behind that goddamn soundproofed door? And what's important enough for him to do the unthinkable and abandon his guests? He held his finger on the button again until Rudi responded.

"I told you . . ."

"Yeah, and now I'm telling *you*. There aren't any guests, there aren't any caterers. There's just me and these fucking hounds and there's the matter of this fire in these goddamn decorations you were no doubt too cheap to have fireproofed. You get your ass down here and help me."

A long, bored sigh floated through the speaker box. "All right," the voice finally said. "We'll be right down."

We? Chuck repeated to himself as he swung out through the kitchen door. Who's *we?* Rudi wouldn't be having a little sexual scene up there, would he? No, that wasn't his style, and that room was sacred turf. The study was for business, all those business pies Rudi had his hands in. . . .

He'd been drinking continuously since before dinner and big stretches of the evening were complete blanks, but Chuck had the sense that some of the faces that had swum past him (without speaking to him, he didn't think, but then why would they bother?) were faces he'd been surprised to see, that didn't belong to the usual idiots, that didn't belong here. *But of course they did!* he remembered. He had invited them! He was sure he'd seen the old actress and the funny man and a politician who *really* didn't fit in, and . . . Walking slowly across the dining room with his head down, he tried to dredge them up. Mario and Patrick, of course, but they had nothing to do with Rudi, did they? No, they were part of what he was fighting off at the moment. Carole Todd, he thought, out in the greenhouse with some overdressed babe who looked faintly familiar. Hamilton McKinnon, looking very stern, very dark. But he hadn't invited him, had he? Anyway, that had been much later, maybe even after Mario had gone? Or *did* Mario leave? And — just a glimpse, but so strange that it left a strong impression — Frances McKinnon. He'd find out for sure in a minute, of course, but right now he was willing to bet that one of Rudi's chickens had come home to roost.

The dogs came racing up to him, whining, their brows puckered in worry, just as he turned into the foyer and saw the glow from the living room. He ran toward it, skidding on the marble floor, water slopping from the pitcher he carried, and then he paused at the door in awe. The Christmas tree was a perfect cone of fire; the drapes at either end of the windows were firefalls; and the garlands framed the entire room with lovely red flames. He thought it was very beautiful, and he had to force himself to move to the intercom, force his finger to hit the Study button. When there was no answer, he was very, very angry. He'd have to be *responsible*. He'd have to walk away from this fascinating, heartbreaking beauty and trudge upstairs to pound on the door, and even then that sonuvabitch might not come out and help him.

He thought he'd only stood there a few seconds, half a minute at most, and when he turned he was amazed by the speed, the deviousness, of the fire. It had slipped past him, carried along merrily through the door and into the foyer by the garlands, already racing along a path to the dining room. Halfway to the stairs, he stopped to wonder how it had found time to throw itself at the other boughs, the ones twisted round and round the banister rail, and then onto the thickly carpeted steps themselves, and he knew it was never going to let him past. He walked calmly back to the living room and dialed 911, and he was proud of himself for speaking so clearly. He tried the intercom again, and when that failed he couldn't think of anything else to do. These boring responsibilities were over, and he let himself relax. He'd done everything he could, hadn't he? Well, then, Daddy's best little junior fireman deserved a drink. The room was getting very smoky and hot and his throat was very, very dry.

Leaning on the mantelpiece with his bottle, he looked down into the fireplace, its logs still blazing, and it struck him as, first, sad and then awfully funny. "You are redundant," he said to it, and he began to laugh.

His eyes were wet with tears, he gasped and coughed from the smoke and from all the new things he suddenly found to laugh about. Funniest of all was a pun he made, something he remembered thinking a few minutes ago, an old-fashioned expression he'd used to himself. "Your chickens are coming home to *roast,* Rudi," he said to the ceiling, and then he collapsed onto the sofa in giggles.

Far away, at the other end of the house — on this floor, it sounded like, not upstairs — a girl screamed. He sat up quickly, giggles forgotten, and when it came a second time, he knew it was Maggie. He began to crawl along the floor where the smoke seemed a little friendlier. Maggie was trapped somewhere and he had to find her and help her.

28

CAROLE TODD VASQUEZ stood at the open window and looked out to the pale green shimmer of Central Park, sprinkled here and there with the whites and pinks of trees in flower. She was supposed to be making a guest list and she had a pen and pad in her hand, but all she wanted to do was drink in this first real spring day. It is possible, she was thinking, that I will never again in my life be as happy as I am at this moment. But of course part of her happiness came from the expectation that there would be many more moments just like it.

Her mood was mostly because of Tony, naturally. He'd come back in February, and they'd flown to Aspen and been married quietly on Valentine's Day. He'd left the next morning to deal with some postproduction problems on the Coast. By the time he got back to New York, she was in Scotland for a cameo in an Ivory-Merchant film. Then he was in Rio to scout for locations for his next project, then she . . . but it was always going to be like that, she knew now, and she wouldn't have it any other way. She'd told herself she wanted to settle down with him, and she had, in her mind. This was the kind of life they were going to lead until they were very, very old, and anything else would be a farce. They believed they'd found something solid in each other, something all this dashing in and out would never change, and they would always have this beautiful home base.

Even with the sheer contentment that had come to her in the form of Tony, though, she knew she couldn't be feeling this way if she had to wonder when the next letter might arrive. That was finished. She'd felt the first rush of freedom when she glanced at the *Post* the next morning, New Year's Day. There had been a grisly picture on the front page, the kind she disapproved of usually but which she couldn't help but relish this time. Two bodies in shiny black plastic bags, being carried down the front steps of that house past a fascinating collection of neighbors in dressing gowns and evening gowns. If she'd been there, she was sure, she would have spat on the one that contained Rudi.

She and Martha had gone on to the party at Tables and stayed for an hour or two, congratulating themselves for pinning down their man. They'd managed to ignore the fact, and it became easier after a few drinks, that they'd never found him again, never had a second talk with him, but they had a great, drunken time thinking of ways to get him to confess. Pulling out his toenails, one by one, had been Martha's suggestion, but Carole thought that was too obvious — hadn't the Germans or the Japanese already done that? — and she had various other ideas that included electric wires and genitalia. They'd shuddered and shouted with laughter and hiccupped like schoolgirls.

They couldn't be positive, at first, that they were safe. Didn't he say, in his very first letter to each of them, that he'd made provisions, that even if he died the letters would never stop, that there were second copies, backups, whatever? When the deadline for the payment — the last-straw demand that had made them so obsessed with finding him — came and went, they relaxed a little more. They decided, now that they knew it had been Rudi, that he wasn't the type to trust anyone that much, even in death. He hadn't left a will — they made sure of that — and now, months later, they told each other their secret had died with him. Even if it somehow started up again, they'd know where to begin looking. All those years, it had been the complete anonymity that was the worst horror. Now it had a face, and that face was, as far as they knew, dead.

She lowered her eyes to the pad she was holding, and slowly, dreamily, she began to write out a guest list for the housewarming party she and Tony would be giving next month.

* * *

Chuck was resting between lessons on the roof of the Metropolitan Athletic Club, and the sweat was pouring down his face on this first warm day. He supposed this must be spring, but he'd never been very impressed by spring — he'd grown up in California, after all, where it didn't mean much of anything — and, looking down over the parapet to the park, he thought the trees were nice but not nearly as nice as they were in the fall. The sun, though — that he could appreciate, that he could understand worshipping, like the Aztecs. It soothed him, energized him, made him feel whole, and he didn't need to see a bunch of leaves that were trying to grow up to know the Sun God was blessing him.

More of the kind of thinking I haven't indulged in for years, he said to himself. Not that it's either original or profound, not that I ought to scribble it down and put it in a time capsule as my gift to the future, just that it comes from some part of me that I thought was gone, that I thought was surgically removed a long time ago.

The fact that he wasn't drinking, the fact that he hadn't had so much as a bite of an Amaretto cookie for eighty-three days now, had everything to do with it. It had started on the plane, on his way out to the memorial service in Santa Barbara. He'd gone straight to Maggie's apartment after the single night they'd made him spend in the hospital, and the first thing he did was to pick up the phone and order a case of Stolichnaya, please, liters, please, and make it hundred proof. Then, sitting in her living room and watching the dogs (who evidently weren't so stupid after all, since they'd survived the fire) fight with the cats, he had numbed himself for a solid week.

Anyway, somewhere over Iowa, he wanted to think, because that was the state his pioneer ancestors had deserted for California, the stewardesses had tinkled up to him with the drink trolley, and he heard himself asking for a Diet Sprite. Sipping it, he'd suddenly laughed out loud, and the lady in the next seat had smiled at him cautiously. It had occurred to him that Maggie was watching him from above, not from heaven but from the urn in the overhead luggage compartment, that she thought it was funny too, and that she approved.

Because, after all, she'd given him back his life, and it would have been terrible — the very worst sin of all — if he turned around and threw it away (or, he corrected himself, if he had continued throwing it away as he had for so many years). It was the screams that got him out of the living room that night, that forced him to crawl through the smoke in the foyer and the dining room. He'd never told anyone this, because of course when he reached the kitchen there was no one there, there never had been, but he chose to believe it was more than imagination or vodka or hysteria. He knew it was Maggie who got him away from the part of the house where — the firemen later told him — he would have surely died.

His next pupil appeared on the far side of the roof and he went back to work. The man hadn't taken a lesson for months, and he said what so many others had said lately, which was that he was surprised — oh, pleasantly surprised, of course — to find Chuck still coaching here. People seemed to automatically assume he was rich now, that Rudi must have left at least some of his fortune to his lover, but there was no fortune to leave. The restaurant, the houses, the horses, the mysterious wads of cash in safe deposit boxes — they'd all been rolled into a big ball with the tax audits and liens and second mortgages, and then the ball had swallowed itself. The other source of income, the one Rudi had never declared on any form in any fiscal year, had gone up in smoke. It was exactly the death Chuck had planned for it, that he would have given it very soon, but he wished he'd had the satisfaction of doing it himself.

He'd never liked contemporary art and he'd never paid much attention to the little collection of drawings and paintings in Maggie's apartment, so he'd been amazed at the prices Max Silverman told him they'd fetch. She wouldn't mind — she *didn't* mind, he was sure — that he was putting them up for auction at Sotheby's in June. There would be enough money for him to think about a down payment on a tennis ranch of his own. Maybe in Florida, maybe even in California, but not yet, not for a while. Of all the slogans and jingoes and platitudes thrown around in AA, the one about not making any major changes in his life for the first year made the most sense to him. Enough had happened, in one night, to last him for a very long time.

* * *

Hamilton was being driven across the park from a meeting on the West Side, and the blur of soft pastels in the warm, sleepy air reminded him of how exhilarating days like this had been when he was a child. All the rules about mittens and caps and galoshes were lifted, everything was different, every detail. Even Nanny's white lace-ups — or, sometimes, Mother's spectators — would make a different sound on the pavement from their winter shoes as he and Dorothy and Freddie were walked across Fifth Avenue. Then the tight hold on their hands would be released and they were free to run in circles with all the other children and all the dogs in the world until they fell down, dizzy and breathless, and stained their knees in the grass.

The car passed a pear tree that was in full flower, and he thought of the other one, much older and maybe not even still standing, that grew in the little cemetery in Boston where nine generations of McKinnons were buried. Ten, now that Dorothy lay there, the first of his generation. He hadn't noticed it at the service, but of course that had been deepest winter and he hadn't thought of trying to decipher the black trunks that rose out of the snow. He hoped it was alive, because Dorothy had loved the springtime and all its pale, feminine fluffiness and he liked to think the petals might be softly floating down on her grave.

He still had trouble imagining her at the end, understanding where she'd found the toughness in herself to do what she did. When he didn't see her, as he pushed from room to room at that dreadful party, asking every dark, older man if he was his host and feeling very foolish, he thought she'd already gone home. If he'd realized she was up in the study all that time with precisely the man he was searching for . . . but he couldn't have known, no one had known, and it wouldn't have made any difference anyway.

He'd finally given up, gone back to Tables, and joined Frederick for more champagne than was good for either one of them, and when he was called to the phone he was drunker than he'd been for years. Someone very high up in the police department had decided the death of a McKinnon might be worth something — to himself; to a couple of junior officers, maybe; to some people in the coroner's office, certainly — and he was right. Hamilton put down the phone long enough to take a deep breath and to ask a waiter to please bring his brother to him. Then, willing himself to be sober, telling himself he could mourn later, he picked it up again and began to make the kind of calls a very rich, very powerful man makes when he wants something to be buried very deeply. Freddie took it in just as quickly, and for the next hour they sat side by side in adjoining phone booths and pulled the strings they'd been born to pull.

They had succeeded. So far as anyone but a handful of people ever knew, Rudi Kranovic, the famous restaurateur, and his guest, Dorothy McKinnon Clough, had died in a tragic New Year's Eve fire in Mr. Kranovic's elegant East Side town house, trapped in an upstairs room that, the press was very careful to explain, was a study or a library or an office, not a bedroom. The fact that Rudi had been shot directly between his eyes and was already dead when the fire reached him, the fact that it was Mrs. Clough who had shot him and who had then turned the elegant little pearl-handled gun on herself, was a fact that simply ceased to exist as anything that could ever be proven.

In trying to reconstruct what had actually happened, Hamilton had made two mistakes. The first was to assume that Dorothy had been . . . not quite in her right mind, that some combination of antidepressants and tranquilizers and painkillers and alcohol — everything Freddie had warned him she might have taken — had caused her to do it. People who noticed her or tried to talk to her earlier at the party said she was in a trance, that she stared into space and barely spoke a word. The autopsy, though — the real one — revealed nothing of that sort in her system. And of course drugs wouldn't have really explained the gun, because putting a gun in her purse implied some sort of intention on her part long before she actually used it.

So he and Freddie were left with a picture, not very clear, of her *planning* to kill Rudi, and at that point they decided it must have been because she had done the unthinkable, something for which their mother would never have forgiven her: she had leaked a family secret to someone who would almost certainly pass it on, and she had to stop that from happening. It wasn't very satisfactory as a motive, but it was all they could assume, and it was their second mistake. A week or two after the funeral, when she was helping

Peekie sort through the clothes in Dorothy's closet, Frances had found a videocassette in a shoebox on the highest shelf. She'd instinctively hidden it from Peekie, brought it home, and watched it herself before showing it to Hamilton, thinking it might have been a sad little indulgence of Dorothy's (male strippers from Chippendale's, maybe) that a brother and a daughter would never need to worry about.

Frances and Freddie (they never showed Peekie) didn't understand how Dorothy could have had such a record of what was obviously a criminal act on Spence's part, but they would never know *exactly* how it had come into her hands. Hamilton knew: it was the same transfer of film to video, the same brand of cassette, as what his blackmailer had sent him. He was very, very sure that Spence had been paying for this for years, and that Dorothy had continued the payments. He was also positive that, somehow, she had discovered that Rudi — her friend — was the one who was bleeding her. He didn't blame her for what she did. He had been prepared, after all, to do the same, and he hadn't been betrayed by someone he had believed cared about him.

* * *

Frances had come back to New York earlier this afternoon from a few days in Palm Beach, where the next Trish Green Boutique would be, where it was always spring if not summer, and the haze of green in the park confused her. She felt as if she'd missed something — the overture to a musical, maybe, or the first few pages of a book. Standing on the roof of the apartment, just outside the glass box that was her office, she was giving herself a very short break from all the work that waited for her inside.

She had spent nearly every spring of her life in New York, but it was an exception that days like this always brought to her mind. There had been an afternoon in Boston, about a week after her baby was born, when she walked slowly along the river past these same colors, through this same air. She had told herself not to be so sad, that she was going to be fine, that this new life beginning all around her was a message, a symbol, that even though it was a little obvious, it was something she mustn't ignore.

It occurred to her that spring was never going to carry memories of Mario with it. Certain crisp autumn afternoons, yes — those would remind her of him for the rest of her life — but not this kind of day, not this season that seemed to be reserved for the young. She had thought it would go on forever and ever, and it ended so suddenly she hadn't known it, hadn't recognized what had happened, until afterward.

The moment it died for her was the moment she sat in her dark bedroom and listened to Chuck Wetherby's words on the phone. It wasn't that what he said was true, as it turned out, it was that it *could* have been true, that what had always been there, deep in her mind, was brought to the surface by just a few words. In the horror she'd lived through in the days following that call, a wall had been built that she could never tear down, or a trench had been dug that she could never fill in — she had struggled to find the right image, once, in explaining how she felt to Trish, and she'd finally given up. She knew there weren't any words to express it.

They might have started again, it might have continued for a while until her feeling caught up with her, if it hadn't been for Maggie. She thanked God she hadn't found Mario at Rudi's house that night, that she'd only heard the next morning, when there was all the ghastliness of Dorothy's death and everything that had to be done for Hamilton and for the rest of the family. It would have been unbearable for Mario to face her in his first hours of grief. It would have been unbearable for her — if she hadn't found the honesty in herself at that moment to admit what had already happened to her — to see what would have been in his face, what she now believed to be true, which was that he had lost the woman he would sooner or later have gone back to.

Accepting that it was over and why it was over was easier for her, in a way, than knowing how it began, how it had ever burned so fiercely in the first place. It had been love, though, she was sure of that, and it was to be respected and cherished as such, and maybe, probably, it wasn't to be understood. Sometimes she thought it would never have lasted for even those few months if it hadn't been for the restaurant, that Tables had been both their passion and what their passion had brought into being, at the same time. Their child.

Hamilton came up to find her, to welcome her back from her trip, and she held on to him for a long while before she let go, even then keeping her arm around him as they stood side by side and gazed out on the park. She seemed to need his touch far more often in the past few months, the reassurance that he was *there,* and she knew he needed the same from her. Whatever it was they had survived was behind them, and it had brought them closer together, but it had left its mark. She didn't think she would ever stray so far away from this man she loved so deeply, and she was very sure she didn't want to.

* * *

Frederick climbed out of the cab in front of the trattoria in one of the old parts of town, the Vecchio Naviglio, and sniffed the air. He had come straight here from the train station and he hadn't noticed till now — there was a lovely Seicento house across the street and he could see the trees in its courtyard — that it was already spring in Milan. This morning, up in the snowfields of the Dolomites, it had been winter.

He always did things in this order: skiing first for a week or so — staying in one village or another, wherever the snow was best — then coming down here as if it were an afterthought instead of the real reason he chose to ski in this part of Italy two or three times a year rather than Switzerland or Vermont or Colorado.

Pushing through the bright plastic strips of the portiere, he stood for a moment to let his eyes adjust. Then, at the other end, he saw her springing up with a single, lithe movement, smoothing her skirt and running her hand through her hair, and it was those gestures — more than the beauty that was so evident even from here — that made the other girl live once again for him.

Frances had believed him, of course, when she had asked him about her child for the first time in all those years, but she still hadn't asked him how he could be so positive that Mario Fermi couldn't be her son, and he didn't think, now, that the question would ever be asked and he approved of that. He was the only one who knew every piece of the story, and he supposed he would die without telling anyone. Mario couldn't be her son because she didn't have a son. She had a daughter: this girl, woman now, who'd been raised here in Milan, who'd grown tall and slim and heartbreakingly lovely.

She knew that Vittorio and Gabriella Ortelli weren't her parents, but so many papers had been forged or altered or destroyed that, even if it occurred to her to look, she'd never be able to trace her birth. And it would never be possible for Frances to know any more than she did at this moment. Vittorio was an old, old friend who was a teaching assistant at Harvard when Frederick was an undergraduate. He and his wife returned to Milan when he was offered a curatorial position at the Brera, and Frederick and his wife always stayed with them on their way to the skiing holidays they'd both so much adored. Because the Ortellis couldn't have children of their own, they had adopted two boys, and that was what gave Frederick the idea. They were very comfortably well off. They were highly cultured. They were more liberal, more modern, than many Italian *alto borghese*. Most important, he had seen how warm and loving they were to the two little boys they'd taken into their home.

He had lied to Frances because he loved her. Maybe, missing his wife so badly in that first year after she'd died and entranced by this girl Hamilton had asked him to help, he had actually been in love with her, as what man wouldn't be? Whatever his feelings were, he couldn't stand to see her in any more pain, and he had silently gone about doing whatever he could to ease her grief. She had wanted a boy so badly, she had been so convinced that she *was* carrying a boy, that he'd made up his mind, long before the baby was born, to make her believe it if her child turned out to be a girl instead. He thought he understood why it was important to her, even though he knew it was based on a kind of stubborn hysteria. She was still in love with Michael and if she was carrying his son, a miniature Michael, then that love was still with her in a way it wouldn't have been if it were a girl. And then there was the reason she herself had given him — which wasn't in the least bit true, of course — that a boy, even a tiny baby boy, would be stronger, not so helpless, less in need of the mother who was pushing him out into the world.

When Hamilton married her — and Frederick had to lie to his own brother, too, once he resolved that nothing must ever slip, that she must never know unless she chose to know — he had gone back and made doubly sure all the tracks were completely obscured.

Frances, at the moment of her marriage, was no longer a sweet, beautiful girl from Little Italy who depended on him for help, whom he loved and would always love. She was a McKinnon, and the stakes were much, much higher. So a nurse could comfortably retire to Florida a few years earlier than she'd hoped. A doctor could build a big summer house out on the Cape. A small private hospital suddenly found itself with a new wing. Several people at this end could buy new Lancias.

He saw Frances's daughter at least twice a year — at her parents' house for dinner or at her own apartment or sometimes, like today, in a place for lunch she'd chosen because it was near the publishing house where she was the art book editor — and every time, he was struck by her resemblance to Frances. It wasn't so much her face: she was very beautiful, but her features were arranged differently from her mother's. It was the way she moved, the way she was so obviously *someone,* an independent, intelligent woman of spirit. As she threw her arms around him and kissed him on both cheeks, he congratulated himself once again for doing the right thing.

* * *

Mario was driving down the Connecticut Turnpike with the top down in the old MG he'd bought a few weeks before, imagining he was traveling not through space, not from Boston to New York, but through time, from season to season. The weekend he'd just spent up there had been cold and damp, and what had only been a hint of spring in the air, a vague promise of green, was now fulfilling itself as he drove south.

A commercial on the radio for contact lenses made him laugh as he remembered the tinted ones his cousin wore and then the scene with him this morning. Tom had slapped him on the back and congratulated him on his success, as if his words a few months ago had never left his mouth. Now he was all smiles because the restaurant hadn't gone down the tubes and now Mario was a boy wonder and he'd obviously be starting to pay back the bank soon, and the company's stock would be freed up in another year and a half, and the family could buy him out. When Mario told him he was going to roll the loan over, when he told him about his new idea, the one that would leave the stock tied up for at least another year or two beyond the original date, he'd been sure he could see murder behind those very contact lenses.

His mother had been so sick that he hadn't even tried to explain it to her. He'd simply sat by her bed and listened to her ramble, let her wander down whatever paths the morphine was leading her. At one point, on one of her trips to the past, she'd been talking to an old lady who'd lived in the big house on the corner, not in Belmont but farther back than that, when they'd all been in the North End together. She'd been angry with Mrs. Roncalli because she was sure Mrs. Roncalli was only pretending she didn't know who the father of Teresa's child was, only lying when she said Teresa hadn't told her before she died. She, Mrs. Fermi, had a right to know if anyone did, she said, or, rather, the drug said.

Mario suddenly knew who his mother, the woman who had borne him, had been. He could barely remember the Roncallis but he knew they were one of the handful of neighborhood families whose affairs no one ever mentioned in anything above a whisper. The old widow had always been very kind to him whenever he saw her in the street and sometimes she'd given him candy, or a quarter. There were two or three sons who drove beautiful cars when they came to visit their mama on Sundays, and one of them had once given a five-dollar bill to Johnny for polishing his hubcaps. There had been a daughter, Teresa, who'd died on a visit to the Old Country when she was very young — sixteen or seventeen, maybe. He wouldn't ordinarily have wondered about her or even known anything about her, because it had happened when he was very little, only a baby, but her name was on a plaque in front of the library her mother had built in her memory and he used to trace the letters with his fingers when he waited there for Johnny to collect him and walk him home.

He was trying to visit his mother as often as he could these days, not only because she seemed to be failing so quickly, but because his new plan would keep him away for weeks at a time. After the service for Maggie, after he and Chuck and her bewildered parents had taken the little family sailboat out into the Pacific with her ashes, he'd stayed on the Coast for a few days. He drove down to

L.A. and checked into the Chateau Marmont, the big old stucco hotel on the Strip. He sat in his room or down by the pool and he didn't speak to anyone but the waitress in the coffee shop across the street and he tried to think.

Patterns, reasons, moments when it all could have been reversed — he looked for them everywhere. *If* I hadn't done that, he would say to himself, and *if* that hadn't happened then and *if* there hadn't been wild cards like Chuck or Jim or Rudi. He blamed her parents, he blamed her, he blamed himself most of all. He would never stop wondering what might have happened if the little plane hadn't gone down, if she'd shown up at Tables the way he was sure she'd intended. It was easy to think now that he'd have wrapped her in his arms and told her he loved her and that he'd never leave her again, but he wasn't sure. He didn't know; he would never know; but he was positive, if the grief he felt meant anything at all, that he and Maggie would have been together again. Maybe not that night, but soon.

And Frances . . . even before Maggie was killed, Frances had taken a giant step back from the place where they'd been together. He had thought their love would go on and on, or else it would explode — he remembered using exactly those words to himself — and instead . . . instead, what? Had it had just . . . ended? While his back was turned? When he was first so frenzied with the restaurant, and then when he was in so much pain he'd been incapable of noticing anything at all? No, it couldn't have been so simple. There had been something else, something had come between them, and he would never know what it was. It was over, but it had *been,* it had existed.

Back at work, seeing what he'd already known — which was that Tables was doing phenomenally well and that his manager was as competent as he himself had been at Rudi's — he relaxed enough to let an idea enter his mind and then to encourage the idea to grow into a plan. He was going to spend some time, fill some time, whatever, in L.A. He was going to look very carefully for exactly the right part of town for a second Tables.

And he was going to ask Frances to design it for him when he found the right spot and he was sure — as the friend he hoped she would now become — that she would. Whatever they had had was gone — evaporated or burned away or any of the words he'd used to himself to try to understand it — but it had been the purest, most intense, most dangerous passion he had ever felt or ever hoped to feel.